CW00632023

The Dangerous Edge

THE DANGEROUS EDGE

EDGE

Tim Renton

HUTCHINSON
London

© Tim Renton

The right of Tim Renton to be identified as Author
of this work has been asserted by Tim Renton in
accordance with the Copyright, Designs and Patents
Act, 1988

This edition first published in 1994 by Hutchinson

Random House UK Ltd
20 Vauxhall Bridge Road, London SWIV 2SA

Random House Australia (Pty) Ltd
20 Alfred Street, Milsons Point, Sydney, NSW 2061,
Australia

Random House New Zealand Ltd
18 Poland Road, Glenfield, Auckland 10, New Zealand

Random House South Africa (Pty) Ltd
PO Box 337, Bergvlei, 2012, South Africa

A CiP catalogue record for this book is available from the
British Library

ISBN 0 09 179151 0

Set in Plantin Light
by Deltatype Ltd, Ellesmere Port
Printed and bound in Great Britain by
Clays Ltd, St Ives plc

Our interest's on the dangerous edge of things,
The honest thief, the tender murderer,
The superstitious atheist. . . .

Robert Browning

I am very grateful to Her Majesty's Ambassador to the Lebanese Republic for her kind hospitality in October 1992. I would like to thank most warmly Captain Adam Fergusson for his technical advice about many aspects of Tornado F3s and Mrs Margaret Holloway who typed and printed my manuscript with care, enthusiasm and constant encouragement.

Any resemblance in the text to personalities from real life is entirely accidental.

For Alice, my best friend
and wisest critic.

1

Tuesday 25 June: Morning

Jock looked across the Cabinet table and wondered what sort of mood the Prime Minister was in. He would have to play him accordingly. The moods could vary enormously. Sometimes a great gale of anger rose the first instant the Prime Minister guessed what the Foreign Office was driving at, a blast that was likely to blow a junior minister in tatters straight out of the door.

At other times the Prime Minister seemed desperately reasonable, softly spoken and leading his interlocutor into a snare step by step, logic turning almost imperceptibly into false logic, reason into exaggeration, fact into distortion, until the victim found himself arguing for a position that he knew to be rubbish. Sometimes, the Prime Minister was just plain sensible. Jock felt profoundly uneasy with the man but, ambitious as he was, he tried his hardest to disguise his feelings. He felt sweat rising in the palms of his hands and he brushed them nervously down the side of his trousers. He said:

'The first message, Prime Minister, which we intercepted on Sunday evening reads:

WE HAVE TWO PRIZES. SEND US YOUR INSTRUCTIONS.

'The reply from Tripoli which was intercepted last night and which GCHQ Cheltenham decoded two hours ago, reads:

PREPARE TO RECEIVE A NEW EMBASSY CAR. IT WILL REACH YOU SHORTLY.

'At least, we imagine that it's a reply and we think we've got to work on that assumption. Of course, it could be just what it says it is, a notification to the Libyan Embassy in Beirut that they're being sent an extra diplomatic car. But the coincidence is too great. We're assuming that the car is connected with the two prizes.'

'Who,' growled the Prime Minister, 'is "we"?'

For a second or two, before replying, Jock gazed at the portrait of George III, hanging above and behind the Prime Minister's head. It was a bad portrait, ill-lit and dirty, a rather bloated face, framed with powdered curls, debauched and suffering. To Jock's eyes, by comparison with the Rt Hon. Bruce Gordon PC, Prime Minister and First Lord of the Treasury, it was the face of a saint.

' "We" means the Foreign Office,' Jock began hesitantly. 'I've consulted the Foreign Secretary on the telephone. Alastair Crichton, the Under Secretary, has spoken to MI6. The experts at GCHQ will do a re-run of the intercept but, at the moment, they are convinced they've got the decoding right.'

'Where does that take us to? How do you read the situation? I want your own views, not those of your civil servants.'

'Well, Prime Minister,' Jock started slowly and carefully. 'As I see it, the two hostages, Bob Janes and Les Harrington, were grabbed two days ago, on Sunday. From what those who saw the kidnapping have told our people in Beirut, they were bundled off the pavement at gunpoint into the back seat of a large American-type car. No one got a record of the number plate. No one, among all the terrorist groups, neither the PLO, Al-Fatah, Hizbollah nor any member of the Islamic Jihad has claimed responsibility. There has been total silence. That's very unusual for Lebanon.

'Then, as I've said, two days ago, GCHQ intercepts this first message from Beirut to Tripoli.' Jock pushed a flimsy copy across the Cabinet table. 'Then last night, they intercept this one.' Again, he pushed a copy across the table. 'Your office has, of course, had copies already but, as you see, it's from Tripoli back to the Libyan Embassy in Beirut. The transmitter is in their Special Services building, and GCHQ have bugged the building for some time.

'Of course, it could be a coincidence, but we have to work on the probability that it isn't. That means that they are planning to send a specially equipped car to Beirut which will be used to smuggle out the two hostages, the prizes. They will presumably be bound and drugged and put in the boot of the car. The car could arrive either by ship or by air freighter. It will, I imagine, have CD plates on it, and it will be imported into Beirut with minimum customs formalities. The same would happen when it was exported.'

'But what excuse are they going to make for sending the car back to Tripoli?' The Prime Minister glared at Jock, who took a deep breath, gathered his wits and ploughed on.

'Well, in fact it wouldn't have to be the same car. They could say that they had brought out a new Embassy car in order to replace one that was getting too old, and now they were sending the old one back. Alternatively, if the car being sent out is specially equipped with air-holes into the boot so that the hostages can breathe, they could pretend that it had proved faulty in some way and they were sending it back to Tripoli for urgent repairs. I don't think that side of things would be difficult. After all, they'll have friends in the Lebanese customs, or they'll bribe them.

'And then, when the hostages arrive in Tripoli, Gadaffi will put the poor devils into show-cages, boast about them to Arafat and all the Arab extremists, and extract confessions from them with which he'll blackmail us.'

Jock Meldrum-Ross faltered. He had had a lengthy briefing with Crichton and his other civil servants before coming to Number 10, but the sense of certainty which that had given him was starting to evaporate before the Prime Minister's scrutiny.

The Prime Minister gazed expressionlessly at the two flimsies that Jock had pushed across the table at him. On his right was Roderick Turner, his principal private secretary. Turner was the only other person in the long panelled and pillared room. He had been taking copious notes as Jock spoke and now openly read the deciphered messages over the Prime Minister's shoulder.

The Prime Minister blew out his cheeks and then let the air escape gently from his lips, a soft breeze rather than a hurricane. 'How long is Robert away for?' he asked.

3

'The Foreign Secretary will be back in five days' time, on Saturday. He only left Nairobi for Harare last night and then he's going to Mozambique and then . . .'

'I know, I know,' the Prime Minister interrupted him irritably. 'The Foreign Office has kindly let me know where the Foreign Secretary is travelling to. Indeed, he himself sometimes asks my permission to leave these shores – when he remembers.'

Jock kept quiet. There was a long pause and then Bruce Gordon said: 'Well, you were quite right to ask to come and see me. There's no need to tell Robert to come back to England at this stage. Let him get on with banging the drums with the tribal chiefs and carousing with those who are, mistakenly, called freedom fighters by the liberal press.' He paused and suddenly smiled across the table. 'Yes, indeed, you were right to ask, Jock, to come and see me.' The Prime Minister turned to Roderick Turner.

'Roderick, see that the Chiefs of Staff and Security Chiefs personally receive copies of these messages. Advise them that, at first sight, this looks like an attempt to get these two men out of Lebanon into Gadaffi's hands in Libya. Tell Cheltenham to make a top priority of deciphering all the message-trade between Beirut and the North African capitals, Cairo and Algiers and Tunis as well as Tripoli. I don't want them coming to us and saying: "Funnily enough we got this one a few days ago but we didn't think it important and we've only just deciphered it." And by then it will be too damn late. I know their form, those brilliant, what are they called, cryptographers, socialists, who think that terrorism is a game of chess, to be played only between nine in the morning and five at night.' The Prime Minister paused and looked straight across the table.

'What else, Jock?' Jock felt a surge of relief, of positive pleasure.

'I'll keep our Ambassador in Beirut fully advised, of course,' he replied. 'I'll ask him to use all his few remaining staff to pick up any crumbs of information they can get. We must be ready for press enquiries and perhaps a Parliamentary Question. The press have been very quiet so far but they're bound soon to start demanding that we send a Guards battalion into Beirut to rescue these two decent Britons who were both working to help the down-trodden Lebanese.' Jock's confidence was returning in leaps and bounds, and he allowed himself a touch of mocking exaggeration.

'Quite right. Roderick, is Eddie Ford back from his jaunt with the Washington press yet?' Roderick nodded. 'Good. I want him to work closely with the Foreign Office press office and make sure that they tell the same story to the press, for once; lies if necessary, but not different lies. Jock, I expect you to keep a personal eye on all of this. It could be nothing, it could be extremely important. I shall be watching you. If it develops, if you want to come and see me again at any hour of the day or night, just ring Roderick and tell him and he will arrange it. That's all.' He gave Jock a friendly half-conspiratorial look.

Jock got up from the table, and walked down the long room into the anteroom. There was a small gaggle of civil servants surrounding and listening deferentially to his friend and political ally, Angela Fawke, the Secretary of State for Social Security. She moved over to talk to him but he waved gently at her and walked on down the long corridor, past the Frink head given to the Prime Minister by his grateful Constituency Association, past the small, dark portrait of Gladstone and out into the front hall. There, one of the uniformed guards instantly opened the door for him. As he stepped out into Downing Street, two photographers behind the low railing five yards away took pictures of him – an automatic reflex, thought Jock. They would take pictures of the milkman coming here on his early morning round in the hope that he might one day turn out to have been sleeping with the Prime Minister's secretary. He swung to his left, towards the Whitehall end of Downing Street, and then turned into the side door of the Foreign Office. It's the first time, he thought, the Prime Minister has been even remotely polite to me since we first shook hands at the Conservative Conference fifteen years ago.

Jock Meldrum-Ross was fifty-one. All his life, he had had difficulty in reaching decisions. On matters concerning his career, sex, his position in the Conservative Party, he had sat on the fence waiting for chance or fate to force his hand. His mother had desperately wanted him to be a boy, his father a girl. The first seven years of his life, his father had given him dolls that spoke, sang and danced, and beautiful, tiny cooking-sets on his birthday. His mother, almost in protest, placed a catapult under the Christmas tree when he was four, an air-gun when he was five, and a .22 rifle, with a very short stock so that his small finger could reach the trigger, when he was eight.

He found himself boasting to his mother of the number of rabbits he had shot, and asking his father about the pretty pattern on the miniature cups that had been brought back from a diplomatic trip to East Germany.

His mother relaxed when he was dispatched, at the age of eight, to a puritanical and deeply masculine prep school.

'We pride ourselves on the three "capital Ss", the headmaster had said to her portentously – Jock's father was, as usual, abroad on official business. 'Scholarship, Mrs Meldrum-Ross, Sport and Scripture.' Unsurprisingly but inaccurately, he did not add sodomy.

Jock, a pretty, dark-haired boy, was seduced within a week of arriving at the school, by the prefect in charge of his dormitory. Their beds were next to each other, and the prefect, on a cold Sunday evening, suggested that Jock would be warmer in his bed. Jock padded over in his slippers, got into the prefect's bed, and, in a few short minutes, his virginal innocence was gone. Thereafter, the invitation was frequently renewed but some hidden, un-suspected sense of judgement stopped him telling either of his parents of these sexual adventures which he came to enjoy in a passive sort of way.

Jock had a naturally good eye and, in the holidays, shot so many rabbits with his .22 that his mother saved from her own small flow of dividends to buy him a shotgun on his thirteenth birthday and followed that up with a clay-pigeon trap for Christmas.

At Cambridge, Jock was cheerfully and dispassionately ambi-dextrous. One term, he found to his amusement that he had gone to bed with other, occasional young men on Mondays and Fridays, and with eager, energetic girls on Tuesdays and Thursdays. On Wednesdays, he regularly worked all night writing his essay for a weekly tutorial the following morning. To his surprise, in his third term, his tutor had leant over from the depths of his armchair and, without interrupting his discourse on the poetry in Gilbert Murray's translation of Sophocles's choruses, had started undoing Jock's fly-buttons. Jock was feeling exhausted as only a handsome undergraduate can. With a detached air he removed his tutor's wrinkled hand and returned it to the lap where it belonged. In exchange, he was offered a large glass of Tio Pepe sherry which he accepted with pleasure.

Jock just missed getting a first in Classics – he had worked hard and knew and loved the Greek and Roman dramatists, but he lacked the spark of originality in his compositions. On the strength of his degree, he was offered a number of jobs and spent some months trying to make a choice between potential employers. In the end, he decided on ICI. His first boss, who was in charge of a factory at Runcorn making caustic soda, found it hard to make full use of his management trainee's talents.

'A queer sort of fellow, full of charm and some ideas, but bad at moving matters forward,' the Works Director wrote in his first report.

After fifteen relatively happy and undemanding years, Jock and ICI tacitly agreed that enough was enough. He had been working at ICI headquarters in Millbank for five years and, for the last four of these, he had been a councillor in Chelsea. On a whim, he put in for the parliamentary candidacy at Kensington and Fulham after the elderly Conservative MP had announced his forthcoming retirement. To universal surprise, including his own, he shone at the final selection evening and made the Committee, who were thoroughly bored by the platitudes offered them by the other candidates, laugh at his description, in answer to a question on his knowledge of British industry, of his early days at Runcorn. To many of the Committee the industrial Midlands were more foreign than the coast of Turkey.

He was selected as the prospective Conservative candidate by a large majority, won the seat at the next election and, twelve years later, after behaving studiously well on the back-benches, alienating few but making only a handful of close friends, he found himself a junior minister at the Foreign Office.

To Jock, this was like coming home. For the first time since his university days, he found himself working with colleagues with whom he could exchange puns in Latin, and he became increasingly fond of Robert Huggins, the Foreign and Commonwealth Secretary. Unconsciously, he had fallen into the habit of regarding Huggins as a father-figure whose brand of liberal conservatism and sense of detachment from the hurly-burly of politics coincided with his own views. Mary, his wife, sometimes teased him at home and called him Robert's little lamb but she was delighted that, at last, he had found a niche where he was usually at ease.

Today, as he walked past the Foreign Office doorman, encased in his cubby-hole of bullet-proof glass, he felt pleased that he had been wearing one of his most vivid colour combinations when talking to the Prime Minister. Nestling under a deep blue suit, was a shirt of variegated dark brown and deep yellow stripes adorned by a black tie decorated with chains of pink flowers. His hair flowed gently, not excessively, over the tops of his ears and the back of his collar and he was dressed in what he regarded as slightly unconventional shoes – black, very well-polished, no laces and little black tassels where the tongue of the more traditional shoe would have been. Dressing well gave him a sense of individuality, of not being just one of the crowd, of being able to stand up to anyone whether he was a British Prime Minister or a Lebanese terrorist.

Jock climbed quickly up two poky flights of steps and turned right down a narrow corridor, through the little door that had been driven through the wall when the old Home Office, at the Whitehall end of the building, had started to talk with the Colonial Office at the St James's end. He strode past numerous portraits of nineteenth-century governors of remote states in India and Australia, and turned right into his private office.

Two men and one woman were working at their desks. One of the men stood up as soon as Jock came into the room.

'There are two more telegrams from Beirut on your desk, Minister,' he said promptly. 'Also, a note from Parliamentary Section saying that Mr Copper has put down a Private Notice Question for this afternoon asking for a statement on the disappearance of the two Britons in Beirut. We haven't heard yet whether the Speaker has allowed the Question.'

Jock pursed his lips together angrily. 'Damn,' he said. 'That's the last thing we need today. When will we hear from the Speaker's Office about the PNQ?'

'In about thirty minutes. It's now a quarter past twelve. I've told the Near East Section to stand by and come and give you briefing over a sandwich if the question is allowed.'

Jock didn't reply. He knew that he needed more time to think, more time to get ready to answer a hostile House of Commons. He suddenly felt nervous and would like to have said 'shit' at the top of his voice. But that wasn't part of the Foreign Office tradition. And one of his private secretaries was a girl who'd only been in his office for a few weeks, so he restrained himself.

He opened the heavy mahogany door and walked into the high-ceilinged, heavily Victorian room that was his personal office. He loved this room with its ornate panelling, the watercolour of Beirut in 1855, painted by Edward Lear, and the five oil paintings of nineteenth-century East Indian potentates, rampant with coloured silk jodhpurs, fancy coats, swords and medals, that he had managed to borrow from the old India Office collection. There was a broad view from his windows over Horse Guards Parade and, if he squinted to his right, he could see the red brick of the Chief Whip's house. Usually, his office and its grand pictures and view added to his feeling of self-esteem but there was no time for any of that today.

'Fuck, fuck, fuck,' he muttered as he walked to his desk.

'What did you say, Minister?' said his principal private secretary, following him into the room. 'I didn't quite catch.'

Peter is an ass, Jock thought crossly. If I said 'fuck' to him, he wouldn't know what it meant. It's not in the diplomatic hand-books. He looked up at Peter Pirelli as he sat down at his desk and muttered, 'Nothing important. I'm worried about the PNQ. I'd better read these telegrams quickly.'

The Foreign Office has the quaint habit of describing every message that is not a letter as a telegram, no matter whether it is sent by telex or radio signal. The two messages on Jock's desk had come in code by radio signal from Beirut to the Foreign Office's receiving station where they had been automatically decoded. The first, timed two hours previously, confirmed that the Ambassador and the Defence Attaché would spend all day checking their contacts in Beirut for information about the hostages. The second, timed only thirty minutes earlier but headed 'FLASH – FLASH – FLASH' in order to ensure that it got priority over all other decoding, read:

MOBERLY REPORTS PLO CONTACT CLAIMS TO KNOW THAT JANES AND HARRINGTON ARE BEING HELD IN OUTSKIRTS OF BEIRUT. BOTH ALIVE. DELICATE NEGOTIATIONS MAY BE POSSIBLE FOR THEIR RELEASE. KEEP STRICTLY CONFIDENTIAL. ADAMS.

'Peter, is Moberly the Defence Attaché in Beirut?'

'Yes,' said Peter. 'He's been there some years. He knows the form very well. The Ambassador, Benedict Adams, has a lot of respect for his contacts.'

'Having a lot of respect for bloody Palestinians doesn't seem too appropriate,' said Jock.

Pirelli winced. 'I'm sorry, Minister. I meant that the Ambassador knows Moberly has got very good contacts.'

'Of course, of course,' muttered Jock. 'But is Moberly himself any good? Or is he useless, like most Defence Attachés?'

'Well, Minister, he has a reputation for getting things wrong. Someone at the MoD told me that he once failed to recognise the PM at a party and asked him to tell him the way to the nearest loo. The PM exploded.'

'God!' said Jock. 'Just what we need. Check that copies of the second message, the urgent one, go over to Number 10 as soon as possible. Are the Near East Section getting an Answer ready for me to the PNQ?'

'Yes.'

'Ask them to send up a draft of it as soon as it's done. Tell them also to prepare briefing on all the possible Supplementary Questions, including the question of who is actually holding Janes and Harrington. What's the precise Question that Copper has asked?'

'It's on the piece of paper on your desk, below the telegrams.'

Jock looked and saw a flimsy white sheet headed 'Parliamentary Section' and timed 11.30 am Tuesday 25 June. Underneath were the words:

Mr Gerry Copper MP to ask the Foreign Secretary: whether he has any information about the whereabouts of two British voluntary workers in the Lebanon, Mr Bob Janes and Mr Les Harrington, and whether he will make a statement.

Jock had hardly finished reading the flimsy when Anthea Wheeler came rushing in from his Private Office.

'Minister, I'm sorry to interrupt, but the messengers have just brought round the midday *Evening Standard*. Look, on the front page, there's a headline about the two men in Beirut.'

Excitement mixing explosively with the oxygen in her lungs, Anthea pushed the *Evening Standard* across his massive desk and pointed half-way down the front page. Jock's heart sank. There was the headline: 'Missing Brits alive in Beirut'. He read on: 'News has just reached me from a reliable Palestinian source, reports Leonard Friend from Beirut, that the two British Aid workers, Bob Janes and Les Harrington, are being held hostage close to the centre of Beirut. They are alive and have been well treated.

'Janes and Harrington have not been seen since Sunday, when they went for a swim and a picnic lunch with some Lebanese friends. In the evening, as they said goodbye to their friends, they

11

said they were planning to walk through West Beirut down to the harbour. Their local friends strongly advised them not to because of the increase in terrorist activities.

'Bob Janes and Les Harrington had been working on water-improvement projects for the UN Rehabilitation Agency for the last two years. Their work has taken them to many parts of Lebanon and they have made many friends in this battle-torn country.

'But fears are mounting rapidly that their silence for the last two days means that they have been grabbed by one of the many anti-Western groups.' Jock's attention started to wander.

Anthea Wheeler, his new private secretary, was looking at him with the air of a faithful dog that has brought its master an enticing bone.

'Thanks, Anthea. I thought the press were bound to start stirring it up. The Speaker is certain to grant the Private Notice Question. Warn Number 10, tell the Foreign Secretary urgently wherever he is, cancel my lunch at Brooks's, order me a sandwich and a soft drink and get that draft to me as soon as possible.'

'The sandwich and an apple,' said Anthea, hopeful of winning an approving smile, 'are outside.'

The telephone on his desk rang. It was Nick Prout, the third member of his Private Office.

'Minister, sorry to bother you but the Parliamentary Section has just rung. The Speaker has allowed Mr Copper's Private Notice Question, so it will be taken at three-thirty, immediately after Prime Minister's Questions.'

'Prime Minister's Questions,' repeated Jock. 'That means it'll be a full House.'

'Yes, Minister, and a lot of the press there in the Gallery.'

Just what those two poor damned hostages need, he thought, but it's a great opportunity for me, if I get it right.

At about the same time, Mary Meldrum-Ross parked her red Fiat in South Audley Street. She got out of her car, looked into her purse and wondered idly whether she should try and slip one of the 200-Lira coins lying in the bottom into the meter. Sometimes they worked, sometimes they didn't. She decided against. There was always a danger they would jam, and then she would have to search for another parking space. She pushed two one-pound coins into the slot instead, checked that the clock had moved on and walked along the road to lunch at the Egyptian Embassy.

Mary was greeted warmly, even affectionately, by the Egyptian Ambassador and, with a glass of champagne in her hand, she looked round the ornate tall-windowed drawing room and smiled to herself. She thought she had arrived at the perfect moment: about twenty minutes after the time stated on her engraved invitation card. The room was already full with around twenty guests, most of whom she knew from similar occasions over the past eighteen months. Interspersed among the Arabs was a sprinkling of white European faces, all with a certain glossy look – an unconscious sense of well-being, of being fed regularly at good watering-holes. For a second or two, Mary remembered the scrimping of her student days, the difficulty she'd had in living on her scholarship and local authority grant as she followed her chosen course of Arabic Studies at Manchester University. I've moved on a bit since then, she thought.

Before she could luxuriate any further, a hand grasped her elbow and she felt herself gently turned, to be greeted with a kiss on the cheek by a woman wearing an elegant chestnut-brown suit, a large string of pearls and massive earrings in the centre of which nestled brown stones that Mary could not instantly recognize.

'Darling, how lovely to see you. I thought I was going to be awfully bored by myself. Charles, as always, is away for his bank doing some dreadful business in the Gulf.'

Mary smiled at Lady Herbert. They had last met only two evenings before at a party given by the Kuwaiti Ambassador at the Dorchester for a visiting Foreign Minister. The Herberts lived in a comfortable, warm house where an aura of discreet wealth permeated the curtains, carpets and sofas. Even the wastepaper baskets appeared to have been custom-made. They frequently asked Jock and Mary to the elaborate meals they gave for visiting Arab Ministers and businessmen. Mary sometimes wondered by what multiple – five, ten, twenty – Sir Charles Herbert's annual income must exceed Jock's, but the four of them had become good acquaintances and Mary picked up the thread of conversation where she had left it at the Dorchester.

'Diana, I'm so glad you're here. I've only just arrived. I didn't want to stand around for hours before lunch, drinking bad champagne and eating pistachio nuts, waiting for the guest of honour to turn up.' Mary smiled and then went on reflectively, 'Last time Jock and I came here, I remember my tummy rumbling like Vesuvius erupting before we were finally allowed to go into the dining room.'

'It's the Lebanese Ambassador whom our Egyptian friends are treating today, isn't it?' queried Diana Herbert.

'Yes,' said Mary. 'I remember last month being asked to attend an exhibition of Lebanese goods – wines, tinned fruits and things like that – in the Arab Centre in Belgrave Square. Jock was abroad and I went, standing in for him.

'We were asked there for eleven. I arrived at eleven-thirty and the Ambassador didn't turn up until well after twelve. He walked round the exhibition very slowly, examining every tin with minute care, and then gave us a thirty-minute speech. It was delightful, full of elegant references to the past connections between Britain and Lebanon and all that sort of thing, but – she paused – we were all horribly late for lunch.'

'Perhaps, he'll remember his diplomatic etiquette today,' said Diana. 'I do hope he does. I'm in a terrible rush this afternoon.'

'Tomorrow there will be apricots,' said Mary, quoting the old Arab proverb. But at that moment the double doors were opened and a small man, immaculately dressed, grey hair smoothed and neatly parted, hurried into the room. He walked straight up to the Egyptian Ambassador, put his arms round his shoulders and pecked him on both cheeks.

'*Le voilà, je crois que je suis arrivé au moment juste. Pour moi, c'est peu banal, çà.*'

'*Félicitations, mon ami,*' said the Egyptian Ambassador. He smiled. 'By your standards you are very punctual. But, perhaps, if you will forgive me, we will go straight into lunch. Some of my guests may have meetings in the afternoon. The Minister was not able to come but I have put Mrs Meldrum-Ross on your right.'

'*Mille fois merci. Elle est une femme très charmante.*'

'She speaks Arabic as you know, but your English is getting better all the time. You must practise it.' The Ambassador spoke in a tone of mild rebuke to his diplomatic colleague. Then he turned and beckoned the other guests towards the double doors as, with mingled feelings of exasperation, relief and hunger, they settled empty glasses on side tables and stubbed cigarettes into the slim, recumbent form of Nefertiti, modelled into the bases of numerous enamel ashtrays.

After the sweet – layer on layer of pastry, all dripping with honey – had been served, the Lebanese Ambassador turned from the guest on his left to Mary and, speaking in slow, careful English, asked her how her husband was. Mary had eaten well and had drunk two glasses of red wine with the inevitable main course of chicken nestling in a bed of rice, peppers and almond nuts. Now she held a glass of sweet white wine in her hand as she looked at the Lebanese Ambassador.

'Very busy as always,' she said. 'It is most kind of you to ask, Ambassador.'

'Ah, I'm always interested in you and the Minister. You both bring such skills to our Middle Eastern affairs. We are – *comment se dit il?* – fortunate to have you as our guardians, looking after us. All of us in the Corps Diplomatique think that.'

'You flatter us, Ambassador,' said Mary. Almost despite herself, she felt pleased at the compliment.

'And you, you have a family as well, I think? Three sons.'

'Your Chef de Protocol has briefed you well,' Mary replied.

'Ah, alas,' the Ambassador smiled wistfully. 'I have too small a staff in London to have a Chef de Protocol. Would that the relations between Beirut and Whitehall were more strong, that there was more business between us. Then perhaps I could persuade my Minister for Foreign Affairs to allow me more people.'

15

'I think you do very well with the team you have,' Mary found herself saying to her surprise. It was not a matter to which she had given any thought but she felt the urge to respond to the charm of the man by her side. 'Often, when I go abroad with Jock, I find the smaller embassies work better, are more . . .' she paused and wondered what was the word she wanted, 'united, thoughtful – they have a better esprit de corps than the bigger ones.'

The Ambassador in turn paused before replying. 'And you, Madame, with your excellent knowledge of Arabic, would you like to have served with your husband in the Corps Diplomatique in place of the political life?'

Mary smiled a touch ruefully and took another sip of her wine before replying. She had often thought that life would have been much easier for them and the boys if Jock had been a diplomat rather than an underpaid politician and Minister, but she felt it hardly tactful to mention this to the Ambassador. She put her fingers round the stem of her glass and twirled it.

'An interesting question, Ambassador, and I am not sure that I know the answer. I think, perhaps, I might have enjoyed the diplomatic world more than my husband. He likes the life of Westminster and Whitehall.'

'But you, perhaps you would like to travel more, take your boys skiing at Christmas, go to the Caribbean Islands at Easter?' The Ambassador looked enquiringly at her but Mary did not rise to the bait. She went on considering the intricate crystal pattern of the glass in front of her. And then, almost reluctantly, she said:

'Yes, I think that's right. I would like that.'

There was a pause, and then the Ambassador said, half-hesitatingly, like a bullfighter making his first pass, 'I remember with pleasure the speech you made at our little exhibition last month. We were very impressed by your knowledge of Arabic.'

'I used to be a trilingual interpreter,' Mary spoke with a touch of pride in her voice. 'French – Arabic – English. But there's a lot of competition. A great many of your compatriots, as you will know, are now in London, Ambassador. They've had to leave Beirut and they're looking for the sort of work that I do.'

'I'm sorry, Madame. I did not realize the life of an interpreter had become quite so difficult.' Mary changed her glass from one hand to the other but did not reply. A tic started to make the Ambassador's left eyelid twitch as he went on: 'Perhaps, Madame, we might be able to use your skills from time to time. We may have another exhibition shortly. I am most anxious, during my service in London, to build up the connections and the trade between our two countries. Britain and Lebanon used to be . . .' he paused and searched for the right word, 'friends, partners; we always regarded you as an important protection against the ambitions of the French at the eastern end of the Mediterranean. I only have a few people here in my office.' He gave a dismissive shrug of his shoulders. 'And we need some assistance in establishing ourselves at a higher level. You, Madame,' he paused again, 'you have such knowledge, so many friends, such charm. It would be an honour for us . . .' He let the words die away, as if he were embarrassed at having said so much, and did not try to finish the sentence.

Mary looked at the line of the moustache on the Ambassador's upper lip. How hard, almost wiry, those little grey hairs looked.

'More coffee, Madame?' a butler in a white coat bent over her right shoulder and directed a well-polished silver coffee pot towards her cup.

'No, thank you,' said Mary. At that moment, the Egyptian Ambassador rose to his feet and, in a gentle sing-song voice started to thank his friends for joining his wife and himself for a simple meal in his humble residence.

On their way out, the Lebanese Ambassador made a point of coming up to Mary and emphasizing how much he had enjoyed her company at lunch.

'I do hope, Madame,' he said, 'we will meet again soon. I found our conversation most interesting.' He took her hand and raised it towards his lips.

Mary said goodbye to the Egyptian Ambassador and walked quickly back to Grosvenor Square. She swore vigorously when she found a yellow ticket tucked neatly under the wiper on her windscreen. She looked at her watch, saw that it was well after three, and that she had exceeded by nearly thirty minutes the two hours for which she had paid on the meter. Blast, she thought. A £30 fine. She wondered whether there was any way in which she could get the Foreign Office to pay: after all, she'd only been at the lunch as a diplomatic duty. But she knew she had no chance of persuading Jock to add the £30 to his expenses claim.

2

Tuesday 25 June: Afternoon and Evening

There is a formidable ritual about Questions in the House. The first Question, the text of which the Minister has in advance, is always routine. 'When does the Minister plan next to visit Newcastle?' Or, 'What are the Prime Minister's engagements for today?' The Minister, in turn, has a prepared Answer ready which he reads out from the Despatch Box. But these are simply part of the preliminary skirmish, like sumo wrestlers snorting and throwing salt on the sacred ground before they charge in at each other. The real battle begins with the one Supplementary Question that is allowed to the Member of Parliament who asked the original question. Provided that the Supplementary remains fairly relevant, it can range far and wide. And then the interrogation is thrown open to other Members of the House, with questioners alternating between the Government benches and the Opposition. If the subject is of little interest, the Speaker will only allow one or two other MPs to ask Supplementary Questions, but if it is of good, topical interest then the Speaker may allow ten or more, with the process of questioning and answering taking up to twenty minutes.

Jock knew that he was in for a long grilling. The BBC News at one o'clock had been full of talk about the possible fate of Bob Janes and Les Harrington. Various experts had been wheeled before the microphone – news correspondents from Beirut, experts from the Arab Institute in the Cromwell Road, ex-Ambassadors speaking from their retirement homes in Gloucestershire – all of whom had pontificated on whether the poor devils were alive and, if alive, where they were being held and by whom. The BBC newscaster had ended the item with words that sank into

Jock's heart: 'The Government are expected to announce in the House of Commons this afternoon what action they propose to take to secure the immediate release of the hostages.'

The House was full. Jock, as he walked in through the double doors behind the Speaker's Chair, heard the infernal babble. 'If that is the attitude the Opposition are determined to adopt, then the country will see that they remain in opposition till the turn of the century,' shouted the Prime Minister as he sat down. Loud cheers from the supporters around him, raucous laughter and cries of 'roll on the millennium' from the Labour benches. Jock squeezed into the end of the Government Front Bench and heard the Speaker call one of the Conservative knights of the shires. Sir John Williamson rumbled to his feet.

'Has my Right Honourable Friend any news about the possible whereabouts of the two British relief-workers, Mr Janes and Mr Harrington, who disappeared in Lebanon on Sunday? If they have been taken hostage, will he give the House categoric assurance that, no matter who is holding them, he will, if necessary, send in British troops to right the grievous wrong done to two well-liked and decent British citizens?'

'Hear, hear, hear,' gargled the colleagues around Sir John as he sat back on the green bench, deeply conscious of a difficult job well done. Then there was a short silence as the Prime Minister got to his feet.

'I share with my Honourable Friend,' said Bruce Gordon, 'a deep concern about the whereabouts of Mr Janes and Mr Harrington who were doing thoroughly worthwhile jobs for a United Nations Agency in Lebanon. I understand that my Honourable Friend, the Minister of State at the Foreign and Commonwealth Office, will answer a Private Notice Question, Mr Speaker, in a few minutes' time on the subject. Perhaps the House would like to wait to hear what he has to say.'

Thank you very much, thought Jock. I've nothing specific to say, no detail to add, and you know it. Thanks for the help.

The clocks above the back-benches moved on. At 3.30 precisely, the last Question was asked of the Prime Minister. As he was on his feet answering it, Jock, stooping in order not to block the views of other MPs, walked past his fellow ministers towards the Despatch Box. Space was made for him by the Prime Minister's side. He sat down. He usually answered Questions well and easily, but, now, his stomach turned over with nerves and he quickly poured himself a glass of water from the jug by the Despatch Box and had a sip. Prime Minister's Questions ended and, unusually, every Member of Parliament stayed in his seat instead of trooping out of the Chamber.

'Private Notice Question,' boomed the Speaker from his high-backed chair. Gerry Copper MP a junior member of Labour's foreign affairs team, rose to his feet, moved to the Despatch Box on the Opposition side and said: 'I wish to ask the Minister of State at the Foreign Office a Question of which I have given him notice: whether he has any further information on the whereabouts of the two British voluntary workers in Lebanon, Bob Janes and Leslie Harrington and whether he will make a statement about them.' Copper sat down with a smug smile on his face. No matter the tragic reality behind the Question he was asking, he had the attention of the whole House and of a large number of the world's press, and he had a splendidly insulting Supplementary Question prepared and carefully learnt by heart.

Jock Meldrum-Ross got to his feet and put his file of papers on the Despatch Box, the prepared Answer to Copper's Question on the top.

'Since the possible disappearance of Mr Janes and Mr Harrington in Beirut was reported to us,' Jock stumbled over the first few words but then his voice gathered strength, 'we have been in constant touch with our Embassy to try and establish their whereabouts. So far, we have received no concrete information. The whole House will, I am sure, share my concern that these two British subjects, who are engaged in worthwhile relief work in Lebanon, should return to their homes safely as soon as possible.' Jock sat down. There was a pause, a positive sense of breaths being held, of disappointment; even his friends on the Benches immediately behind him were silent. They wanted to hear positive and more encouraging news.

21

Copper sprang up as if the Despatch Box would disappear into thin air if he did not grab it quickly.

'Does the Minister realize that he has just given us a most unsatisfactory answer?'

'Hear, hear.' 'That's right,' yelled the ranks from behind him, and Copper's voice gained further confidence and spite: 'Is the Foreign Office these days not capable of safeguarding the lives of even those British citizens abroad who are working for the United Nations? Can the Minister of State tell the House whether he has received any information, any information at all since Sunday about the possible fate of these two poor souls? Or is this yet another case of the Foreign Office shilly-shallying whilst British lives and interests are lost?' Copper bounced back on to his bench.

'Well done, Gerry.' 'Sock it to him, typical Foreign Office smoothy,' shouted the supporting benches opposite. 'Knows nothing. Where's Huggins? Bring him back,' the militant members on the green leather bench below the gangway roared happily. Jock hesitated. He could say nothing about the inter-cepted messages – they were strictly secret – and telling the House too much of what the British Ambassador had radioed could just lead to the deaths of the two men. But, equally, he could not lie to the House; that had been the undoing of many a Minister. He had to temporize.

'The Honourable Member must realize . . .' he started and then stopped, trying to decide just what the Honourable Member should realize. The members on the benches opposite sensed his hesitation and pounced on him.

'Get on with it. Ass. Doesn't know what he's talking about,' they shouted. The Tories were silent. The Speaker started to look restless and to drum his fingers on the side of his black breeches.

'The Honourable Member must realize . . .' Jock tried again, 'that we are doing everything in our power to ascertain the whereabouts and to ensure the safety of Mr Janes and Mr Harrington, but we only have a small Embassy staff in Beirut and it is not possible for them to cover the whole country thoroughly.' He sat down, conscious that this sounded very lame.

The Speaker called a Tory MP who tried to help Jock. 'Can my Honourable Friend assure the House that he has instructed our Ambassador to do all that he possibly can to find out the whereabouts of these two men? Has he yet spoken to the Lebanese Ambassador in London, expressing his concern for their safety, and has he made contact with the Head of the United Nations Development Agency to ask for the assistance of all their officers in the Lebanon?'

God, thought Jock, that's what I should have done but I haven't yet. I just haven't had time. He rose to his feet. 'I can assure my Honourable Friend that our Ambassador is under strict instructions to make contact with all of those in the Lebanon who may be able to help, if the two Britons have been taken hostage. As for the second half of his question, I shall myself be making contact with both the Lebanese Ambassador in London and with the local Head of the United Nations Development Agency later today.' Still an uneasy, unfriendly silence as he sat down.

'But surely the Minister of State must be able to tell the House whether or not he has received any information regarding their whereabouts? He seems very evasive on this point. Perhaps he's been too busy to read all the Foreign Office telegrams yet?' questioned a Labour MP who himself had been a Foreign Office minister some years before.

Jock flushed with annoyance. 'I can assure the House and the Honourable Gentleman opposite that I have read all the necessary telegrams,' he started. Some members snickered with laughter and Jock realized that he was digging himself further into a hole. 'As regards further information, I have nothing more to tell the House beyond my original answer. I cannot go further than that.'

'But really, my Honourable Friend must know that his answers so far are very unsatisfactory,' boomed the soldierly Sir John Williamson. 'Both sides of this House will be deeply worried at the apparent failure of Her Majesty's Government to secure either the safety or the release of Mr Janes and Mr Harrington. Can the Minister reassure us that the Foreign Office is not being quite as dilettante,' Sir John emphasized each syllable of the word, 'as it

23

appears and that, if necessary, he will talk to his Right Honourable Friend, the Secretary for Defence, about the use of troops to ensure the safe return of these two gallant British subjects?' Soldiers have always hated the Foreign Office, thought Jock as he struggled to his feet. They want to shoot it out; we try to talk it out.

'If it seems appropriate, we will of course talk to ministerial colleagues in the Ministry of Defence but I hardly think it has come to that yet.'

And so it went on for another ten minutes. Jock stalled, lost his customary smoothness, hesitated, as he tried both to conceal the information that he had and yet not to deceive the House of Commons. Bruce Gordon sat grimly by his side throughout the inquisition, staring ahead. On Jock's other side was Greg Stevens, the Chief Whip, mentally noting all Jock's hesitations and filing them away for future reference.

The last question was the worst. It came from a Tory MP who had long resented Jock's ministerial appointment, thinking himself a good deal more intelligent than Jock and regarding himself as an expert in foreign affairs.

'As soon as my Honourable Friend gets back to his office, in between catching up on those Foreign Office telegrams that he has not yet read,' – a pause for supporting derisive laughter – 'will he send a message to the Foreign Secretary asking for his instant return to London? It is clear that, in the Foreign Secretary's absence abroad, a potentially dangerous situation, in which the lives of British subjects are involved, is likely not to receive the careful attention that it deserves.'

Jock flushed as he rose to his feet and gripped the Despatch Box. He started angrily: 'I resent what my Honourable Friend . . .' but then changed his mind and said: 'I can assure my Honourable Friend that the Foreign Secretary has been kept closely in touch with all the developments on this very difficult issue. We will continue to keep him fully advised.'

The Speaker announced the next piece of business, a debate on the problems of transport in south-eastern England. Members rose to their feet and ambled towards the various exits. Jock swept

24

together his various bits of paper and moved back along the Front Bench towards the doors behind the Speaker's Chair. Other Ministers and the Whip on the Front Bench looked at him in silence and no one spoke to him until he had passed into the long corridor behind the Speaker's Chair. And then the Prime Minister, who had followed him out of the Chamber, muttered to him, 'You fool. All you had to do was say that the whole House would understand if you didn't share with them the information that you had because of the delicate situation. You didn't have to commit yourself to having any information at all, but that would have let you off the hook and got the House with you. I'm disappointed. A poor performance; not like you. You can do a lot better.'

The Prime Minister moved quickly away across the corridor towards his own room, followed by a covey of civil servants and private secretaries. Jock stood for a moment, stranded in the middle of the corridor, horrified at what Bruce Gordon had said to him but realizing that it was perfectly true. If he had taken that line with the House, asking for the House's sympathy in not being pressed too hard to reveal secret information, he would have got away with it. His face burnt. His private secretary, Peter Pirelli, came up to him.

'That was pretty difficult, Minister, but I thought you did as well as you could under the circumstances.' Loyal fellow, thought Jock. That's a polite way of saying I did bloody badly.

'How was it?' asked Anthea anxiously of Peter, the moment the Minister was back in the Foreign Office and on the other side of the door between his room and the private office.

'Awful,' replied Peter. 'It wasn't the Minister's fault. Of course, he couldn't tell the House anything positive and they wanted to hear that the men were safe and sound or that we were sending in the tanks to get them. Even so, he made a hash of it. The Prime Minister was there all the time listening, and looked grim, and so did the Chief Whip.'

'Oh dear, poor Jock,' murmured Anthea. 'He'll mind tremendously. He worries such a lot.'

'He'll have to get used to it on this one. Everyone always gets stirred up about hostages. They're dynamite.' Peter had been in the private office for nearly three years and remembered the agonies that Jock's predecessor had been put through when a holidaymaker had disappeared near Tyre a year before. He had turned up three days later after a long and exhausting stay in a Lebanese brothel, but not before the Foreign Office had been bombarded with questions by his constituency Member of Parliament, his wife and the national press.

Peter sighed and moved towards the stacks of files on his desk, some neatly tied with pink ribbon. He picked up the one on top, and, summoning up the resources of an orderly mind, concentrated on the protocol problems of a visit from the King of Morocco to the United Kingdom.

Jock did not get home until after eleven. He had had to vote at ten o'clock and again at 10.20 and, to his extreme irritation, yet again at 10.40. The second and third votes were formalities and the Government won with a huge majority, most Opposition MPs having already gone home after the first vote. Jock had asked the Whip responsible for pairing if he would let him go home, too, pointing out that he had an enormous lot of work to prepare for the next day. But his request had been sharply refused, a reflection, he thought, on his wretched performance at the Despatch Box that afternoon.

'Bugger the Whips,' he said to Angela Fawke, the Social Security Secretary of State, when he bumped into her in the corridor by the library. 'They're nothing but little Hitlers in depressing grey suits.'

'Don't be petulant, Jock,' said Angela. 'They're only doing their job. How did you get on with the PM this morning?'

'Better than I expected.'

'What were you seeing him about?' asked Angela.

'Can't tell you, I'm afraid, but the PM was almost civil.'

'Perhaps he fancies you,' Angela's mouth twisted in a half-crooked smile which Jock found strangely attractive.

'Don't be silly,' he said. 'I'm not his type.'

★

He was tired and irritated when he let himself into the flat in Warwick Gardens and his irritation increased as he heard Mary in full flood down the telephone in the drawing room, her voice rising and falling and sounding fraught. He pushed the front door noisily shut and heard the telephone being quickly replaced on the receiver and Mary rushing down the passage to greet him.

'Darling,' she started, but Jock interrupted her.

'You're always on the telephone,' he said grumpily as he put his two red boxes down on the floor, 'and usually to the Continent. It plays havoc with the telephone bills.'

'Oh, come off it, darling. I bet you spend far more at your Club and you wouldn't want me not to talk to my friends.'

'I spend very little at my Club,' said Jock pompously, 'and I can't really afford to be a member.'

Mary noticed the bleak look on Jock's face, but she smiled warmly at him, put her arms round him and gave him a long hug.

They had been married for fifteen years. Mary had entered into Jock's political battles with zest. A complex person herself, she enjoyed the simple duels of political life when everything to do with the opposition is bad and everything on your side is good. She urged Jock on to verbal onslaughts at election time that he found faintly embarrassing, and she used her own platform as President of the Kensington and Fulham Conservative Women's Club to pour torrents of sarcasm over the Socialist Party, Animal Rightists and Ban-the-Bombers. If asked what she believed in, she always replied: 'God, the Conservative Party and Jock.' She was deeply ambitious for him and regretted that, particularly now their two eldest boys were both at Westminster, Jock's old school, they could not afford to give dinner parties to which Jock could ask his ministerial colleagues and influential figures from the Conservative hierarchy. She loved eating out in fashionable restaurants and covering her elegant figure in glamorous clothes, but the wife of another minister, with whom she sometimes played tennis in Vincent Square, had introduced her to Pandora, the up-market

27

second-hand clothes shop, a few years earlier and she had quickly acquired the talent of making the nearly new look as if it had just been unwrapped from tissue paper within a large, olive-green Harrods' box.

Mary took a metaphorical deep breath, put her arm through Jock's and led him along the passage towards the drawing room. She knew from long experience that she would have to wheedle him out of his grumpy mood.

'How did it go?' she asked. 'I heard you were answering questions in the House about those poor men in Beirut. I bet you did it well.'

'No, I didn't,' Jock contradicted her. 'I made a mess of it. Let's have a drink.'

'I'd love one. I've been waiting for you to come home.'

They walked together into the high-ceilinged drawing room, a room that Jock loved, with its two comfortable sofas, masses of bookshelves and four good contemporary English pictures on the walls. The fact that the fire was imitation – gas burning bogus coals – didn't bother him too much. He poured Mary a small glass of whisky which he topped up with orange juice. For himself, he poured a large one to which he added a small amount of water. They sat down on the sofa, close to each other, and slowly, painfully, as if she was extracting a tooth, Mary got out of him all the details of the disastrous Question Time in the House of Commons.

'I made such a bloody fool of myself,' Jock said, and he explained about the messages between Beirut and Tripoli and the new diplomatic car, and his meeting with the Prime Minister at Number 10 that morning. He never held anything back from Mary, however secret, and, sympathizing, she urged him on as he went over the detail of the dilemma in which he had been placed in the House. When he told her of the Prime Minister's rebuke, she squeezed his arm affectionately and assured him, however much she didn't believe it, that the Prime Minister was far, far too busy and would have forgotten all about the incident by the following morning.

As he talked, and as the whisky permeated his body, some of the tension eased and the bubbles of anger within him began to subside.

None the less, when they finally went to bed and Mary, in a friendly and comforting way, pushed her body up against his and started to soothe him, gently stroking his cheek and running her tongue round the inside of his ear, he muttered:

'I'd better get to sleep as soon as possible. Sorry. Awful lot of work tomorrow.'

'Of course. I understand, darling,' said Mary. 'Goodnight. Sleep well, my love, and don't worry too much.'

3

Wednesday 26 June

The sky that had been totally dark showed a first, gentle dusting of light. Cocks started to crow, that most archaic of sounds, dogs to stir, birds to move in the trees. The muezzin, loud at first and then sinking to a plaintive murmur, began reminding the faithful to pray. The call was picked up, echoed and repeated from loudspeakers, new additions to old minarets, throughout the city. What had been quiet and empty was suddenly noisy, strident, full of human endeavour with its undertone of agony and strife.

Bob struggled to turn over from his right side to his left. Hands roped together and a chain twisted round his ankles, a rag blindfolding him, he managed only by rocking backwards and forwards until he gathered enough momentum to roll from one side to the other. The thin heap of straw on which he lay scratched his back through his cotton shirt. He smelt vile. Urine had soaked through his trousers and wetted the dirty straw beneath him. He felt more alone and deserted than he had ever felt before. Suddenly, he heard the sound of footsteps, coming up the stairs to the room in which he had been held since Sunday evening. He raised himself and drew himself up so that his back was propped against the concrete wall.

He heard a stiff lock being turned, and a door pushed open. The steps came towards him and automatically he turned his face in the direction where he supposed another human to be. The butt of a rifle hit him violently between neck and shoulder. He felt the crack of a bone and pain flooded down his arm into his fingers, overwhelming him. As he gasped, the rifle hit the other shoulder in the same place. He cried out. There was another sharp, violent, agonizing thud on his shoulder and instinctively he jerked on the rope, trying vainly to put his hands up to protect himself. Tears flooded into his eyes as he gasped for breath, and pain coursed so violently through his body that he started to retch.

'That's to stop you moving about, English bastard. Lie down on the floor till we come to fetch you in the morning. Go on. Lie down, flat.'

'I can't,' sobbed Bob. 'I can't move at all.'

'Yes, you will.' The rifle butt jammed against his collarbone and pushed. Bob imagined lumps of bone grinding against each other. He gasped and sobbed. The rifle was turned, like a screw-driver forcing its way into his body, and he was pushed down relentlessly, until he collapsed, a pathetic bundle, on to the straw.

'Here you stay till we decide what to do with you,' murmured an ugly Arab voice, threatening, rising and falling in anger. 'One day, one month, one year, Inshallah. We shall see.'

'Where's Les?' Bob struggled to get the words out.

'Leys? Leis?' the Arab voice mispronounced absurdly. 'Leis who?'

'My friend. The one you took with me.'

'There is no Leis. You are alone. If you try to escape you will be killed. Probably you will be killed anyway, by those we give you to. We shall see. You will be brought some food this evening.'

'I must . . . I must shit.'

There was silence. Bob sobbed again. 'I must go to the toilet.'

'Toy-let? Toy-let?' The Arab voice laughed. 'When you do not eat, you do not shit. Soon you will not need to shit.'

Suddenly, out of the black blindness, a boot kicked Bob on the side of the stomach. Then again. And again. He didn't scream, but he gasped for breath, and fought against being sick. The kicking stopped.

'That, English bastard, will make you think, not just about shitting. You and your friends have helped the Jews steal our land. You have stood and watched while Jews and Christians killed Muslims. You have brought Israel into Lebanon, now you will share some of our pain.'

Steps moved away to the door, a hinge creaked, a key turned

31

in the lock and the steps, further retreating down the stairs, died away.

Pain and misery filled every corner of Bob's being and overwhelmed his mind. He struggled to think of Sally, his wife, and their children but there was only the silence with which to share his pain. The muezzin sounded clear and loud from nearby, and he stumbled into the prayers that he knew. He started to repeat: 'Our Father . . .' but when he came to 'forgive them that trespass against us,' he gagged and tears poured down his cheeks. There were only shadows in the room with him.

The headlines were rude.

MINISTER DITHERS OVER HOSTAGES said the *Daily Mail*. FOREIGN OFFICE COCK-UP said the *Mirror*. *The Times* was more guarded in its approach: FEARS FOR SAFETY OF TWO BRITONS IN BEIRUT. But the text below was unkind:

Foreign Office Minister, Jock Meldrum-Ross MP, failed to dispel worries in the House of Commons yesterday afternoon about the fate of the two British aid workers, Bob Janes and Les Harrington, who have now been missing in Beirut since Sunday. Mr Meldrum-Ross, in a hesitant appearance in the Commons, was heckled by both sides of the House as he refused to give any clear answers to persistent questioning. The impression increased in Whitehall yesterday evening that the Foreign Office were uncertain whether or not the two men had been captured by terrorists. But the overwhelming view in Beirut is that they are now the prisoners of one of the many militant Arab groups, probably Hizbollah. A number of extreme statements in recent weeks, accusing Britain of taking sides with the Maronite Christian party in Beirut, have been attributed to this group.

No one has yet claimed to be holding the two men but a number of witnesses have come forward, saying that they saw the two men being bundled into a large car around 6 pm local time, (4 pm BST) on Sunday. They are likely to be used as bargaining-counters between local terrorists, in association with the PLO or the Syrians, and the West.

Jock's reading was interrupted by Peter Pirelli entering the room. In his hand he had two flimsy pieces of paper which he put on the desk in front of Jock. The first was an urgent telegram from Harare. It read:

FOREIGN SECRETARY HAS DECIDED ON IMMEDIATE RETURN TO LONDON. HIS PLANE WILL LEAVE HARARE AT TEN HUNDRED LOCAL TIME THIS MORNING AND SHOULD ARRIVE AT NORTHOLT AT EIGHTEEN HUNDRED BST. ROBERTSON.

John Robertson was a fussy High Commissioner in Zimbabwe. Jock remembered him as a diplomat who spent more time with his wife drawing up elaborate guest-lists to celebrate the Queen's Birthday or the arrival of a group of British businessmen than considering Britain's long-term relations with the country to which he was posted. His nickname in the office was Long John, as he was rumoured never to discard his heavy woollen underpants, even in tropical climates. He will be furious, thought Jock, at having his well-laid plans for the Foreign Secretary messed up. I bet that means the end of a large drinks party and of a pompous, black-tie dinner at the High Commission tonight.

The second flimsy was headed 'Top Secret'. The message said:

GCHQ Cheltenham report the following decoded intercept from Tripoli to Beirut. AIR FREIGHTER WILL ARRIVE IN BEIRUT AT 2000 TONIGHT, LOCAL TIME, CARRYING THE NEW EMBASSY CAR YOU REQUESTED. ESSENTIAL THAT YOU ENSURE THAT CUSTOMS FORMALITIES ARE WAIVED. CABLE CONFIRMATION OF SAFE ARRIVAL OF VEHICLE AND THEN AWAIT FURTHER INSTRUCTIONS.

Jock had hardly finished reading the message when his private secretary walked back into the room.

'Minister, Number 10 have just been on the line. The Prime Minister is calling a meeting about the Beirut hostages in one hour's time, at ten-thirty. He expects you to be there. His private secretary says that the Service Chiefs will also be present, and

Spacemead, the SAS Commanding Officer. Anthea is organizing your briefing.'

'Oh, God,' said Jock. He paused, then said: 'All right. Postpone the visit of the Egyptian Ambassador until later today. Make certain you've got in the brief all the Middle East and Near East overnight telegrams that are relevant. Ask Mr Crichton to come and see me and get hold, as soon as possible, of the head of the London Office of the UN Rehabilitation Agency. You know, the people that Janes and Harrington were working for.'

'Yes, Minister.'

The private secretary walked out of the room and the heavy door swung shut. Jock leaned back in his chair and gazed at the ornate Victorian ceiling. He followed, for a second or two, the intricacies of the moulding and wondered how it was that the Victorians had had time to create such elaborate buildings when, at the same time, they were conquering a large part of the world in the name of Trade and Christianity. Then his mind switched back to the meeting an hour ahead. I've not met the head of the SAS, he thought. I wonder whether he is as tough and wiry as they are all made out to be . . . Despite the bloody morning papers, it's fun to be involved in this in Robert's absence, but what the hell will happen next . . . Those poor buggers in Beirut . . . Where will the terrorists move them to? The Muslim lot don't usually kill their hostages. They've kept them all alive so far . . . They must be scared out of their wits. I must find out where their wives are. His thoughts were racing on as the door swung open, and Alastair Crichton walked into the room with Peter Pirelli.

'Sit down, Alastair, Peter,' said Jock.

They sat in two chairs on the other side of his desk. Jock looked across and noticed that Alastair was looking more immaculate than ever. The knot of his Brigade of Guards tie nestled between the snowy wings of his starched white collar. Right in the middle of his tie, not a fraction of a millimetre out of place, was a diamond horseshoe tie-pin with a small ruby in the heart of the horseshoe. A striped blue-and-white shirt under a dark charcoal-grey suit, with a deep red handkerchief pouring lavishly out of the top pocket, completed the Under Secretary's outfit. His cheeks were shaven to a beautiful smoothness and there was a faint whiff of Royal Yacht surrounding well-combed brown hair. The Under Secretary looked as if he had not a care in the world, and Jock found it hard to decide whether that was indeed the truth or a pretence put on for the benefit of passing ministers. He felt almost jealous.

'The meeting with the PM starts in precisely fifty minutes, Minister,' said Alastair. 'You've seen all the telegrams. There's nothing new to report. Adams, our Ambassador in Beirut, has not picked up any further sign of Janes and Harrington since his message to us yesterday that they were alive and probably being held in Beirut. Beyond that, they seem to have disappeared off the face of the earth.'

'Are their wives in Beirut?' asked Jock.

'Yes, they are. Both men are married, and with young children. The Ambassador's been in touch with the wives – he told me so on the telephone yesterday afternoon – but they haven't received any messages from anyone since the two disappeared on Sunday evening. They haven't heard a word.'

The telephone rang on Jock's desk.

'It's Jerome Smitherman on the line for you, Minister,' said Anthea Wheeler from his private office. 'He's the London head of the UN Rehabilitation Agency.'

'Put him through,' said Jock.

Seconds later, he heard the strong American accent of Mr Smitherman greeting him. He asked whether the Agency had any news of the two men.

'Christ, no,' he was told. 'We've put out feelers all over Beirut. We've told our fellas in Damascus to keep their ears wide open. Every UN post in the Med's been alerted. So far, not a smell nor a hint. Even our usual sources are about as useful as suntan oil in December.'

Jock winced and said: 'Let us know as soon as you hear anything.'

'You bet. They're good guys, we don't want to lose them.'

'Will you give my personal good wishes to their wives in Beirut, and tell them that all of us in London are thinking about them and will do everything we possibly can to find their husbands?'

'Yes, sir.' Mr Smitherman accented the 'sir' so heavily that Jock wondered if he was being mocked.

'Do you think the wives are in any danger? Should you fly them back to London, or to New York, to the Agency Headquarters?'

'Not necessary at this moment in time. But if they get threatening letters from one of the terrorist groups, if anyone says they're going to bomb their apartments or shoot the kids, then we'll have to think again.'

That's small comfort, thought Jock. 'Well,' he said. 'Remember to keep us in touch if you hear the slightest suspicion of a piece of news, and if you want any help from us, if there is anything you think we can do, let me know personally.'

He put the telephone down and told Alastair Crichton and Peter Pirelli that the UN Agency had no more information than they had, indeed, rather less, as they had not even picked up the rumour that they were alive and in Beirut.

'Why is the Foreign Secretary flying back, Alastair?' asked Jock.

'I don't know, Minister. His private office haven't told me anything special. Presumably he thinks this is going to blow up and get worse, so he had better be here in London rather than in a distant corner of Africa.'

'I suppose so,' said Jock pensively. 'It doesn't seem like him to break off an important trip that has taken months of preparation just because two of our people have been taken hostage.'

'The Foreign Secretary has a sixth sense for trouble,' said Crichton enigmatically. An unusual glint came into his eye, as if the thought were a pleasant one.

'Well, prepare for it now. I can't believe that the meeting at Number 10 will be an easy one. They rarely are,' said Jock.

The Foreign Secretary's plane left Harare airport fifteen minutes before the meeting at Number 10 began. Robert Huggins sat in the front row of the RAF VC10, and wished that government ministers had a faster and more comfortable plane to fly in. He had tried to get the Prime Minister to buy a long-range Boeing 747 for the use of the Foreign Secretary in his constant trips around the world. But that was another of the many battles that he had lost.

'You can't be seen arriving at Canberra or Ottawa in an American plane, Robert,' the PM had said. 'What was good enough for Peter Carrington or Alec Douglas-Home is good enough for you. If the VC10 is a bit slower, it really doesn't matter. You and your Foreign Office colleagues can't get up to much mischief when you are thirty thousand feet above the earth.'

The Boeing, thought Robert, would have got him back to London in six to seven hours instead of the eight that the VC10 would take.

An RAF steward came up and offered him a drink. He thanked him, asked for a glass of orange juice and started to open one of the three black briefcases, all embossed with a rather faded royal coat of arms, that his private secretary had piled on the seat beside him. He was in the habit of working on government papers at every moment of the day and night, even as he fell asleep in bed, or between munches of toast, butter and marmalade at the breakfast table. His wife found it irritating, but Robert had been a minister for nine solid years and she had got used to having only the periodic personal conversation with him.

Then Robert stopped, as his hand fell on a thick bundle of papers. He looked out of the aeroplane window, saw that all the clouds had dropped away and they were flying north in a clear blue sky, and he asked himself just why was he returning to London four days earlier than planned. It had caused a lot of irritation to his hosts in Harare. Parties had been cancelled. Important meetings with the President and a number of senior ministers had been postponed. The High Commissioner's wife had burst into tears and he had had to placate her with a half-promise that her husband would get a knighthood next year. He hoped he had not been too specific about that.

It had been hard for him to give a clear reason as he did not know what it was himself. His political nose warned him that trouble lay ahead with the disappearance of the two Britons in Beirut. But he could perfectly well have left Jock Meldrum-Ross to deal with that. One of his private secretaries had rung him from London the previous evening, briefed him on the doings of the day and told him of Jock's difficulties at Question Time in the House. That did not particularly concern Robert. He knew how easy it was to get the mood of the House wrong, especially when there were critics from one's own Party as well as from the opposition. Jock was competent enough even if indecisive.

Huggins was an honest man and his motives for taking the sudden decision to cancel his African trip puzzled him. Was it that he was fearful that the man he had come to dislike so much, the First Lord of the Treasury, his own prime minister, might take the wrong decision and put the lives of the hostages into greater danger? Was he genuinely anxious about the Prime Minister's judgement or did he feel that, as Foreign Secretary, he must be present and be seen by the Party and the press to be in clear command of his office? He knew that, for the past few months, he had been concerned that key decisions had increasingly reflected Bruce Gordon's impetuosity and bad temper. He remembered the recent visit of the French President when, at the state banquet in his honour, the Prime Minister in his speech had sympathized with the President over recent violence in the streets of Paris and assured the President that he would not allow the perpetrators to reach Britain via the Channel Tunnel. The President became so angry at this unnecessary and public reference to his domestic troubles that he got his speech notes in the wrong order and muddled the elaborate compliments he paid to the Queen. His official visit was terminated half a day early and Huggins winced at the memory.

From the copy telegrams that had been sent to him in Harare, he guessed that a Cabinet committee would have to consider using the SAS to try and rescue the two Britons. If that went wrong, he mused, and such things usually did go wrong, that would put

Bruce Gordon into a bad light. The press would portray him as a rash, intemperate man, who was not suitable to lead the country for another five years. Huggins could try and divert the attention of the press, as he knew he had often tried to do in the recent past, or, this time, he could just let the dogs bark and not bother to stop them. The election was now only four or five months away. It had to take place by 15 November. Many thought that it would happen in October. Labour were now a few points ahead of the Conservatives in the polls. If this Beirut business gets really cocked up, thought Huggins, and if it is clearly Gordon's fault, that will put us another point or two down in the polls. It's just possible, only just possible, that the Parliamentary Party might then force him to resign before the summer holidays. With all the bad economic news, there's certainly many an MP who thinks he should go before the election is right on top of us. Damn difficult, though, to get rid of a PM in an election year. It leaves too much blood on the carpet, too many open wounds.

Huggins felt a twinge of personal ambition. After the election, he thought, if we win, and that's by no means certain, that will strengthen Bruce's hand. The new MPs will never vote against someone who's just won an election. I bet he will make a point of going to all their constituencies during the election campaign, speaking in their church halls, buttering up their wives, promising them that, within a year or two, they will have a ministerial job as he finds them so extraordinarily talented. I've already got my eye on you, that's what he will say, and they'll smile back at him. God, he's as bad as Lloyd George bribing the young members with his patronage. If I'm ever going to beat him, it has to be this side of the general election. I'll be sixty-one next year, soon they'll be looking for someone younger to lead the Party. Yet I think I've got so much to offer the country.

Robert Huggins' thoughts raced on and on, down tracks that he had only recently started to explore. The RAF steward reappeared and this time he asked for a glass of whisky as a replacement for his orange juice. When it appeared, he thanked the steward and contemplated the glass reflectively before raising it to his lips. His growing dislike of Bruce Gordon gnawed at him and had started to keep him awake at nights. Only a month ago, he had been publicly humiliated at the European Union summit when the Prime Minister had corrected him in front of journalists, saying that his views on the possibility of a single European passport were very much his own and did not represent those either of the majority of the Cabinet or of most British people. They were, what was the word Gordon had used? Yes, 'idiosyncratic'.

Huggins spluttered to himself as he remembered the incident. He was a courteous man, not at all given to bad temper. Indeed, many of his friends wished that he would spark more readily, stamp on his opponents' fingers and curse his enemies widely and vividly. But once the slow-burning fuse had been lit, it smouldered indefinitely and with intense heat.

He took a handful of crisps out of the bowl in front of him and, aimlessly, crunched his long, slender fingers round them until they were reduced to crumbs. Then he rubbed his palms together and squeezed the remains on to the floor. At least, he thought, lots of our MPs dislike Gordon much more than I do. They've been snubbed by him for some reason or other in the past year, treated as lobby-fodder and never as friends and helpers. Perhaps I've been too loyal to him for just too long. He caught the eye of the passing steward, and asked for another whisky.

'A large one and bring me some nuts with it, will you?' he said. The steward walked back along the gangway to the galley and shook his head as he poured the whisky. He liked to see cabinet ministers buried in their red boxes.

A solemnly quiet group entered the Cabinet Room and sat down with their backs to the long windows and to Horse Guards Parade. The Prime Minister was already seated in his chair in front of the fireplace with three civil servants around him. Immediately to his right was Roderick Turner, his principal private secretary. On his right again was Sir Peter Trout, a retired Ambassador, now attached to the Cabinet Office. The Prime Minister particularly liked his advice as he would anticipate the way in which the Foreign Office was thinking and, thus, advise the Prime Minister in advance how to counteract the arguments the Foreign Secretary would put forward. Like a successful chess player, he always knew a few moves ahead what those on the other side of the table were thinking and would slip the Prime Minister notes pointing out the flaws in arguments that they had not yet even advanced. He was extremely unpopular with Foreign Office officials, being seen as a Peter who had turned into a Judas Iscariot, and he revelled in this.

On the Prime Minister's left was Neil Hawthorne, a bright young man attached to the Cabinet Office from the Ministry of Defence. His job was to ensure that the military did not fool the Prime Minister with any of their arguments in favour of excessive amounts of equipment, men or money.

On the other side of the table, the Defence Secretary, Tony Castle, sat in the middle, Jock Meldrum-Ross, standing in for the Foreign Secretary, on his left, and beyond him Alastair Crichton. On the other side of the Defence Secretary was General Briggs, one of the Chiefs of Staff, and a small sparse man who had introduced himself to Jock in the anteroom as Colonel Spacemead, the new Commanding Officer of the SAS. He had taken over the command a month earlier. Beyond the Colonel sat two other men, neither of whom was known to Jock. He assumed that they were from GCHQ and M16. Everyone else in the room appeared to know them well, but never referred to them by name. The third man and the fourth man, thought Jock. At least, we no longer have to pretend that they don't exist.

The Prime Minister did not look up as they took their seats. He went on reading a dossier of papers, occasionally marking some of the typed lines with a red pen. The long thin room, with its elegant panelled walls and cluster of pillars at the anteroom end, was filled with an air of nervous expectancy. Jock had been to a number of meetings at Number 10 before, standing in for the Foreign Secretary, but he always hated these anticipatory moments; despite his experience, he could not help wondering whether he had all the right papers in the files that his officials had prepared for

41

him, whether he would find the right paper at the right time and whether he would manage to put the Foreign Office points to the Prime Minister without a cold douche of sarcasm being poured over him. He reached for the plain carafe of water in front of him and poured himself a glass.

'Is everyone here?' asked Bruce Gordon.

'Yes, Prime Minister,' Roderick Turner replied.

'Good. The position seems to be becoming a little clearer. Have you all seen the latest telegram from the Ambassador in Beirut? I was handed it ten minutes ago.'

'What is the reference number on it, Prime Minister?' asked General Briggs.

'3707, dispatched at eleven hundred local time this morning,' intervened Turner quickly.

Jock looked quickly in his file. Damn, he thought, I haven't got it.

'I don't seem to have that one,' said General Briggs.

'Nor I,' muttered Jock, looking angrily at Crichton who was engaged in studying the picture above the Prime Minister's head with the air of a connoisseur.

'Ah,' said the Prime Minister. 'The Foreign Office is out of date, as usual. I thought your department ran the communications services to our Embassies. It's certainly a large element in your budget.' He looked at Jock who did not reply.

'Roderick,' the Prime Minister continued. 'Get everyone a copy of this latest telegram. Meanwhile, I'll read it out to you:

PLO CONTACTS TODAY ADVISE JANES AND HARRINGTON STILL IN BEIRUT AND NEGOTIATIONS UNDER WAY FOR THEIR POSSIBLE TRANSFER TO LIBYANS. WILL CONTINUE SEARCH FOR WHERE-ABOUTS. LARGE AIR FREIGHTER WITH LIBYAN MARKINGS RE-PORTEDLY ARRIVED BEIRUT AIRPORT IN THE LAST HOUR. WILL ADVISE FURTHER. ADAMS.

'Roderick, read it to everyone again so that they can write down the contents,' ordered the Prime Minister as if he were leading a class of schoolchildren.

As the message from Beirut was read out once more, Bruce Gordon surveyed the men sitting opposite him. His usual sense of knowing more than anyone else filled his mind. He always made a point of being better briefed, better read, more up-to-date than everyone else present, whether it was a full Cabinet, a Cabinet committee or an unofficial meeting. This gathering came into the last category. It was an ad-hoc group that was not governed by Cabinet committee rules, called together by the Prime Minister's office in order to give him a range of opinions. He either agreed with these or not, at his own preference, but he would in due course tell the Cabinet what he had decided. Tony Castle, the Defence Secretary, was the only Cabinet member present. The Prime Minister was not very close to Castle. He had rarely invited him to Chequers but he had an increasing respect for him. He found that Castle, as he got to know his job better, was increasingly ready to contradict the opinions of the Chiefs of Staff, and their incessant demands for more money. Castle had better start the ball rolling, thought Gordon.

'Defence Secretary, what do you make of it?'

'The PLO are friends with the Libyans?' asked Castle, looking at the man from MI6.

'Yes,' he replied. 'They go up and down, but at the moment they are quite close. Gadaffi, of course, gives a lot of money to the PLO and to many of the terrorist groups in Beirut, except when there has been a row between them. Currently, the relations between Tripoli, Arafat and most of the Islamic Jihad are good. I think the Foreign Office would agree with that.'

'Yes,' said Jock. 'Our friends in Beirut recently reported a large increase in the money coming from Gadaffi either directly or through the PLO. PLO leaders have been seen in Tripoli recently. So there is good reason for close contacts between the Libyan Embassy in Beirut, and the PLO, and some of the Muslim terrorists.'

'Why has the Ambassador, Adams, bothered to mention in this telegram the arrival of the Libyan air freighter?' asked the Defence Secretary.

'We radioed to Beirut copies of the messages that we intercepted between Tripoli and Beirut a few days ago, so they will have understood the importance of the air freighter,' said the man from GCHQ. His tone implied that he regarded his companions round the table, with the possible exception of the Prime Minister, as ignorant fools who would have difficulty in understanding a standard opening move in a game of chess.

'Could our messages not have been intercepted in turn?' asked Castle.

'No,' said GCHQ. 'Beirut has our latest decoders. So we used the most up-to-date ciphers.'

'This isn't getting us very far,' said the Prime Minister impatiently. 'We now know that terrorists have got Janes and Harrington. We don't know precisely why they have got them. We have confirmation that a large Libyan air freighter has arrived in Beirut. We don't know why it's there. It's possible that it will have the new embassy car inside it that has been referred to in the earlier intercepts. We don't know, if so, why this car has been sent to Beirut rather than asking their embassy to buy another car locally. Is it because it is specially reinforced against terrorist bullets or bombs, or is it because it has been specially designed to smuggle the two Britons out of Beirut back to Tripoli? What do you think we should do now, General Briggs?' the Prime Minister snapped.

The General gawped across the table. He gave the impression that he wished anyone in the room had been asked to answer rather than he. His file was held up nervously in front of him, and if he could have used it as a shelter and hidden behind it, he would have done so.

'Well, I don't know, Prime Minister. Actually, there are a great many questions. We don't know why Janes and Harrington have been captured. As you said in your, if I may say so, masterly summing-up just now, there are few points to which we have clear answers. I think, on balance . . . I think we should wait until we have further news from Beirut about the aeroplane and its contents, if we can actually find that out.' There was an awkward pause round the table.

'Colonel Spacemead, your view?' asked Gordon.

'I have to disagree with General Briggs,' said the head of the SAS, with considerable relish. 'We don't have long. If there is a car inside the air freighter, and if it is intended to take Janes and Harrington back, presumably drugged, to Tripoli, this could happen pretty soon. I assume there is still some negotiation to be done between the Libyans and whatever terrorist group is holding them. They'll want a high price in money and arms for these two hostages, running into millions of dollars. I suspect we have a maximum of three or four days, so we can't afford to wait for decisions.'

While Spacemead was speaking, Crichton wrote a note and pushed it in front of Jock, suggesting that he support the Colonel. Jock cleared his throat and, as soon as Spacemead finished, caught the Prime Minister's eye.

'Minister of State,' said Gordon.

'Prime Minister, hm . . . I think . . . hm,' Jock coughed and then plunged in. 'I think Colonel Spacemead is right, Prime Minister. From the reports we have on previous negotiations about the release of hostages, we would expect the terrorists to hold out for a few days whilst they negotiated the highest possible price from the Libyans for the two men. Presumably Gadaffi wants them as some sort of reprisal for the air-raid of a few months back. He may intend to parade them through the streets. In any event, he will make full use of their being held in Libya. The terrorists will recognize their high value, but we can't be certain that these negotiations will take very long. If we are to try and intercept the air freighter with the car and the hostages on board as it flies out of Beirut, in my judgement we will have to take some decisions today.'

'In your judgement, or the Foreign Secretary's?' asked the Prime Minister.

'In mine. The Foreign Secretary is coming back from Harare, but he won't be here till six or seven this evening.'

'How very good of him to decide to return precipitately to these cold shores from sunny Africa and to give us the benefit of his wisdom and military experience.' The Prime Minister made this sound like the opening of a mayoral speech in Manchester City Hall, but Jock winced at the sarcasm that underlay the words.

'I agree with the Minister of State's line of thinking,' said the Defence Secretary quickly, almost defensively. 'I don't think, General Briggs, that we have time to sit back and wait for further messages from Beirut.'

'Very well, sir,' said General Briggs uncomfortably. 'In that case we have a plan of action ready which my staff prepared overnight, working in conjunction with Colonel Spacemead. It involves two of the SAS platoons setting off from Brize Norton by six o'clock this evening. They will fly to our military base in Akrotiri in southern Cyprus. They will take the minimum amount of equipment with them in two VC10s. They will be followed by heavier equipment in a Hercules. Two hours after they have left, a squadron of Tornado F3s, will fly from Coningsby, their station in Lincolnshire, to Akrotiri, where they will arrive within sixty minutes of the SAS. They will fly in what we call ferry configuration with drop tanks and full weapons load. The tanks will be jettisoned at Akrotiri, and the squadron of F3s will then be on quick reaction alert. Their objective will be to intercept the Libyan freighter after it has flown out of Beirut over the Mediterranean. Having intercepted the freighter and forced it to return and land at Akrotiri, the SAS will use appropriate methods to enter the plane and remove the hostages by force if the Libyan captain does not agree to open up the plane. That, sir, is a brief summary of the action plan at this stage. I have fuller details here if you would like those round the table to see them.'

'Yes, there's no reason why not,' said the Prime Minister. 'Everyone's cleared for security.'

Roderick Turner, the principal private secretary had just re-entered the Cabinet Room with copies of the Beirut telegram in his hand. He walked round to where General Briggs was sitting, picked up copies of the action plan from the Chief of Staff and distributed those along with the telegram.

'Are you in agreement with all of this, Defence Secretary?' asked the Prime Minister.

'I think it's a hideously risky exercise,' said Tony Castle. 'There are an awful lot of unanswered questions, but time really is not on our side. We've got to decide today whether we want to get the Tornados and the SAS in place in Akrotiri. We can take the decision here in principle to commit them to action. From what the Minister of State and MI6 have said, it's almost certain that we then have time for that decision to be confirmed at Cabinet tomorrow morning.'

The Prime Minister grimaced involuntarily. He did not like to have his decisions formally confirmed at Cabinet, but he wanted to keep the Defence Secretary on his side.

'Yes. Yes, that's important, of course.' Gordon paused and then added: 'Let's have a look at the detailed plan that General Briggs has given us.'

A sense of involvement in an extraordinary decision gripped Jock as he sat and studied the action plan. He was amazed to find himself reading this document and playing a part in the decision. He had been on dummy runs and training exercises with the SAS before, when their combat routines had been tried out, with himself as a fascinated bystander. This, though, was real, terribly real, and full of risk. As the air freighter flew west out of Beirut, it was clear to Jock from reading the plan that the Tornados out of Akrotiri might have very little time within their operating limits in which to engage the air freighter and force her back northwards to Cyprus. What did the Tornados do if the air freighter, a civilian plane, simply flew on? The same thought struck others.

'It seems,' said the Defence Secretary, 'that, depending of course on winds and the flight-path the Libyan plane takes, after leaving Beirut for only about fifteen minutes, possibly twenty, the Tornados, having intercepted the air freighter, will fly parallel to it, westward. That is on an assumption of normal speeds for the Ilyushin-18 freighter, if it is one of those. The plan also assumes that the planes will meet approximately one hundred miles west of Beirut and have either to separate or to turn north to Akrotiri

together approximately two hundred miles west of Beirut. That
could be the limit of their fuel capacity, depending on whether, at
any time, they have to fly at supersonic speeds to catch up with the
Ilyushin. If the Libyan air captain is stubborn, it gives precious
little time for negotiation. Is that right, General?' Castle had
spoken clearly and carefully, and this gave confidence to General
Briggs.

'Yes, Defence Secretary, that's correct. They will have to use
warnings over the radio and then their cannon in front of the plane.
They will also be carrying Sidewinder and Sky Flash missiles, in
case of hostile intervention by either the Libyans or, indeed, the
Egyptians. If they were to have to use these on the Ilyushin, and
actually to shoot it down, that would not achieve our aims.' Briggs
paused, looked across and saw the look of contempt flitting over
the Prime Minister's face. He added quickly: 'Of course, that is a
statement of the obvious. The plane would fall into the sea with the
hostages in it. All the crew and the passengers would be killed.
Indeed, we'd be unlikely to know whether the hostages were ever
actually in the plane or not.'

A chill silence fell over the room. Not since the end of the Gulf
War, had there been discussions in this room about battle plans,
gambits that would consciously lead to the deaths of a number of
people. Jock had never participated in such a discussion before in
all his life. He had worried routinely about hostages and those
dying from starvation in the Sudan, another part of his area of
responsibility, and those being beaten up and tortured in refugee
camps. But he had never taken part in a decision in which death
was clearly one of the likely results. He felt immensely excited but
in no hurry to condemn or commend the plan of action.

'What do you say, Colonel Spacemead?' the Prime Minister
asked.

'I don't think our part of the action should be too difficult, sir.
Once the Ilyushin has been grounded, we would treat it as a
regular hijack situation. We would attack the plane on either the
first night, or, possibly, on the second or third. By that time we will
have a clearer idea of whereabouts on the plane the two Britons are

– we should be able to establish that by bugging the plane once it has landed. We would expect to know exactly how many there are in the crew, and where they are standing or sitting. We'd then use our usual methods for entering the plane. Our aim, of course, will be to get the two Britons out alive, if necessary at the expense of the captain and the Libyan crew. That we cannot say in advance. We have practised on a mock-up of an Ilyushin-18. It doesn't present any unusual difficulties to us.'

There's a man I like to hear, thought Jock. He is treating this as if it were a shopping expedition to Sainsbury's, calm, detached, and he aims to get to the check-out when there isn't too long a queue.

'There'll be an enormous row, Prime Minister, when we intercept the plane. I imagine all the Arab countries will protest and some may threaten a trade war against us. And that'll be nothing compared to the row if we shoot the plane down, either accidentally or on purpose.' Sir Peter Trout, the Prime Minister's foreign affairs guru, spoke quietly but with great authority. Everyone round the Cabinet table listened intently to him. 'What is being suggested amounts to an act of piracy on the high seas. What the Defence Secretary and the Chiefs of Staff are putting forward will be seen by a great many of our friends throughout the world, not just the Arabs, as an armed attack on an unarmed plane based on a suspicion, no more than that, that two British hostages are on that plane and are being taken against their will to Libya. But it won't be any more than a suspicion. From what I've heard so far, there doesn't seem any chance of our having concrete evidence that Janes and Harrington are on the plane.' Sir Peter paused and then went on slowly in his prim but decisive voice: 'I have to say, Prime Minister, that I would advise against adopting this plan. I think the risks are far too great.'

There was a long pause and then the Prime Minister turned to Tony Castle. 'Defence Secretary, what do you think?'

'Prime Minister, I don't think we have any option but to adopt the plan, but only in principle at this stage. We authorize the SAS and the Tornados to move to Akrotiri as a first step. Whether they are used or not can wait until a later meeting of this committee or the approval of a full Cabinet. But we've got to get the planes and the men into position quickly so that they can be fully briefed and ready for action, if that's the final decision.'

Jock was impressed. Castle spoke decisively and evidently had no difficulty in making his mind up.

'Minister of State, what's your view?' the Prime Minister spoke softly, almost purring as he put the question to Jock. Jock paused, looked at Crichton who gave him a barely perceptible nod and then plunged in.

'Yes, I mean, hm, actually I haven't had a chance to consult the Foreign Secretary . . .' Jock's voice started to trail off.

'But you're sitting here in the Foreign Secretary's place,' said the Prime Minister. 'Presumably you have some ideas.'

'Yes, and I'm sure . . .' Jock paused before he said the final words, 'the Foreign Secretary would in principle support what the Defence Secretary has said. Of course, he'd want to study all the details with great care, but we're very anxious in the office not to let British hostages anywhere in the world be used as bargaining tools by their captors.'

'Quite,' said the Prime Minister and then paused and reflected for a moment. 'Very well, that's decided. We will accept the clear recommendation of the Foreign Office, supported by the Defence Secretary.' The civil servants scribbled in their notebooks. 'And we'll agree in principle with the action plan that the Chiefs of Staff have put forward.' He nodded towards General Briggs. 'As a first step, the SAS will embark this evening for Akrotiri and they will be joined there by a squadron of fully armed Tornados from Lincolnshire. I'll inform the Cabinet of this tomorrow, Defence Secretary. The actual use of the planes can be approved later, if necessary by consultation between us all over the telephone if there's not enough time to call an urgent meeting.' The Prime Minister looked around him as he gathered up his papers and then gazed across the table directly at Jock. 'I hope the Foreign Office is right,' he said. 'As the Defence Secretary commented, it's a very risky business.'

4

Thursday 27 June

A hand shook the Prime Minister's shoulder. He struggled to wake. Climbing out of a deep, comfortable pit of warmth and forgetfulness, he opened his eyes and saw a uniformed attendant standing apprehensively, head forward, in front of him.

'What time is it?' he growled.

'Just after six, sir. I am sorry to wake you, but your instructions were to be told if any telegrams came in from Beirut. The duty clerk at the Foreign Office has just sent over this one.'

'Give it to me. Get me my dressing gown . . . please,' he added, as a reluctant afterthought.

The other half of the bed was empty, with a second duvet lying unrumpled over the mattress. Although the Prime Minister's wife had been dead for a few years, he continued to sleep in a double bed, on the same side of the bed as he'd always slept in when his wife was with him, and her duvet remained in place almost as a memorial to her. The small table by that side of the bed had four books on it. A book-marker protruded from the top one showing the page which his wife had been reading a short time before her death.

The attendant brought over his dressing gown and held it out for him. He struggled to put it on, getting his arm caught half-way down the sleeve, and the attendant moved quickly to help him.

'That's all right. That's all right. Leave me alone, will you?' he growled. He walked over to his dressing table between the windows overlooking Downing Street, sat down heavily on a chair and read a long telegram from Beirut, signed by Adams, that the attendant handed him. This told how the Defence Attaché, Colonel Moberly, had seen a black Mercedes driven down the

ramp of the air freighter, an Ilyushin-18 carrying the colours of
Libyan Airlines. It had driven straight across the tarmac and the
exit barriers had been raised for it with no checking. There'd been
one passenger sitting beside the driver, wearing Arab dress and a
red headscarf. The Defence Attaché had not recognized either the
driver or the passenger but he had recorded the registration on the
number-plate and he was now following the Mercedes on the road
back to Beirut from the airport. The telegram was timed 0700
local time.

They're two hours ahead of us, thought the Prime Minister.
Moberly, whoever the hell he is, must have been out all night
hovering round the airport. He handed the telegram back to the
attendant and asked him to make certain that it was in his morning
box. Without another word, he turned back to his bed. I bet the
bugger loses him, he thought as he sank below his duvet and then
his memory started to prick him and he tried to grasp the straw
which was floating around at the back of his mind. Moberly,
Moberly. Why did the name have such an unpleasant ring about it
for him? Had the man fouled something up at some stage of his
career and that was why he was now stuck in Beirut? Gordon
seemed to remember being very angry with Moberly. He tried to
grasp the memory and put it into concrete form but he couldn't
visualize the incident. He had a growing, uncomfortable feeling
that Moberly was a fool. Had he shouted at him in front of his
senior officers or told his private secretary to send someone a
memo refusing him promotion? He was sure the man was an ass.
Perhaps he should get Roderick Turner to ask the Ministry of
Defence about him, but would they tell him the truth? He tossed
and turned under his duvet, put out a hand instinctively towards
the empty side of the bed and then withdrew it. He fell asleep
wondering why the name of Moberly irritated him so much.

At much the same time, 2000 miles to the south-east, Bob woke
quickly. His shoulders ached violently. The smell of the straw
under him was nauseating and his clothes stuck to his body. He felt

dirt soak through him from chest to spine. The night before, he had been given an old metal bowl with some lumps of chicken, boiled vegetables and rice in it, surrounded by slimy grease. He had eaten it with his fingers. He longed to shit, and he thought he would soon burst into his trousers.

The key was turning in the door and steps came towards him. This time he did not move. He lay as he was, his body flinching in anticipation of a kick, of more bloody pain. Like sitting in a dentist's chair, he thought. You don't know when the pain will begin.

Then a shoe started nuzzling against his bruised side. He froze.

'Wake up! Wake up!' said the purr of an Arab voice. Bob groaned aloud.

'I am awake,' he said. 'I need to shit. For God's sake don't kick me any more. But I must shit.'

'I will bring you a bucket, and then we will talk.'

The steps retreated. Talk? thought Bob. Talk? Better talk than kick. I mustn't cry out this time. I mustn't yell. I must hold on to myself. I will say prayers, anything. And he stumbled for the words of the Lord is my Shepherd.

The door swung open again, and steps came towards him. 'Turn your head to the side,' said the Arab.

Bob turned, his body stiff, expecting thudding pain some-where. He clenched his hands, fingers touched the back of his head, and he flinched.

'Let go,' murmured the Arab. 'Unlike the fanatics in Hizbollah, we do not want you to know us only by the sound of our feet. We are not frightened of your seeing our faces, so I shall untie the blindfold round your head.'

The knot was undone, the chain removed from his ankles, and Bob blinked in the half-light. He looked first at the pile of filthy, smelly straw beneath him, and then looked up. He saw an Arab of medium height, thick black hair, moustache, long nose, a scar down the right cheek, wearing a brown, open robe with trousers under-neath, an old black belt into which a revolver was stuck, and a red-checked headcloth with two black bands around the top of his head.

53

'Here's your bucket, and some newspaper. Do what you need to do.'

Bob struggled, but couldn't raise himself.

'My shoulders hurt too much, and I'm too stiff to get up.'

The Arab slipped behind Bob, roughly put his arms under his armpits and in a strong heave, raised Bob to his feet.

'Christ,' said Bob, feeling faint. 'That hurt.'

'But you are standing on your feet. Better that than lying dead. Go into the corner over there and do what you need to do.'

Bob took the bucket and stumbled off. He shat, urinated, turned and looked out of the window. He saw a grey house on the other side of the road, its concrete walls dirty and windows covered in dust. He heard people walking in the streets below and, over to the right, the top of a line of pine trees. In the distance, he heard the heavy sound of lorries or buses and heard car horns being blown. The sun was half-way up the sky to his left. Bob guessed it was around eight. It was already hot. We must be in South Beirut, somewhere off the road to the airport, he thought. He turned round, put the bucket down on the floor and shuffled back towards the Arab who was looking at him all the time.

'Do not think of shouting. Our friends are all around us and you will only be hurt. Yesterday, I brought you pain. I could make it much worse,' said the Arab. 'Today I want to ask you some questions and I have brought you coffee, to help your memory, wassab, as they say in Lebanon, medium sweet, as the English like it.'

He pointed towards a rough table with four chairs standing round it a few feet away. He sat down in one of the chairs and Bob moved hesitantly over and sat down with him.

'My name is Faisal. I am a Palestinian,' said the Arab. 'I hate the English for giving my homeland to the Jews, for allowing Christians to worship in holy places where there should only be Muslims. You I hate even more for you have been working for the Americans who are helping the Israelis to kill us in Sabbra and Chatila. Why have you spied for them?'

'But I haven't,' protested Bob. 'I am a relief-worker for the UN Rehabilitation Agency.'

'You lie,' said Faisal. 'We have been following you and your friend. When you visit the Bekaa Valley, when you go on to South Lebanon, you are always taking notes, writing details in your little book.'

'But we've got to do that,' Bob protested. 'My job is to map and then to improve the water-supply to the villages. We can't do that without asking for information. I am a water-resources specialist. My friend, Les Harrington, is a civil engineer. Ask around, you will find that we have helped many who grow fruit and vegetables to sell in the Beirut market. Our office . . .'

'I know where your office is,' said the Arab angrily. 'We have watched you, and we have seen where you go. But we know you send long radio messages to Geneva and to New York. You are sending details of the Palestinian forces, saying how we are to be shelled and bombed.'

'Never!' shouted Bob. 'Never! Never! If we ever stumbled on military information, we never sent it back to our headquarters. It doesn't interest us – it's not our business. We are here for the United Nations. We are here to help the people of Lebanon by bringing them more water. You must believe me, for I am telling the truth.' Bob paused and then said urgently: 'And now you must get me a doctor because I think my collarbone is broken. It needs setting, and I just can't stand the pain. And I want to know where Les Harrington, the one you captured with me, where he is. Is he all right? Is he dead? I want to see him.'

Faisal looked at Bob for a long time. He held Bob in his gaze and searched his face. Then he said: 'I am going to tie your hands in front of you. That will give you less pain. I will talk to my friends and you will think whether you are telling me the truth or not. I will be back this evening, and you will search your mind in order to tell me all the truth. If you lie to me you will suffer horrible pains.'

'Is Les alive?'

'He is, at the moment, alive.'

The Arab got up and crossed Bob's arms in front of him. Bob jerked with the sudden pain, but his wrists were held closely together and rope was tied round them, and double-knotted. Faisal did the same to his ankles, then he moved in front of Bob and stood looking at him without saying a word. A minute or so passed and then the Arab walked away, opened the door and went out, turning the key in the lock.

The two leading motor-cyclists swept to the right into the narrow street at the end of which, on the left-hand side, stood the Residence of the British Embassy. Immediately behind, tyres squealing, came the Ambassador's Jaguar. It took the corner at thirty miles an hour. The car was armour-plated, as protection against bomb attacks. This added nearly half a ton to its weight and Morris, the driver, had to tug at the steering wheel in order to take the corner smoothly. Immediately behind the Jaguar were another two armed motor-cyclists. They leaned gracefully over into the curve and then followed the Jaguar up the short tree-lined street as it zigzagged between concrete blocks. On both sides of the street were high wire fences and barricades, turning the street into a cul-de-sac. If a terrorist threw a bomb at the Residence, he would then have to turn round and go out the way he had come, passing the guard houses 200 yards back. The intention was that he should not get out alive.

Benedict Adams, CBE, Her Majesty's Ambassador and Envoy Extraordinary to the State of Lebanon, bent to get out of the car, and then walked quickly past four guards, all carrying automatic rifles, up the steps to the front door of the Embassy. As he reached it, it opened, pulled back with split-second timing by an Arab messenger, wearing an immaculate white shirt with the royal coat of arms sewn on to the breast pocket, and neat, dark blue trousers.

'Is Colonel Moberly here?' the Ambassador asked.

'Yes, sir. He's waiting upstairs, outside the quiet room.'

The Ambassador ran up two flights of steps, walked along a short corridor and turned into the third door on his right. He walked through another brilliantly lit room and found his Defence Attaché sitting in a chair. He was reading a copy of *Country Life*, and smiling to himself. As he saw the Ambassador coming into the room, he pushed the magazine away and jumped quickly to his feet. The chair fell backwards on to the floor with a loud clatter.

'Good morning, Ambassador,' said Colonel Moberly, and bent over to pick up the chair.

'We'll go into the quiet room,' said the Ambassador, without acknowledging Moberly's greeting.

He walked to the far end of the room, pressed a catch, and a piece of shelving lined with fake books swung away, revealing a bulky door with a large combination lock. The Ambassador twiddled the rings on the lock for some seconds, got the numbers into the right places, pulled the large steel door-handle downwards, and the door swung open. Inside was a brightly lit room that looked like a cabin on a boat. It had no outside windows, two supporting columns in the middle, a narrow table between the columns and four chairs. The ceiling was low on account of the insulated lining that completely surrounded the room. No listening device, however powerful, could pick up the details of conversation that went on in the room.

Moberly ducked his head and followed the Ambassador inside. The Ambassador shut the door, sat down and motioned to Moberly to do the same. Despite the heat, Moberly was dressed for a day at the races at Goodwood. He was wearing beautifully creased light grey trousers, suede shoes, pale blue shirt with a faint herringbone pattern on it, a Rifle Brigade tie and a Greenjackets blazer. His expression was one of near-permanent happiness as if he knew the horse he had backed was about to win the race. He sat down opposite the Ambassador and waited.

'Get on with it,' said the Ambassador. 'For God's sake, what happened?'

'I'm sorry, Ambassador. The buggers got away. Seven am, I chased the black Mercedes from the moment it left the airport. It wasn't going very fast, I suppose because of the amount of armour plating on it. We went along the autostrada, went over the green line by the Museum crossing, through the Bois du Boulogne and into South Beirut. He was driving in the direction of the sea. I was following all the time, trying not to get too close. Then an American car, a Buick, I think, overtook me and got between me and the Mercedes. A boy ran out into the road – I had to brake to avoid hitting him.'

The Colonel paused, apparently enjoying the suspense that he was trying to build up.

'A pity one isn't allowed to smoke in the quiet room,' he said.

'You know perfectly well you're not allowed to smoke in here. Nor am I. Nor are any of us. It's hot enough and smelly enough without fumes being puffed around.'

'Of course, Ambassador. It's just that I've had a bad night. A cigarette would have helped.'

A well-groomed hand took a cigarette case out of his pocket, tapped it and put it inside again.

'Well, go on, man. What happened then?'

'The boy slipped on the road in front of me. Most unfortunate. I had to brake violently, and eventually he got up and walked on. By that time, I had lost sight of both the Buick and the Mercedes. I went down the road as fast as I could, looked up the side streets to the left and the right, but there was no sign of the Mercedes. Eventually, I turned up a street to the left and I asked some young children who were playing at the side of the road whether they had seen the two cars go by, but they all shook their heads. I don't think they understood my Arabic. I tried the same thing on children on the other side of the main road a bit further down, but again, with no luck. A damn shame.'

'Are you sure you got the number of the car right? London will be trying to check on its provenance.'

'Yes, sir.' The Defence Attaché pulled out his diary, flicked over the pages and repeated a seven-figure number. 'It had CD plates as well, as you would expect. I could hear that it had a diesel engine, and from the way in which it took the corners and appeared to have poor acceleration, I certainly imagine that it was carrying a lot of protective weight.'

But, none the less, you lost track of it,' said the Ambassador.

'Yes, sir, I'm afraid I did,' said Moberly. 'But there was nothing

I could have done about that, without running over the boy, I mean. And he was quite young,' he added inconsequentially.

'Do you think it was a put-up job? The boy walking in front of you, I mean, and making you slow down? And then slipping on the road?'

'Lord, d'you think so, Ambassador? I hadn't thought of that.' Moberly paused. 'Clever buggers, aren't they?' he added.

The Ambassador looked carefully at Colonel Moberly, and wondered by what evil chance the Ministry of Defence had managed to send him a man of such well-meaning incompetence. Here they had had in their grasp the possibility of tracing the car to the spot where the two British hostages were being held. It was no more than a possibility, but it was certainly a chance. That chance had gone, and the Defence Attaché didn't seem to realize what a golden opportunity had slipped through his fingers. The possibility of having him transferred on promotion had also gone. The Ambassador momentarily wondered whether he could send him away on sick leave.

Colonel Moberly's hand again slipped down into his left blazer pocket and pulled out the cigarette case. He looked thoughtfully at it, and left it lying as a talisman in front of him. Then he opened the case, picked out a cigarette carefully, knocked the end of it gently twice on his thumbnail, looked at it, and put it back in the case again.

The Ambassador was becoming increasingly irritated. He was longing for a cigarette himself.

'Did you notice anything strange about the car other than its apparent weight?' he asked.

'No, Ambassador. I can't say that I did. It appeared to be a fairly recent model of Mercedes, but I must say that most Mercedes look the same to me. It's like their Volkswagens. The Krauts go on turning out the same car year after year; you know, it's very hard to tell the difference between their models, even when one is twenty years older than another.'

The Ambassador winced. Time for Moberly to take early retirement, he thought.

'Is there anything more you can tell me? Anything that could possibly be of significance?'

The military forehead wrinkled, stayed that way for some seconds of intense thought, and then went smooth again.

'No, sir, I really don't think so. I've been worrying a good deal about it. If there is anything more that comes back to me, I can ring you from my flat and tell you.'

'That's very good of you, very good indeed,' the Ambassador felt with irritation that his voice was starting to tremble. 'Meanwhile, I'll send a message to London, saying that you lost sight of the Mercedes on the southern outskirts of Beirut.'

'I'll keep looking for it, Ambassador, as I drive around. One of us might just pick it up again.'

The Ambassador sighed to himself, got up, opened the door, and re-set the combination lock after Colonel Moberly had followed him out. He went downstairs to his study on the first floor, facing backwards into the hill. The security experts had judged that it was less likely that he would be attacked, either by bomb or by bullets, from the garden at the back than from the road in front. So he had had to give up his large, airy room at the front of the Embassy and move to the smaller room at the back. There were heavy mesh curtains across the windows to catch splinters of glass in the event of a terrorist attack. This meant that the electric light was kept permanently on, giving it the appearance, he thought, in his gloomier moments, of a dental surgery.

The Ambassador slumped down at his desk, picked up a pen and started drafting a telegram for the communications officer to encode and send back to London.

FLASH, he wrote at the top.
DEFENCE ATTACHÉ FOLLOWED BLACK MERCEDES, REGISTRATION 8374071, FOR SEVERAL MILES TO SOUTH BEIRUT. CAR WAS EVIDENTLY ARMOUR-PLATED BUT HAD NO OTHER DISTINGUISHING MARKS. IT CARRIED CD PLATES. CAR WAS LOST SIGHT OF ON THE SOUTHERN PERIMETER OF BEIRUT. ITS DESTINATION THEREFORE

UNKNOWN. WILL CONTINUE TO KEEP WATCH FOR IT. ADAMS.

He wondered whether the hostages' lives could have been saved if Moberly had kept the Mercedes in sight, if the boy had not run out into the road, if he had a quicker-witted Defence Attaché. If, if, if . . . it's no use thinking like that, he thought. It would only drive us all mad. But those poor devils, Janes and Harrington. How many more hours will they be alive?

Mary had been lying awake for what felt like several hours. Probably, she thought, it's only fifteen minutes. She watched the sky turn from dark to paler blue; obviously, it was going to be a gloriously hot day, and her mind turned back to swimming in the bay in Beirut encircled by grand hotels and comfortable yachts where she could reasonably be expected, as a pretty girl, to be invited on board for a glass of sweet wine and a bowl of salted almonds. Those were carefree days, she thought. All changed now. Beirut looks like Dresden, bombed to bloody bits. Man's inhumanity to man.

Jock was lying on his back. His mouth was half-open and Mary, looking at his clear profile, noticed the stubby hairs growing out of his nostrils. I must get at those, she thought, with my tweezers. That's not Jock at his most attractive. What would he look like with a beard or a moustache? She had often wondered whether that would give him a stronger, more defined face and she reached over and started, with the index finger of her left hand, gently tracing the line of a moustache along his upper lip. Jock's nose twitched. He sleepily raised a hand to brush away an imaginary fly, and then his eyes opened, he smiled at Mary and reached instinctively for his watch.

'God,' he said, 'it's already ten to seven. I'd better start on my boxes.' He reached down, pulled up his pyjama trousers and started to get out of bed.

'Wait a moment, darling,' said Mary. 'Can we talk?'

'I suppose so,' said Jock. 'What is it?'

'Give me a kiss first.'

Almost grudgingly, Jock slipped back between the sheets, leant over and kissed Mary on the cheek.

'What's the problem? I can guess from your voice you've got one.'

'Nothing, really. I've been lying awake thinking how I was going to fill my day after the boys have gone to school. For once I don't have any Foreign Office duties. I don't have to be the Minister of State's sophisticated, elegant, well-dressed wife.'

Jock raised his eyebrows and smiled at her. 'Is it really all that much of a bore?'

'Sometimes yes, sometimes no. You know that as well as I do. You couldn't expect it to be roses, roses all the time.'

She rolled close to him, pulled him on to his side, put her hand on the back of his head and started, reflectively, to stroke his hair down to the nape of his neck.

'I was thinking that I should try harder to get a part-time job. You know, interpreting, translating work with one of the Embassies, using my languages, that sort of thing.' She brought her hand forward and, resting her palm on his chin, with one finger softly stroked his lips.

'I thought you said that's very hard to get at the moment,' Jock muttered.

'One or two Embassies have hinted they might be able to find me something,' Mary said.

'Oh, well, you'd have to get security clearance if it was with an Embassy. You know that.'

Mary slid her hand down and started stroking Jock's right nipple with the tips of her fingers. She felt it harden.

'Would that be difficult?' She wondered whether to tell him about the Lebanese Ambassador's overtures two days earlier.

'Depends on which Embassy it was. Some would be impossible. I don't know why you bother.'

'Well, sometimes I'm bored. Then I want to keep my languages going. And it would all help with the school bills; they don't get any smaller.'

She felt Jock stir restlessly, and he pushed her hand away.

'Couldn't you try something brand new, darling? What about arranging elegant walking holidays in the Dordogne, or letting other people's chateaux to our rich friends? That might be more dignified.'

'You're always worrying about dignity and pompous things like that,' Mary muttered.

'I've got so many big things on my mind at the moment,' Jock said defensively – 'hostages, the SAS, the Prime Minister. I'm getting really worried about those two in Beirut. We don't think now they're being held by the Syrians but by one of the extreme Muslim groups, and they're absolutely unpredictable, and we don't know why the two men were grabbed in the first place.' He paused, and then turned and sank his head in a loving, conciliatory way on to Mary's shoulder. And then the radio clock started quietly. They heard the familiar time signal. Jock settled back on to his pillow as the BBC voice intoned its regular introductory sentences, as familiar as the mass.

'Got to listen to this,' he muttered. 'May be important.'

Mary sighed and turned her face to the window. He's hopeless, she thought, he doesn't understand about real life but he's got lots of worries on his mind. She heard the newsreader say:

'The Foreign Secretary, Robert Huggins, cut short his visit to Africa last night and returned to London from Zimbabwe some days sooner than expected. He gave no reason for his early return to our reporter who met him at the airport, but it is generally understood that it was concern about the lack of news regarding the two Britons who have disappeared in Beirut, Bob Janes and Les Harrington, that brought the Foreign Secretary back to Britain. There will be a regular Cabinet meeting this morning, and our political correspondent is on the line to tell us what will be discussed at that meeting. Here is Martin Jevons.'

'Normally,' said Martin Jevons, with that air of complete certainty that characterizes the political guesses made by the BBC, 'economic news and thinking would have dominated this morning's Cabinet. The Chancellor will tell the Cabinet that, thanks to continuing pressure on sterling and the strength of the Deutschmark, it may be necessary for interest rates to be increased in the near future, and the Secretary for Trade and Industry will comment on the poor balance of trade figures that are expected to be announced on Friday. The Employment Secretary will report on the continuing up-trend in unemployment.'

'What an awful word, "up-trend",' Mary remarked.

'Shhh, darling. This is important,' said Jock.

Jevons's modulated tones continued: '. . . attention will focus on the Foreign Secretary's early return from a very important African trip. The Foreign Secretary would not have cut short this visit if he were not extremely worried about the fate of the two Britons, Bob Janes and Les Harrington, who disappeared in Beirut four days ago. There is growing political unease at the Foreign Office's inept handling of the situation. In the Foreign Secretary's absence, the House of Commons has been given the impression by the Junior Minister, Mr Meldrum-Ross, that there is little knowledge in the Foreign Office about the hostages' where-abouts, and very little certainty as to what the next steps should be . . .'

'Bugger them. Bugger them,' said Jock, jumping out of bed. 'How dare they talk like that, the bloody BBC simply doesn't know what it's talking about. And I gave that rotten man, Martin Jevons, lunch two weeks ago. Ungrateful sod,' he muttered as he walked towards the bathroom.

Mary lay in bed for a few more minutes, thinking and listening to the BBC, and then got up and, in her dressing gown, went to wake their boys and to get breakfast ready for them all.

Secretaries of State like, on arrival each morning at their offices, to summon their junior ministers, their most senior civil servants and their press officers to discuss the day's headlines and the likely major events of the next twenty-four hours. In Whitehall, such meetings are known as 'prayer meetings', perhaps remembering the days when the senior minister started off with a prayer, perhaps reflecting the private entreaty to the Almighty of those attending that the tabloids should not have decided to choose them as their victims for today's revelations.

The Foreign Secretary was no exception. Whenever he was in London, he held his prayer meeting at 9.15 am precisely in his large office overlooking Horse Guards Road on one side and Horse Guards Parade on the other. Jock had asked the Under Secretary responsible for the Near East and the Middle East, Alastair Crichton, to be present and, as they trooped into the Foreign Secretary's room from the private office outside, Jock asked him whether there was any further news from Beirut that might not yet have reached his desk.

'I don't think so, Minister. You saw the message saying that a black Mercedes had definitely come off the air freighter from Libya?'

'Yes, I did, but I haven't yet seen whether the Defence Attaché or anyone else managed to tail the Mercedes successfully.'

'This arrived on my desk just a minute ago, as I was leaving to come to this meeting.' And Crichton showed him the telegram from Beirut, reporting the Defence Attaché's unsuccessful attempt to follow the Mercedes.

'Damn,' said Jock. 'That's not what we need. It's not going to help the poor devils, is it?'

'No, it won't. It may have been our only chance of finding where they were.'

The Foreign Secretary took his prayer meeting quickly and efficiently. Everyone round the table reported on the events from their part of the world that were causing most trouble or that were likely to be raised at Cabinet later that morning. Jock brought the Foreign Secretary up to date on the latest position regarding the two Britons in Beirut, and the press officer reported on the stories in that morning's press that most concerned the Foreign Office. After twenty minutes, the meeting broke up.

As everyone dispersed from the large table that dominated the further side of the room, the Foreign Secretary said: 'Jock, wait behind for a moment, would you?'

Jock turned and went and stood over by one of the armchairs in front of Huggins' desk. The junior private secretary went out, closing the door, and Huggins said: 'Sit down.'

Jock sat and turned towards the Foreign Secretary. Huggins looked at him over his glasses, rearranged the pencils on his desk and then said:

'I'm getting very worried about the mischief that the PM may stir up about Beirut. I'm not at all certain that I trust his judgement any longer. He's becoming more edgy and irritable all the time.' Huggins paused and looked speculatively at Jock. 'He's worried about his own position. He does not want any sort of leadership challenge until he has a favourite son in place, and, in a strange way, I think that he feels that if he can show up the Foreign Office as being either weak and wet, not defending the lives and interests of Britons abroad, or as rash and irresponsible, that puts him in a stronger position both inside the Party and out. He's almost more at ease attacking us at the Foreign Office than attacking Labour. There's nothing that will get the press so excited as the thought that the Foreign Office, whom they love to hate, has failed to save the lives of two Britons, lives that could possibly have been saveable.'

'But we are doing our damnedest,' interjected Jock, angrily. 'You've heard about the SAS and the Tornados going out to Cyprus. Obviously, you and the Prime Minister will be getting final clearance for the use of the Tornados at Cabinet this morning. I don't see what more we can do.'

'Yes, but that's not public knowledge and what's-his-name, Moberly, could have tailed the Mercedes more successfully.'

'Yes, but the fact that he didn't isn't our fault,' said Jock.

'Some will see it as our fault. Some see everything that happens abroad, from football hooligans to muggings on the Costa Brava, as our fault. Look, I know you're very conscientious, Jock, but watch this one very carefully indeed.

'I expect we'll have another meeting later today about the use of the Tornados and the SAS, and we must agree the fine print of the operation. But it's more than that.' Huggins paused and then said: 'I'd really like to take you into my confidence.' He looked at Jock who nodded his head in agreement. 'You know well enough that the Prime Minister and I don't exactly see eye to eye? He thinks I'm after his job. Fair enough. I'm five years younger. We're unpopular in the country and I think it's time that he handed over to me or to someone else. But he'll fight terribly hard before agreeing to that. And I just suspect that he'll try and use this awful hostage issue as a means of throwing mud at me.'

'It's terrible to use the lives of these two Britons for his political ends,' said Jock.

'The ends justify the means but it's not as simple as that, is it? It wasn't his fault that Moberly failed to tail the Mercedes earlier this morning, any more than it was ours. But if there is any sign of us slipping up, of the Foreign Office failing to respond the right way, of us showing ourselves as vulnerable, I am sure Number 10 will leak that to the press and we'll be hounded. The election is only a few months away.'

'Of course, I understand,' Jock said. 'I'm flattered you've told me. I've been wondering,' he paused. 'You know, Robert, I'll do everything I possibly can to help.'

'Thank you, Jock.'

Jock got out of his chair and walked quietly to the door, and out of the room.

A straightforward chap, thought Robert, but an innocent still. He doesn't yet know just what a nasty business politics is. He'll learn. He went back to his desk, pulled over the heavy, stiff blue file with the royal crest on it, and started to study the papers for the Cabinet meeting at eleven o'clock. Robert Huggins had learnt to leave as little to chance in politics as possible. The Prime Minister aside, he wanted to be sure that he impressed all his Cabinet colleagues with his detailed knowledge of their worries as well as his own. After all, they might some day soon have to make a choice of leader between Bruce Gordon and himself.

★

It is only a hundred yards down Downing Street from the Foreign Secretary's personal entrance to the Foreign Office to the black door of Number 10. Robert Huggins had walked that hundred yards more times than he cared to remember over the past four years. When Bruce Gordon had first appointed him Foreign Secretary after the last general election, the walk was tinged with pleasant anticipation. Huggins loved his job, and he looked forward to sharing details of his most recent discussions with the American Secretary of State or the German Foreign Minister with Gordon. They had been in the House together for seventeen years, they had neighbouring parliamentary seats in the South of England, which they had held with small majorities after recent boundary changes. In opposition in the early Eighties, they had put together and led the policy groups that produced the pamphlets and literature on which the Party's new thinking had been based. As soon as the Conservatives returned to power, they had entered the Cabinet at the same time as Secretaries of State for Environment and Employment respectively, and, when two years later, the Prime Minister had a sudden massive heart attack and died, Huggins had been the second of the two names on the piece of paper that went to the chairman of the all-powerful 1922 Committee, the committee of Tory backbenchers, proposing Gordon as the next Leader of the Party, and therefore, subject to the Queen's constitutional discretion, the Prime Minister.

But somewhere, a few years after that, things had started to go sour. Huggins had often wondered as he travelled incessantly round the world in aeroplanes, and went from one international conference to another, just what it was that had started the rot. For rot it had certainly become.

There is always hostility and suspicion between the Foreign Office and the Prime Minister's Office. Each office has a different set of officials who are ready to prove to their ministers that they are right in their judgement of events and their counterparts across the road, wrong. Heads of government go visiting, and expect to speak only to other heads of government. Foreign Secretaries attend such meetings by invitation, not as a matter of right. But when it is a question of an exchange of visits at the next level down, then it is the Foreign Secretaries who are the cocks of the walk. They know each other, stay in each other's magnificent government houses, call each other by nicknames, and understand each other's foibles while planning treaties that may, sometimes, change the face of the world. It is not surprising that Foreign Secretaries, particularly those who have been years in their jobs, come to think how much easier and more sensible foreign affairs would be if they could be settled directly between them without the interference and contradictory decisions of heads of government.

Huggins, though, knew that the growing coldness between Bruce Gordon and himself went far beyond the normal, institutional, almost natural difficulties. He found Gordon increasingly rude in front of their colleagues at Cabinet meetings, and more and more prone to snub him at summit meetings and international conferences, particularly at the gathering with the press that came afterwards. The press came to lick their lips, exaggerate and gloat over the way in which the Prime Minister put down his Foreign Secretary.

They drifted apart in their views of policy. Huggins was all for more open encouragement to liberal movements in the Third World. He thought they were a necessary preliminary to democracy. Gordon would have none of this, regularly referring to such groups as terrorists. By and large, despite a sceptical press, people trusted Huggins and felt, as he travelled the world and reported in the House on his travels, that he was trying to arrive at reasonable solutions to intolerably difficult problems. As Foreign Secretary, he was distanced from the day-to-day bloodletting over patients waiting months for operations, blocked motorways and foreigners getting social security benefits.

He always came top, or near top, when the newspapers sampled a few thousand voters on which cabinet minister they had most confidence in. By contrast, the media laughed when Gordon's ratings for honesty and competence fell below the annual rate of inflation.

Gordon's wife had died on Christmas day. She was fifty-five, beautiful, witty and a very good hostess at all the Downing Street parties for Tory backbenchers. Gordon and she had been married for twenty-five years. They still held hands on conference platforms, kissed in public and were evidently in love. She died of a sudden and extraordinarily painful cancer, leaving Gordon a widower with no children and only the contents of his interminable red and black boxes to worry about.

After her death, he retired from sight for nearly a month, during the Christmas recess, was reported to have drunk himself into a stupor on some solitary evenings at Chequers, and then re-appeared a few days after Parliament reassembled in mid-January. He never was heard to mention his wife again to any of his political colleagues.

But some sort of iron had entered his soul. His knowledge of detail became greater, his fear of being caught out, not knowing the answer, almost obsessive. He found it harder and harder to leave Cabinet colleagues in charge of intricate problems, so he set up committees of which he was the chairman the moment that a difficult, challenging question started to attract media attention. Whilst other Secretaries of State caved in and trotted meekly round to Number 10, Huggins, as an old friend and near contemporary, stood up to him and protested and sometimes refused to send him copies of departmental working papers.

'Typical Foreign Office arrogance,' the Prime Minister would mutter whenever Huggins tried to explain this to him. 'You lot are just not interested in Britain.' And, increasingly, Huggins, in recent months, had given up trying.

He walked across the road, over the pavement, and up the steps into Number 10, at the same time as Tony Castle, the Defence Secretary.

'Good morning, sir. Good morning, sir,' said the policeman on the door, first to the Foreign Secretary and then to the Defence Secretary. 'A lovely morning, sir.'

Huggins smiled at him, but Castle replied cheerfully: 'Much too lovely to be working.' They passed through the door together and walked through the wide hallway down the long passage towards the Cabinet Room. As Huggins passed the picture of Ellen Terry, he stopped and admired her profile as he had done so often before, with its long wavy, reddish hair and eager face, looking out towards Downing Street.

'She's better-looking than any of our colleagues,' he commented.

'You've come back early from Africa, haven't you?' said Tony Castle, standing at his shoulder. Huggins regarded Castle as a friend whom he had grown to trust and on whose judgement he increasingly relied.

'Yes, I have,' he said. 'I don't quite know why, but I was getting more and more worried about these two hostages in Beirut. I thought the PM might muck things up while I was away.' Castle smiled. He had heard Huggins sing this tune before.

'We've had several meetings about them,' he said.

'I know, I've read the minutes. It will all come up at Cabinet.'

'Yes, of course,' said Tony.

At that moment, they were joined by Piers Potter, the Home Secretary, and Angela Fawke, the Social Security Secretary. Their conversation stopped, and they walked towards the anteroom, talking and laughing softly, like acquaintances who know each other well going into a meal together. There were already eight other Cabinet members gathered in the anteroom, four talking seriously around the table on the left side of the room, one stressing a point to Roderick Turner, the Prime Minister's principal private secretary, and another looking shifty as he talked to the Chief Whip, Greg Stevens. Someone's missed a vote, thought Huggins, and is trying to make his peace with Greg.

Other members of the Cabinet joined the various groups and people moved from one group to another, quickly settling points of business that affected their departments until, after a few minutes, a bell rang quietly. The uniformed attendant immediately opened the white door into the Cabinet Room and stood by it. Everyone filed into the long Cabinet Room and sat in their customary seats, the Home Secretary sitting directly opposite the Prime Minister who was already seated in his central chair in front of the fireplace, with three private secretaries standing around him. They moved away as the Cabinet took their seats. Robert Huggins, as was his custom, sat immediately on the Prime Minister's left. This was the position to which he was entitled as the most senior Cabinet Minister, but the physical nearness was tangibly embarrassing at times, as if each found the other suffering from bad breath. It made the sparks between the two men fly more quickly, like electric current jumping between two metal rails.

As usual, there was no written agenda. The Prime Minister first checked that everyone was present except for the Secretaries of State for Scotland and Northern Ireland, both of whom had asked for permission to be away on ministerial engagements. He then asked the Chancellor of the Exchequer to introduce the discussion on the state of the economy. In a gloomy monotone, Ross Macintosh, Chancellor for just over a year, pointed out that the pound had been under continuing pressure from the Deutschmark, and had also been very weak against the dollar. Indeed, if the Bank of England had not supported sterling heavily over the last two days at considerable cost to the reserves, it would have gone below the levels that the Treasury felt right.

'I'm afraid, Prime Minister,' he said, in the tone of a headmaster telling a parent that his loved son is about to be dismissed from school, 'we have no alternative but to put up interest rates after the market closes this afternoon. The market is expecting an increase of a half per cent, and that is allowed for in today's inter-bank rate. However, I think it would be better to put it up by a full one per cent.'

There was a perceptible intake of breath from his Cabinet colleagues. He continued, 'That will certainly strengthen sterling and the foreign banks will start buying. It should mean that there will be no possibility of another interest rate rise between now and the election in the autumn. It would obviously be most embarrassing if we had to have a half point rise today, and another one, say, in September or early October, just as we were going into an election.'

A long and bitter discussion followed. Several members of the Cabinet thought it would be far better if the Bank continued to support sterling for a few more days and if the Chancellor appealed to his colleagues on the Continent and in Washington and Tokyo to join in supporting sterling.

'If we put up interest rates now,' said Angela Fawke, the Social Security Secretary, 'it will have a disastrous effect on the young home owners, who are already so far behind on their mortgage payments. The number of repossessions will increase, and unemployment is bound to rise further. That will have a bad effect on my budget which is already under pressure. I would have to ask the Chief Secretary for a supplementary vote. I really do think, Prime Minister, that we should try and hang on for a bit longer for the sake of the young families with heavy mortgages.'

She looked across the Cabinet table at Robert Huggins. He often supported her, but on this occasion, he was deep into his file of papers and did not raise his eyes. The Defence Secretary came to her help.

'In my judgement, the Social Security Secretary is absolutely right, Prime Minister. I think it would be electorally disastrous to raise interest rates by even half a percentage point and I'm sure more can be done to help sterling through these difficulties. I think we must hang on.'

But Piers Potter, the Home Secretary, took the Chancellor's side. He was an ex-Chief Secretary of the Treasury himself, and always took the view that the Treasury was much more likely to be right than any of the spending ministers such as Defence and Social Security.

'The Chancellor has had the opportunity to study this much more closely than any of the rest of us,' Potter said crossly. 'I am sure, Prime Minister, that we should back his judgement. Of course, it will be unpopular to put up interest rates by a full point, but the Chancellor is right about the tactics. To have to put them up again by another half point just as we are getting near the election in the autumn, would be much worse.'

The argument continued. The Employment Secretary, William Ford, sided with Angela Fawke and Tony Castle, emphasizing that, on Friday, he would be announcing a sharp increase in unemployment. Anything that made the relentless approach towards a figure of two and a half million unemployed more inevitable was to be avoided. Others came down on the Chancellor's side. Economics became mixed with politics, reason with passion, old enmities started to surface. After half an hour, the Prime Minister summed matters up.

'We've had a thorough discussion. On balance, more members of Cabinet are in favour of putting up interest rates this afternoon than not, and again the majority favour the Chancellor's difficult but, I am sure, correct decision that the increase should be a full percentage point.'

He paused, and the private secretaries to his right continued scribbling as fast and as accurately as they could in their large schoolboy notebooks, trying to take down every word he said.

'We have to face the fact that the election has to take place by mid-November. As you know, I have not yet decided when we ask Her Majesty the Queen for a dissolution, but it is most important that the run on the pound should be stopped firmly and now, without any possibility of it coming back to hurt us just before election day. Chancellor, you will see that the announcement is made at five pm, after the market closes. Presumably, you will want to make a statement in the House tomorrow, despite the fact that it is a Friday?'

'Yes, Prime Minister. I will have to do that at eleven tomorrow morning, in the House.'

'Do you see any difficulties with that, Chief Whip?' asked the Prime Minister, looking down the table to his left to where Greg Stevens was sitting.

Stevens had written in front of him a list in two columns of those who had spoken. According to his piece of paper, there was one more voice against putting up interest rates that evening than there were in favour of this course of action, but he did not think it his business to say so at a full Cabinet meeting. He might mention it quietly to the Prime Minister afterwards, once the decision had been formally taken.

He looked at the Prime Minister and said: 'Friday isn't the best day, Prime Minister, for a statement, but I'll get some of the faithful among the London members to turn up and make supportive noises. I have to say, though, a rise of a full point in interest rates is bound to be unpopular with our colleagues as a whole. I think many of those with marginals will be desperately worried, and will voice their unhappiness to you, Prime Minister, or to me.'

'Well, there'll be nothing unusual about that,' said the Prime Minister. 'What are your Whips for but to see that the Parliamentary Party fall in line? Most of them don't understand a thing about economic realities.'

There was a half laugh, sycophantic in tone, from one or two members of the Cabinet. An angry frown passed over the Chief Whip's face, but the Prime Minister went on.

'That's settled, then. Now, Foreign Secretary, we have spent too much time talking about the economy. I want you to tell us about the real world of Foreign Affairs. Welcome back from your long trip to Africa.'

Huggins felt the colour rising rapidly to his cheeks. This was a spontaneous reaction to hostility that he had had since his childhood. Like any experienced politician, he could control his voice, his smile and his eyes. Unfortunately, he had no mastery over the colour of his cheeks.

Huggins described the purpose of his African visit, told his colleagues which Presidents and Foreign Ministers he had seen and what negotiations he had conducted. A perceptible feeling of greater calm fell over the room as, in a reassuring voice, he went from one African capital to the next. Then he switched to the subject of the hostages in the Lebanon. Huggins told his colleagues that he believed Janes and Harrington were alive and being held by Muslim terrorists and that a black Mercedes had arrived in Beirut from Libya in which they might be hidden and shipped back to Tripoli.

'Yes,' said the Prime Minister, interrupting him, 'and our marvellous Defence Attaché in Beirut followed the Mercedes and lost it in a traffic jam. If he had been more on the ball, we could have learned where the hostages were being held.'

'I don't know that it was the Defence Attaché's fault,' objected Tony Castle quickly. Before the Prime Minister could interrupt again, he told Cabinet of the squadron of Tornados that had flown out to Akrotiri the day before, and the two platoons of the SAS that were now in Cyprus. They were, of course, studying the layout of the air base and getting extensive briefing on local conditions.

'If the Tornados have to intercept the Libyan air freighter with the Mercedes on board, and succeed in forcing it to divert to our base at Akrotiri,' continued Castle, 'then the SAS will storm the aeroplane in order to get the two Britons out.'

'Good God,' said William Ford, the Employment Secretary, quite audibly, from the right-hand end of the Cabinet table.

A strained look came over the collective face of the Cabinet, and those at the two ends of the long table leaned forward in order to pick up every word that Tony Castle said from his chair next to the Home Secretary.

'It's going to be tricky, because there will be a relatively short time in which the Tornados, flying out of Cyprus, will have sufficient fuel to intercept the air freighter and bring her back to Cyprus. They will have a normal weapon and fuel load, including missiles in case those are necessary. A lot will depend on their radar picking up and identifying the plane at a very early stage in her flight. Alternatively, Akrotiri may get a message from our people in Beirut that the freighter has left with the Mercedes on board. That would give them a little more time.'

'Not very likely that they'll get such a message,' said the Prime Minister. 'Not from the incompetent way in which the Beirut Embassy have handled this matter so far.'

Huggins couldn't hold back his anger.

'Really, Prime Minister, I think that's totally unjustified. It was they who picked up the fact that terrorists were holding the hostages and that they were still in Beirut, and they sent us a message about that straight away. I've no doubt that they are using all their contacts to try and discover exactly where the hostages are being held, even if they weren't able to follow the Mercedes yesterday.' He paused and then added solemnly: 'It is extremely dangerous being a diplomat in Beirut at the moment.'

A stillness had fallen on the Cabinet Room: the quiet that comes before a thunderstorm.

'I think that your people have made asses of themselves almost from the moment that Janes and Harrington were taken,' said the Prime Minister. 'They've failed to get us any of the really hard information that we need. On the other hand, I have to say that your Minister of State was quite competent at our meeting yesterday.' The Prime Minister, looking directly ahead, then said quietly: 'Sometimes, I find that junior ministers know more about what is going on than do their Secretaries of State who are so busy travelling round the world.'

Huggins arranged the four pencils that were on the table in front of him. He put them neatly in order with all their points facing towards him. Then he turned them around so that the sharp ends faced outwards.

'I don't think that in nine years of attending Cabinet meetings virtually every week, I have ever heard a ruder or more unnecessary remark.' He leant forward and moved the pencils around so that they pointed back at him again.

A long silence followed. Then the Prime Minister said: 'I take it that Cabinet agrees with the general outline of the plan to intercept the Libyan air freighter, the use of the Tornados and, if necessary, the storming of the Libyan aeroplane by the SAS. Obviously, that may cost lives, and lead to a final breakdown in our relations with Libya. Perhaps with Egypt and some of the other Arab states as well. Is everyone prepared to accept that?'

He paused and looked round the table. No one said anything. A few heads nodded.

'Very good, then. I will appoint a small Cabinet sub-committee to go over the details of the operations plan under my chairman-ship. The Chiefs of Staff will be on that sub-committee, also representatives, of course, from the Security Services, the Defence Secretary, the Foreign Secretary and . . .' the Prime Minister paused, 'the Minister of State at the Foreign Office responsible for the Near East and Middle East. I don't think there is any other business. The meeting is concluded.'

The members of the Cabinet put their papers into their stiff folders, some dark blue, some bright red, all embossed with the royal crest and with the titles of their offices stamped beneath. They filed silently out of the room as the Prime Minister turned to his right and talked confidentially to his private secretary.

'That bloody man,' said Huggins, boiling with anger, to Tony Castle, as they walked back down the long ill-lit corridor to the front door. 'He gets worse every day. He'll have to go.'

The door was opened for them, and across the street was the usual gaggle of photographers and press reporters waiting for the Cabinet to end and for ministers to come out into the street.

'Any news, Mr Castle?' shouted one of them.

'All happy and serene,' said the Defence Secretary, giving a half wave and settling himself into his government Rover.

Huggins passed by the reporters without a word and turned to the right, on his way back to the Foreign Office.

'Like a ray of sunshine, isn't he?' muttered the *Daily Mirror* to the *Telegraph* next to him.

'Yeah. Guess he caught Aids in Africa.' The *Telegraph* had never approved of Huggins' open approach to foreign policy.

5

Friday 28 June

The military base outside Akrotiri resembled a cross between Cairo and Aldershot. Barracks, stores, lorries, empty metal barrels were everywhere, dumped in the dust. Aeroplanes were parked at odd angles, casually, as if their pilots had found a slot where there were no double yellow lines and had jumped out quickly before they were told to move on. The night was hot and still; the earth seemed to be taking a breather from the intensity of the day, giving out strong smells of oleander and jasmine, and gathering its strength again before the violent heat of the morning. Dogs barked sharply and incessantly and ran between the shadows under the trees, finding holes in the perimeter fence that, twenty years ago, had been built to keep them out, but that had now abandoned the attempt.

Colonel Spacemead, walking around in the small hours, absorbed his surroundings like a sponge, and gave the appearance of assuming there to be order and efficiency around him, even if it was not as apparent as he would like it to be. Squadron Leader Snowling was with him, in charge of the squadron of Tornados from Lincolnshire. Together they strolled towards a distant end of the tarmac, and then swung off down a thirty-yard stretch of concrete that led to a large hangar, its wide doors open, a few piles of stores inside. On one side of the hangar was a belt of cypress trees, watered by a rare, little stream. Close to the hangar were a number of sheds that contrasted in their newness with the shabby, rusty metal and concrete building, and by the sheds were two large caravans, their roofs decked with radio antennae and satellite dishes. There were lights on in the caravans, and, as Spacemead and Snowling walked past, they could see three young men, two of them with earphones on bowed over desks and the third talking down a telephone.

'The telecoms are working all right,' said the Squadron Leader, 'and we are picking up signals from Beirut clearly at the moment. That's just as well, because it's going to be a very hairy operation. If we don't get advance warning from our security people in Beirut, we will have to try and identify the Libyan air freighter on our radar within a few minutes of her take-off. In any case, we'll have very little time in the air to negotiate. We may have to shoot at them almost as soon as we see them.'

'That's the way the SAS always operates. How are you going to argue with them thirty thousand feet up?' asked Spacemead.

'Hard to say whether that'll be easy or bloody difficult. We know the VHF radio bands they normally use. The problem comes if the Libyan captain doesn't speak good enough English to understand what we want, or if he's just plain bloody-minded and goes on flying back towards Tripoli. Then do we shoot or don't we? That's the question . . .'

'You'll be more in the limelight than my lot,' said Spacemead. 'I know we can get into the plane. We can blow our way in with explosives. We've done it often enough in trial exercises. Our problem comes after that. If the Libyans fight and shoot, how many of them get killed and how many of my boys get killed? Can we get the two hostages out alive? There's no probability ratio. You just have to go in and use stun grenades and smoke-bombs and act extraordinarily quickly. You can have a hideous casualty rate, or none. There's no knowing.'

The two men had come to the end of the concrete and on to the dusty grass. They peered at the water trickling slowly under the cypress trees, and then turned back. They were both deep in their thoughts, and there was a long silence until Spacemead murmured, almost to himself: 'Death or life. That's the sort of calculation that politicians never make. They have an aim that they see they must achieve for whatever reason, whatever the cost. The pride of Britain, our relations with Arab countries, or their own personal position and prestige. Who knows? But they tell us to go in, and it's we who get killed, not them.'

'You sound like my grandfather talking about the 1914 war. But, all the same, you in the SAS, you'd be very disappointed if you didn't, sometimes, have to use all those extraordinary skills that you train your men in.'

Snowling thought he was being rather cheeky to a superior officer, but he could not resist making his point.

'True enough, I wouldn't have volunteered to join the SAS, nor would any of the men, if it was all about theory and training exercises,' said Spacemead. 'Of course, we want to see how we perform in real life. Everyone who opts to join the SAS knows that he may get killed, and he is warned of that at his first interview. He may get killed on a training exercise, quite apart from real action. But I don't know how much thought our political bosses give to all of this. Look at the present exercise. I'm very sorry for those two Britons. From all I've heard, they were doing a good job for a United Nations agency. But, all the same, they've been taken hostage. I don't know whether they were taking too much risk or not, but does it really matter now whether they're held in Beirut or in Tripoli? What difference does that make to them? Very little. I'd have thought they'd be hostages in both places. Yet we're told to take part in a risky exercise that could lead to lots of deaths, and I wonder whether this is to save the face of the Foreign Office or whether it's because there's an election in a few months' time, and, if we succeed, it will be a feather in the Prime Minister's cap.' The last words almost tumbled out.

'I thought colonels in the SAS never speculated along such lines,' said Snowling.

'Officially, we don't, as you know very well.' Spacemead smiled in the dark. 'But even the toughies in the SAS are allowed to have some inner thoughts,' he said.

The two men had reached the quarters where they were to sleep. They turned off the concrete path, opened a door in a darkened building, and walked down the corridor towards their rooms.

'It probably won't happen,' said Snowling. 'We'll get a message saying the Libyan air freighter has left without a big black car in it at all, or something like that. And we'll all be called back home.'

'You're wrong,' replied Spacemead. 'I am sure it'll happen, and one or other of us will have to use our guns. I just don't know what the outcome will be.'

A few hours later, Bob Janes was woken by a tap on his shoulder. He stirred painfully out of his sleep, muttering to himself, as he woke up, about the nastiness of life. Then a hand undid the rope around his wrists and gently began to untie his blindfold. A voice said quietly in his ear: 'It's me, Les. They've put me in here with you.'

The blindfold slipped off Bob's head and he turned in the half-light and saw, to his astonishment, Les Harrington, five days' growth of beard on his cheek and chin, kneeling beside him. He put out his arms and instinctively hugged Les to his chest. Then pain once again flooded through his neck and shoulders, and he pushed Les away.

'Where the hell have you been?' he asked. 'Did they hurt you? Are you all right? I've never been so pleased to see anyone in my life. I didn't know whether they'd killed you. Where did they take you?'

'A mile or two from here, I guess. Of course, I was blindfolded but I think it might have been West Beirut, Mazraa perhaps.'

Bob saw that Les was shaking. He put a hand on his arm and said, 'God, it's good to see you.'

'I need a fucking cigarette,' said Les. He was quiet for a minute or two and then seemed to steady himself and went on: 'When they bundled me out of the car, they pushed me into a building and up the staircase. I counted them – forty-nine steps up a staircase that turned clockwise. I thought that might be important. Everywhere, there seemed to be empty buckets which I bumped into and a lot of shit lying on the landing, I could smell the filth.

'On the second floor, we stopped going up, they pushed me over a bare floor and then told me to lie down. I thought they were going to kill me there and then and I had a strange feeling of a cold pistol being pressed against my head when there wasn't one there.

'There was a mattress on the floor, horribly dirty and smelly. They shoved me on to that and they passed a chain round my stomach and another over my feet and ankles.' Les paused again and looked round. 'I'd give anything for a smoke,' he said. There was silence between the two men and then Les went on: 'On the second day, they took away my blindfold. My room had no windows but I guess there must have been a balcony just outside, as I could see the sunlight under the door getting brighter through the early morning and then fading in the evening. There was an enormous amount of hooting and noisy blaring from the road. I tried to picture where I was in case there was a chance of finding the building later but . . .' his voice broke and he buried his head in his hands and muttered, 'I was so shit-scared all the time, Bob. I couldn't believe this was happening to me. After all we've heard about other people being kidnapped, and now there was I, fuck it, chained up like a bloody murderer. Kidnapped. A hostage. I was terrified. My mind went round and round. Why me? What've I done to deserve this?

'One evening I cracked. It was the third day. The hours had gone on and on, dragging by so slowly. I suddenly couldn't stand it and I yelled and yelled and yelled. One of the guards came in from the next room and I swore at him. I told him in all the Arabic that I knew, to let me go. He looked down at me and, first, he kicked me and then he stopped and asked me whether I'd ever been in Chouf. God, was I glad to tell him. "Yes," I said, "I've often been in Chouf." "Why?" he asked me. I explained about our work together. He told me that he lived in the village in Chouf near Beiteddine. You remember, where you and I worked on the water supply last year.'

'Of course I remember,' Bob interrupted. 'We were there for several weeks. That's where the village water was getting contaminated from sewage seeping through from that awful municipal pit into the watercourse of their underground stream. There had already been one case of typhoid and the doctors told us there'd be an epidemic soon, but the lorries kept on coming from Beirut and dumping their loads of waste into the pit. So we tapped the water upstream and got all the villagers to build a surface canal by-passing the sewage pit. We were local heroes,' he smiled as he remembered.

'That's right,' said Les. 'They gave us a great feast one evening before we left. My guard had been at it, and that's how he recognized me.

'The next evening,' he went on, 'I heard a tremendous argument next door. You know that my Arabic's pretty bloody good, but I couldn't understand half of that row. They were arguing among themselves about what was going to happen to you and me. They talked of handing us over to the Libyans who, they thought, would pay a lot of money for us, or to Hizbollah, who've got the other hostages and are being paid by those arseholes in Teheran. The one I talked to, his name was Ahmed, stood up for me and said I'd done good work in his village. The row went on and on. Typical Lebanese, more and more names being thrown around. Amal, Walid Jumblatt, Nabih Berri, Aoun, the lot. I thought they'd never stop but they couldn't make up their minds. Backwards and forwards. They started shouting at each other but I heard one say that it was bad for Lebanon for ordinary sods like us to be kidnapped. Another said that it was all our own fault as no one had asked us to Lebanon in the first place.

'In the end, I just fell asleep, still with chains round my waist and ankles, on to the rings in the floor. God knows how I slept, but I did. Other nights, I'd talked myself to sleep, having imaginary conversations with Helen and the children, but that night, I couldn't think of anything. An hour later, I was wakened. An Arab was brought into my room to whom Ahmed showed great respect. He questioned me in good English, and I told him all about our Agency and our work. He asked me whether I was working for either American or British Intelligence. And of course I said: "Fuck that for an idea." I must have given him something to chew on as he went away looking worried. Then, early this morning before dawn, Ahmed came into the room and told me that I was going to be brought here and that I'd be with you. I think they considered your place was safer and a bit quieter than mine.

'So I was blindfolded again, taken down the stairs and shoved into the back of a truck. I tried to look. I'm sure we turned south to the airport and then left after Sahat Salamat into that dirty tumbledown area before the golf course. You might like to know that you're on the second floor of a breeze-block house, ugly as sin, and the road outside is a shambles. I guess you're plumb in the centre of Shiiteville.'

Bob laughed. 'After Sally,' he said, 'I'd rather see you than anyone else in the world.' The two spent the next few hours crawling over every detail of what had happened since the previous Sunday. Les had obviously had the easier time. Apart from the odd shove and kick, he had not been seriously hurt and he'd been better fed with chicken and rice in the evening and mezze and salad every morning. Despite that, Bob felt Les was suffering and in far greater panic than he was himself.

'You know, Les,' Bob said, 'I'm sure we're going to be all right. I feel it in my bones. Then we'll see Helen and Sally and the kids. We'll have a party and be famous and write books and make lots of money.'

Les looked away. 'It's no good,' he said quietly. 'You know, as a kid, I hated being shut in a cupboard. If I was, I'd panic straight away and scream and scream. At school, the others got to know this and they started threatening to shut me into the cellar or the boiler room, and I'd get frightened before anything even happened.

'I feel the same way now. Every other second I start panicking about what's going to happen next.'

Bob looked at him and, with great gentleness, said: 'Shall we try and pray together?' He saw tears falling down Les's cheeks.

'I want to pray, but I can't. I bloody can't,' sobbed Les. 'I've tried, but it doesn't work. Bob, I'm scared out of my mind and I just don't know why this sodding awful business has happened to me.'

'And me,' added Bob.

'And you. Sorry. I'm sure I'll never see Helen again. A hundred per cent certain of it.'

'Don't talk like that, of course you will,' argued Bob. Their talk died down and both men sat on the floor looking out of the window at the hills stretching away in the east. At one moment, Les wandered over to the window and started testing each in turn of the four steel bars that were let into the stone. As he expected, they were firmly cemented. He shook each of them, but none so much as quivered.

As he turned back to where Bob was sitting, the door was quietly unlocked and two Arabs came in. Bob immediately recognized the one with the moustache and the scar on the right cheek; it was he who spoke first.

'I did not come to see you last night, because my friends and I have been talking about you both for many hours. We decided you should be together.' He paused, and there was a long silence while he and the other Arab stared at Bob and Les. The Arabs, normally noisy and talkative, had a capacity for sudden quietness that eluded most Europeans. They stared and thought without any trace of emotion crossing their faces. Bob felt his heart beginning to beat faster. Memories like single shots in a film slipped through his mind. As he looked up at the two Arabs, he remembered his mother, last seen in London two years before, entreating him to be more careful. She had held his hand tightly as he said goodbye to her before leaving for the airport, and had urged him, looking him straight in the eyes, not to take any risks that could be avoided.

'I can't go to Lebanon without taking risks,' he had replied, 'and I must go back there. There is so much useful work to be done.'

A flash came back to him of Sally, his wife, saying the same sort of things to him three weeks before, as they had sat on the tiny balcony outside their flat in the evening up in the Metri hills, looking down across the blocks of flats and noise of Beirut to the inky, solid calm of the Mediterranean. A few ships moved, their minute lights pricking holes in the dark, as Sally repeated the fears and the pleas of his mother.

'I'm sure you don't have to go to all the remote places you and

Les travel to,' she had urged him. 'Do you ever think of me and of our children? What would it do to us if you were taken hostage and killed, or just held prisoner for several years? I think we'd all go mad.'

Bob grimaced instinctively, and wished he had been able to quieten Sally's fright. Then the pain in his body came back at him, and he looked up angrily at the two Arabs, and said: 'We've told you our story. I know that Les has told you exactly the same as I have. So why don't you release us? You know we are not spies for the CIA. And, Christ, my shoulders hurt!'

The Arab who had already spoken, and who was taller and more heavily built than his companion, said again: 'We have talked a lot about you. We have talked with our General. We have to speak with him again. It is a complicated matter and it is very difficult to arrange. There are many people to be consulted.' He spoke in a careful voice, with no emphasis on individual words, as if reciting a text that he had learnt by heart.

'How long will it take you to make a decision about us?' Bob asked.

'Not long. Inshallah. We will do what we can but there are many others who wish to decide about you.' The Arab paused, looked as if he would say some more, but then turned away.

'At least, take me to a doctor,' said Bob. 'I'm sure my collarbone needs setting.'

'Very well. I will take you with me to see a doctor, so that he can look at your shoulder and neck. Come with me now,' said the first Arab turning to Bob.

Bob was lifted to his feet by the two Arabs. The chain was unlocked from around his ankles, a blindfold was tied round his head and they walked him towards the door of the flat.

'Goodbye, Les,' said Bob. 'I'll be back soon. Don't eat all the breakfast.'

'What breakfast?' said Les. 'I don't see any. Good luck.'

'We will bring you some soon,' said the second Arab. 'Be glad that you are alive and can talk to each other.'

Les took a string of beads out of his pocket, as soon as the door

87

was padlocked. He tried to recite poems, prayers, anything that he could remember, something for each bead, down the anchor-chain, link by link, stretching his memory, past his marriage back to school and his childhood. He had done this so often in the past five days, determined to keep himself balanced and sane, but every time he ended up with a great wave of depression sweeping over him. Each day, this seemed to come sooner and sooner and he felt himself staring down into a black pit in which there was no hope and no light. Tears came into his eyes and he threw himself on to the straw and buried his head in it.

6

Saturday 29 June

Chequers, and Chevening, two great houses, the one standing in the flat, fertile land of Buckinghamshire, the other with the Kent hills on one side and a lake on the other. In recent tradition, Chequers has been the country home of the Prime Minister, Chevening that of the Foreign Secretary. Chequers is an Elizabethan house that has been added to on many occasions. The rooms are comfortable, panelled and dotted with Tudor and Stuart portraits. It is a family house.

Chevening, by contrast, is much grander. The home of the Stanhope family for many generations, the rooms are tall and of Georgian elegance. A hanging staircase leads from ground floor to first and second floors and all the way up the walls are the muskets and pikes of an old Kentish regiment, acquired by a past Earl Stanhope for a few hundred pounds when the regiment was disbanded in the nineteenth century. Huggins, dressed in light grey trousers with an open-necked blue shirt, walked down the Chevening staircase with Jock Meldrum-Ross by his side.

'I often think of picking up one of those pikes when I go to London on Sunday evenings,' said Huggins cheerfully, 'and taking it into Number 10 with me and putting it through the Prime Minister as if it were a spit. Then, like some medieval general, I would carry him out into Downing Street, show his writhing body to the world's press corps, and say: "Look, this is my Attila the Hun, this is my Pedro the Cruel, this is my scourge, my enemy. I have killed him, and the world is mine." '

'I don't think the chairman of the 1922 Committee would like that,' said Jock. 'It's not the way we choose the leaders of our Party these days!'

'Bring back the old days. Chevening shall triumph over Chequers and it'll be a lot quicker than running round, sucking up to all those boring back-bench MPs.'

Laughing, they both arrived in the big hall, swung to the right, and walked towards the white-panelled drawing room that runs down the north side of the house. There were sixteen guests there: two ambassadors and their wives, a famous newspaper editor and his girlfriend, and a sprinkling of young MPs and their spouses. Huggins greatly enjoyed showing off Chevening on a Saturday, and knew that his invitations were prized by a wide range of people.

His wife, Perdita, greeted her husband and Jock as they walked into the room.

'There you are at last. Everyone has arrived for lunch, and we wondered what on earth had happened to you. Jock, go over and ask James or Jacob for a drink.'

Jock wandered through the guests to the far end of the room overlooking the lake, where the two white-coated butlers were standing by a table covered with bottles, large crystal glasses and a big ice-bucket.

'Good morning, Mr Meldrum-Ross,' said one of the butlers. 'What would you like? A glass of wine?'

'No. Can you mix me a Bloody Mary, Jacob?' asked Jock.

'Certainly, sir.'

As Jacob poured vodka and tomato juice and then added Worcester sauce, pepper and pieces of lemon into a glass jug, Jock turned back and looked at the guests. He thought that he knew all of them, and made a mental note to go and talk to an elderly man of small stature and medium-brown skin, who, unlike any of the other guests, was immaculately dressed in a double-breasted navy suit.

The Lebanese Ambassador, thought Jock. I wonder why Robert invited him. It must be something to do with the hostages.

As he waited for his Bloody Mary, Jock saw a uniformed attendant come into the room, walk over to the Foreign Secretary and whisper in his ear. Robert Huggins listened, nodded and then turned and beckoned Jock over to him. Jock threaded his way between an armchair and a sofa, past the plump newspaper editor who was boasting proudly to a well-dressed woman of his circulation increases. She, in turn, was looking over his shoulder at the Canada geese on the lake.

'Jock,' said Huggins, in a very low voice. 'I'm told a telegram has just arrived from Beirut. They've put it on my desk in the study. Would you go up and have a look to see if there's anything special in it? Let me know if you want me to come up and look at it as well, otherwise, if you're satisfied, I'll leave it till after lunch.'

Jock nodded, left the room, and walked up the hanging staircase into the tapestry-lined room that the Foreign Secretary used as his study. On the blotter, in the middle of the desk by the window, was a neat bundle of Foreign Office telegrams. Jock picked up the one on the top, which was headed: FLASH – FLASH – FLASH and stamped in red TOP SECRET. He saw that it had been sent off from Beirut two hours earlier. He read on:

YOUR MESSAGE 8317/85 REFERS. WILL DO UTMOST TO ARRANGE FOR DEPARTURE TIME OF LIBYAN AIR FREIGHTER TO BE ADVISED TO YOU AND AKROTIRI BUT CANNOT GUARANTEE. ANONYMOUS TELE-PHONE CALL ADVISES AL-FATAH HOLDING JANES AND HARRING-TON AND IN DISPUTE WITH OTHER TERRORIST GROUPS ABOUT THEIR FATE. CALLER STRESSES ESSENTIAL, REPEAT ESSENTIAL, AL-FATAH'S NAME NOT MENTIONED PUBLICLY. THIS COULD PREJU-DICE DELICATE NEGOTIATIONS. ADAMS.

Jock read the message again, and turned to the flimsies underneath. To his surprise he noted that the copy for Number 10, marked traditionally *'For the Attention of the Prime Minister's Private Secretary'*, was attached. He thought that the Duty Clerk must have made a mistake, and he slipped it into his pocket, intending to see that it was returned to Number 10. Below were other Foreign Office telegrams that had come in from other parts of the world. There was nothing of urgency among them, and the same locked box and the same motor-cycle rider had been used to bring these down to Chevening as had brought the message from Adams.

Jock walked back down the stairs and into the drawing room. He picked up his Bloody Mary from the inlaid rosewood table on which the butler had placed it and walked straight up to the Foreign Secretary's side.

'Possibly good news from Beirut,' he said. 'Al-Fatah are holding the hostages. Nothing firm yet. There's nothing urgent in the other telegrams. They'll all wait till after lunch.'

'Thanks, Jock,' said Huggins. He looked across at his wife, who, with antennae honed by years of political experience, was eyeing him and Jock and wondering whether her lunch party was about to be ruined by her husband being summoned to Westminster or to Chequers. Robert nodded across the room to her. She nodded in turn to Jacob, who had left the drinks table and was standing by the door to the hall. He threw out his chest and announced in elegantly modulated tones that luncheon was served. Jacob never lost an opportunity to remind the guests at Chevening that he had served as head butler at the Embassy in Paris, and then as majordomo at the High Commission in Delhi. For him, Chevening was a backwater.

Jock made contact with Mary, who had been dutifully chatting up one of the impressionable young MPs.

'I was telling Roger Stable here,' she repeated the name, slowly and in full in case Jock had forgotten it, 'how carefully the Foreign Secretary always chooses his guests for his Chevening lunch parties. He is always most anxious, isn't he, Jock, that everyone, the Ambassadors, the press men, the MPs, should all fit in and contribute to the discussion, as well as having a good time.'

As she said this, Mary's mouth twisted into a cross between a grimace and a smile. For fifteen years she had worked hard and conscientiously to help further Jock's ambition, and she knew that his success so far was intertwined with that of Robert Huggins.

'That's right,' said Jock. 'That's why you were asked to the lunch today.'

Roger Stable looked very pleased.

'I didn't know that anyone in high places even knew I was Secretary of the All-party Anglo-Lebanese Parliamentary Group, but of course, I have met the Ambassador once or twice already.'

He nodded across the room at the small, dark-suited gentleman who was moving towards the door with his wife, and then he turned to Mary.

'Weren't you in the Foreign Office yourself before you and Jock married?' he asked, remembering an earlier conversation with Jock and hoping, perhaps, to impress the Minister's wife with his knowledge of her past.

'How clever of you to know that,' Mary smiled. 'Yes, I was, and I was an Arabist, too. But there's been so much change since then, especially in Lebanon. It used to be the country where everyone wished to be posted, but now it's a tragedy. You never know who's on which side.'

Roger started to tell her but Jock interrupted, 'Come on. Mary's being modest. She's an expert Arab speaker, and she keeps herself up to date. She's got lots of Arab friends and all the ambassadors love her. But we must go into lunch or everyone'll be furious with us.'

They walked across the room, through the hall, and into the heavily panelled dining room with high windows looking across a series of lawns and walks down to the lake. There was an air of pleasant, unworried expectancy in the room. Twenty people were looking forward to eating a good meal in interesting company and with few apparent worries between them. Roger Stable gazed round the room determined to remember the details in order to write them up in his diary that night and noticed that Mary, across the table from him, was already in deep conversation with the Lebanese Ambassador. She's frowning, he thought. Perhaps he's suggesting a dirty weekend when Jock is away on one of his endless trips. He smiled to himself, tucked into his tomato and avocado salad, and turned to his neighbour on his right.

A different sort of lunch party was being held at Chequers, ninety miles away to the west. There, four men had already sat down at a small, round, painted circular table, a few feet away from the main mahogany dining table. Their table was close to the double doors that led on to the rose garden. The doors were open, and on the brick wall outside, stood the empty tumblers in which the four men had had their pre-lunch drinks.

Once the butler had served them with cold chicken, cucumber and watercress salad and new potatoes, he left the room. There was an open bottle of English white wine on the table. Bruce Gordon refilled his guests' glasses and then went on with his political exposition. Scenery painting, he called it.

He wondered how they were going to get themselves into a position in which they had any chance of winning the election in the autumn. They were five points below Labour in the latest opinion poll published in the *Telegraph* that day. 'Never believe opinion polls,' he muttered, but, still, the one-point rise in interest rates had been badly received both by the press and in the House of Commons on Friday. Even the tabloids had turned against them, and there was no doubt, in his mind, that the next opinion poll would show a further fall in the Government's rating and in his own personal popularity. Unemployment was up, going up further and the Scottish Tories were in hopeless shape, all arguing with each other. The House would rise for the summer recess in four or five weeks' time, and there were no evident cards that the Government had left to play before then.

He was, he said, feeling gloomy, and he just wanted to have a talk with three close friends in order to clear their minds about all the options. Bruce Gordon took a long sip from his glass of wine and looked across the table at Piers Potter, the Home Secretary, who was sitting opposite him.

'You know,' he added. 'I've always hated English wine. I think it's thin and expensive. It's a tradition that we've got into here at Chequers. I suppose it's a sort of loyalty thing. We feel that we must be supporting our home producers. On the same basis, I imagine we'd eat English caviare and smoke British tobacco, if that sparkly fellow, the Minister of Agriculture, were ever to devise a means of producing them.

'Before I leave Chequers, I'd like to lay down a firm rule that we never have anything especially British either to eat or drink here unless it's clearly the best. I'm not going to sacrifice my liver to the pretensions of the National Farmers' Union.'

He paused, and took a further drink from his glass. He noticed that, at the very suggestion of his leaving Chequers, an imperceptible current had passed round his three colleagues. He went on: 'As I said, I wanted us to discuss all the options, but I should tell you, in the strictest confidence, I've thought seriously whether the Party would be helped if I announced now that I was giving up the leadership. After all, I'm sixty-five, and I have done quite a few years.'

He stopped again, and gazed out at the roses that were in full bloom in every bed. He thought that he liked the dark red ones best. What were they called? John S. Armstrong? Baccarat? His wife would, of course, have known. Pushing that thought urgently away from him, he re-focused his attention on the three men sitting around him.

'I've decided that it's now too late for that. It would be impossible for any of you to become properly established in the minds of the Party and the country before November, and I'm also very worried that, if I were to give up now, the Party, our parliamentary colleagues, that is, would choose Robert Huggins. I couldn't stand that. I don't think that he's the right man to step into my shoes, and as Foreign Secretary, his judgement has got much worse, much flabbier, over recent years. However, that's no secret to all of you.

'When I go, I'd much rather that it was either you, Piers, or you, Ross, who took over from me. One or other of you – that's what I'd like.' He gazed at the two men, his eyes turning from one to the other, weighing them up and down as if he were Justice holding them in her scales.

'But, sadly, I'd have to say that I think you'd be beaten by Huggins, both of you, at the moment. So the real question is whether there is anything we can do on the economics front in the next few weeks that would turn the election-tide in our favour. For

95

example, Ross, could we, in the light of the interest-rate rise, put up the tax relief on the payments of mortgage interest? Cut the rate but double the ceiling? I know that'd be going against the tide. But house prices are very high and we could argue that, because of the current high interest rates, it was particularly necessary for young couples in their first homes. That should please Angela, our Madonna of the Social Services, and I think it'd help us in a lot of the marginal seats in London and the South-East. Not to mention the South-West, where those damn Liberals are thriving.'

The Prime Minister stopped talking. There was a long pause, and then both Ross Macintosh, the Chancellor, and Piers Potter, the Home Secretary, started talking at once. Neither was anxious to let the other have the first word. The Prime Minister stopped them, and then asked Ross to give him his views about the possible increase in mortgage-interest relief.'

'It's worth examining,' said Ross. 'I've been looking at something like that for a while in the Treasury. Of course, it will infuriate the Labour Party who will say it's just an election bribe, but that doesn't matter. I was quite equivocal in my last Budget speech as to whether or not we were going to keep the present ceiling for ever. Most people took that to mean that I was planning to bring it down, or about to abolish the tax concession altogether. It would be amusing to see the look on the faces of the financial editors if we go in the other direction. But first, I'd have to get the Treasury and the Bank of England to do a run-through on the likely effect on sterling. And I think we should also ask Central Office to let us know what precise effect there would be on the marginal seats. There is no point in taking this risk unless it is clearly going to keep five or ten dicey marginals in London and the South. That's where it will help most.'

'I declare an interest,' said Gordon. 'My seat is desperately marginal.' He looked across at the Home Secretary. Piers Potter noted that Ross had said nothing about the Prime Minister's intention not to resign. When he had been telephoned on Friday evening and asked to cancel his Saturday engagements and come, instead, to lunch at Chequers, he had wondered whether the

Prime Minister was going to tell him in confidence that he would be resigning within the next few days. He could not think of any other reason for the sudden summons and, throughout the night, he had been working in his mind on the sort of speech that he would make to the back-bench MPs that he would ask to support him. He had slept only in patches, and had kept on waking up with new turns of phrase on his lips that he remembered one moment and forgot the next.

His wife had finally rebuked him and suggested that if he wanted to go to the lavatory, he should do so, rather than keep tossing about in the bed. He had got up with a conscious attempt at dignity, relieved himself, and then come back to lie between the sheets, trying not to wake the shrew by his side, but still wondering how he, a solid supporter of capital punishment, could win the votes of those who had always campaigned and voted against its return. He belonged to a right-wing club called Behind the Bars, and at a dinner of theirs in the House, he had once described the abolitionists in the Parliamentary Party as 'ponces who hadn't learnt how to pounce'. It had seemed funny at the time, but the remark had appeared in Londoners' Diary two days later, and he had regretted it ever since.

Piers Potter's mind turned round and round the question of whether he was more likely to beat Robert Huggins and Ross Macintosh for the leadership, if Bruce Gordon stood down now or if he resigned in the autumn after losing the election. He found it hard to make up his mind, and played for time.

'I think your suggestion that we should examine the ceiling on mortgage-interest relief is a good one, Bruce. It will, of course, be seen as a political gesture, but none the less I believe it will be quite popular in the Home Counties. It could make an important difference. I don't frankly see why it should have much effect on sterling as the tax concession can't cost us that much.'

Ross Macintosh shook his head in disagreement, and muttered something about a billion a year being a high price to pay for a handful of marginals. Piers continued:

'In any event, that's all to be examined both by the Treasury and

97

at Central Office. I'm sure that's right, and I suggest we get a report – a confidential report – on this proposal by next weekend. As to your generous view about resigning,' he paused and wondered whether generous was the right word to use, 'obviously, I'd like to be a candidate in the next leadership contest. I've told you that frankly in the past, and I do agree that timing is enormously important. Dominic is closer to the Parliamentary Party than any of us, and I wonder what his views are.'

All three men looked at Dominic Anderson, the Prime Minister's parliamentary private secretary. Large, florid, tall, and with a clear imprint of whisky on his face, Dominic revelled in the fact that he was more subtle than he looked. Many was the backbencher who had blurted out some marital indiscretion or profound doubt about government policy after two or three glasses of Black Label with Dominic, little knowing that the information would be stored meticulously, for eventual use when needed. The Prime Minister trusted his judgement more than that of anyone else in the Party, and knew that, if Dominic thought he had become a loser, he would tell him so.

Dominic looked at the three men, took a packet of cigarettes out of his pocket and lit one. He drew in the smoke with evident pleasure, paused and then puffed it out around the table. He had arrived at Chequers half an hour before the Home Secretary and the Chancellor, and the conversation so far had followed precisely the lines that he had suggested to the Prime Minister. He now told his colleagues that any suggestion that the Prime Minister should stand down before the summer recess should be stamped on firmly, as it would cause great division in the Party.

'It'd tear us apart like hounds on to a fox,' he said.

In his judgement, if there were to be an immediate leadership election, it would probably be won by Robert Huggins, but the greater danger was that the uncertainty would lead to further falls in the markets and thus make another rise in interest rates inevitable. That would be immensely damaging to the Party's electoral chances.

'We've got to stop Huggins,' said Dominic. 'I've no doubt about that. He's not the best person for the Party. But it will take us more time to ensure that happens. We need a scandal of some sort. Couldn't he divorce his wife and be found with a bimbo? I don't know if the Chief Whip has got anything sexy on him, but he isn't letting on to me.'

The tension went, and all the four men laughed.

'I don't think the Chief is all that sound,' said Bruce Gordon. 'I wonder if I shouldn't replace him when we come back after the holidays, and perhaps have you as Chief instead, Dominic.'

'You don't have to have me as Chief Whip, Bruce, to get all the dirt and gossip out of me. You'd better keep Greg Stevens where he is for the moment. You need all the friends that you can get.'

'I don't know that he's a friend,' said Ross Macintosh. 'I often think that he'd rather see Robert Huggins as Prime Minister than you, Bruce.'

The four men started discussing in earnest the divisions within the Cabinet. The butler came back and offered them all cheese and fruit. That was refused, but both Piers and Ross had a glass of brandy. By the time that that had been drunk, the Cabinet was evenly split in their discursive analysis between those that supported Bruce Gordon and those who would prefer to see Robert Huggins in his chair. Dominic Anderson refused to say how he thought the Parliamentary Party would divide, but repeated that it would be total folly for Bruce Gordon to give even the slightest hint of resigning before the election.

'I must get back home,' said Ross Macintosh, after another half hour of discussion in which junior ministers were moved across an imaginary board as if they were pawns in a chess game. 'I haven't been home for two weeks and even my wife must be wondering what's happened to me.'

The men laughed. Bruce Gordon led the way back through the hall and to the front door. He walked with his guests down the short flight of stone steps to the two black government Jaguars that were waiting on the gravel sweep. The Chancellor of the Exchequer got into the first, the Home Secretary into the second, and after perfunctory waves between passengers and their host, the chauffeurs drove out of the gates, down the drive and then turned right on the road towards Heathrow.

'Poor Piers,' muttered the Prime Minister to Dominic. 'He did look on tenterhooks when I mentioned the possibility of my resigning.'

'And then you squashed his hopes so brutally. He does wear his ambition on his sleeve. He's like the envious Casca, longing to stab his Caesar but anxious for others to start the bloody process,' said Dominic.

'That's very literate of you, Dominic.'

'I read all of Shakespeare at school. I find it very helpful, with parliamentary colleagues. It teaches me how they are likely to act. And their wives, too.'

'And do you think we've put to bed the idea of my resigning before the summer recess?' asked Gordon.

'I don't know. If there's to be trouble, more trouble in the weeks immediately ahead, for example, over these hostages in Beirut, then the possibility of your going before the end of July will come back.'

'If there's trouble about the hostages, I'll damn well see that it lands in Huggins' lap. I'll see that the shit hits his Foreign Office fan, not mine.'

Dominic looked enquiringly at Bruce Gordon, but the Prime Minister said no more.

'What have you got in mind?' said Dominic.

'I think Huggins might over-reach himself over the hostages,' said Gordon ambiguously, and then walked firmly towards Dominic's car, which was parked modestly at the far side of the gravel sweep. He opened the door of the Ford Granada.

'Thanks, Dominic. Thanks very much for disturbing your Saturday and coming over. It was helpful to have you here.'

'It was a pleasure, even if it ruined my day of golf. I'll see you on Monday morning at the usual time,' said Dominic as he settled into the driving seat.

'Have a good weekend, or what remains of it.'

The Prime Minister waved and Dominic raised his right hand in return. As he drove down the drive and past the police in the little guard-house towards the main road, Dominic thought of the Prime Minister playing off the ambitions of the Chancellor against those of the Home Secretary. He smiled happily to himself, inserted a tape into his car radio of Gielgud reading King Lear, and turned left out of the drive towards Buckingham, his golf course and his home.

The Prime Minister walked slowly back up the stone steps and turned towards his study. There he sat for a time contemplating, leaning back in his chair, his eyes almost closed, and then he leaned over, picked up the telephone and asked the switchboard to find Eddie Ford, his press secretary, for him and to get him on the line.

7

Sunday 30 June

Sunday was the only day of the week when Jock and Mary took a long time over breakfast. They had all the Sunday heavies and spread the various sections at random over the kitchen table where they ate, dipping in and out like seagulls scavenging on a beach. As Jock scooped out the first mouthful of a boiled egg, his eye fell on a front-page piece in the *Observer* by Toby Renulf. It was headed: WHEN WILL THE HOSTAGE ROT STOP?

Renulf pointed out that, over the last few weeks, two professors from the American Lebanese University, David Malik and Tom Schiavi, had both been kidnapped, two Frenchmen had been abducted and an American plane, TWA 930, had been hijacked. First it had been diverted around the Mediterranean, from Algeria to Italy to Greece, and finally it had been allowed to land at Beirut. One hostage, Julius Landers, had been shot and his body dropped out of the aeroplane on to the airport tarmac. Thirty-nine other passengers remained hostage. The hijackers were demanding the release of Shiite prisoners held in Israel as well as the release of seventeen Arabs in Kuwait. The hostage crisis had reached a new level of intensity.

Renulf wrote:

Western governments appear paralysed and incapable of action. The British and American governments in particular behave like rabbits, frozen into immobility by the stare of a hostile snake. Since Bob Janes and Les Harrington were grabbed in Beirut a week ago, there has been no indication of serious planning or of strategic thinking. Whilst the Foreign Secretary was in Africa on one of his usual jaunts, his Minister of State, Jock Meldrum-Ross, bumbled through a difficult Question Time in the Commons, clearly embarrassed at not being able to give

102

any positive answers to anxious Members of Parliament on both sides of the House.

But this is the sort of inertia that will seriously damage the Government. One prominent Tory backbencher told me last night that the Prime Minister himself was very concerned at the inability of the Foreign Office to come forward with any new ideas regarding the British hostages. Downing Street thinks that the Foreign Office is, as usual, over-anxious to pacify Arab opinion. 'A Saudi Prince only has to twitch his white robes and the Foreign Office falls over to kiss his feet,' commented a Downing Street source.

Egg forgotten, Jock read on. His cheeks flushed when Renulf concluded his article with a sentence saying that the ministerial team at the Foreign Office was undoubtedly weak and would have to be radically changed if the Conservatives won the next election.

The telephone rang, and Jock reached over the newspapers to pick it up. He heard Robert Huggins' familiar voice at the other end, and he had hardly time to wish him good morning before Huggins burst into a storm of protest.

'Have you seen today's *Sunday Telegraph?*'

'No,' said Jock. 'I was just reading the *Observer.*'

'Forget the bloody *Observer*. None of our voters read it. Look at the *Telegraph*, page three, a special piece by Brewster Godden, and you'll find "sources close to Downing Street . . .", those creeps, saying that the Prime Minister thinks that I should go before the election, as I am out of touch with Tory philosophy. What bloody nonsense! I'll bet every penny I have that that line comes directly from Gordon himself through Eddie Ford, the Press Officer.'

'I don't know,' said Jock. 'Godden could have made it all up.'

'Never,' said Huggins. 'He wouldn't be allowed to. He must have convinced his editor, Polly Plowman, that this was a genuine unattributable leak from Number 10, or she wouldn't have printed it.'

'The stuff about the American airliner is bad, isn't it?' said Jock, trying to divert his boss away from the treachery of Number 10.

'Yes. I've already had George Swithin on the 'phone from the State Department asking whether we would make our facilities at

Akrotiri available for fuelling and suchlike, in case they decide to send the Marines over. I agreed.'

'The last time they tried to rescue hostages by force, it was a total disaster,' said Jock.

'I haven't forgotten that.' The voice at the other end of the telephone line was still angry. 'But if the Americans want to make fools of themselves, I can't stop them. In any event, they think that Hizbollah are behind the hijack of the TWA plane, and they're usually more dangerous than the lot holding our two men.'

'Did you tell him about Al-Fatah?' asked Jock.

'No, I didn't. I wouldn't trust the Americans not to blurt it out.'

They talked on for a while, agreeing that hostages, British and American, were bound to be headline news throughout the days ahead, and then Huggins rang off.

'What's Robert so cross about?' said Mary, looking up from the *Sunday Times*. Jock told her in full and angry detail, until she looked at her watch and said:

'Are we going to church? The boys are all away with your parents.'

'Yes, we should go,' said Jock.

'Well, you'll have to hurry and put on a tie and a coat.'

Jock got up from the table, pushed his uneaten egg to one side and walked with Mary to their bedroom. He pulled a pale yellow tie off a rack in the cupboard and then followed it with the same coat that he had worn the day before. Slipping his hand into the pocket, he pulled out a flimsy piece of paper.

'What's that?' asked Mary, turning away from the mirror to make sure that he was dressing with speed.

'Blast. It's Number 10's copy of a telegram that went to Chevening by mistake. I meant to send it on to them yesterday evening, but I forgot. I suppose they'll have got another copy of it by now.'

'Is it important?' asked Mary. 'Do let me see it.'

Jock was busy tying the laces on his well-polished brown shoes and gave no sign of hearing, as Mary picked up the telegram and read it. She raised her eyebrows in surprise and asked:

104

'Why is it so important for the Beirut Embassy to radio the moment the Libyan air freighter leaves?'

'Oh, darling,' said Jock crossly, as he turned to the mirror and took his coat off the back of a chair, 'it's all to do with the Tornados catching the air freighter off Cyprus. They'll have precious little time to spare.'

'So that's all decided?'

'Oh, yes, provided we're as certain as can be that our two hostages are on the plane. If we attacked it and they weren't on board, it'd be disastrous.'

Mary screwed up her lips and looked out of the window. A clock sounded in the distance.

'Jock,' her voice sounded sharp. 'We're going to be late again. I can't stand walking into that church during the first prayers and having everyone turn round and stare at me. For goodness sake, stop tying your laces in huge knots like a small boy and hurry up.'

'It's not my fault, it's Robert's. He shouldn't have telephoned and talked to me for so long on a Sunday morning.'

As they walked out of the front door, towards their car, Jock went on telling Mary of the Foreign Secretary's fury at the leaks from the Number 10 Press Office.

'I always think that "sources close to Number 10" make it sound as if the rumour must have come from either Number 11 or Number 9,' said Mary.

Jock laughed. 'You're being generous, darling. "Sources close to Number 10" means Number 10.'

Two hours later, around three o'clock Beirut time, Colonel Moberly left a large and elegant lunch party at the Spanish Ambassador's residence in Hadath, got behind the steering wheel of his Rover, and drove off into West Beirut. He had enjoyed the gathering. He had liked chatting about the intricate problems of the Lebanese and discussing which of the innumerable political parties would win the next election, whether money from the Gulf would start rebuilding central Beirut or whether the endless fighting between Jew and Arab, between extremist and moderate, would deter every foreign investor.

As he worked his way through the many dishes of mezze and aubergine, spinach fatayer, red mullet and lamb on rice dotted with currants and red and green peppers, he had quietly revelled in impressing the attractive, heavily jewelled and scented women around him with his knowledge of the endless convolutions of Lebanese political life. They bolstered his confidence and gave him more of a feeling of being a personality than he ever had at home or in the Embassy.

'You must come and have dinner with us at our house up the coast near Byblos,' said one of them as he left, 'or come for lunch and a swim. Do you water-ski? My husband has just got a new boat and he is longing to show it off. A pity your wife is not here with you.'

Moberly had accepted the invitation with pleasure and tucked it away for future use.

Underneath his Sandhurst exterior, however, he felt deeply indignant at the way the Ambassador had rebuked him the day before for losing sight of the black Mercedes that could have led him to where Janes and Harrington were being held.

Moberly was a desk-top soldier. He had read books of military history. He had been through the Strategic Studies courses at Staff College. At a pinch, he could talk about Clausewitz' philosophy of war or Tolstoy's theory on generals, but he had never fired in anger except at a low pheasant that he had already missed with his first barrel. He longed to put this right and to be involved in action with noise, bullets, bodies and blood. Yesterday, as he followed the Mercedes, he had heard tunes of glory and dreamt of medals and congratulations from commanding officers. He knew it was not his fault that he had lost the Mercedes but he was determined to find the hostages' whereabouts if he possibly could.

Moberly drove to the shabby, ruined area of South Beirut where he had last seen the Mercedes. In the bright Mediterranean sunshine, with the sun seeming to be hanging, static, overhead, he drove past houses with holes in their walls and shell-craters in the ground but with small shops still trading, their goods and fruit and fish spilling out on to the pavement. He passed a café where he could see Arabs sitting inside around white metal tables, drinking from cloudy bottles of orange juice or sipping minute cups of coffee.

It was steaming hot, and Moberly felt the sweat start soaking through his cream cotton shirt into the lightweight blazer that he was wearing. He drove twice round the block where he had lost the Mercedes and then came back, parked the Rover opposite the little café, took off his coat and walked over in shirt sleeves to the other side of the road. He had no clear plan of what he was going to do, but he noticed one of the Lebanese sitting at a café table, looking closely at him. Then he got the impression that the Lebanese half nodded at him. There were empty places at the table, so he sat down and ordered a glass of lemon juice from the waiter. Some minutes passed, and then the lemon juice appeared, accompanied by a carafe of water and an extra glass. Moberly thanked the waiter, diluted the juice with some extra water, drank and waited.

The Lebanese leant over the table and said in a quiet voice, 'You are a European. There are not many Europeans these days in this part of Beirut.' He spoke slowly and with a strong accent, but with no searching for words.

'It's a pleasant afternoon. I had not much to do, so I thought I would drive through South Beirut,' said Moberly.

There was a long silence. Moberly poured himself a glass of water and drank alternate sips of water and diluted lemon juice. He again got the impression that the Lebanese was eyeing him inquisitively as if not certain whether to say more. The silence continued, but without strain. It had no particular stress or pregnancy. It was just an Arab silence, suited to the heat and to thought and to waiting, a silence for those with plenty of time.

Then the Lebanese leant over the table and said quietly: 'South Beirut is not a safe place but you drove up the street and then down again. You are, I think, looking for something.'

Moberly paused for only a second, and then said: 'Yes, I am. I am looking for two men who were captured a week ago.'

107

'Why have you come here to look for them?'

'I think they are in this part of Beirut.'

'Why, my friend? Why should they be here?' The voice of the Lebanese seemed to get softer and slower.

'I have my reasons.' Moberly spoke pompously but wondered immediately whether he had gone too far. The words had slipped out and there was nothing he could do to call them back.

'Reasons? Reasons? Persuade me of your reasons and perhaps I may be able to help you.'

Moberly paused further, and then, impetuously, suddenly thinking that his luck might be turning, he went on:

'Yesterday, I was following a black Mercedes. I think it was connected with the kidnapping of the two Britons last weekend. I thought that it could lead me to where the hostages were being held, but unfortunately, two blocks away from here, a boy ran in front of me and slipped. By the time that he got up, there were other cars in front of me and I lost the Mercedes.'

'So you came back today to see if you could pick up the scent?' There was a harsh note in the voice. The Lebanese suddenly sounded as if he were interrogating, and Moberly froze. Fool, he thought. I have already gone too far. At that moment, he noticed the Arab opposite him turn his head away and look through the open door at the back of the café. Almost immediately, three men in camouflage denims came in through the door and started moving across the café towards Moberly's table.

Without pausing for thought, he jumped up, pushed his chair backwards, and ran towards the roadside. The Lebanese sitting at his table shouted in Arabic at the three men and they started to chase after Moberly.

He tore across the street, dodged between cars, opened the door of the Rover and locked it immediately from the inside. As he shoved his key into the ignition, a pistol shot rang out from across the street and the toughened glass by his side rang with a loud smack, crazed but did not break. The car started instantly and jerked forward as Moberly pressed his foot hard down on the accelerator. He felt a body bump into his rear door and grab for the handle, but the car pulled away quickly and the door did not open. More shots rang out but Moberly kept his foot flat down on the accelerator and the Rover surged through its automatic gears. What a bloody fool I was, he thought. I can't think why I blurted all that out to a stranger. He turned to the right and to the right again. He looked in the rear mirror to make certain that he was not being followed but saw no sign of any suspicious car. So he settled down in his driving seat, turned back north towards his flat, and started to bend his mind to the difficult question of what he would say to the Ambassador and how he would explain the crazed glass on the window.

Two kilometres away, and an hour later, the Lebanese who had sat opposite Moberly told his side of the story to Ahmed and Faisal. They sat around a table on the ground floor of the house where Janes and Harrington were now held. There was a pile of old cans, bottles and rubbish in a corner. Under the table were scraps of food with which a leggy, ginger cat played unenthusiastically, and flies buzzed round the windows. Heat permeated the stale air, giving every smell a tangible quality as if it could be analysed, savoured and absorbed.

Faisal shook his head with disapproval when he heard of the three Arabs coming out of the café and chasing the Englishman across the street.

'Why did you summon them?' he asked.

'I thought we would try to capture the Englishman. He knows something about the hostages. It would have been useful to question him and perhaps to keep him.'

'But you did not succeed. He got away, and now he will tell those for whom he is working that the hostages must be in this area. Otherwise, you would not have attempted to try and capture him.'

There was silence, and then the sound of a car arriving. The three got to their feet. Faisal went to open the door and they were joined by a short, heavily built Arab with a thick, black moustache covering the centre of his upper lip. He wore a khaki uniform, the colour of fresh mud, and had three rows of medal ribbons and two

109

stars and a crown on his shoulder flashes. Faisal explained to the new arrival what had happened, addressing him as Colonel and treating him without deference but with cautious respect.

'You were fools,' said Colonel Karam, 'to allow this Englishman to be chased and then not to be captured. That was careless.'

The story and the explanation were given again. The Colonel listened with evident impatience and anger.

'The wolf will stay near the chicken coop,' said the Colonel. 'Certainly, we can now expect the Lebanese forces sniffing around all of this area, and perhaps they will be joined by Syrian troops as well. There is far too much activity since Hizbollah hijacked the TWA aeroplane last week. Then there are journalists everywhere looking for hostages, and they are even more trouble. We will have to release these two; they are good men and we will make the best of it. Today, we will tell the Libyans we are not interested in handing over these two. They will try to negotiate with us but, later, we will say they escaped by mistake. That madman, Gadaffi, will become even more mad!'

The Colonel paused and thought for a while. Then he said: 'Bring the Englishmen down here.'

Ahmed walked across the room and disappeared. The others could hear him through the thin walls as he climbed up the stairs and unlocked the room on the second floor. A few minutes later, he appeared with Janes handcuffed to him, and Harrington following behind. Both the Englishmen were dirty, with week-old beards; the spark had gone out of them and they stood, heads hanging down, as they faced the Colonel.

'Take off those handcuffs,' said the Colonel. 'There is no need for them. You two, you know well enough that if you try to run away we will shoot you.'

He tapped the pistol holster that was strapped to his left hip. Janes and Harrington each gave a half-nod. The handcuffs were unlocked and removed and Janes moved cautiously rubbing his wrists in relief still aware of pain in his shoulders despite the heavy strapping which now bound and supported them. They gazed about them, taking in the filthy room and looking across at the door out on to the street. They could hear sounds of people walking past and chattering in the street outside.

The Colonel followed their gaze.

'Don't go on thinking where your escape route might be and planning how to get away.' He spoke in quick, peremptory English, reflecting a military training at British hands.

'You will not have heard this, as you have been held now for one week, but for the last few days, the Americans have used all their resources to get the release of thirty-nine passengers from a hijacked TWA plane. One passenger was shot. Hizbollah would like to do the same to the other thirty-nine unless Shiite prisoners in Israel and Kuwait are released. But the Amal militia have got hold of the airline passengers and crew, and we expect that they will be freed tonight. That will make the extremist groups very annoyed. Hizbollah have already told us that they would then want to use you as suicide bombers.'

The Colonel paused, looked out through the window, as if he were searching for some sign of salvation in the dusty heat outside, and then turned back to Janes and Harrington. Panic was showing on their faces.

'You wonder what would happen to you. You would be tied down on the back seats of two cars, each driven by one of those mad young girls whom Hizbollah have taught to believe that they will win perpetual salvation by driving themselves and their cars filled with explosives into the frontier posts of the South Lebanese army. They blow up the posts, they kill themselves, but they kill hundreds of the Jews and the Lebanese traitors at the same time. And, perhaps, they kill Americans, too. They are, of course, mad, but they have been taught that such suicide leads to salvation. You two, trapped in the cars and blown up at the same time, would,' he paused, and chose his words with extra care, 'be an added spice. Dead, you would gain headlines all round the world, and so would the Hizbollah girls.' He paused again. 'We are not an extreme group.' He pointed to Ahmed and Faisal. 'I hope they have not been unkind to you.'

Bob Janes remembered the brutal kicking that he had received

111

earlier in the week, his broken collarbone and the bruises that were still all over his shoulders, but he said nothing. The Colonel went on:

'We have investigated you two. We do not think that you are here to spy for the Americans or for the United Nations. We are told that you have been doing good work in bringing water into our distant villages and in improving the water supply where it has been damaged and is full of disease. Allah is merciful, and we have decided to follow in the steps of Allah and to show mercy to you.

'One night very soon, when we have finished our arrangements, we will drive you into central Christian Beirut and allow you to escape from the car. You will be able to get back through the streets in the early morning, either to your Embassy or to your homes or wherever you wish. But there is one condition. You must make it clear that you have run away, escaped. You must never say that we released you. That would cause us Palestinians great problems with our patriotic comrades, with Hizbollah and with others in the Islamic Jihad. We would certainly be killed by them as they would think we had betrayed the Arab cause, and, if you are still in Lebanon, you and your wives will be killed, too. Do you understand me?'

He stopped and looked at Janes and Harrington. They looked at each other, and a feeling of incredible relief flooded through them. Each waited for the other to speak, and then Bob burst in:

'Thank you,' he paused and added: 'Sir . . . I, I, we can't thank you enough. It's, it's bloody incredible. Isn't it, Les?' He turned but Les was looking the other way. Bob spoke more emphatically and slowly, as if he were making a formal statement.

'As we have said to you, we are here only to do good for the Lebanese people through a United Nations agency. We've worked to help the poor people in Lebanon by improving their water and by stopping them getting terrible diseases through filthy water. We are grateful to you for trusting us, and we will give you our solemn word that we will always say that we escaped by luck rather than by your letting us go.'

He looked at Les who had tears running down his face.

'I just can't believe it,' said Les. 'I'm, I'm . . .' he searched for words. 'I don't know what to say – I, I never thought you'd let me go. I thought I'd had it.' He turned away and sobbed, not trying any longer to conceal his tears which were mixed with nervous laughter.

Colonel Karam and the other Arabs looked intently at Janes and Harrington, as if trying to gauge the honesty of the two of them, and wondering how long that honesty would last. Eventually the Colonel said:

'You swear this to me, that you will keep silent about Al-Fatah releasing you, by the most solemn promise in your religion?'

'Yes,' said Bob, and then added: 'By all I hold true, I promise. I realize you're putting great trust in us.' Les nodded his agreement.

'And you will stick to this story when you are talking to your wives, your families, the press, your Ambassador here in Beirut? And your employers at the United Nations?'

'Yes,' Les and Bob spoke at the same time.

'Very well,' said the Colonel. 'We will now plan in detail how this escape is to happen. It will be soon because there will be great pressure on us when Amal release the hostages from the TWA airliner. Hizbollah, who are fanatics, murderers, paid for by the thugs in Teheran, will want to make an immediate gesture to show that they cannot be bullied by the West, and you would be part of that. Your deaths as suicide bombers would suit them well.' He paused. 'I'll come back or I will send Faisal and Ahmed when we have arranged matters.'

The Colonel turned, gestured to the three men around him and went on speaking quietly for some minutes in Arabic to Ahmed and Faisal. They both nodded their heads a number of times in agreement, and then the Colonel walked away towards the door. A short while later, they heard a car start up and then drive off at a slow speed. Bob imagined the Colonel's driver picking his way between piles of garbage, potholes and passers-by, all mixed in a narrow, dusty road.

Faisal turned to the two Englishmen and said in his careful English and soft voice: 'We must shut you back in the room upstairs, but we will no longer handcuff you or tie you up to the chains, so you will be more comfortable. Do not try and escape, for if you do, I will still shoot you with pleasure. But the Colonel, he is a kind man. He is to be trusted. Within the next night or two, he will arrange for you to get back to your homes.'

'Thank God,' said Les instinctively, and he and Bob walked out of the room, looking as if burdens of care and doubt had just fallen off their backs. Upright and cheerful, they talked noisily to each other as they walked back up the stairs until Faisal gestured to them to keep quiet.

8

Monday 1 July

'If you play your cards right, and we win the next election, in a year or two, you could be Foreign Secretary.'

The Prime Minister looked across the small table at Jock Meldrum-Ross. He smiled inwardly as he noticed the Foreign Office Minister of State was simultaneously excited and uneasy. Jock, in turn, looked up at the Prime Minister with a half-supressed gasp of surprise, and then his eyes fell to the cheese and water-biscuits on his plate, and he went through an elaborate motion of cutting three little bits of cheddar and arranging them on his biscuit. He is really a typical Foreign Office worm, thought Bruce Gordon. You put him on a hook and he wriggles a bit, then goes limp and subsides, but he's good-looking.

'Yes, you could, Jock,' went on the Prime Minister, in his most paternal voice. 'You're the right age, you've got the brains and the experience. You've got a lot of friends in the House. I know that – the Chief Whip tells me. If we win the election, what I'd like to do is get you into the Cabinet immediately at a junior level, say at Employment, or Chief Secretary. Would Chief Secretary at the Treasury do you? Are you tough enough to fight Environment, Health and Social Security on their ghastly budgets?'

The Prime Minister was enjoying himself. He had always been a bully and had found pleasure in making people junior to him squirm with embarrassment. To this, he had added in recent years a brutal touch of sadism. Many times he had threatened young MPs with the total ruin of their future careers if they crossed him by not voting for his policies.

He enjoyed seeing a young hopeful back away from an assurance, made to his constituency executive and the local press the previous weekend, that he would stand up and vote the way his conscience demanded whatever the pressure from the Government. Principle faded quickly and was replaced by the moth of corruption as the Prime Minister purred about the bright future ahead for those whom he could totally trust to support the policies about which he had tossed and turned and agonized for many sleepless hours.

He had long ago come to the conclusion that all his parliamentary colleagues were venal. The only difference between them was that some could be bought for minor posts with a hideous overload of work and few prospects; others needed seats in the Cabinet, and plenty of junior ministers under them who would make the tiresome daytime journeys to the provinces for them, and take the late-night debates in the Commons afterwards. He was not yet certain into which category Meldrum-Ross fell.

'Have some coffee, Jock?'

'Yes, please, Prime Minister.'

The Prime Minister got up and walked over to the low shelf on which a percolator was bubbling gently. He poured two cups.

'Cream? Sugar?' He looked over at Jock, who was still studiously regarding the biscuit crumbs on his plate.

Ass, thought Bruce Gordon. He's embarrassed, or he's trying to protect Huggins. If he had any spunk, he'd have already jumped at my offer of a Cabinet seat.

'Cream, please, Prime Minister. No sugar.' The Foreign Secretary was away in Brussels for the morning, at a European Community Foreign Ministers' meeting. When Anthea Wheeler had burst into his office at mid-day and gushed that Number 10 were on the 'phone and asking if he was free to lunch with the Prime Minister, Jock had assumed that the purpose of the lunch was to talk about the hostages in Beirut. He had meant to put in his pocket Number 10's copy of the telegram that he had removed from Chevening on Saturday, as he felt he should show it to the Prime Minister, but he could not find it anywhere. Perhaps that was as well. It would be hard to explain why he had hung on to it for forty-eight hours.

116

'I don't think Chief Secretary would suit you. You are not really a figures man; you are an ideas person. Someone who deals in strategies and concepts. I've seen that in the way you approach the problem of these two men who got themselves caught in Beirut, silly fools. They shouldn't have been wandering up and down West Beirut the way they were. No wonder they got grabbed by some bloody Arabs. We'll hear from the terrorists soon, and they will demand that our men are swapped for arms or those prisoners in Kuwait. That's the way it always is.

'You didn't do well in the House last week, but we can all make mistakes like that. What I like is the way you kept your head on the position in Cyprus. That's going to be tricky. We can't afford to make any mistakes. If we shoot down a Libyan plane, or if we force it down and there are no hostages in it, there will be hell to pay throughout the Middle East. I don't think your boss understands this. He's just too wrapped up with his friends in the Community, and then he goes off on these dreadful trips round the black African countries, when all they want is more money and more aid from us. The begging bowl is always out, and Robert Huggins is always the man to fill it up from the British taxpayer's purse.'

Bruce Gordon paused, took a long sip from his cup of coffee, and wondered whether he was going too far. No, he thought, if ever I am going to get hold of Meldrum-Ross this is the moment to do it. And I may need him in the days ahead. He gestured round the small kitchen in the flat at the top of Downing Street in which they were sitting.

'That's why I asked you to lunch with me privately up here. We're going to be under real pressure about the hostages from now on. Last night the Americans got their thirty-nine released from the TWA aeroplane, and today every madman in the House will be demanding that we do the same for our two. You saw the leader in *The Times* this morning quoting that ass, Swithin – "You are back, and America did not compromise its principles to get you back." That's a load of balls. I bet he promised the Iranians, the Syrians, the Palestinians and everyone else in sight a cargo of the latest American weapons. But then, of course, the leader-writer turns on me and insists that I achieve the same result without compromising our principles. What does *The Times* think we all are? A bunch of choirboys?' Gordon was becoming indignant.

'But your Foreign Secretary, your master, Huggins, hasn't got a clue, not a clue, how to get a deal. The terrorists may bump them off if we don't come up with some ideas soon. Or they will get killed in the Libyan plane.

'Now what I want you to do may be a bit unconventional but hard times demand hard solutions. I want you to ring Martin Jevons at the BBC, and arrange to meet him somewhere private tonight. At your home, I suggest. I want you to tell him frankly that you are concerned about our gung-ho attempts to get our hostages back, leak to him the story about Akrotiri, and the SAS, and the squadron of Tornados that we have sent there. Tell him not to use this information until something breaks, but say that you're worried that the Foreign Secretary is going to go over the top and that there is a danger that a Libyan plane will be shot down and our two hostages killed.

'Paint it hot and strong. Say that it's all part of Huggins' mania to show himself a man of action and to get himself a good press before the election. That's why you're so concerned about it.' Bruce Gordon paused again and looked over the table at Jock. Jock had stopped fiddling with crumbs and was gazing with rapt attention directly at the Prime Minister. Gordon noticed for the first time that he had very clear blue eyes. 'Martin Jevons won't be surprised to get a telephone message from you. He has been alerted to the possibility,' the Prime Minister added cryptically.

There was a very long silence. Jock's mind twisted this way and that. His father had been an Ambassador, in Copenhagen, Brussels and, finally, Rome. Jock had been brought up in the atmosphere of polite, secret plots, of conversation that could only be understood by the initiated. That was part and parcel of the Foreign Office. He had always longed to be Foreign Secretary, ever since he was a small boy and he remembered the Foreign Secretary coming to stay with his parents at the Rome Embassy and the deferential way in which he had been treated by everyone, his mother and father included. Mary had stirred and poked the slender fire of Jock's ambition. She thought Jock was wasting his time as a junior minister and wanted him either in the Cabinet and in the newspaper headlines every day or out of government, earning a good lot of money. She was witty and quick and enjoyed putting over her views about Middle East Christians and the problems of the Palestinians on the West Bank to admiring Ambassadors who were sometimes pleased, sometimes alarmed to find a sharp mind on top of the pearl necklace, but she was bored easily.

'But isn't that a bit like . . .' Jock paused and gulped, 'treachery?' The word hung in the air and Jock stared straight at the Prime Minister. At least he doesn't duck looking at me, thought Bruce, feeling a twinge of old homosexuality.

'No it isn't, Jock. It's pragmatism. It's being a good Jesuit. It's using appropriate means to achieve a necessary end. Here is Martin Jevons' telephone number; it's his direct line.' He held out a piece of paper and, as Jock reached to take it, his hand rested on Jock's for a second or two longer than was necessary. Jock looked at him, smiled instinctively and put the paper in his pocket.

Colonel Moberly had been wondering all night how to explain the cracked glass on the window of his car to the Ambassador. The Ambassador was so finicky, he was bound to notice.

He wondered whether to pretend that a stone had been thrown at him and that had caused the damage. As he tossed and turned in his bed indecisively, he thought how awful it would be if he were found out and sent back to the small house in Surrey where his wife and two young children were soldiering on in his absence. Better come clean, he thought. The Ambassador can't shoot me. So, with shoes newly brushed and wearing his best uniform with a shiny Sam Browne belt, he walked from his office to the Ambassador's around six o'clock that evening. He hoped the Ambassador might open his drinks cupboard and offer him a gin and tonic and that would put everyone in a more genial mood. He found the Ambassador looking excitedly at a piece of paper in his hand.

'I'm sorry to disturb you, Ambassador,' Moberly started pompously, 'but I thought I should let you know that I had a bit of bother in South Beirut yesterday afternoon.'

'Did you?' the Ambassador interrupted him. 'You shouldn't have been in South Beirut without an escort. Never mind, Moberly, as long as you weren't doing anything foolish like looking for those hostages. Look at this, it's just come in from London. They have intercepted another message between the Libyan Embassy here and Tripoli. Read it.' The Ambassador bubbled with evident excitement as he handed the paper over to Moberly. Moberly read slowly, almost spelling out the words audibly.

URGENT. PRIORITY. LONDON 1330. MESSAGE INTERCEPTED FROM BEIRUT TO TRIPOLI AT 0930 THIS MORNING AND DECIPHERED AS FOLLOWS:

SERIOUS MECHANICAL TROUBLE WITH NEW EMBASSY MERCEDES. THEREFORE WILL SHIP MERCEDES BACK TO TRIPOLI TUESDAY USING AIR FREIGHTER STILL AT BEIRUT AIRPORT. EXPECTED TIME OF DEPARTURE 1500 LOCAL TIME.

'There it is, Moberly, we're in business at last. At last!' The Ambassador sighed with relief. 'You must go to the airport tomorrow morning in civilian clothes, take the VHF radio and send us a message when the car arrives and as soon as the freighter takes off. That will give the signal to Akrotiri to start things moving. Now, what was the trouble you wanted to tell me about?' The Ambassador was excited, delighted that, after months of inaction, his little team was going to take part in a real exercise that could be of great importance. Before Moberly could answer, he leant back in his swivel chair, turned towards the drinks cupboard behind him and pulled out a large bottle of Gordon's gin, two finely-cut glasses and two bottles of Schweppes tonic. 'We must drink to the success of the Tornados and the SAS. I'm sorry there's no ice or lemon.'

120

Moberly waited while the Ambassador filled his glass with a generous quantity of gin and topped it up with tonic. The saliva glands in his mouth moistened and he poured a large slug of the gin and tonic down his throat.

'Excellent. I'll be there, Ambassador. I'll take the radio and my binoculars and I will let you know everything I see. About my car . . .'

'Forget about your car, man. Provided it's in good enough shape to get you to the airport, that's all we need. But you can't transmit in code on the VHF radio, so just send us the absolute essentials and put it all cryptically, just to confuse anyone who is listening. How about referring to the car as a laundry basket and the freighter as a van? You could say that the laundry basket has arrived and is safely in the van, and so on.' The Ambassador smiled and could not help thinking how ridiculous this all sounded.

'Good idea, Ambassador. I'll do just that. Basket of laundry – van. Excellent. Must get it the right way round, though. Can't afford to drop the ball in the slips.' A look of pain crossed the Ambassador's face, and Moberly drained down the rest of his gin and tonic and decided that it would be a mistake of timing and propriety to refer any more to the damaged window in his car.

An hour later, as Jock was putting his papers together to go to the Cabinet sub-committee meeting on the Akrotiri interception, he got a message from the Foreign Secretary's private office asking him to walk along the passage and to see the Foreign Secretary before the meeting began. He bundled the papers into a file, shoved it under his arm and walked through his private office, telling them that he expected to be back in around an hour.

'I hope it goes all right,' said Anthea. 'It'll be a very worrying meeting, Minister, committing the aeroplanes, and the SAS and all.'

'These things have to be done, Anthea,' said Jock piously. Even as he said it, he wondered whether that was true. He walked down the corridor, past the murals of the Triumphs of the British

Empire, past the open door of the Ambassadors' waiting room and into the large private office, with its windows full of sun and overlooking the trees and the water of St. James's Park.

'The Foreign Secretary is waiting for you,' said one of the private secretaries, nodding towards the door. Jock walked into the Foreign Secretary's room and found him sitting at his desk which looked like a small work-centre in the middle of the room, surrounded by a large conference table and empty sofas and chairs.

'Sit down, Jock,' said Robert Huggins. 'I've just got back from Brussels. I left before the last three items on the agenda, including a ludicrous proposal from the Luxembourgers that the Community should start and finance a European Contemporary Dance Company. It'd make Bruce pee in his pants if I agreed and promised a million pounds for young Europeans, in jeans and tutus. He'd chase the little sods all over the place.' He laughed and went on. 'But that's another story. I felt I had to come back for the Cabinet sub-committee. There are a few things I want to rehearse with you.'

His voice became serious. 'First, it's extremely important that, depending of course on Cabinet's final decision, clear and precise instructions go to Akrotiri, committing us to engage the Libyan air freighter and to force it to land in Cyprus. Once we've made up our collective mind, we can't afford to have any doubts. If the car is driven on board tomorrow morning, and we get a message that it is on board, we will just have to assume that Janes and Harrington are there as well, even if they haven't actually been spotted. Otherwise, we will give muddled instructions and probably let the air freighter slip away and back to Tripoli.

'Then . . .' Huggins paused and chose his words carefully, 'as I said to you before, I'm worried that the Prime Minister is somehow going to use this affair to get at me and undermine my position. I don't know how he proposes to do it but I want you, this evening, to get hold of someone from the press or the BBC, someone you know well and whom you can trust, and go over all the details with him, explaining carefully why we have to be committed to this interception and make it quite clear that the Prime Minister and, indeed, the whole Cabinet are fully involved. Do this on a confidential basis, on lobby terms, not to be used until after the interception takes place. But, then, the information can be used and spread around at once.' Huggins paused again. 'I want to be absolutely certain that my side of the story is clear and well known. I can't trust our own press officer here. All the press officers are in cahoots, and they take their instructions from Number 10 anyway. So I want to use you as my messenger. Who do you think you should talk to?' He looked enquiringly at Jock.

Jock paused. A great feeling of loneliness suddenly washed over him. He realized he was approaching his own crossroads at which he would have to decide where his final loyalties were. It was not an experience to which he was accustomed, and he did not feel ready to make his decision.

'I suppose I could talk to Martin Jevons of the BBC. I know him well and I can trust him not to leak the story before we've got the Libyan air freighter down on the ground.'

'Martin Jevons?' Huggins looked surprised. 'Why not Sandy Gorman of the Press Association? He would have better access to all the other journalists.'

'Perhaps, but I couldn't be certain that he wouldn't spill the story too soon. After all, it's an enormous scoop for someone.'

'That's true,' said Huggins. 'All right. Use Martin Jevons. Tell him I asked you to do so.' Huggins paused. All his political life, he had been loyal to his party leader and all those above him in the Party hierarchy. Ever since he had become a member of the Government, he had been studiously faithful to the Prime Minister in public, however much he disagreed with him in the privacy of his heart or in private conversation with friends. Now he realized he was going over the brink. Like a Jesuit leaving his order, he had to shed garments that had been part of his way of life for many years.

'Jock, I know this isn't easy for either of us but, if you do this well, and if we get rid of Bruce Gordon, I'll look after you. I'll see that you're in my first Cabinet.'

Jock coloured and got to his feet. 'That's very good of you, Foreign Secretary,' he said formally. 'I'd love to serve in any Cabinet where you were the Prime Minister.' He looked at his watch. 'It's time that we went to that committee meeting or they'll have started without us and agreed a plan that we won't be able to amend.'

The two men laughed, and Robert Huggins picked up the telephone and told his principal private secretary to join them. Together, the three walked down the private staircase and out of the Foreign Secretary's entrance. They turned right and climbed up the steps into Downing Street. With barely a glance at them, the policeman at the top turned the key in the lock and opened the heavy iron gates for them.

'Good afternoon, Foreign Secretary, a lovely afternoon,' he said. Huggins smiled and, remembering the policeman's fondness for racing, asked if he had any good tips for that afternoon.

'John's Joy,' said the officer promptly. 'Each way, the four-thirty at Brighton.'

'Remember that, Jock,' said Huggins and then walked on briskly towards Number 10, hands deep in his pockets, a myriad thoughts in his mind.

The same group was waiting in the Cabinet Room as had been there at the meeting the previous Wednesday, with the exception of Colonel Spacemead. Tony Castle was already sitting down facing the fireplace, with the windows behind him. Two seats away on his right was General Briggs and beyond him, the anonymous men from GCHQ and MI6. Opposite General Briggs sat Neil Hawthorne, the Cabinet Office Defence expert, and Sir Peter Trout. Robert Huggins sat down in the empty chair between Castle and Briggs. Jock sat on Castle's left. Huggins's private secretary disappeared to the far end of the table and immediately pulled out a notebook. He intended to keep a thorough record of everything said as this would be a valuable check on the official Minutes produced by the Cabinet Office later.

The Prime Minister bustled through the double doors and into his seat, followed by Roderick Turner and a further three dark-suited civil servants in his wake. All of them sat down on the Prime Minister's right, and the stage was set, as traditionally as a chess board, for the meeting and discussion that were to follow. Jock thought, with relief, that, as Huggins was present, he was unlikely to be called on to say very much and he settled down into his chair and started to relax.

'Has everyone seen all the telegrams from Beirut, including the intercepts?' asked the Prime Minister. 'I seem to remember that last time there was a little trouble. The Foreign Office had lost some of them.' There was a pause. No one said anything.

'The last telegram that I have is the one to Beirut about the GCHQ intercept this morning,' the Prime Minister continued. 'The one in which we're told that the Embassy car will leave Beirut by the Libyan air freighter at lunch time tomorrow.'

'Yes, Prime Minister. That's the last one I have as well,' said Huggins.

'Good. My office and yours are working in their usual harmony. Now, Defence Secretary, will you brief us on any last-minute changes in the action plan that we looked at last Wednesday? Are there any new details?'

'Yes,' said the Defence Secretary. 'Quite a few new points since we learnt that Al-Fatah were holding the two men, and I'd like to ask General Briggs to take us through these.' The Chief of Staff visibly inhaled a lot of air, picked up his papers and started to read monotonously from the typed sheets in front of him.

'Prime Minister, I would first like to advise you that the squadron of Tornados has arrived successfully in Akrotiri and so has the SAS platoon with Colonel Spacemead personally in charge.'

'I know all that, man,' muttered the Prime Minister. Briggs continued as if the needle were firmly wedded to the track of the record. 'Routine exercises have been undertaken, a location for the Ilyushin freighter within the air base has been determined and the SAS have conducted a mock exercise in the vicinity of that location. From the point of view of men and equipment, we are therefore all ready to go.' A tiny note of triumph crept into the

General's voice and then wavered and disappeared. 'But serious logistical problems have emerged about the timing of the interception, and I have been asked by my Air Force colleagues to make these plain to the committee today.' Briggs paused and picked up the second page from the bundle in front of him.

'A great deal depends on whether the Libyan plane heads straight out to sea from Beirut or decides, for tactical reasons, to hug the coast. If the latter, we could be in real trouble.

'Depending on the speed and direction of the wind, we calculate that the Tornados might then have only enough fuel for ten to fifteen minutes of interception and combat with the Ilyushin air freighter. This is based on the prevailing winds for this time of the year, which are south-westerly. We need therefore to send a clear authorization to Squadron Leader Snowling, telling him after how many warnings he and his pilots can fire at the Ilyushin. One, two or three? If the Ilyushin continues to fly on, are they to shoot it down into the sea? Even if the Ilyushin pilot states categorically that he hasn't got our hostages aboard, are they to continue firing at the plane until it dives into the sea? In fairness to the pilots of the Tornados, we cannot leave anyone in doubt on these points.'

There was an impenetrable silence for some seconds. Then, 'Fair questions,' said the Prime Minister. 'What is your view, Foreign Secretary?' He looked enquiringly across the table at Robert Huggins.

'It's a very difficult question but I'm fairly clear that if we get a message from Beirut telling us that the Mercedes is on board the Ilyushin, we have to intercept. Obviously, we must avoid shooting it down if that's at all possible,' Huggins replied with some hesitation, 'but we can't allow it to fly on to Tripoli.'

'You realize that you are potentially condemning Janes and Harrington to death,' said the Prime Minister, 'if they're aboard the plane, that is.'

'I don't think it will come to that,' said Huggins. 'I'm sure that after one or two bursts of warning fire from the Tornados, the Ilyushin captain will do what he is told and turn towards Akrotiri.'

'But if not?' the Prime Minister pressed his point, 'is it possible for the Tornado pilots to shoot to cripple the plane, causing it to make a forced landing in the Mediterranean, rather than shoot it down in flames?' Huggins turned towards Briggs and asked him.

'Very difficult,' said Briggs. 'You never know when a fuel line is going to catch fire and how quickly the fire will spread and there's the real danger of losing pressure in the cabin. It's not like shooting at the legs of a running man.' There was, again, silence round the Cabinet table.

'I can see why Squadron Leader Snowling needs a clear instruction,' said the Prime Minister, 'especially if we can't agree amongst ourselves. Defence Secretary, do you want to add anything?'

'I see the dilemma but, on balance, I think the Foreign Secretary is right. I think we should give the maximum number of warnings, three or even four. The maximum number that the fuel capacity of the Tornados permits. At the end of that, though, they will have, if necessary, to down the Ilyushin. We should have some boats from Cyprus on hand to pick up the survivors. We will need to have helicopters in the area as well.'

'It is out of flying range for any land-based helicopters,' said General Briggs, 'and the nearest ships carrying helicopters are in the Gulf. We couldn't get them to the area in time. However, assuming that this might be the committee's decision, we have made arrangements for two torpedo boats to be in the area. They would be there to pick up survivors. Provided the Ilyushin doesn't catch fire in the air, I'm told there's a reasonable chance it could make a forced landing on the water without breaking up. If the pilot's up to it, of course. He'd have to come down very quickly if the plane starts to lose air pressure in the cabin.'

No one round the room was in a hurry to pick up the discussion and coax it to a conclusion, for they all, especially Huggins, could sense the gamble that the Prime Minister was being asked to endorse. If it went wrong and if the Ilyushin were shot down, killing all those on board, and if there were no hostages but simply a large, black Embassy car to be recovered from the bottom of the Mediterranean . . . The consequences would be horrendous.

Libya would ask the other Arab nations to impose sanctions on
Britain, Saudi Arabia would cancel defence contracts worth
billions of pounds, there would be an embargo on trade in North
Sea oil, sterling would tumble, interest rates would go up further.
Like a hand grasping a bare wire, the minds of the politicians
fastened on to these horrific possibilities and started to twitch.

'You haven't given us the benefit of your opinion, Minister of
State,' said the Prime Minister quietly.

'I think we have to take the risk,' Jock paused and then replied.
'It's not as rash as it sounds. I don't believe the captain of the
Ilyushin or his crew will want to die. After a few bursts from the
cannon on the Tornados, once the Libyans realize that the threat is
for real, and that the choice is between turning for Cyprus and
being shot down into the ocean, they'll opt to go where the
Tornado captain tells them. The Libyans are not made to be
martyrs, Prime Minister, they are not like the Iranians or the
suicide bombers of the PLO, and if we don't take this action, and
the hostages are then put on a show trial in Tripoli by Gadaffi, we'll
be blamed day after day for not rescuing them.' Jock fell silent and
wondered if he had gone too far, if he had been too definite.

The Prime Minister was silent. Then he turned again to the
Foreign Secretary.

'At the end of the day, Foreign Secretary, you and your office are
supposed to know more about how to deal with the Libyans than
anyone else. Do you agree with the psychological insight into the
Libyan mentality that your Minister of State has just given us?'

Huggins choked with exasperation and stared across the table at
the Prime Minister. He gathered his thoughts together and finally
said: 'Prime Minister, this is a very difficult decision. I don't think
it helps to fuel division and hostility between your office and mine.
The Minister of State gave a fair assessment of his view of the way
the Libyans would react. I think he's right, so I believe does the
Defence Secretary. All of us, after careful consideration, would
advise you to take the risk and intercept the Libyan aeroplane
provided we know that the Mercedes is on board. The Tornados
will have to use threats when they intercept but, for the avoidance

of doubt, our battle orders to the base at Akrotiri must make it clear that, if the Ilyushin is shot down into the sea, the pilots of the Tornados will not have exceeded their orders.' Huggins fell silent. He felt desperately worried about the decision but did not want his anxiety to show.

The Prime Minister looked enquiringly round the table, but no one wished to add anything. He picked up his pen and twiddled it in his fingers thinking that, on this decision, finally hung his political career. If he got it wrong, badly wrong, his Party would lose the next election. If he got it right, and could make a personal triumph out of it, he had a very good chance of leading the Party into victory and staying Prime Minister for a few more years.

For a second or two, he saw himself as a golfer. He had survived many holes, despite going into bunkers or driving the wrong side of trees into thick undergrowth, from where he'd had to drop the ball at arm's length and accept penalty strokes. Now, he was on the green and he could see the hole very clearly three or four feet away from him, but it looked unusually small. There were spike marks in the grass and a sharp angle falling away from the hole. Near though it was, it was also a light year away. He felt choked. His head began to ache and he wondered whether he would have time for some sleep before the four evening engagements, formal dinner party and after-dinner speech that lay ahead of him. If the meeting ended quickly, he might be able to snatch half an hour.

'Very well, Foreign Secretary. I very much wish your office had been able to come up with something more subtle, less gung-ho, but you haven't. On your head be it. The collective view of the committee is to go ahead with a plan over which I, personally, have little doubt, provided that you have worked out all the details properly. General Briggs, you will, indeed, ensure that there are torpedo boats in the area to pick up survivors. Your command instructions to Akrotiri will make it clear that interception is permitted when we have clear knowledge that the Embassy car is on board. The Tornados may take all necessary action to force the

Ilyushin to divert to the base at Akrotiri. We certainly do not wish the Ilyushin shot down, but if that happens as a consequence of the interception . . .' Gordon paused, and pronounced the next words very carefully, 'no one in the Tornados will be blamed. I cannot say the same for the rest of us. Assuming that the Ilyushin lands safely at Akrotiri, the SAS is authorized to take all necessary steps to board the aeroplane and to release the hostages. Fatalities are, of course, to be minimized, but the SAS will be using live ammunition. It may not be possible to avoid some deaths.

'I want there to be constant and immediate communication to my office on every detail and incident. The sub-committee will meet again if that is necessary. You have all of that down, Roderick?' He turned to look at his private secretary.

'Yes, Prime Minister. What about a press line?'

'Eddie Ford will be in charge of that but we'll talk further about that as and when developments start happening tomorrow. That is all, gentlemen.'

Bruce Gordon rose immediately to his feet. He passed a hand over his forehead and noted that he was sweating and his hand was shaking. He hoped Huggins had not seen this. He walked towards the door and felt pain grip his stomach, so much so that he had difficulty in not crying out. God, he thought, I musn't get another bloody ulcer. An ulcer again, at this moment. Just what I don't need. The doors miraculously swung open as he got near them and he turned left in the hall outside and headed quickly, past the portrait of Harold Macmillan, for the staircase leading up to the first floor and then to his private flat.

'And some to Mecca turn to pray, and I toward thy bed, Yasmin.' Les stared out of the barred window and he struggled to remember Flecker's poem which he had learnt at school. He had recited so much poetry to himself in the last week, but he had failed to keep the devil of despair away, and every morning he had woken up feeling sick with fright.

It was dark outside, and there was little noise in the street. There was no moon, and only a gentle breeze pushed its way between the walls, causing the occasional piece of loose corrugated iron to creak and rattle. The endless barking of dogs had stopped an hour before, and something of the ancient peace had fallen over Beirut.

'Christ, Bob, I want to see Helen so much. I want to kiss her and hold her and make love to her. She must be worried stiff and I just miss her so much.'

'Another day or so and you will see her, lucky bugger. I wouldn't like to be in the flat when you two get into bed together, thumping and bumping about,' said Bob. 'You'll have another baby in nine months' time and that'll make sure you always remember your days as a hostage.'

'I'll never forget them. Never. Ever,' repeated Les and then added in a tone of self-reproach, 'It's the first time in my life I've been near death. For the first day or two, I couldn't stop shaking.'

'Once,' said Bob, 'I remember, we were driving up the Ml in my dad's car. I was a kid of seven or eight and a track rod broke. We veered all over the motorway, swinging from side to side and I just didn't know whether we were all going to be killed. I suppose it lasted only for ten seconds, but it seemed bloody endless. As soon as it was over, I was ashamed to find I had dirtied my pants.

'Last week, seven days, I just never knew from minute to minute whether I was going to be shot. I tried to pray, to think of Sally and the children, but I found it very difficult. I kept on thinking of all the things I hadn't done in life that I would like to have done – you know, driving a fast car round Silverstone, having a weekend of sex with Sally in a five-star hotel, drinking champagne with no clothes on.'

A half-smile broke reluctantly on Les's face. He pulled out of his pocket the pack of cards that he'd been given by Ahmed a couple of nights before and started playing patience on the dirty floor of their room.

Through the quiet of the night, steps could be heard coming up the stairs. By now, Bob had the contours of the staircase firmly in his mind and he imagined each corner, each individual step, as the footsteps advanced. A key turned in the lock, the door was pushed open, scraping on the floor, and Colonel Karam walked into the room. He paused, then announced with a touch of solemnity: 'It has been finally decided by our High Command. There were those who thought differently but General Haddad has agreed. Tomorrow night, or early on Wednesday morning, we will drive you into Central Beirut. You will be allowed to escape from the car. You will make your way quietly to your homes and, as we said before, you will tell them that you escaped. You are lucky. Others would still like to use you in suicide cars or, at least, to hold you to make a bargain for weapons or money, but General Haddad has decided against them.' He pointed at the cards on the floor. 'You have one more day in which to play cards and do nothing. Then you will be family men again.'

Bob thought he heard a tone of sympathy in the Palestinian's voice.

'That's fantastic news. Bloody marvellous.' Tears came into his eyes, and he fought to push them back. An extraordinary, bubbly feeling of relief poured through him and he felt like embracing the Colonel, but a laconic twitch of the lips under the Arab's thick black moustache persuaded him not to.

'Think, Les. In a day, we'll be home with Sally and Helen and the kids. We'll have a bloody great party. We'll be free, free, free.' Bob jumped up, playfully threw a punch at Les, and then stopped, his collarbone and shoulders twanging with pain from the quick movement.

'If it all works,' said Les quietly.

'Of course it'll work,' said Bob. 'Why the hell shouldn't it work?'

'But remember your side of the bargain,' said the Colonel. 'You do not know who was holding you. You never heard the name of our group. You escaped, we did not set you free.' Colonel Karam turned and, without looking back once, walked, a short, upright figure, to the door, let himself out and locked the door behind him.

'Why aren't you cheering, Les?' asked Bob. 'You'll see Helen tomorrow night. She just won't believe her eyes when you walk in the door of the flat and the kids will be over the moon. Then you'll get into bed and have some splendid sex.'

Les's face crinkled. 'Of course, there'll be sex, Bob, and lots of it, but I can't believe that it'll really work. I don't know. I suppose it just seems too good to be true. I'm still frightened out of my wits.' He turned back to his pack of cards, reshuffled and dealt another game of patience. The Queen of Spades was the first card he turned up. 'Oh, Christ,' he muttered and, fear rising like bile through his stomach, he buried his head in his hands.

Jock stood at the bar in his Club and eyed Martin Jevons with a good deal of caution. He was in a torment of indecision and had been ever since the Cabinet committee ended some hours before. Which horse should he back? Torn between stirring ambition and long-standing loyalty, he was altogether uncertain how to mention the Cyprus operation to Martin and whether he should hint that, if it went wrong, it would be the Prime Minister's fault or the Foreign Secretary's. He wished he had not agreed to speak to Martin, but there the man stood, propping up the bar at Brooks's, elegant Georgian windows behind him, a large gin and tonic in his hand and a bowl of nuts in front of him.

'Lovely club, Jock,' said Martin. 'It must be the most elegant club in London.'

'Oh, it's elegant all right,' said Jock. 'What with the big subscription room and the original card table where Charles James Fox gambled and lost fortunes and the pictures of the Hell Fire Club, it's elegant but boring. I know lots of members but they never seem to come here.'

'You'd better join Groucho's,' said Martin. 'That's full of journalists and politicians and actors. It's noisy and friendly and it's the best place for political gossip I know, better than the Garrick.'

'I've been to lunch there,' said Jock, 'with that very attractive fair-haired girl from *The Times*, Emily something-or-other.'

'Emily Sutherland,' said Martin. 'She does the big pieces on the centre page about electoral reform, a Bill of Rights, Whither the Constitution, and all that stuff. I'm told she's very good in bed.'

'You're a typical over-sexed journalist, Martin, even though you work for Granny BBC,' laughed Jock. He paused. This seemed as good a moment as any to raise the subject of the hostages, so he looked quickly behind him, saw that there was no one nearby and, picking up a handful of peanuts from the bowl by him, said quietly: 'Martin, I wanted to break something to you privately. I'm not telling anyone else, but because you're the BBC and we've known each other a bit for years . . .' Martin nodded his head encouragingly, 'I thought I'd let you in on the act on the strict understanding that this is off the record until the news breaks officially.'

'Okay,' said Martin, 'off the record, lobby terms for the moment, but when do you expect the news to break?'

'Wednesday or Thursday.'

'So this is a sort of background briefing?' asked Martin.

'No, it's more than that. I'm a bit caught in this one between the Prime Minister and the Foreign Secretary, and I want to see justice done when the news comes out.'

Martin wondered what on earth Jock was driving at, and, to hide his surprise, raised his glass of gin and tonic and poured a large measure down his throat.

'Go on,' he said, 'you have my word. This is off the record but I haven't the faintest idea what you're driving at.'

Taking another handful of peanuts, Jock replied, 'It's about the two hostages, Bob Janes and Les Harrington. We think that an attempt is going to be made to smuggle them out of Beirut in a Libyan air freighter, probably some time tomorrow. The idea is to take them to Tripoli where Gadaffi will put them on show.'

'How do you know all this?' asked Martin.

'GCHQ intercepts,' said Jock, and Martin nodded.

'Robert Huggins with Tony Castle has worked out a plan for the plane to be intercepted by a squadron of Tornados as it is flying west from Beirut. If all goes well, the Tornados will escort the Libyan plane back to our base at Akrotiri in Cyprus. There, if the captain refuses to release the hostages, the SAS will storm the plane and try and get the hostages out alive.'

'What happens if the captain refuses to switch the plane's course?' asked the BBC reporter.

'It'll be shot down if necessary.'

'God, what a gamble, what a crazy idea,' Martin reacted violently.

'It's not a crazy idea, but it has serious flaws in it,' said Jock in his most Foreign Office voice.

'You can say that again. If you end up with a Libyan plane in the Mediterranean and the hostages inside, dead, your boss will be for the high jump.'

'But we have got to do something,' anguished Jock. 'After the success of the Americans in getting their hostages off the TWA plane, we simply can't leave these two to stew. We have information that they're going to be on this plane tomorrow. We've got to do all we can to get them off it. If we succeed, it will be a great coup.'

'Okay. I still think it's a fantastic risk. But what's the problem between the Prime Minister and the Foreign Secretary?' asked Martin.

'As you well know, they don't get on. In fact, they hate each other's guts. They've been fighting like wildcats over this plan, and I think . . .' Jock paused and then said slowly, 'that's one of the reasons for the weaknesses in it. There is so much tension in the Cabinet Room that the Chiefs of Staff have not been able to give the matter the detailed care they should. They haven't come up with any alternatives.' Jock hesitated before going on. 'The Prime Minister wants to be more cautious and that makes Robert even more ready to take risks. On balance, I think the Prime Minister's caution is right but he's been unable to convince Robert Huggins of that.'

'And that's what you wanted to tell me?' asked Martin. 'If it goes wrong, it's Huggins' fault?'

'I'm afraid so,' Jock hesitated again and added as an after-thought, 'much as I respect and like the man.' He paused and then said, 'Have another gin and tonic.'

Little bastard, thought Martin. He owes all his promotion to Huggins. He said: 'Tricky situation, three months before an election. If the shit hits the fan, you could all have egg on your faces, to coin a mixed metaphor. No more drink, thanks. I've got to get back to Broadcasting House. I'm doing *Newsnight* tonight and I'm interviewing Tony Castle about the next round of defence cuts. I've got to do some thinking first.'

'Not a word about this,' reiterated Jock.

'No, not a word until I read from the tapes that there has been an intercept of the Libyan plane. Then, anything goes.'

'Anything goes,' echoed Jock as he walked his guest out of the bar, turned right through the hall, past the glass box in which a uniformed attendant, acting as doorkeeper, sat and down the steps into St James'. A taxi came by within a short time. Martin hailed it and, as he got into it, turned to Jock and said: 'Many thanks, Jock, for the drink and for the tip. You're skating on very thin ice, you know.'

Jock grimaced, waved his hand at the departing Martin and got into his office Vauxhall as his government driver pulled up in front of him.

'We'll go home, Joe,' said Jock. 'I've got time to have supper with my wife before the ten o'clock vote.'

As he sat in the back seat on his way back to his flat, the word 'duplicitous' kept on coming into Jock's mind. It was a satisfying word with lots of short syllables in it. It would fit the end of a Latin pentameter well, thought Jock. He was being duplicitous and was letting down a very old friend and patron. Did that really worry him? Jock wasn't quite certain. He was still pondering the question as he inserted his key into the Ingersoll lock in the flat door, only to find the door being pulled open before he had time to turn it.

Mary was on the other side. She threw her arms round his neck, kissed him hard on the lips and said, 'I heard you coming up the stairs. I've got a feeling that you've had a very exciting day and, on top of that, you smell of gin.' Taking him by the hand, she led him down the passage and into the drawing room. She pushed him down on to the sofa and walked over to the drinks trolley where she poured both of them a heavy mixture of gin and tonic in large tumblers. She added ice and a slice of lemon to each glass, brought them back and sat down by Jock on the sofa.

'Go on, Jock, tell me all about it. I find real political gossip very exciting.' She curled up close to him and put his gin and tonic into his hands. 'I want every detail. I rang you at some stage in the day, about lunch time, but your office told me you were with the Prime Minister. How grand. What were you doing?'

As Jock drank and rattled the ice-cubes in his glass, he told Mary every detail of his conversation with the Prime Minister.

'The old bugger,' Mary murmured appreciatively. 'He wants you to help him ditch poor Robert before the election. Go on.'

Jock went on and described the whole afternoon. When he got to his conversation with Martin Jevons at Brooks's, Mary stopped him again.

'You need another drink.' She got up and poured him one and another for herself. 'You are a devil. After all of these years of marriage, I didn't know you had it in you to be so devious. You are Iago, and I've often thought of you as a mildly heroic Malcolm. Go on.'

'Well, there isn't much more,' said Jock. He looked across at the dove-grey and blue wallpaper that ran in narrow stripes up from the low marble fireplace opposite him to the ceiling, and he thought how untrue that remark of his was. He hadn't told Mary about the perceptible pause during which the Prime Minister's hand had lingered on his. That was a side of his past that he kept to himself. He hadn't told her the half of the confusion that he found himself in, caught in the wounding hostility between the Prime Minister and the Foreign Secretary and trying to find the thread of his own future as his long-standing loyalty to Robert Huggins cracked.

'You're in a muddle, aren't you, darling?' said Mary. She came up close to him on the sofa and kissed his cheek and then reflectively started to undo his shirt buttons. 'You've always been loyal to Robert, and I've loved you for it but this is the moment when you've got to shape your own career. The Prime Minister is the better bet. He's tougher, wilier and, above all, he's in possession. I think it's very flattering that he has trusted you so much even though he knows you're a great friend of Robert's.'

Her hand slid inside his poplin shirt and her finger nails gently raked across his rib cage and then the palm of her hand settled on his nipple which she caressed backwards and forwards.

'At some stage, you're going to have to break away from being a pupil of Robert's,' she muttered. 'I guess that the time has come as I think Robert's on the way out.'

Jock leant back on the sofa, his shirt half undone, glass half full of gin and tonic in his hand. He partly closed his eyes and turned and smiled at Mary.

'You are leading me astray.'

'Yes I am.' Mary smiled. 'Politics excite me and supper won't be ready for at least fifteen minutes.' Her right hand slid, flat and slow, over Jock's stomach and she turned closer to him and with her left hand started to undo his belt. Jock grinned and leant forward and put his glass down on the floor.

'As long as I get to the ten o'clock vote. It's a three-line whip,' he murmured, 'pairing's not permitted.'

9

Tuesday 2 July: Morning

Colonel Moberly had had another restless night. He had tossed and turned, caught between dreams and wakefulness. He had looked at his watch almost every hour, on the hour, and had felt a rising sense of tension inside him until the knots formed in his stomach and he rose and went to the bathroom, and filled his mouth with indigestion tablets. Like a small boy about to play in a vital school match, he felt that the day ahead was of key importance to him and, this time, he had to get it right. On this would depend the Ambassador's report on him at the end of term.

He longed to move to a bigger embassy where red-tabbed staff officers would fly out from the Ministry of Defence and consult him, the expert on the spot, on how best to deal with the local generals. He saw himself conducting a delegation of British weapons manufacturers to a specially reserved conference room in the Hilton International, where the Defence Minister would greet him by his Christian name and he in turn would introduce the visiting managing directors from General Electric and Ferranti and British Aerospace. With a pointer in his hand, he would stand in front of a white board on the platform explaining to a rapt audience, in which the visiting British business men were interspersed with dozens of local delegates, the importance of orders for ground-to-air missiles being placed with British manu-facturers. Only in this way, could the growing threat from the fundamentalist movement and its threat to the whole stability of the Middle East be contained . . .

Trring . . . trring . . . trring. Moberly groaned, leant over and hit the top of his old-fashioned alarm clock which promptly stopped and fell on the floor. The glass broke on the clock's face. Moberly groaned again. It's going to be one of those days, he thought. He got up slowly, went to the bathroom, shaved, cut himself, put a piece of cotton wool on the cut, dressed and made himself a cursory breakfast in the little kitchen of his flat. With a cup of coffee in his hand, he wandered over to the flat's one balcony, opened the windows and stepped out. Already it was hot and muggy as he stared westward and downhill at the concrete skyline of modern Beirut. Over the blocks of flats and the hotels and the ugly, rectangular offices, he could see the blue haven of the Mediterranean. Already there was a hubbub of noise rising from the streets below him. Cars hooting, the sirens of police cars and of ambulances wailing and, immediately to the right of his block of flats, a policeman trying to direct traffic and blowing piercingly on a whistle. The thought of the heat and effort ahead began to make Moberly's determination evaporate.

'Come on,' he muttered to himself in a half-encouraging manner. 'This is going to be a big day, a great day, a successful day.'

Four hours later, he was sitting in his car under a short line of palm trees overlooking the perimeter fence of Beirut Airport. There was no air-conditioning in his car, so he had opened all the windows but the car was still unpleasantly hot and he had taken off his jacket and his tie. These were lying on the seat beside him, along with his binoculars and his VHF radio transmitter. Twice already, at ten and at eleven, he had sent a routine message back to the communications officer in the Beirut Embassy saying that there was no sign of either van or basket. He had identified the Libyan Ilyushin freighter about 800 yards away across the tarmac but, all morning so far, there had been no sign of anyone coming and going from the aeroplane.

He picked up his glasses again and, wearily steadying his elbows on the window ledge of the car door, focused the binoculars at the distant plane. This time he noticed that the big door in the tail of the plane was open and that a ramp had been lowered to the ground. Sweat started to form on his forehead and this trickled down into his eyes, making it impossible for him to get a clear picture through the glasses.

'Bugger,' muttered Moberly to himself, wiping his forehead frantically with his handkerchief and then polishing the eyepieces of his binoculars. 'Bugger. I just must get a clear picture of what's happening now.' He raised his binoculars again, screwed up his eyes and peered with all the concentration that he could muster. He saw a large, black car – he thought it was a Mercedes but could not be sure – emerging from a shed about 400 yards behind the Libyan plane and driving slowly towards it. Two Lebanese soldiers were running along by its side, each holding a rifle and acting as some kind of a casual guard. Sweat again clouded his vision and the car disappeared through a steamy haze on his glasses.

Shit, thought Moberly. Don't let it all fog up. I really mustn't lose sight of the Mercedes now. Please, God, let me see it get clearly into the plane.

He wiped his forehead and eyes once more, and put the glasses back in place and saw to his relief that the car was now only about fifty yards from the ramp of the freighter and the two soldiers who had run ahead were standing on either side of the ramp and beckoning the car towards them. Then the car stopped, and the soldiers walked back towards it.

Moberly put his binoculars down, picked up his radio set, looked at his watch and keyed in his personal identification number.

'This is the Master calling the kennels at eleven fifty-five. I've seen the basket approaching. It's very near the door of the van now.' Moberly, feeling relieved and cheerful, made up more and more of the impromptu code as he went along. 'And it looks as if it will enter the van any second, but I can't possibly tell whether the dogs are inside the basket or not. I will radio again once the basket is clearly inside the van. It's come to a halt just now. Over and. . .'

The car door was jerked violently open and a hand slammed down on the VHF transmitter, pushing it on to the car seat between Moberly's legs. Moberly looked up instantly and saw a furious Lebanese officer looking at him. The officer brought his swagger stick sharply down on Moberly's hands as they clasped the transmitter and he turned to the two soldiers behind him and barked an order in Arabic. The soldiers moved in and, without a word, pulled Moberly out of the car, banging his head against the door-frame as they did so.

'Don't do that,' muttered Moberly as, like a limpet being prised off a rock, he was extricated from the car and then prodded by the soldiers with their rifle butts into an upright position. He clutched his transmitter as though it were a baby. Looking at his captor, he saw a well-dressed Lebanese police colonel, neatly turned out, tie immaculately knotted and a foot shorter than Moberly himself. The two soldiers continued to clasp Moberly's forearms and to hang on to him as if they expected him, like a balloon, to disappear into the air above.

'Colonel, tell your men to let go of me at once. I'm not going to run away.'

'You are under arrest,' said the Lebanese in slow, precisely modulated English. 'You have been here for over three hours and you appear to be spying on military movements. You will come with me to the police headquarters where you will give a full account of your actions.'

'You cannot do that, you cannot arrest me,' said Moberly. 'I am the British Defence Attaché and I have diplomatic immunity.'

The Lebanese Officer slowly ran his eyes over Moberly, who shifted uncomfortably.

'You can argue about that with Captain Hessayan. I do not care whether you have . . .' he stumbled over the words and said them very slowly, 'diplomatic immunity. You have clearly been spying and for that, in my country, the sentence is execution.' The Lebanese muttered a further order and the two soldiers pulled the transmitter out of Moberly's hands and then started to jostle and push him towards a jeep which he now saw was parked off the road behind the trees fifty yards away. He looked again through the perimeter fence and could just see the black car standing, like a beetle on the ground, by the ramp of the Libyan freighter. It had not moved since his last message to the British Embassy.

The Lebanese Colonel turned and, whilst the soldiers pushed

Moberly towards the jeep, examined the radio transmitter closely. He pressed some buttons on it without any sense of purpose and then, putting it down, got into Moberly's car, turned the ignition key, and drove it down the road to join up with the jeep. As he drove, the transmitter started to bleep and a green light on the top of it flashed but the Lebanese could only look at it and drive on.

The communications officer took off his earphones and wiped the sweat off his face. It was hot and stuffy inside the heavily insulated cubicle in which he sat to send and receive radio messages. One of the prices of safe communications, he had often thought, was headaches. The more sophisticated your equipment became, the more the walls of the room in which it was installed were filled with lead or cork or concrete in order to try and stop the other side picking up what you were saying, the more you needed to have a bottle of Disprin with you. Beirut was now so run-down as a post that he had no full-time assistant, either. Another source of complaint. So he switched off the VHF set, left the teleprinter on automatic hold, opened the door in his stuffy cubicle and walked along a passage, down the stairs and then along the corridor to the Ambassador's private offices. He walked in and was greeted by the Ambassador's secretary, Lillian Curtis, who sat behind her desk looking clean, fresh and dressed for a garden party in Surrey. She removed her gaze from the large desk diary which she had been studying as if it were the Holy Writ and gazed critically at the communications officer.

'You look hot, Charlie,' she remarked.

'I am hot, I'm sweating all over, I don't feel great and I should be paid double time for sitting in that rotten little box upstairs. Can I see the Ambassador straight away? It's urgent. Is he in?'

'Yes, he is. I'll ask him.'

Lillian Curtis picked up the telephone on her desk, pressed a button on the receiver, waited for a green light to appear and then told the Ambassador that Charlie Campbell was anxious to see him. She listened for a few seconds, put the receiver down and said,

'You can go straight in. His Excellency sounds a bit distraught.'

Charlie Campbell walked through the connecting door and into the next room. This was lined with books on two walls, heavy fat volumes that had an air of complacency, even smugness about them. Autobiographies of past Foreign Secretaries jostled with critiques of Lawrence of Arabia and histories of the Middle East College of Arabic Studies. On the wall behind the Ambassador's desk were the required pictures: a fine Edward Lear of Beirut in the 1840s with the harbour in the foreground and then a medley of low buildings, beautifully drawn, and in the distance the range of high mountains that bound the Lebanese plain. On either side, signed photographs of Heads of Government in whose countries Benedict Adams had served and then, larger than the others, coloured photographs of the Queen and of Bruce Gordon, both with standard messages of support and good wishes inscribed in the bottom right-hand corner.

On the Ambassador's desk was a large glass tray full of innumerable pencils, several rubbers and a Swan fountain pen. To its right a handsome cut-glass Georgian inkpot with a crested silver top, to its left a medium-size photograph of Mrs Adams and the four Adams children, two boys and two girls, all looking like possible entrants for the Foreign Service. There was not a single paper on the Ambassador's desk, and His Excellency was gazing pensively at a virgin sheet of blotting paper, lodged in a well-tooled open leather folder, when Charlie Campbell came into the room.

Campbell paused as he walked towards the desk.

'Sit down, man, sit down. No ceremony here,' said Adams. 'What's the news?'

Campbell sat down in the chair on the far side of the Ambassador's desk. He filled him in on the detail of the messages radioed by Colonel Moberly from his car, right up to the time when Moberly seemed to have been violently interrupted.

'I guess he was surprised and caught by someone,' said Campbell. 'I tried sending a message back to him a few minutes later but got the wrong answer-sign from his end, so I can only guess that someone else was tampering with his set.'

'Silly fool. I suppose he got himself arrested by being too damned obvious,' muttered the Ambassador. 'I'll have to go and make a formal protest to the Foreign Minister about his arrest and he will chew my balls off for spying and there will be a hell of a row. We might even have to send Moberly home.' He paused and realized that an instant spark of hope had passed through him. The question was whether the office in London would allow him a replacement Attaché or whether he would have to do without one altogether. That was the key point to consider.

'Now, where have we got to?' he said fussily. 'We know that a black car, that looks very like the one that arrived in Beirut a few days ago, is parked just by the Libyan air freighter. The cargo hatch is open and the ramp is down. It's reasonable to assume that the car is going to be driven on board the plane.' He paused and looked enquiringly at Charlie Campbell.

'Well, it's none of my business,' muttered Campbell, 'but yes, I think that's right, sir. From all that the Colonel said, it's fair to suppose that the black car would be driven on to the plane any minute.' Charlie Campbell was much fonder of Colonel Moberly than he was of the Ambassador, and he felt an instinctive need to put Moberly's case as clearly and as favourably as possible.

'But we've got no idea whether the hostages are in the car or not.'

'That's right, Ambassador. But it's obviously, from what the Colonel said, a big car. They could easily be drugged and hidden away in the boot.'

The Ambassador opened the right-hand drawer of his desk, took out a packet of cigarettes and inspected its contents carefully, like a shopper considering which peach to select from the box on the fruit counter. He picked out the second cigarette from the right, gazed at it, put it back in the packet and chose the fourth from the right instead. He lit his cigarette and filled his lungs from it with evident, long-drawn-out pleasure. Then quickly remembering the formalities, he retrieved the box from the drawer, opened it again and offered it to Charlie Campbell.

'No, Ambassador, thank you, I don't smoke,' said Charlie. He must be in a dither, he thought. If I've told him once, I've told him a hundred times that I don't smoke.

'Charlie, I'll draft a short message to London telling them where we've got to so far. They will certainly instruct me to go and protest at Moberly's arrest, but that can wait, if necessary. The key thing is to find out and to tell Akrotiri and London the moment the plane takes off from the airport. It's vital that we do that, but the trouble is that we haven't got anyone else from the Embassy to send to the airport. We can't ask any of the Lebanese staff to do it. They'd be terrified and, if they were caught and arrested, we would never see them again. You could go, but I need you manning the communications room, particularly for the next few hours.'

'I think you'd manage the VHF set all right yourself, sir. But how good would you be at coding and sending on any messages to London?' Charlie enquired.

'No, I don't think that's exactly my form,' said the Ambassador. 'I've had one or two communication lessons and that sort of thing in my time but I never really got the hang of it. You'll have to stay here. It's typical that John is away on leave at the moment. He's never around when I need him.' John Barker was the Consul at the Beirut Embassy and also doubled up as Commercial Councillor. He was the Deputy Head of Mission and, as a Foreign Office career man, was senior to Moberly and the only other expatriate male on the permanent staff. Unfortunately, his long summer leave had begun just a week before and he would not be seen again in Lebanon for two months.

'I don't think I can go myself. The Embassy car with the security outriders would be a bit conspicuous,' said Adams. Charlie Campbell suppressed a smile. The old boy must be worried, he thought. He's really spilling it out to me. 'And if I got arrested, then the British Government really would be in trouble. That could do permanent damage to our relations with the Lebanese. Lasting damage,' he repeated to impress himself and his audience of one.

The Ambassador paused and gazed at the small chandelier in the ceiling as if he expected inspiration to strike him in the shape of an illuminating beam direct from one of the light bulbs. The silence lengthened and deepened, and Adams took a long puff from his cigarette, changed his gaze from the chandelier to Charlie Campbell sitting opposite him and suddenly said:

'We're in a fix. Have you any ideas, Charlie?'

'If you don't mind my saying so,' said Charlie, hesitatingly, 'what about your wife? I think she's got a little car of her own and I don't think it would be at all dangerous. If she was arrested, you could presumably get her out of prison quite quickly.' The Ambassador puffed furiously at his cigarette, and then said, 'Good idea. I'll ask Lillian to find her.'

He picked up the telephone, pressed a switch and instructed Lillian Curtis to find his wife urgently and to put her on the telephone to him. Two minutes later, Lillian rang back with a message that Mrs Adams' car was in the garage but there was no sign of her. The housemaid thought she had gone out about an hour before. She was wearing tennis clothes and carrying a racquet, so probably she had been picked up by the wife of one of the other Ambassadors and they were now playing tennis together.

The Ambassador thought for a moment. 'Do you drive, Lillian?' he asked down the telephone.

'Of course I do, Ambassador.' Charlie, from where he was sitting, heard the indignant tone in the voice. 'But I wasn't allowed to bring a car to Beirut with me. The Chief Clerk's office said it would be too expensive and there was no safe garage space left for me.'

'Never mind about that now. Could you drive my wife's car?'

'Yes. Mrs Adams has lent it to me once or twice already. Very kind of her.'

'All right. Come in quickly, will you? There is something I want to ask you to do.'

Lillian came into the room and Charlie looked at her appreciatively. Nice girl, he thought. He wondered if she would come out for a drink and a meal with him one evening. Perhaps he might even score as she must be quite lonely and bored. His thoughts began to wander lustfully over the intimacies of Lillian's body and then were summoned back as the Ambassador asked him, in the middle of a series of detailed instructions to Lillian, what code number she was to use on the VHF transmitter. Charlie told her and said that he would get another set straightaway from the communications stores.

'Excuse me, Ambassador,' he said as he walked towards the door, 'but you do know how to work the VHF don't you, Lillian? I gave you a lesson when you first arrived here.'

'Yes, of course I do, Charlie,' said Lillian. 'You press the transmission button, wait for the green light, press in the digits of the code number and then start talking.'

'Yes, but remember I can't transmit to you while you're speaking to me, so you must say "message ends" or "over and out" at the end, every time you're speaking, and press the transmitting button again when next you start speaking.'

'Yes, I remember all that,' said Lillian.

As Charlie left the room, he heard the Ambassador repeating to Lillian that the only important message she had to get over was to tell them when the Libyan airliner took off. That was, the Ambassador emphasized, of major importance, indeed it could make a good deal of difference to British–Lebanese relations. He was, Charlie thought, sounding confident and pompous again.

'And what shall I say I'm doing if I'm arrested?' Charlie heard Lillian ask, but he had shut the door before he could hear the Ambassador's answer.

Every Tuesday and Thursday during the parliamentary term time, the Prime Minister answers questions for fifteen minutes and every Prime Minister hates it. Bruce Gordon was no exception. He cursed the custom that had grown up of Prime Ministers, under the guise of supplementary questions, having to answer, quickly and punchily, about any subject under the sun without prior warning. From lunch-time onwards on those days, he was always deeply tetchy.

On Tuesday 2 July, the routine was as usual. He had lunched

sparingly in his flat, reading the background notes to the questions and adding handwritten thoughts of his own, and now Roderick Turner, his principal private secretary, Dominic Anderson, his parliamentary private secretary, and Eddie Ford, the Number 10 press officer, joined him in the low, comfortable drawing room under the eaves of Downing Street to run round the course once again.

They each had an identical volume containing, behind each question, first the prepared answer, then notes of the possible supplementary answers, arranged alphabetically subject by subject, and finally a page of personal notes on the Member of Parliament asking the question and on his constituency. The Prime Minister had already been through his copy twice and had highlighted the points among the supplementaries that he had thought most worth making.

The four men sat in comfortable chairs, covered in material with a large bold print. Bruce Gordon's wife had chosen this material shortly before she died, saying that the room desperately needed brightening up. The new chair covers had been fitted some weeks after her funeral and, Bruce occasionally thought, were a memorial to her liveliness. She had not enjoyed Number 10 much in the short time she had been there, he knew, but she had been determined to make it as much like a home as possible.

'Well, Dom, do you see anything special about the PQs this afternoon?' He turned to Dominic Anderson who, unlike his boss, had enjoyed an excellent lunch at White's and had been only sorry that, as always on these occasions, he'd had to leave before he could share a decanter of port with some of his oldest friends.

'No, Prime Minister. The Chief Whip tells me that he has arranged for some good, supportive supplementaries from our side on the first and third questions. They'll all be asked by friends and, for the first, we'll try and concentrate on Health, and for the third, on Education. I expect that the Leader of the Opposition will come in on number one and, as Education is in all the tabloids today, he'll probably have a go at that as well. But you can concentrate on the drop in the waiting lists and the three contracts for new hospitals that have been let in the last week. The details are all in the folder.

'Number two is a Labour constituency question. Jarrow and shipbuilding. Not much to say, but there are one or two bull points about new orders from the Ministry of Defence, particularly the two new frigates. If you felt like it, you could say that another Socialist government would certainly mean another march for the unemployed from Jarrow. That would bring a cheer from our side. But the one I worry about is number four, John Williamson: "When does the Prime Minister next expect to visit the Middle East?" You remember, John was very rude to Jock Meldrum-Ross at Question Time last week. He thinks the Foreign Office have been very incompetent about the hostages, and that you should have sent the army in to rescue them. He'll probably quote the success of the Americans in getting their hostages off the TWA plane last Sunday and ask why we haven't done something similar.'

'But that's very tricky,' interrupted the perfect civil servant, Roderick Turner. 'As you know, Prime Minister, that's a very sensitive subject at the moment and there could be developments within the next few hours.' Dominic Anderson's eyebrows shot up and he looked enquiringly at the Prime Minister. Bruce Gordon said nothing but nodded his head in agreement.

Turner went on: 'You would have to be very careful in what you say about that, Prime Minister. You could, perhaps, say that we are exploring all the possible avenues but that we cannot possibly give in to threats, nor are we going to do any deals, supplying arms or releasing other prisoners in return for the release of our hostages.'

There was a silence. 'All the usual guff,' muttered Bruce Gordon. 'That'll bring them out cheering.'

'But, Prime Minister, this is the one that the press will pick up,' said Eddie Ford. 'At our twelve-o'clock press briefing this morning, all the usual people, the *Mail*, the *Express*, the *Sun*, the *Mirror*, they all wanted to know what action you were going to take. One of them, I think it was Pete Brodie from the *Express*, said that his editor wanted him to write something very rude, accusing us of cowardice, inertia, ignorance, being in the pay of the Arabs. All the usual stuff. If we just let the Americans get their thirty-nine hostages released and fail to do anything similar, there'll be hell to pay in the tabloids. You must surely have some information you can leak about who is holding them or why they're being held and what progress has been made in the negotiations. Something for the pack to bite on.'

Eddie Ford sounded desperate for he hated losing his daily tussle with the press. Like Dominic Anderson, he knew nothing of the Tornados and the SAS waiting at Akrotiri. The Prime Minister shared this knowledge only with Roderick Turner, so the conversation went backwards and forwards, dealing in points of mood and style, turning on the question of how John Williamson could be kept happy and loyal, and firmly on-side, while half those present concealed their scant information from the other half.

At 3 pm precisely, Roderick Turner looked at his watch and pointed out to the Prime Minister that it was time for them to go round to the House. The bullet-proof Jaguar and the two cars of escorting policemen were waiting at the Number 10 doorstep. And precisely fifteen minutes later, at 3.15, the Prime Minister got to his feet to a murmur of supporting applause from his back-benchers, in order to go through the routine of answering questions.

However well-prepared and well-rehearsed he was, Bruce Gordon knew very well that the winning trick, at Question Time, lay in appearing spontaneous, in being funny at the expense of his opponent and in being subtly supportive and complimentary to his own parliamentary colleagues. Afterwards, he might wander with Dominic Anderson along the corridor to the tea-room and there, drinking a cup of tea and surrounded by friendly faces, hear the words that were always music in his ears: 'You were in good form, Prime Minister, this afternoon. Excellent form.' Bruce Gordon knew well that the Chief Whip, however much he might get backbenchers to ask supportive questions, could only persuade a very few to utter direct compliments that were not heartfelt.

Health was duly dealt with. Statistics regarding new hospitals, carefully memorized, were trotted out without any obvious reference to the folder lying on the Despatch Box. The Leader of the Opposition was satisfactorily squashed, to roars of supporting approval, by odious comparison between the meagre spending record of the previous Labour government and that proudly led by Bruce Gordon. Jarrow was sympathetically dealt with, support for the unemployed being mixed with a strong hint of British naval pride in reference to the contract for the new frigates. The patriotism card was always a winner.

All in all, thought Eddie Ford, sitting two away from Roderick Turner, in the civil servants' box behind the Speaker, it all seems a doddle. Gordon may be tired, old and cynical, but he's still a master at Question Time. Ford decided to try and run the frigate story and wondered what marginal seats might benefit from new orders for ships from the Ministry of Defence. He hardly heard the Prime Minister assuring his honourable and gallant friend that he intended to visit the Middle East as soon as opportunity and his busy diary allowed. If there were not time before the general election – at the slightest mention of those two words, MPs twitched nervously and shifted their buttocks on the green-leather benches – the Prime Minister would certainly plan to visit the Middle East, where he knew his honourable friend had very considerable experience, after an election victory in the months ahead. A quiet swell of approval, allegro moderato, from the Conservative benches.

But Sir John Williamson was too old a hand to be fobbed off that easily. It was nearly a year since he had asked a question of the Prime Minister, and he, too, was standing for re-election and he thought a bit of publicity – perhaps even a slot on *Newsnight* that evening – would do him no harm.

So he rumbled back to his feet: 'I am grateful to my Right Honourable friend for his full and typically courteous reply to my question, but could he tell the House what action he proposes to take to ensure the release of the two hostages, Mr Janes and Mr Harrington, who have now been held in Beirut for the last ten days? Is it not intolerable that the United States should succeed in releasing thirty-nine hostages last Sunday, without any apparent concessions on their part, whilst we have failed to release any?' The Speaker started to gesture from his chair at Sir John, emphasizing that he had already asked two questions and that was surely enough. But Sir John was in full gallop and was not to be put off by the Speaker who, after all, had come into the House a few years after him. 'And has my Right Honourable friend no information at all as to who is holding these two brave men or why they are being held? If he has no information, has not the time come for a change at the Foreign Office where ministers seem better at giving out aid to our enemy than in obtaining the release of British captives?'

Sir John sat down to a few loud cries of 'Hear, hear' but no great swell of approval. This was too near the knuckle when a general election was only a few months away and the Chief Whip, from his seat on the front bench by the gangway, turned and glared openly at Sir John.

The Prime Minister was unabashed. He glanced at the clock opposite him, saw that the time was 3.29 and knew there was only a minute to go before questions ended. If he gave a fairly expansive answer to Sir John, he might well avoid having to answer anyone from the Opposition on the subject of the hostages. So he rose to his feet, stood at the Despatch Box and, without glancing at any of the notes in his folder, assured Sir John of his deep concern for the hostages, shared his sympathy for their wives and children, and reiterated the daily efforts that he, personally, was making to ensure the release of Mr Janes and Mr Harrington. That, he thought, was not quite good enough to win his troops, and the digital clock still stood at 3.29. He remembered the remark which the Defence Secretary had dropped that morning in Cabinet about Al-Fatah, and he added:

'I can advise my honourable friend that we have now obtained information that these good men are being held by what I believe to be a Palestinian organization known as Al-Fatah. We think it is possible that Al-Fatah were not aware of the helpful work being

153

done by the two men with their UN relief agency and I have instructed our Ambassador to use all the means at his disposal, and every possible contact, to try and persuade Al-Fatah to return the men unharmed to their wives and families as soon as possible.'

The Prime Minister sat down to a warm hum of approval from the benches behind him. This sounded like a new and positive development. He looked up at the clock. It was 3.30, and the Speaker moved on to announce the next piece of business, a backbencher's Bill being introduced under the ten-minute rule. Dominic Anderson leant over from the bench behind and muttered to the Prime Minister:

'Well done. The lads will like that.'

As the Prime Minister got up and walked down the row of ministers sitting on the Treasury bench, he was immediately followed by Robert Huggins. As soon as they were through the double doors behind the Speaker's chair, Huggins, red with anger, moved forward and said:

'Prime Minister, you've blown it. Why on earth did you mention that Al-Fatah were holding Janes and Harrington?'

'Why not? It showed the House that we were working hard on their release and had some positive information as to who was holding them.'

'But you must have seen the message from Beirut saying that Al-Fatah insisted that their name was not mentioned publicly. Your civil servants must have shown you that.' Huggins looked at the unmoved face of the Prime Minister. He saw no trace of regret on it, so raised his voice in anger:

'Prime Minister, what you've done is unforgivable. It may well put the lives of those two men at risk.'

Members of Parliament were starting to spill out from the Chamber and to walk past the Prime Minister and the Foreign Secretary. A few, who were close to them, were startled to hear Bruce Gordon say:

'Robert, I refuse to be talked to like that. If the Foreign Office have failed to give me any necessary information, it is the Foreign Secretary's fault.'

154

Bruce Gordon turned and walked quickly away. His protective gang of private secretaries encircled him like bees surrounding their queen. As he turned down the narrow corridor past the Chancellor of the Exchequer's office towards his own, a junior secretary came out to meet him carrying a flimsy piece of paper in his hand.

'Prime Minister. You must see this immediately. It has just come over from Number 10.'

The Prime Minister read on. The message was headed:

FLASH-FLASH-FLASH 1705 BEIRUT
INFORMATION JUST RECEIVED FROM OUR PEOPLE AT AIRPORT.
LIBYAN ILYUSHIN FREIGHTER AIRBORNE FIVE MINUTES AGO.
ADAMS.

The Prime Minister walked quickly through the private office to his own room overlooking New Palace Yard and Parliament Square.

'Get me the Chief of Staff immediately,' he said over his shoulder to Roderick Turner. He sat down at his desk in the alcove of the L-shaped room and waited for the telephone call. It did not take long. The telephone rang and the girl in the office outside told him that General Briggs was on the line.

'General, I've just seen the message from Beirut. Have the Tornados taken off from Akrotiri?'

'Yes, Prime Minister. They were airborne fifteen minutes ago.'

10

Tuesday 2 July: Evening

Squadron Leader Snowling was a happy man. He had a wife, who as far as he knew was faithful to him, and two children all safely tucked away at Royal Air Force Coningsby in Lincolnshire. He also had a small moustache, a Jaguar XK140 and all his hair. Some of his colleagues, regularly involved as he was in low-flying exercises 250 feet above the ground at 500 miles an hour, had gone quite bald. The stress and the tension, the constant reliance on electronic equipment which inevitably went wrong at crucial moments, had caused nervous breakdowns among the pilots. Some marriages had broken up: other pilots, after years of intensive training, had left the service and gone back to dull civilian jobs flying airliners for British Airways.

But Snowling was not of that type. Sometimes he found it hard to understand why his colleagues got so uptight about low-level flying, why they worried about the technical shortcomings of their aircraft when flown to the limits, and why they developed an increasing tendency to black out under the physical strain of combat manoeuvres. Snowling had never had such problems. Perhaps, he thought, he lacked imagination, but his greatest worry was what he would do when his time with the Royal Air Force ran out. He hated the thought of applying to British Airways for a routine pilot's job. Sometimes he thought that he might sign on as a mercenary pilot and fly jet fighters for Third-World countries and teach them how to do the job properly. Meanwhile, he flew as many hours each month as he possibly could, made love contentedly to his wife between flights and taught his children how to do high dives and backward flips in the station swimming pool.

Snowling's Tornado carried four Sky Flash and two Sidewinder air-to-air missiles, and the 27-mm cannon was loaded with live ammunition. The other four aircraft in the flight were similarly equipped. He and his fellow aircrew had had a final meteorological briefing three hours earlier and had gone over again the detailed instructions for the mission. Snowling had been surprised to learn that it was code-named Icarus but one of the other pilots had pointed out that Icarus was a classical Greek character who had tumbled out of the sky into the sea, so it all seemed quite appropriate.

Snowling hummed to himself as he flew south. They had got the scramble signal at 1710 local time and they had been airborne within four and a half minutes. Good work, that. The sun lay half-way down the sky on his right as he flew southward. He had never seen a more beautiful evening. There were fringes of grey-white cumulus cloud beneath him and these gave detail and outline to the great cavern of blue all around him. The sea glistened 30,000 feet beneath and, to his naked eye, looked faintly wrinkled, like walnuts, he thought, or my skin when I'm eighty years old. The wind was from the west and getting stronger all the time.

Snowling looked again at the airspeed indicator among the dozens of dials on the instrument panel in front of him. Six hundred and fifty knots. His navigator in the seat behind confirmed that they were now seventy miles south of Akrotiri. The Libyan air freighter had been airborne, according to the message copied and flashed directly from Beirut to their air base, fifteen minutes before them. Assuming it was travelling on a west-south-westerly course to Tripoli at 350 knots, they would meet it 150 miles out from Beirut and eighty miles south of Cyprus, but there was no contact yet on the radar. Of course, if the Libyan plane wished to avoid detection, it would be flying very low over the sea, or it could have turned south-west and be following the Egyptian coastline. He pressed the radio transmit switch on the control column,

'Falcon Section. This is Falcon 1. If the target was heading direct for Tripoli, we would have radar contact by now. I'm descending low level with Falcon 2. Remainder maintain this level and search further south.'

157

The four other pilots confirmed the order over the radio and Snowling pulled the throttles back, lowered the nose and sent the Tornado plummeting towards the sea closely followed by Falcon 2. As he passed through 15,000 feet, the radio clicked in his helmet.

'Falcon 1, this is control. Report your position.'

'Falcon 1 is one hundred miles due south of Akrotiri. No contact with target. Two aircraft carrying out a low-level search. Remainder now looking further south.'

'Control. Roger, out.'

Snowling levelled off at 500 feet above the Mediterranean, peering into the twilight while his navigator continued the search, eyes glued to the radar screen glowing green in the rear cockpit. The radio clicked again.

'Falcon 1, this is control. The weather deterioration that was forecast has now reached Akrotiri, with occasional wind gusts above thirty knots.'

Snowling acknowledged and looked out of his cockpit over his right shoulder. True enough, the little bands of white cumulus were thickening into heavier cloud. The cloud was still all above him, but the ceiling was coming down rapidly. If they did not pick up the Libyan plane soon, it would be hard to argue with the Libyan captain when surrounded by banks of impenetrable nimbus.

When his tactical air navigation system indicated that he was 140 miles from Akrotiri, Snowling started to turn right to re-intersect the Libyan's direct track for Tripoli. His good humour began to dissipate. Bloody Libyans, typical wogs, he thought, they're probably running along the coast in order to try and keep out of trouble. His suspicions were compounded a minute later.

'Falcon 1, this is Falcon 3. We've got slow-moving contact south-east at forty miles, high level.'

'Roger. We're on our way,' Snowling answered as he applied full power. The aircraft surged forwards, his navigator already calculating a heading to close on the target. The Tornado thundered skyward, bursting back from dark clouds into the sunshine. To his left, Snowling could see his wingman climbing back into bright, clear light, and further away the vapour trails of the remaining members of the Falcon Section converging with him on to the suspect aircraft. A minute later, his navigator announced that he had radar contact with the target.

'Falcon Section, this is Falcon 1. I have radar contact. Falcon 2, stay with me for interception, remainder give us top cover.'

Snowling was now rapidly approaching the target under the detailed directions, second by second, of his navigator. Forty seconds later, he saw the evening sun glint off a shiny fuselage.

'Control. This is Falcon 1. In visual contact with suspect aircraft at one hundred and eighty miles on a bearing of one hundred and seventy degrees from base at twenty-seven thousand feet. Continuing with interception.' The adrenalin started to pump through his veins for, in all his life with the Air Force, he had never fired a weapon in anger. Was he now going to see if those expensive missiles actually worked? Hours of training, hours of practice, interminable drills. He looked down at the weapon systems control panel, the switches sprung and gated to prevent any inadvertent selections. He smiled nervously to himself and wondered whether the armourers had put everything in the right way up.

The Ilyushin was now a few hundred feet below him. He looked at the clock on the instrument panel and saw that it was 1750, thirty-five minutes since they had left Akrotiri. He throttled back to 320 knots to keep pace with the Libyan and read out the markings aloud to the operations room at Akrotiri.

'Control, this is Falcon 1. Good visual contact with an Ilyushin freighter marked "Libyan Airlines", Libyan colours and numbered Lima Bravo eight three eight. I am about to commence radio contact with the Libyan captain. Over.'

The earphones crackled back at him: 'Control, Roger. Do not waste time. Your fuel situation is not brilliant. Good luck. Out.'

Snowling switched his radio set on to the international emergency VHF frequency, and took station just ahead of the nose of the Libyan plane, keeping it on his starboard side, and transmitted: 'This is Falcon 1 of the Royal Air Force. I am speaking urgently to the captain of the Libyan freighter Lima Bravo eight three eight. Can you hear me? Over.'

Within a few seconds, a strong, angry voice came back through the earphones: 'This is Captain Proudian to Falcon 1. I have your message. Explain immediately why you and one other RAF plane are crowding round me. Over.'

'I have an urgent instruction to you from the British Government,' radioed Snowling. 'You are to follow me to the Akrotiri Base in Southern Cyprus, approximately one hundred and eighty miles distance.'

His earphone crackled with anger. 'I certainly will not follow you and I object to being ordered. I am on course to Tripoli and will follow that course.'

'That is not acceptable,' Snowling radioed back. 'You have on board two British hostages kidnapped in Beirut. I am instructed to rescue the hostages by requiring you to follow me to Akrotiri.'

'You are talking nonsense. There are no hostages on board this plane. It is a Libyan freighter. We are carrying perishable goods from the Lebanon and an Embassy Mercedes for repair. You must cease your interference immediately.'

What, Snowling wondered briefly, was the definition of perishable goods? Did it include hostages?

'I repeat. I am under instructions to convoy your aeroplane back with us to Akrotiri in order that the British hostages can be released. There are five Tornados in this flight. We are all armed with missiles and live ammunition. I am under instructions to use my weapons if necessary to force you to follow me.'

There was a squeak of violent indignation into Snowling's ear. Captain Proudian's voice lost its edge of professional calm and he protested that he was being threatened with an act of international piracy. He was innocent, there were no British hostages on board, but if force was used against him, he threatened, the British pilots would be tried in an international court, there would be war between Britain and Libya. In between, without switching his microphone off, Proudian could be heard shouting in Arabic at the other members of his crew. Then he spoke again in English to Snowling:

'We have a recorded tape of all that you have said. This will be given to our authorities who will tell the world of your threats. I am not going to speak any more. I shall continue flying on my course to Tripoli.'

Snowling looked at his watch. Another five minutes had passed and they were flying south-westerly away from Cyprus. In the far distance, over his port wing, Snowling thought he could just make out, in a hazy line, the coast of Egypt. Perhaps he was imagining it.

'I must warn you formally, Captain Proudian, that unless you change course and follow me northward, I will fire at your plane. This will be on my government's instructions in order to release our hostages.' There was no answer.

Snowling ordered the pilot of Falcon 2 to fire from above the Libyan plane a short burst of tracer, well in front of the nose of the freighter. He watched as the stream of light shot through the air in a fiery line and disappeared; just like the films, he thought.

His earphones crackled. 'You are mad, you British. You have gone off your heads. You are behaving like pirates.' The anger and incredulity in the Libyan's voice came through all too clearly.

'Falcon 2, give the Libyan another longer burst a bit closer in,' ordered Snowling. A long stream of light flashed past the nose of the Libyan plane. The plane appeared to quiver and then Snowling heard Captain Proudian's voice calling Cairo airport and releasing a furious stream of Arabic.

'Captain Proudian,' Snowling transmitted, 'I shall shoot your plane down if necessary. Those are my orders. I give you one more warning before using live ammunition on your plane. Bank to the right and start following a course due north.'

There was no reply from the Libyan and the planes continued to fly towards the south-west. Six o'clock had passed and Snowling noted his fuel state, calculating that he would have to turn the Libyan in the next five minutes. He switched his radio back to the operational frequency.

'Control from Falcon 1.'

161

'Control, go ahead.'

'We have fired two series of warning shots at the Libyan aeroplane without any effect. Our fuel situation requires that we must turn him back within the next five minutes. I shall now shoot at the plane, despite the risk of decompression.'

There was a perceptible pause and Snowling could imagine the controller at the other end putting down his earphones and shouting across the operations room. Then the impersonal voice said in his ears: 'Understood. You know your instructions.'

For a final time, Snowling switched over to the emergency frequency and said: 'Captain Proudian. I repeat, this is your last warning. If you do not turn to the north immediately, I will fire at your aircraft.'

Once again, there was no reply. Snowling transmitted: 'Falcon 2, drop back. I'm going to engage him.'

As his wingman moved away, the Squadron Leader manoeuvred his Tornado behind the Ilyushin. He waited for fifteen seconds and, as he waited, he found himself praying against all his normal habit that he would see the starboard wing of the freighter dip and the nose swing round towards the north. 'Please God,' he said to himself, 'let them see sense. Turn your bloody plane round . . . now.' But nothing happened and he reluctantly armed the cannon.

Through his gunsight he could see the tail and fuselage but, knowing that his 27-mm shells would penetrate the length of the aircraft and all within it, he gently pushed his right rudder pedal and moved the sight on to the starboard wing. Fuel tanks, he thought. A further adjustment placed the inner starboard engine in his line of fire. Thankful for the Libyan's smooth flight path, he made a final check of his aim, squeezed the trigger on the control column and fired a half-second burst into the turbo-prop engine.

He felt the Tornado shudder and was surprised both by his accuracy and the result. The propeller disintegrated, the engine violently oversped and sprayed its turbine blades through the cowling, like shrapnel ripping into the fuselage aft of the cockpit. Debris flashed past his canopy and then he saw the stricken engine belch white smoke as the internal fire extinguishers were activated. God, he thought, what am I doing? There was a yell in his ears:

'Your rounds are killing our people,' a voice screamed. He did not know whether it was Captain Proudian or not but, as the scream died down, the Libyan aircraft wallowed for several minutes and then sluggishly turned right, settling on a northerly heading.

Thank God, thought Snowling. He switched his radio over to the other pilots in the Falcon Section.

'Falcon 3, 4 and 5, we are on our way back to Akrotiri. Stay at thirty thousand feet and follow us back. If we need you, I will let you know. Falcon 2, take up a position on his starboard wing. We should get back to Akrotiri with five minutes' fuel in hand.'

'Well done, Boss,' said the pilot of Falcon 3.

'Thank you. With any luck, no one was hurt,' said Snowling. He passed a message back to Akrotiri, telling the Base to expect them in about sixty minutes as they were now only flying around 200 knots when he heard Captain Proudian's voice cut in on the emergency frequency:

'You will be pleased, you British assassins. You have killed one member of my crew and another is bleeding to death. I think she will be dead by the time we reach Cyprus.'

Snowling felt time stop in his cabin, and his heart stood still. Christ, he thought, and then, with all the feeling he could summon up, he said over the radio:

'I'm very sorry about your crew members, Captain. I'm deeply sorry. I did my utmost to shoot only at the engine where I thought no one would be hurt, but my orders were to turn your plane round. What about the hostages? Are they all right?'

There was no reply.

It was six o'clock in the evening in London. Jock received an urgent message, asking him to come round from the Foreign Office to Number 10. When he arrived at the front door, the policeman nodded to him cheerfully and told him that he was expected in the flat upstairs. He walked down the corridor to the lift, pressed the top button and wondered what on earth was going to happen now. As he opened the lift door, he heard the Prime Minister's voice shouting: 'Jock, come along to the drawing room. I am doing some work there.' Jock walked along the short, brightly-lit passage and turned into the low-ceilinged, cheerful drawing room with its mass of contemporary political cartoons on the wall, some of them funny, some of them rude, and all of them featuring Bruce Gordon prominently.

Bruce Gordon stood up from the desk in the corner as Jock walked in and said: 'It was good of you to come round so quickly, Jock. I gather that you're free for half an hour before your next appointment. I thought we might have a quick word about developments in Akrotiri. Have you seen the latest telegram? Would you like a drink?'

Without waiting for an answer, Bruce Gordon moved over to the silver tray sitting on the top of the low bookshelves at the end of the room where Jock was standing.

'Thank you, Prime Minister. I'll have a gin and tonic, not too large.' Jock paused and then said with a smile, 'I've got a lot of work still to do this evening and I'm going to two Ambassadors' receptions before dinner.'

'Which ones?' asked the Prime Minister as he placed large ice-cubes in round glasses, engraved with a sketch of the front of Number 10.

'The Israelis and the Saudis. Luckily, they are talking to each other at the moment so I don't have to pretend to one that I haven't been to the other.'

'I'm sure you're very good at that. It's all part of the Foreign Office expertise and lots of what we used to call charm, but I think that word's gone out of fashion.' The Prime Minister handed Jock his full glass and waved to him to sit down on the sofa.

'So far, the Akrotiri affair seems to have gone all right,' the Prime Minister commented. 'The car's definitely on board, thank God. We've got the pilot's own confirmation for that. Two Libyans dead, perhaps, but that's not the worst news in the world. The vital question is whether the hostages are there or not. The captain of the airliner is, of course, saying that they're not, but he would say that, wouldn't he? If they are on board, the hijacking of the airliner over the Mediterranean, for that's what it is, will be justified and we will make the most of it politically. My press office has got the tabloids all lined up. The headlines tomorrow should be tremendous. But . . .' he paused, 'if they're not on board – that nasty little word, *if* – we're in real trouble.

'So far, Jock, your estimate of the Libyan psychology has been right. The captain did turn round, and fly his aeroplane to Cyprus rather than be shot down into the sea, just as you said at the Cabinet committee yesterday. I congratulate you.'

'Thank you,' the combination of gin and compliments made Jock feel more relaxed. 'The key point always seemed to me that the RAF should not shoot down the plane by mistake. Rounds into the petrol tanks, for example, which would burst into flame and destroy the plane just as the pilot was trying to turn and follow the Tornados.'

'Yes, that was a problem. We wanted it a runner, not a dead bird. Fortunately, they're trained to be good shots.' The Prime Minister paused, clinked the ice-cubes round his glass, looked carefully at the lines engraved on it and then turned and, from his end of the sofa, stared straight at Jock. 'Your boss is furious about my remark in the House this afternoon when I said that we had information that Al-Fatah were holding the hostages. He was extraordinarily rude to me outside the Chamber in the presence of a number of our colleagues. I have to say that it was intolerable behaviour from a colleague; I shouldn't be saying all of this to you, Jock, but you seem to be becoming quite a friend, and I wouldn't be surprised if the lobby correspondents got hold of some of the row and put it in the papers tomorrow. That's just what we don't need at the moment.

'But I've had my office check it all out and it seems that there was a telegram from Beirut last Saturday, making the point very clearly that Al-Fatah's name should be kept secret. A copy of that never got to Number 10. Do you know anything about that?'

Is this man a friend or an enemy? Gordon mused to himself as he waited for Jock's reply. Is he, as Margaret used to say, one of us or is he against us? A quick wave of loneliness swept over Gordon as he thought how many of his real friends, those in whom he could always trust, were now either out of the Cabinet or dead or both. Dominic Anderson, whose family he had fished and shot with in Scotland ever since he was at university, was one of the few left who would tell him the truth, however unpalatable. He hadn't really got the feel of his new Chief Whip, Greg Stevens. Perhaps he would, in time, but, for the moment, he didn't know where the man's true sympathies lay. What an amazingly good profile Jock had and his face was marvellously unlined. His thoughts started to wander, and he wondered whether he could possibly ask Jock to stay at his little house near Southampton for a weekend without his wife. They could go for a long walk over Corhampton Down. He supposed it would be a risk but it might be worth it. He heard Jock's voice talking through a distant dream and he pulled his thoughts back.

'Sorry, my thoughts were wandering to pleasant occupations,' he smiled. 'What were you saying, Jock?'

Jock looked surprised. Is the old bird really gay, he wondered? He's got that embarrassed look on his face that always led to disaster at Cambridge.

'Prime Minister, sorry, you were just asking about the missing message from Beirut. My office told me that yours was enquiring about it after Question Time this afternoon. I can't think what happened. I certainly saw one myself over the weekend, perhaps in my Saturday box.' He paused and then plunged on.

'It may be unfortunate, or it may lead to nothing, but certainly it did say categorically that the name of Al-Fatah was to be kept out of the public view. I imagine that they are worried about their relations with the other terrorist organizations, they're all at each other's throats in Beirut all the time.' Jock looked down at his glass and took a long drink from it. He noted with relief that, as far as he was aware, there had been no tremor in his voice. The missing copy of Saturday's message from Beirut had finally disappeared altogether. He had looked for it in the flat the previous evening but couldn't find it and he assumed that Mary, the careful, tidy Mary, had torn it up and disposed of it.

'I know, Beirut is a bit like the Wars of the Roses,' said the Prime Minister. 'A new faction appears every day and you don't know whose side they're on, whether they're supporting the Christians or the Muslims, the Syrians or the Iranians, the Palestinians or the Israelis but, Jock, if mentioning Al-Fatah's name causes trouble, you must know that I shall hold Robert Huggins wholly responsible.

'Missing message or no, I regard it clearly as his job to see that I was fully briefed about all the intricacies of what was happening in Beirut before Question Time this afternoon. He has let me down.' Gordon paused again and moved slightly along the sofa. He gently rested a hand on Jock's knee and said: 'But I don't suppose that'll do you much harm, Jock. Indeed, it can only help you get that job in the Cabinet that I've promised you after the election, not Foreign Secretary yet, but sitting at the top table.' He squeezed Jock's knee and smiled at him as a returning smile hovered discreetly over Jock's lips.

'Well, Jock, you must get on to your diplomatic carousel. First the Israelis then the Saudis. What fun! No drink, I suppose, at the Saudis?'

'Oh, no,' said Jock. 'The Saudis are quite grown-up about that sort of thing now. Champagne and whisky all over the place. And smoked salmon and quails' eggs.'

The Prime Minister laughed as he started to walk towards the door.

'That can't be too bad. The key thing now is what happens to the hostages. Let's hope to God that they're in the plane and that the SAS'll get them out all right. I gather from the Chief of Staff that the SAS plan to go in around midnight, local time. That's ten o'clock our time. If they're quick and effective, we could just make *Newsnight*. That would be a real shot in the arm.'

★

167

'You know,' said Jock to Mary as they walked up the drive to the Israeli Embassy in Hampstead, past the police who were insisting that all cars be parked at least 400 yards from the Ambassador's residence, 'you know, I really think Bruce Gordon may be going gay. To use an old-fashioned university phrase that our children certainly wouldn't understand, he seems to have a crush on me.'

'Don't be silly,' said Mary. 'He's as old as the hills and he must be quite past it.'

'I don't know. We were sitting on the sofa in the flat at Number 10 thirty minutes ago and he was dishing the dirt at poor Robert about the hostages and he gave my knee a positive squeeze. It was just like the old days with Crabtree, my tutor at Cambridge. I've often wondered whether, if I'd gone to bed with Crabtree, he'd have helped me more to get a First.'

Mary laughed as they approached the steps up to the Ambassador's residence. There were other guests around them and she turned close to Jock and dropped her voice:

'You know, Jock, that's one thing about you I've never worried about. I may have worried about your being weak, or bullied by your civil servants, or bossed around by your constituency chairman, but I've never, never thought of you as gay. But scrap dinner and I'll test you out in bed.'

Jock smiled. 'We can't,' he said, 'after this, we've got to go and chat up the Saudis.'

As Jock and Mary left the Saudi reception, their government driver had just turned on the radio for the news.

'There's a great fuss going on, sir,' Joe, the driver, said. 'Gadaffi, the Libyan fellow, is saying that we've hijacked one of his aeroplanes over the Mediterranean and killed two of the crew. I can't believe it really, but he's threatening blood and thunder, and he says he's going to bomb London. Of course, he couldn't do that?' Joe ended with a hopeful note of query in his voice.

'Of course not,' said Jock but he asked Joe to turn up the radio and he listened to the tail-end of the news report:

'Official government sources have confirmed· that a Libyan Ilyushin air freighter was escorted by RAF Tornado jets to the

Akrotiri Base in Cyprus a few hours ago. This was, the official spokesman added, on the basis of certain information that had been received regarding the airliner, but he was not prepared to make any further comment.

'Our diplomatic correspondent said that, although our relations with Libya could not get any worse than they are at present, the apparent armed interception of the airliner could win a great deal of support for Colonel Gadaffi from some of our traditional Arab allies. Their first reactions are beginning to be received and they are, without exception, very hostile. There will be further coverage on our final news bulletin at midnight.'

'Thank you, Joe. Switch it off, could you?' Jock turned to Mary who had snuggled up alongside him on the back seat.

'Oh my gay diplomat,' she murmured. 'Are you sure that I'm your sort?'

Jock frowned and muttered: 'Ssssh.' He nodded his head forward towards Joe's grey-suited back. 'You know, we've really put the match to the blue touch-paper now. I think I'd better go to the House to see what happens at ten o'clock.'

'All right,' said Mary. 'Time for a quick pizza. I've got one in the fridge at home, but could I come back to the House with you, and you could get me into the gallery? I don't want to miss anything.'

The House was very crowded. Angela Fawke, the Social Security Secretary, was winding up an angry debate on unemployment benefit. Unemployment had recently risen to almost two and a half million, and the Minister was striving her utmost to put over the Government's side of the case. As Jock entered the Chamber and sat at the Speaker's end of the Front Bench, he heard Angela Fawke change gear from the andante of civil service statistics about rates of benefit and percentages of women in work to the fortissimo of her peroration. The electronic clock in the Chamber stood at 9.57, so there was time for three minutes of passion before the debate ended and the vote was called.

'What would happen,' asked the Minister rhetorically, 'if Labour were in power rather than us? We would see

169

unemployment benefit being reduced, as it was in the 1970s, rather than rising in real terms by twenty-five per cent. What would happen if the Liberals . . .'

The world was never to know, as the Labour Shadow Foreign Secretary jumped to his feet and stood at the Despatch Box immediately opposite and four short feet away from Angela Fawke.

'Point of order,' he shouted. 'Point of order, Mr Speaker.' He looked menacingly at the Speaker and then at Angela Fawke. 'Point of order, Mr Robinson,' sighed the Speaker.

Angela Fawke sank back on to the green leather of the Treasury bench whilst Paul Robinson, conscious that he had a full house of members of parliament listening to him, all of them there for the ten o'clock vote, bellowed over the crowded Chamber.

'Mr Speaker, it is widely reported on the radio and television that the British Government has used RAF planes to hijack a Libyan airliner.'

Immediate, angry cries of: 'Rubbish. Not hijack, escort. The Libyans shot first. Sit down, you ass,' interrupted him from Conservative benches.

The Speaker rose quickly to his feet. 'Order, order! The House must listen to the Honourable Gentleman quietly. He has an important point of order.'

Robinson had stayed on his feet all of this time and now, encouraged by the Speaker, he went on even more strongly. 'There are reports that the RAF planes made an unprovoked attack on the Libyan airliner, shot at it and killed two people inside it. Colonel Gadaffi has been on television . . .'

'He is a terrorist. You are supporting a terrorist leader,' thundered Sir John Williamson from the ultimate peak of his back-bench.

'Order, order,' bellowed the Speaker without rising from the chair. Paul Robinson continued, delighted by the uproar he was creating on the Tory side.

'Other Arab leaders, friends of Britain, are threatening to cut off diplomatic relations because of this cowardly, unprovoked hijack of a Libyan plane. The Opposition insist, Mr Speaker, that a Foreign Office minister make a statement immediately after the ten o'clock vote. I see the Minister of State from the Foreign Office has just entered the Chamber' – he pointed across at Jock sitting at the far end of the Treasury bench. 'If the Minister of State has any guts, indeed if he has any knowledge which he usually succeeds in concealing from us,' the backbenchers behind Robinson cheered with happy laughter, 'he will get to his feet now and deny this appalling story which will do so much damage to British relations with the Arab world.' Ten o'clock appeared on the electronic clocks round the Chamber. The Speaker rose to his feet, and, projecting his voice like the good actor he was, boomed:

'I have received no indication that the Government wish to make a statement. The question is that the Bill be now read a third time. Those in favour say "aye", those against say "no".' The Tory benches, relieved to be back on track again, roared: 'Aye.' Labour roared: 'No,' and the House divided for a vote. Paul Robinson sank back on the Opposition Front Bench, thoroughly pleased with himself, knowing the lobby correspondents were hurrying from the press gallery above the Chamber to get his remarks into the final editions of their papers.

'Bloody good. You nailed them. You've got them on the run,' said the Labour members around him. One leaned over from behind and ruffled his hair as if he had just scored a goal.

Jock leaned back and muttered, as Tory MPs trooped past him to vote,

'Avenge, O Lord, thy slaughtered saints, whose bones
Lie scattered on the Alpine mountains cold.'

'What did you say?' said the Whip sitting beside him, scribbling his notes about the debate for his chief to read later that night.

'Oh, nothing,' said Jock, who did not like the Whips either in general or in particular, 'but write it down all the same. I'll give you two more lines. They're very appropriate:

'Forget not. In thy book record their groans
Who were thy sheep . . .'

He rose, turned up the steps in front of the box crowded with

171

civil servants, and walked through the door, held open by a uniformed attendant, towards the division lobby.

Strange fellow, thought the Whip. Snooty. Typical Foreign Office type.

About an hour later, at 11.15 on the Westminster clocks, 1.15 am in Akrotiri, Colonel Spacemead raised his right arm and flashed his torch three times to the sky. Thirty men in black denims, with darkened faces and hands, crawled down ropes already in place along both sides of the Ilyushin airliner. Another twenty raced up ladders leaning against the entrance hatch and wings of the plane. Each man went to a target area that had been previously allocated to him and placed a small charge on the chosen spot. Limpet-like, the charges stuck to the metal of the plane. There were six around the entrance hatch and ten around the big door into the loading bay. Every other porthole had a charge sticking to it like a giant, malevolent snail.

Within thirty seconds, the men were back in their previous positions, either on the ground or on top of the plane. Spacemead again shone his torch at the sky. Precisely thirty seconds later, there was a chorus of small explosions all along the aeroplane. The aluminium fabric of the plane ripped apart with a screeching, tearing sound. Glass burst and shattered. As the noise rang out, the SAS men were back down the ropes and up the ladders. Through clouds of smoke, four wrenched back the entrance door which now hung cracked and half-open on its hinges and, followed by another six, they tore into the airliner, half going forward towards the cockpit and half aft.

Down the main fuselage, others scrambled in through the blown-out portholes and, with a rasping shake, the huge door to the loading bay in the tail first swung half-open and then collapsed on to the ground.

Spacemead stood at the bottom of the ladder up to the entrance hatch and waited, tensely, to hear shots. Every second that passed without gunfire lifted a weight from his mind. He loved his men. They trained with precision, accuracy and speed, and they knew that they were the best in the world, but nothing he could ever do would stop the captain of an aeroplane who waited with his pistol cocked and shot immediately once one of his men appeared in the gangway.

He looked at his watch. Thirty seconds passed, then fifty. He sighed with relief and, at that instant, his second-in-command appeared at the entrance to the plane with his arm locked round the elbow of a short, thick man wearing the uniform of an airline captain. The smoke had started to clear and Spacemead could see the three gold rings on the captain's sleeve and the peaked blue and white cap.

'He says he's Captain Proudian. He has given me his gun without firing it. So far we've found nine crew members as the captain said over the radio, plus two dead. That's a lot of crew. Paul and his team have just started searching the cargo bays; he says that there is a large, black car down there.'

'Thank you, Peter. Well done, everyone,' said Colonel Space-mead. He turned and said slowly and carefully to the Libyan, 'Captain Proudian, would you come down the ladder so that we can talk. It will be easier on the ground. Bring the other members of the crew out and on to the tarmac as soon as possible, Peter, just in case the fuel tanks go up.'

'Of course,' said Peter and turned back into the dark cavern of the plane.

As Captain Proudian climbed slowly down the ladder, Colonel Spacemead stepped back five paces and looked at the Ilyushin with satisfaction. So far, it had gone just as he had planned and hoped. The fuel tanks had not exploded and there had been no detonations near to them. Both the key hatches had come off immediately and there were no deaths. A copy-book operation, he thought. Just what the SAS are trained to do, and we're a hell of a lot better at it than either the French or the Americans. The only question that remained was that of the hostages.

Captain Proudian was now on the ground, his shoulders hunched forward. Even in the darkness, Spacemead could see the sweat streaming off his face. He walked forward two paces and saluted the captain.

'Captain Proudian. I am Colonel Spacemead.' He put out his right hand towards the Libyan but Proudian shook his head violently and half turned away. 'The damage to your plane could have been avoided if you had opened the doors for us as we have requested ever since you landed.'

Proudian bunched his hands together as if he would like to punch Spacemead in the face: 'How can you do this?' he spat out. 'You are British but you behave like pirates, terrorists.'

Spacemead felt himself pushed on the defensive: 'But you know, Captain, that it did not have to happen. If you had followed our Tornados when they asked you, and they warned you repeatedly, there would have been no shots at your aeroplane. If you had agreed to our requests to open the doors of your plane, we would have searched it and, if there were no hostages there, you would have been airborne again, refuelled, within thirty minutes.'

Proudian shook his head in disbelief. He turned and looked at the hulk of his plane with the great holes in the fuselage behind the wing and in the tail.

'I do not understand this about hostages,' he said slowly. 'What hostages? I told you many times, there were twelve people aboard: me and eleven members of my crew. Now, two are dead.' He looked back at the Ilyushin. The smoke had disappeared and the plane stood clearly in silhouette against the night sky, sitting in the quiet corner of the tarmac whither it had been ordered by the control tower on landing.

'Your Government will pay, will pay millions of dollars. Millions and millions. The Muslim world, the Arab League, will fight you. You have killed a woman and a man without excuse.' Proudian looked up and shook his head violently from side to side.

As if on cue, a darkened figure appeared in the hole where the entrance hatch had been and shouted: 'Colonel Spacemead, sir.'

'Yes,' said the Colonel, as the nine crew members started to climb down the ladder towards the ground until they stood a few yards away, with four SAS men behind them, their sub-machine guns in their hands.

'We'll need two body-bags. Paul and his team have finished

searching the hold. From what he can see, the cargo is much as the captain described it over the radio. There are between sixty and seventy different crates, none of them big, but the men are opening them all at the moment. We don't think anyone could be alive inside any of them. There is a large, four-door Mercedes with a particularly big boot, but there's no sign of Janes or Harrington. It's quite empty and there are no obvious signs of anyone having been held in it.'

'Thank you, Peter. I'll send up the body-bags. Bring your men back on to the tarmac and stand them down when you want.' The Colonel turned towards the SAS men beside him and detailed one to take the two bags on to the plane. Then he swung away and stared quietly into the darkness, alone, thinking. Peter came down the ladder from the plane and started to talk to him, but he gestured to him to stop. He felt his sense of achievement, even of triumph, ebbing away into the velvet air. He moved from elation to terrible flatness. No hostages, he thought, that's done for us. What a mess. What a bloody row there will be.

He turned back slowly to face Captain Proudian and said formally: 'I'm desperately sorry, Captain Proudian. Two British hostages were taken by terrorists in Beirut ten days ago. We had every reason to believe that Colonel Gadaffi had given orders for them to be shipped back to Tripoli and our intelligence led us to believe that your aeroplane and the Mercedes car would be used for that purpose.'

Captain Proudian looked at him, uttered a long stream of Arabic, paused and then spat at his feet as he turned away.

11

Wednesday 3 July: Morning

The car sped through the outskirts of Beirut, going north up Kidnap Alley, then turning off the main road to the left, twisting, appearing at times to be going back on the route that it had followed five minutes before. Slowly, the buildings became larger and more important and the streets, still full of potholes and stones and trash, got wider. Ahmed swore under his breath as he ran over a cat that, belly close to the ground, slid across the road in front of him. There was a slight bump as the left front wheel hit the cat, and a lesser jolt from the rear wheel.

'*Illi yajawir,*' he muttered, '*al haddad yinkiwi bi naru.*' They were the first words he had said since telling Janes and Harrington to put on their shoes when he woke them and then instructing them to sit in the back seat of the car and to keep quiet as they drove away from the house where they were held. He now sat alone in the front of the car, slightly crouched and both hands gripping the steering wheel, with his knuckles showing as spots of bone gleaming on top of the padded wheel.

'What did he say?' Bob asked Les.

'It's an old proverb,' Les replied. 'It means something like "he that touches tar will be stained by it". They think killing a cat is very unlucky.' The two sank back in silence and each stared out of the window on his side of the car.

Ahmed entered the Bois de Boulogne, turned left, and then sharp right again at the Museum Crossing. They left West Beirut and drove rapidly towards the Tripoli road.

Bob now knew exactly where they were and felt, as much as saw, the quiet shimmer of the Mediterranean on his left. The night was still, without a breath of wind, and Bob imagined the sound of

176

waves as he recognized his pleasure at being so close to the sea again. It can't be many miles to go now, he thought to himself. Four miles, five miles. If they drop us close enough to the Embassy for us to walk there, we could be there in ten minutes. His heart bumped up inside him and, for a few seconds, he quietly thanked God that he was free and thought that it was totally unbelievable that he was out of that house with the ropes no longer on his wrists or chains on his ankles.

'I suppose Ahmed took us a roundabout way,' muttered Les by his side, 'so that he could be certain we wouldn't be able to tell where we had been held.'

'Christ! I don't care where I was held. It's sheer bloody marvellous to be out and to be free.'

'I can't believe it yet,' said Les. 'I just can't believe it. That cat, it was a horrid feeling running over it.'

They had sat all evening in the small, upstairs room, the door still bolted, waiting for their captors to come. They had been brought no food and, as the night fell and the hours of darkness slipped by, they had both become gloomier, convinced that the plans had gone wrong and they were not going to be released after all. They had got angry with each other, each blaming the other for the carelessness that had led to their capture ten days before. Then they had patched it up, and agreed that it was no good bickering, and, once again, they had got back on to the same old, dirty heap of straw and they had tried to sleep as the night darkened further. And then, when they had given up hope and were dozing off into unhappy dreams, they had heard Ahmed's footsteps on the staircase and, immediately after, the turning of the key in the lock on the door, and his voice urging them to get their shoes on and to follow him.

'I'm so bloody nervous,' said Les, turning to Bob. 'I'm sure something's going to go wrong. The car will get blown up or something like that.'

'Don't let yourself think like that,' urged Bob. 'Look, we're on the autostrada now.' As he spoke, the car speeded up to take advantage of the dual carriageway. They sank back into silence as both men nursed their hopes and counted to themselves the remaining distance as familiar landmarks flitted by. There was the office of the agent for Mercedes cars, then the showroom full of imported Zanussi washing machines. Les started biting his finger nails.

'Another block,' said Bob, 'and he'll turn off up the hill to the Embassy.'

As he said this, a car came up fast from behind them, turned in front of them and, brakes squealing, an arm out of the window gesticulating them to stop, slewed round and braked in front of them, blocking their side of the road. A figure in white shirt and dark trousers hurried out, came round to Les's side of the car and pulled open the door. Bob looked across and recognized Faisal. He started to say: 'What's wrong?' but Faisal shouted at them both, his voice vibrating with anger and violence.

'You have betrayed us. Your government has announced that it is Al-Fatah who are holding you. General Haddad has heard it on the BBC and now your government has hijacked a Libyan plane and killed two of the crew. Get out of the car. We cannot release you.'

He shouted at Ahmed in the driver's seat, who started to open his door and come round to Bob. Faisal pulled his pistol out of his trouser belt and pointed it at Les.

'Get out of the car at once!' Ahmed turned and shouted. Bob opened his car door. He clambered out and saw Les get out on the other side of the car. Faisal came forward, pushed Les hard in the small of the back so that he stumbled and fell. As he lay on the tarmac by the edge of the road, Faisal raised his pistol and put it close to Les's head above his right ear.

Bob turned, saw Ahmed moving towards him, and put out both hands and rushed at Ahmed, pushing him with frenzied strength in his chest. Ahmed stepped back, tripped on a stone and stumbled into the street. Bob charged forward, heard three shots in quick succession from the side of the car where Les lay. There was a pause for five seconds and then an angry shout behind him. Bob reached the far side of the road where there was an untidy row of olive trees and no street lamps. There was another shot and a whizzing noise, wasp-like, went past his left ear. Bob swerved to the right, ducking under the branches of one of the trees, and another wasp buzzed past him. Sucking in his breath, he ran as he had not run since leaving school twenty years before. I'm not fit, he thought as his lungs started to hurt and he panted for breath. My back hurts like hell. I've been sitting around doing nothing for ten days.

There were footsteps along the pavement some way behind him but he didn't dare turn round to see whether they were gaining or not. He heard another pistol shot but this time he did not feel the breath of the bullet passing him. I can do it, he thought. I'm not going to let myself be killed by those bastards. I can do it. Sally, God, Christ, help me!

Fifty yards on, the road forked and, as he ran, Bob thought he remembered that up the right fork, up a bit of a hill, past a petrol station and then again a turning on the right, led to the maze of little streets careering up the side of the Met'n to the Ambassador's residence. A few hundred yards back now, he heard the car starting up but, at that moment, he saw a pathway on his right so he turned off the road and ran up a steep path going straight up the hill and then turned left again. He crossed back over the main road and saw the car going further up the hill, 200 yards in front, so he ran straight across into another alleyway with shuttered houses on either side and turned right at the end. He saw a painted sign saying 4th St and thought he remembered the Ambassador's house was further up the hill on a tree-lined 8th St. He did not dare stop running and he felt his chest heave and heave as though he would be sick if only he had time to stop and vomit. He followed the road up round the curve of the hill. He turned right yet again and then left and then, miraculously in front of him, he saw the barrier across the road at the end of which was the Ambassador's residence, and the little guard-house in which a soldier in army denims was sitting, half asleep. Bloody hell! I've almost made it, he thought and, gasping, gasping for breath, he ran straight past the guard-house. Twenty yards on he was stopped by a shout behind him:

'Stop, or I shoot!' yelled the soldier. Bob turned and, lungs and chest heaving, he saw a sub-machine gun pointed straight at his chest.

'I'm the hostage, Bob Janes,' he sobbed. 'I've just escaped from the terrorists. They're following me in a car and they've shot Les Harrington.'

The light from the guard-house shone out towards Bob and the soldier stared at him: 'Have you got your passport?' asked the soldier.

'Don't be bloody stupid,' sobbed Bob. 'Of course I haven't got my passport. I tell you I'm Bob Janes.' The soldier looked at him closely and suddenly remembered the picture of Janes and Harrington that he had been issued with a week before.

'Stay there,' he shouted. He turned back, went into the guard-house, looked at the photo on the board in front of him and picked up the phone to the residence. Bob stood in the street waiting for the terrorists' car to come by and riddle him and the guard-house with bullets. His breath was slowly coming back and he thought that this was a very, very stupid way to die. But then the soldier came out of the guard-house and said:

'Walk up to the residence. On the left. It's the last door before the barriers. I've warned them you're coming.'

Bob turned and walked slowly under the trees, all sense of pursuit ebbing away from him, towards the residence. The sight of Les lying by the side of the road and the sound of bullets being pumped into his head suddenly came back to him, and tears came into his eyes and he started to cry as he stumbled down the steps towards the door of the residence. As he reached to bang on it, the door swung open and there was the Ambassador in pyjamas, looking as if he had been waiting patiently all night.

'Are you all right?' asked the Ambassador, anxiously. 'Where's your friend? Come in, come in at once. I'll get you a drink and you can tell me what has happened.'

Thirty minutes later, a long telegram was on its way to London. It was marked FLASH and MOST URGENT. It had been carefully drafted by the Ambassador who, at two in the morning, still remembered his syntax and did not waste words, but it told of Bob's escape and the murder of Les in great detail. Even the Ambassador had hesitated for a long time over the sentences which finally read:

JANES MAKES PLAIN THAT THEIR RELEASE WOULD HAVE PRO-CEEDED AS PLANNED IF AL-FATAH'S NAME HAD NOT BEEN REVEALED IN THE COMMONS YESTERDAY. AL-FATAH REPEATEDLY STRESSED THAT THEY COULD NOT AFFORD TO BE REGARDED AS TOO WEAK OR PRO-WESTERN BY OTHER ISLAMIC OR PALESTINIAN TERRORIST GROUPS. THE MISTAKEN INTERCEPTION OF THE LIBYAN AIRLINER OFF CYPRUS IS OF SECONDARY IMPORTANCE. DESPITE THE SUBSTANTIAL FUNDING RECEIVED FROM LIBYA, THERE IS LITTLE LOVE LOST BETWEEN AL-FATAH AND GADAFFI. IT IS AL-FATAH'S STANDING WITH OTHER TERRORIST GROUPS HERE THAT IS OF PARAMOUNT IMPORTANCE TO THEM. THE NEED TO PRESERVE THAT STANDING CAUSED HARRINGTON'S DEATH.

Mary Meldrum-Ross tossed and turned under the duvet spread over their large bed. She had always wanted to have a duvet rather than sheets and blankets, as she thought them much more comfortable and it meant much less time being spent on bed-making. Jock had objected because he said that he liked the comfort of being wrapped up tightly under sheets and with a great weight of blankets on top. Mary smiled to herself as she remembered that Jock had said that he thought bed should be like being inside the womb, warm and tight and confined. But, in the end, she had had her way as in most matters to do with the way they organized and ran their lives. Light was streaming through the heavy double-lined curtain and she rolled over on her right side and looked at her watch. Only a quarter to seven. None the less, if she woke Jock now, he could finish doing his red box in good time for breakfast. She rolled over and gave Jock a gentle shake on his shoulder.

'Jock. I must tell you about an extraordinary dream I've been having,' she whispered near his ear. 'You and I were in bed together and we were having a lovely time, very cosy and very passionate' – Jock murmured with pleasure – 'when that tarty little girl from your office with the big breasts, what's she called?'

'Anthea Wheeler,' muttered Jock, 'and she's not tarty. She got a First at Somerville.'

'That doesn't make any difference. I think she's tarty. In any event, she came into our room and she insisted on getting into bed as well on the other side of you, and I got very jealous and then, and this was really strange, Bruce Gordon came flopping into our room in pyjamas that were all hanging down and he said he wanted to get into our bed, too, and he insisted on being next to you, and he wanted me to roll over and make way for him. I woke up at that moment so I don't know what happened next.' Jock chuckled and stretched his arm.

'It sounds like the Great Bed of Ware. I always imagine there were lots of goings-on in those big medieval beds. What's the time?' Mary told him that it was nearly seven. She rolled close to him and put her arms round him:

'You know, I'm awfully jealous about you and the nearer you get to the top in government, the more exciting I find it. Which shall it be? Sex or the red box?'

'If I'm to get any further in government, I think it had better be the red box,' said Jock, swinging his legs over the side of the bed.

'Damn,' said Mary. 'That shows what a boring minister you've become.' Jock put on a light, silk dressing gown, shoved his feet into his slippers and walked down the passage, past the bathroom and the children's bedrooms towards the drawing room. He picked up his red box where he'd left it the night before, at the side of the desk, opened it with a key on a ring in his dressing-gown pocket and, within a minute, was wholly absorbed in a paper from Alastair Crichton, the Under Secretary, discussing ways and means of getting closer to the ruling sheikhs in the Arabian Gulf. He picked up a red pen and made various annotations and comments as he read through the closely woven text that argued for spending more time and effort on wooing the small states of

Oman, Qatar and Dubai. He had just reached the inevitable suggestion that the Minister of State should himself visit the Trucial States more often, when the telephone by his desk rang. He looked at his watch as he reached for the receiver. It was just 7.30. He wondered who was ringing. Not many people had his private London number.

'It's Martin Jevons here, of the BBC. Just to say that I imagine I'm now free to use all the material you gave me at Brooks's the other night. Of course, I won't attribute it to you, so people won't know that you're the source. As you will know, the story about the botched hijack from Akrotiri is all over the world. We've been running it since late last night and now there's the news that one of the hostages in Beirut has escaped but the other, Les Harrington, has been killed.'

'What? What did you say?' asked Jock.

'Hadn't you heard? That news came here about two in the morning. The World Service has been running it ever since and we first put it out on our six o'clock bulletin.'

'My God! That's awful,' said Jock. 'Harrington killed. No, no, no. How?' Martin Jevons filled him in on those of the details that he knew and then added:

'I'd like to do an interview with you for the *One O'clock News*.'

'Radio or television?' asked Jock.

'Both. This is bound to be headline stuff throughout the day.'

'All right,' said Jock, thinking ahead to his programme for the day. 'Will you get someone to ring my private office soon after nine to make all the arrangements? Can you bring the cameras to the Foreign Office? I'm going to have a very busy day.'

'Yes, of course,' said Martin. 'We'll be there about half past twelve, I should think. We may do some of it live.'

'All right.' He paused, then added: 'Thanks for letting me know about Harrington.'

'My pleasure,' Martin Jevons chuckled down the telephone. 'The BBC is always proud to keep the Foreign Office informed.'

God, thought Jock. No hostages on the plane, the Arab world furious. Harrington dead. What a fucking mess. How the hell will we ever get out of this?

Mary walked into the room, carrying a tray with a pot of coffee and a cup, a large glass of orange juice and a little silver rack full of toast. Butter, marmalade and brown sugar were in small, matching china bowls on the tray. Under her arm, she had a great pile of newspapers, which she dumped on the side of his desk.

'I went out to get you these. I thought you'd want to see them all this morning. They're very rough on Robert.' Jock picked up the glass of orange juice and started to leaf through the tabloids.

'Thanks, darling.' He started to tell her about Martin Jevons' telephone call, and the murder of Harrington, when his eyes caught the giant headlines that blared from the pages in front of him.

'HUGGINS MUST RESIGN' demanded the *Daily Express*, 'COCK-UP IN CYPRUS' thundered the *Mirror*. 'PM DEMANDS HUGGINS' HEAD' said the *Mail*.

'Hey, what's this number? Am I to ring it?' Jock asked. He held up a piece of paper with Mary's handwriting on it that was lying between the newspapers. There was a long telephone number on it with an 010 prefix.

'Oh, no,' said Mary quickly. She paused. 'It's just a friend of mine.' Then she added, 'You remember the French girl I was talking to on the 'phone the other evening when you came home. Remember? Perdita Huggins introduced me to her a year ago at one of her parties for the wives of diplomats. She told me the other day that she might be coming to Britain soon from Switzerland. I liked her and wanted to find out when she might be here. You were so busy talking on the 'phone just now that I rang her from the call box below as I went to get the papers.'

'When is she coming?' said Jock, his eyes and attention wandering back to the press.

'In a day or two. We've planned to meet and have some lunch together. She's dark and very pretty,' Mary added inconsequentially.

Jock did not pay any attention. He had turned to *The Times* and his attention was wholly absorbed in a piece written by Philip Havilland, *The Times*' political editor. Jock knew that Eddie Ford, the press officer at Number 10, had worked with Havilland for years and that, if he ever tried to place anything serious with one of the heavies, it was to Havilland that he turned first. As he read, he drank deeply from his coffee cup and wrinkles, of exasperation, of excitement, of fear, appeared on his forehead. Mary watched him closely and wondered which emotion was uppermost. She knew him so well and yet, at times of stress like this, she had no idea which way he would turn. He put his coffee cup down on the desk without looking, missed the edge and the cup slipped over, spilling its dregs down his pyjama trousers.

'Blast! I'm soaked to the skin.'

'Are you burned?' asked Mary anxiously.

'Nowhere vital. Just wet.'

'Don't worry, darling. I'll get a cloth and I'll mop you up, and the floor.' Mary quickly put the cup back in its saucer, picked it up together with her handwritten note and walked out of the room.

When she came back with a cloth and starting mopping up the coffee on the floor, Jock looked up from *The Times* and said: 'I'm sorry, darling, to make such a mess. I'll read you a bit of what Philip Havilland has written. It's all on the front page. Listen to this:

Sources close to the Government we all know what that means were saying late last night that the Prime Minister was furious at what he sees as yet another initiative by the Foreign Office that has gone seriously wrong. I understand that, when the plan to intercept the Libyan airliner was discussed at a top-level Downing Street meeting, the Prime Minister was very hesitant about its wisdom but was persuaded by the strong views expressed by the Foreign Secretary.

Now it is the Arabs, the traditional friends of the Foreign Office, who are furious at the astonishing events over the Mediterranean yesterday evening. 'It is as if the British have lost their senses,' one senior Ambassador said to me early this morning. 'We will ask for a UN resolution condemning their action and we will be summoning a meeting of the Arab League to discuss economic sanctions against Britain as soon as possible.'

The Labour Shadow Foreign Secretary has told me that Labour will today demand an emergency debate on the whole issue. If they feel that the Prime Minister is personally involved, they will press for a vote of no confidence in the government. Otherwise, they will demand the resignation of Robert Huggins, the Foreign Secretary. With a general election certain within the next four months, this comes at an extremely embarrassing time for the government.

'That says it all, doesn't it?' remarked Jock, 'except that they didn't know about Harrington being murdered. I should think all of that was dictated to Philip Havilland by Bruce Gordon himself via that obsequious, odious tool of his, Eddie Ford.'

Mary pulled up a chair and sat close to Jock. She raised her face, put an arm round his shoulders and kissed him on the cheek and then she looked at him for a long time.

'Darling,' she finally said. 'Darling. You are going to have to decide, aren't you? Gordon or Huggins? You can't love them both and only one of them is going to win. Whose star are you going to hitch your wagon to, so that you can become a Privy Councillor, Cabinet Minister, one of the greatest in the land?' She smiled, then she went on, emphasizing her words: 'What you don't want to do is to fall between two stars so that your wagon is hitched to no one.'

Jock stared at her: 'You know it's difficult, darling.' He paused. 'I've already shopped Robert to Martin Jevons, said he had been too enthusiastic about the Akrotiri plot, and so on. But . . .' he paused again and then said, 'but Harrington's murder makes a difference. Whose fault is that? Gordon's? Or Robert's? Or even mine?' He suddenly buried his face in his hands. 'God, I don't know, love. I, perhaps I killed Harrington.'

Mary took his face in her hands, and pressed it against her cheek. Then she slid her hand round to his neck and slowly, calmly, stroked the nape of his neck as if she were soothing a baby.

'Darling,' she murmured in his ear. 'They're none of them as good as you. You must go for it. If you don't, you'll get nothing. But, if you try, you're much better than any of them.'

Jock looked up at her and smiled for the first time that day. 'I think you'd quite like me to be in the Cabinet, wouldn't you?' he asked.

'Yes, but not just that. Further, much further. I think you're much more intelligent than many of the people there. Tony Castle and William Ford haven't got a brain in their heads.'

'That's not fair, nor accurate. Tony is a splendid person . . .'

'Oh, stop being so loyal, Jock. It's typical of you and boring.'

At noon in downtown Beirut, Bob Janes and his wife, Sally, and Jerome Smitherman, the London head of the United Nations Rehabilitation Agency, walked up the steps on to the platform in the ballroom of the Carlton Hotel. Bob stumbled as he reached the top step and Sally, immediately behind him, put out a hand and caught his elbow to steer him and hold him upright. They both looked deeply tired with dark hollows round their eyes. The flesh on Bob's face was waxen and transparent so that the bone structure shone through, heightened by the oppressive light from the television cameras.

'He looks like King Lear in the Fourth Act,' muttered one foreign correspondent in the well of the large room.

'Not surprising,' said his neighbour. 'He's just seen his best friend killed in front of his eyes.'

Bob sat in the middle of a row of three chairs, with Sally on his left and Smitherman on his right. Ahead of them was a battery of microphones, looking like a cluster of black boxes growing out of a tree of aluminium rod. Bob looked at the microphones and then at the waiting gaggle of 200 pressmen beyond, and his head began to sway. He put his hand up to his forehead and then let it slip down in front of his eyes. He felt, rather than heard, the click and the flash of cameras and light bulbs all around him. He stayed for some seconds in this posture, and prayed silently for strength, strength to bear witness to what had been done to Les Harrington and to ensure that such a tragedy never happened again. He could feel with every nerve in his body – he could not stop it – the thumps of the bullets going into Les's head and, try as he might, he could not get out of his mind the awful image of Les lying on the ground, the pistol pressed against his skull. He remembered running in

187

desperation, his own lungs wheezing until they nearly burst, and the fear that gripped him as he ran, but none of that compared to the noise of those shots. He wondered whether he would ever get that out of his mind. He felt sick all over again.

'You OK, darling?' whispered Sally, the anxiety spilling out of her voice. 'Can you go on or shall we call the whole thing off?'

Smitherman heard this and leant over and said: 'Give it a go, Bob, if you can. I guess I know what's in your mind. Spit it out, tell the world, get it out of your system. Then take a break, and get away from here with Sal.'

Bob thought that Smitherman must be right. He owed it to Les to tell the world how Les had been killed, and that he would do. So he dropped his hands from his face, gripped the edge of the table and looked straight across the chamber at the reporters sitting in crowded rows of chairs, grasping notebooks and pens and, much nearer, under the edge of the little platform, a bank of photographers pointing their long, fat lenses at him and flashing endlessly, without rhyme or reason.

'All right, Jerome, I'll do it. You introduce me and then I'm ready to go.'

Jerome Smitherman held up his hand and the crowded room responded like an orchestra, with those nearest to the platform falling quiet first, and the brass at the back remaining noisy to the last.

Smitherman told the audience that he was the London head of the United Nations Rehabilitation Agency, that he had employed Bob Janes and Les Harrington in Lebanon for the last two years, where they had been engaged on development and humanitarian work and that he, himself, had come to Beirut five days before in order to give any help he could to the search for the two hostages. He said that Bob Janes would make a short statement about the events of earlier that morning and then answer a few questions, but he was under very great stress and the press must be compassionate and generous to him.

As he sat down, he nodded at Bob Janes and Bob, in a slow quiet voice, made all the more dramatic for its lack of rhetoric and histrionics, explained to an audience that got quieter and quieter the full details of his and Les's captivity and how Al-Fatah, slowly persuaded that they were neither of them British or American spies, had decided to release them early this morning, making it look as if it were an escape.

It was all so clearly etched in his memory, and he described the quietness of the streets as they had driven through Beirut early that morning, his excitement as he guessed that the British Ambassador's residence was only a mile or two away, the violent stopping of his captors' car by the man he only knew as Faisal, Faisal's terrible cry that Al-Fatah had been betrayed by the words spoken in the House of Commons and heard all over the world, the bullets being fired at close range into Les, and his own violent escape and race through the streets and alley-ways to the safety of the Ambassador's residence.

The story took much longer to tell than Bob had intended, the cameras stayed on his face for every second as he told it, and then he came to an end and stopped and stared quietly out from the platform into the void ahead of him. He felt totally alone. Silence filled the room. The 200 reporters there, men and women, had never heard anything quite like it before. They were used to boasts of exaggerated deeds at press conferences, of small successes being disguised as great triumphs, and defeats being brushed off as minor inconveniences but, collectively and individually, they had never heard a man's heart laid so bare before, and his total honesty they found embarrassing. It removed from them their own protective armour of cynicism and habitual disbelief.

Smitherman looked at the audience and said that he would take just a few questions, not many because obviously Bob Janes was very tired and should go back to the anonymous hotel where he was now staying with Sally and get some rest as soon as possible. There was a continuing silence from the audience and then a hand shot up from half-way down the hall and a woman's voice asked:

'Are you saying, Mr Janes, that if the Prime Minister had not mentioned in the House of Commons yesterday, that you and Les Harrington were being held by Al-Fatah, you would both by now be free, as you would have been allowed to escape – both of you?'

Bob paused and, as he spoke again into the microphones, was conscious of another round of sheet lightning in front of him as all the cameras flashed and clicked.

'Yes. I don't know who was responsible for the remarks yesterday in the Commons. I've no idea why they were made, but we had certainly been told that our escape depended on us, Les and me, keeping totally silent about who had held us. And that, of course, was the point behind what the man I knew as Faisal shouted at me and Les before he killed Les. He mentioned this other business about a Libyan plane being held up by the British, but I don't think that was that important to him.'

There was a further pause, then a Scots voice from the front row of the hall said directly to Bob: 'Are you saying, then, Mr Janes, that you blame the Prime Minister for Les Harrington's death? You think that what the Prime Minister said killed Les Harrington?'

Bob tried to see the Scotsman's face but couldn't make it out clearly. Then he heard the sound of the shots ringing in his ears again, and he put his head down on his crossed wrists in front of him on the table and his shoulders started to heave as the tears rolled from his eyes down his cheeks. The cameras closed in on him until the zoom-lenses almost touched his face. Sally looked across the table imploringly at Jerome Smitherman, who got to his feet and brought the press conference to an immediate close, saying that he did not think Bob Janes should be asked to answer any more questions. The men and women in the hall got up and walked quickly towards the exit doors and then, with gathering momentum, started to run to their telephones, faxes and type-writers, to send their story round the world.

190

12

Wednesday 3 July: Afternoon

The time for Jock's interview with Martin Jevons had been continually postponed throughout the morning. Anthea Wheeler was the member of his private office responsible for liaison with the press and, from eleven o'clock onwards, she popped in and out of his office, giving him a running commentary on the state of play with the BBC. Like a railway guard constantly announcing further delays in the arrival of a train, Anthea relayed the hesitations and procrastinations of Martin Jevons to her boss.

'What's happening? You must be firmer with them, Anthea. It's intolerable that they should mess me about like this. Who the hell do they think they are? It's lucky that I haven't got an appointment for lunch, but Martin Jevons was absolutely clear that he would be here well before one. It's intolerable the way they treat ministers.' He looked at Anthea angrily and wished that he had given the press job to Peter Pirelli, his principal private secretary. Anthea went out of the room back to the private office, and Jock thought gloomily that, if Mary thought she was sexy, Mary had never seen her flustered at work. He picked up the full file of that morning's telegrams that had been put on his desk by Peter around eleven o'clock and he started to read them through. All the ones on top were from the British Embassies in the Arab countries and they all showed the great upsurge of Arab anger with Britain. The latest telegram from Ryadh said that the Saudi Ambassador in London had been instructed to call on the Foreign Secretary that afternoon on the personal instruction of Prince Khalid; Muscat reported that the Sultan of Oman was considering cancelling his visit to Goodwood; Kuwait said that the signing of a billion-pound order for the new British tank had been cancelled; Algiers advised that

191

there was a double police cordon round the British Embassy building as the Interior Minister had announced that there was a strong possibility of the building being attacked by a hostile mob. Doubtless organized by the Algerian Government itself, thought Jock bitterly.

He was overwhelmed with a sense of not knowing where to go to next and, grateful that he was neither the Prime Minister nor the Foreign Secretary, he picked up a dun-coloured file labelled: 'Possible Future Areas for Co-operation with Morocco' and tried to engross himself in the pros and cons of a cultural conference in Rabat in November. The Assistant Under Secretary was putting forward a strong argument that the British Council should be persuaded to find more money for this conference as it would have a worthwhile effect on Moroccan–British relations. King Hassan was known to be a difficult character and, as he was due to visit the United Kingdom in two years' time, it would be very helpful if . . . the telephone rang on Jock's desk and Jock picked it up to hear the Foreign Secretary's voice speaking directly to him.

'Jock. I'm calling you on my private line. Is there anyone in your office?'

'No,' said Jock.

'Good. You'll have seen this morning's papers.' Jock grunted assent. 'They're really gunning for me and that, of course, comes from Number 10. I understand from our press office that you're going to give an interview to the BBC any minute now. Well, make certain, won't you, that you put over the points you and I discussed the other day? There's a lot at stake.'

'Of course. I understand that.'

'We've got to rub it in about the Prime Minister letting slip Al-Fatah's name and what a fatal result that terrible slip had. We can't let him get away with blaming it all on us.'

Jock was silent and then he heard Robert Huggins' voice from the other end of the telephone: 'Did you hear me, Jock? You heard what I said?' There was a clear note of irritation in the Foreign Secretary's voice.

'Yes, of course, Foreign Secretary,' said Jock formally. 'I was just thinking.'

'Good. Well, don't hesitate, put it over hot and strong. The Cabinet meeting tomorrow morning is going to be a crucial one. I may well want to talk to you tonight. Will you be at home?'

'Yes. I've got to go out to a dinner, thank God, not with one of the Arab Ambassadors, but we should be back home by eleven. There's no vote in the House tonight.'

'That's right. All the same, I've cancelled my trip to Strasbourg as there's too much going on here. I rely on you.' There was a pause and then Jock said: 'Thank you, Foreign Secretary. I know you do.'

'This could be make or break for your career, Jock,' Huggins spoke slowly and with heavy emphasis.

Anthea came running into the room without knocking and, looking at Jock with the appealing eyes of a labrador, she paused just inside the door.

'Sorry, Foreign Secretary,' said Jock, 'but one of my private secretaries has just come into the room.' Jock put down the telephone and looked at Anthea. A line from a musical wriggled, unasked, across his mind. 'I'm as horny as Kansas in August.' No, that's not right, he thought.

'Anthea, really,' he began. She interrupted him.

'He's here,' she gulped. And then she visibly pulled herself together and said: 'I'm so sorry to come rushing in like that, Minister, but I thought you should know Martin Jevons is here to interview you. They've set up the cameras in the Ambassadors' waiting room but we've just heard from our press office that Bob Janes has given a press conference in Beirut. He said that he and Les Harrington were on the point of being released early this morning, they were going to be allowed to escape apparently, but Al-Fatah who were holding them were so angry at their name being mentioned by the Prime Minister in the House that they shot Harrington and would have shot Bob Janes as well if he hadn't run away, and Bob Janes burst into tears in front of the television cameras and nearly passed out and . . .' Anthea paused for breath.

'How did you hear all this?' asked Jock.

'Our Ambassador in Beirut rang through and has been talking to Alastair Crichton. And the Defence Attaché is still under arrest.'

'He's best out of the way. How soon can we get a transcript of what was said at the press conference?'

'I don't know. I think we'll have to rely on the World Service to get us one.'

'The World Service! Christ! Talk about asking our enemies for favours.' Jock paused. 'Oh well, I'll go along to the waiting room and do the television interview, and radio as well if they still want it. I'll have to tell Martin Jevons that I've heard about the Beirut press conference but I don't know the full details. Come along with me.'

Jock got up from the chair, looked at the papers on his desk but decided that he did not need any of them and walked out of the door. Anthea followed at his heel. Jock paused in the corridor and looked at the head of the first King Feisal of Jordan painted in the mural on his right and said, pointing upwards, to Anthea:

'I wonder what he would have thought of all of these Middle East disasters.'

'As long as he got his own kingdom, I don't think he'd have worried about anything else very much. That, after all, was what he came to London for,' replied Anthea, regaining her composure. But Jock wasn't listening. His mind was switched to the interview ahead. He turned right into the Ambassadors' waiting room and found Martin Jevons waiting there with the usual oversize BBC team of three cameramen, a man and a woman adjusting the sound-boom, two men redirecting the powerful arc lights and another two leaning against the wall with their hands in their jeans' pockets. Two chairs had been placed confronting each other, with a small gap in between, and the large mahogany table, covered with periodicals, was pushed into the further corner of the room. The Foreign Office press officer fussed around, looking like a queen bee whose drones were distinctly out of order.

'I'm sorry the BBC are so late, Minister,' he said, flapping a wrist helplessly. 'I've been nagging at them all morning but they wouldn't pay any attention. I do so hope you're not inconvenienced.'

'Not at all. It doesn't matter a bit.' Politics had taught Jock, whenever possible, to be nice to pressmen, particularly when he expected a difficult interview. 'I'm sure that Martin Jevons has had a great many things on his mind.' He smiled at Martin who smiled back at him with the look that one boxer gives another when they shake hands before a fight begins, a look that sums up, that measures and wonders who will be on top in thirty minutes' time.

'Are you ready?' Martin asked the cameramen.

'Yes. All ready to go.'

'Will you, Minister, sit in that chair over there with your back to the window? I'll sit here and then the camera will get a better shot of you than of me.'

Jock sat down, made himself comfortable in the chair as he had been taught to do and smiled expectantly at Martin. He asked:

'When do you expect to use this?'

'Depending on what other news develops, we'll use bits of it in all our news broadcasts tonight, and we may use some sound-bites for the five o'clock and six o'clock radio news as well. Depends on what you say, Minister.'

'What line are you going to take?' asked Jock, trying to keep any hint of anxiety out of his voice.

Martin Jevons looked at him reflectively. 'Well, first, a few questions on the events of the last twenty-four hours, obviously. That's the big story. And then I'd like your judgement on what went wrong and why. And who was responsible,' he added almost as an afterthought. 'The Prime Minister, or the Foreign Secretary, or you, yourself.'

Jock's stomach turned over. So this is it, he thought. I'm going to have to jump one way or the other. There'll be no turning back.

But he smiled guilelessly, keeping up appearances, and asked how long the interview was likely to last.

'The usual,' said Martin. 'Seven or ten minutes. That sort of thing. We'll see how we go.'

195

The Foreign Office press officer intervened and was reassured that he would be sent a full transcript of the interview. Satisfied about this, he in turn settled down at the corner of the big mahogany table a few feet away and put his tape recorder on the edge of the table so that he could catch every word his Minister said. Fussily, he adjusted the little controls several times before he was satisfied.

The cameramen pointed the camera straight at Jock's face and, as the little green light came on at the top of the camera, Martin started to take him through the events of the last twenty-four hours over the Mediterranean, at Akrotiri and in Beirut. The questioning, thought Jock, was full but quite fair and only once, in the first five minutes, did Jock ask for a question to be repeated so that he could re-run and change his answer. Then Martin made the point that the impression given by Number 10 was that the Prime Minister had always had doubts about the interception of the Libyan plane but it was Foreign Office ministers particularly who were in favour of the plan.

'I've been told, Minister, that it was your voice especially, as you are the Middle East expert, that persuaded the Prime Minister, and the Foreign Secretary as well, that there was no risk in the interception of the Libyan plane and that you did not expect any deaths. You were wrong, weren't you?'

Jock was thrown off balance. 'It wasn't quite like that. I was asked my opinion at a Cabinet committee and I said that I thought interception was justified. We didn't want our hostages to be paraded on the streets of Tripoli by Gadaffi.'

'But you said that you thought the plane could be turned away to Cyprus before there were any deaths,' interrupted Martin. 'You expressly recommended the interception on that basis.'

Who's been sneaking, who the hell did he get that from? thought Jock.

'No. What I said was that I doubted whether the Libyan captain, after threats from the squadron of British Tornados, would go on flying until his plane was shot down into the sea. It didn't seem to me that that degree of blind courage was part of the Libyan make-up.'

196

'So you are quite content that, on the basis of your specific advice to the Prime Minister, two innocent people should have been killed in the Libyan plane, including a twenty-year-old air hostess?'

Jock's face flushed angrily and he leant forward quickly in his chair.

'That's not fair. It was inevitable that there would be some risks.'

'But you were the one who said decisively that those risks should be taken,' Martin pressed home his point and then said: 'Let me move on to Bob Janes' press conference in Beirut an hour ago.'

I'll get my own back, thought Jock. I'm damned if I'll carry the can for anyone.

'The clear impression given by Bob Janes in his press conference, and I think you will have heard this from your own press office, Minister, is that a deal had, in effect, been struck between the hostages and the terrorist organization holding them. They would be allowed to escape provided the name of their captor, Al-Fatah, was not revealed.' Martin Jevons was proceeding quickly and smoothly through the background and towards his crunch point. 'Unfortunately,' and Martin paused significantly, 'the Prime Minister by mistake revealed Al-Fatah's name in the House yesterday at Question Time and in consequence, Les Harrington was shot and Bob Janes had to run for his life. Is that correct?'

This is it, thought Jock, and he gulped perceptibly. No turning back.

'Yes. That, I'm afraid, sums it up. Of course, we don't know the precise detail of what was discussed between Janes and Harrington and Al-Fatah in Beirut . . .'

He was interrupted quickly by Martin: 'The point, though, Minister, is that sources closest to Number 10 are saying that they were never told of the embargo on mentioning Al-Fatah's name. It is being implied, in fact, that this information was deliberately suppressed by the Foreign Office, perhaps by you yourself.'

'But that's ridiculous. Why should I do that?' Jock said deliberately.

'I don't know, but why don't you tell me?' Martin said calmly.

'I'm told that it revolves round an important message from Beirut last weekend that Number 10 never saw. Did you hide it?' A tone of insolence crept into Martin's voice.

'This is nonsense,' interjected Jock, anger rising to the top of his voice. 'If there was a message that Number 10 didn't see, and . . .' he paused, 'I don't know that there was, then I'm afraid someone at Number 10 slipped up and forgot to show the message to the Prime Minister.'

Immediately Jock said that, he half-regretted it. The unwritten code for any minister was not to lay blame at the door of the Prime Minister or his office. But there was nothing he could do to withdraw the remark. The Rubicon was now crossed. If he asked Martin to re-run the question so that he could revise his answer, Martin would only be that much more aware of its significance.

'So you are saying, Minister, that, as far as the tragic death of Harrington is concerned, there is no blame on the Foreign Office for that at all. If there is a culprit, and of course I stress the word "if", then that has to be in Number 10. In fact, the Prime Minister himself.'

'Yes, it does come down to that.' The reluctance, the slowness, in Jock's voice was clear, and the press officer took his cue. He got up quickly from the side of the table and, with the pained expression of a referee walking reluctantly between two heavy-weight boxers many times larger than himself, said that he thought the interview had gone on long enough. Fifteen minutes had passed and he was quite sure that Martin Jevons had got all the material he wanted and he knew, he added subserviently, that the Minister had an extremely busy afternoon ahead of him with a great many meetings planned. Martin gloated inwardly and pressed no further. He had got just the statement from Jock that he had been hoping for and, if he hurried back to Broadcasting House with his tapes, his editor might get some of it on to the radio news at 3 pm while the spicy extracts for television were being prepared.

'I quite understand, Minister. You must be very busy and I am very grateful to you for giving me so much of your time.' He turned and told the waiting technicians to get the equipment dismantled as fast as they could so that they need not trouble the Minister any more. 'We don't need a two-shot,' he said. 'And I want to get this to the newsroom as soon as possible.'

Jock thanked Martin Jevons formally, thinking as he did so what a fool he had been to imagine a drink in a smart club might sway the judgement of a journalist, out for the kill. A memory of that drink must have crossed Martin's mind for, as Jock turned to leave the room, Martin said to him:

'You must come to Groucho's one of these days and let me repay your hospitality there.'

'I'd love to,' muttered Jock. Bugger you, he thought to himself as he walked out of the room. I'll see you in hell first. You really have screwed me up.

'I thought that went quite well, Minister. It was difficult but you managed to hold off Martin Jevons successfully,' said Anthea as they walked back down the corridor. She had been taught always to make comforting remarks to ministers after tricky interviews with the press.

'Did you really think that, Anthea?' said Jock. 'If so, I begin to doubt your judgement. I think it will prove disastrous.' They turned together into his private office and Peter Pirelli got to his feet as they walked in and said:

'How did that go, Minister?'

'Not at all well,' said Jock, 'although Anthea kindly thinks otherwise.' Peter Pirelli smiled the smile of someone whose prime concern is to see that the waters run smoothly and said that he was sure the Minister was needlessly worried, and then he added that the Leader of the House would make an announcement at 3.30. The Prime Minister had just agreed to the Opposition's request for an emergency debate tomorrow afternoon on the interception of the Libyan airliner and on the killing of Les Harrington.

'Who will open the debate?' asked Jock.

'I don't know yet, Minister. I don't know whether it will be the Prime Minister or the Foreign Secretary.'

'I'd better go over to the House to listen. Tell Joe to be in the quadrangle at three-twenty.'

'I'd thought you'd want to. I've already told him that and I've put some sandwiches and a glass of orange juice on your desk.'

'Thank you, Peter. You think of everything.'

He walked into his office and sat gloomily at his desk, thinking that the fat was now really in the fire. He tried to ring Mary to tell her his troubles and to discuss how the Prime Minister would react to Jock putting the blame firmly at his door, but the line was constantly busy and, after a few minutes, he gave up trying. He started to eat his sandwiches and looked out over Horse Guards Parade, wondering how much longer he would be in that office enjoying his unique view. Not long, he decided and a great wave of doubt about his future swept over him. He tried to ring Mary again, but the number was still engaged.

At 3.30 prompt, Question Time ended and the Right Honourable Anthony Onslow, MP, Leader of the House of Commons, rose to his feet and stood in front of the Despatch Box. He announced that the Leader of the Opposition had written to the Prime Minister that morning, requesting an emergency debate the following afternoon on the interception of a Libyan air freighter south of Cyprus the previous afternoon and the tragic murder of a British hostage, Mr Les Harrington, in Beirut early that morning. He extended the heartfelt sympathy of the whole House to the widow and the children of Mr Harrington.

'There have been full discussions through the usual channels,' Onslow continued, 'and it has been agreed that the business already announced for Thursday afternoon will be held over. There will be a debate instead, asking the House to approve the action authorized by the Government and undertaken by a squadron of RAF planes, requiring a Libyan air freighter to proceed with them to the Akrotiri Base in Cyprus. This debate will give a full opportunity for the tragic circumstances surrounding the death of Mr Harrington to be fully discussed. The Motion will be tabled by five o'clock and will, of course, be in tomorrow's order paper.'

When he sat down, he had been listened to in almost total silence. There had been a few 'hear hear's when he had announced the emergency debate and a suspended whisper of excitement when he had said that the Motion would call on the House to approve the Government's action. If Onslow had simply said that the Motion would ask the House to take note of the Government's action, it would have been possible for the wording to be regarded as sufficiently neutral for there to be no vote. But the Opposition, thought Jock, will have insisted on a form of words that would be bound to lead to a vote. Labour could not possibly approve of the Government's action. Indeed, they would regard the debate as ending in a vote of no confidence in the Government, and they would do their damnedest to bring the Government down. They will be supported by the Liberals, all the Nationalist Parties and the Irishmen, Jock calculated, but how many of our lot will go into the division lobby with them? I bet it will be tight, he thought.

As one of the ministers involved in the issues, Jock was sitting close to the Leader of the House and he marked in his mental notebook how composed Onslow was at the Despatch Box as he announced a debate and a vote that could lead to the fall of the Government, but the heel of Onslow's shoe was twitching, up and down, against the floor all the time that he spoke.

On momentous, historic occasions, when the collective voice of the House mattered, Jock knew there was little of the ordinary barracking that was such a feature of humdrum days. This afternoon was typical. Royal Air Force planes had apparently been involved in an act of piracy on the high seas against an unarmed Libyan plane, two Libyans had been killed, and, due to a slip by the Prime Minister or an error between the Foreign Office and the Prime Minister's office, a British hostage had been shot while on the point of being allowed to go free.

The collective conscience of a crowded House realized that, for once, they were concerned with matters above the range of normal insults and gibes, that ministerial careers were at stake and so, too, were the parliamentary lives of many backbenchers. Labour were now four points ahead in the latest poll and, if that represented the final result in an election, it meant some fifty Tory MPs losing their seats. Most of those fifty were present in the House this afternoon. Another seventy MPs from all parties had said they would retire at the next election, and most of those were in the House, too. Between all of these, there was an unspoken, common bond of worry about their personal future, of a wish to put off from July that which could be delayed until November, of potential nostalgia for this extraordinary, powerful, argumentative, frustrating chamber in which they now sat.

All of them had been angered at some time or other, by the futility of sitting until late in the night, debating trivialities of no great importance, or the frustration of preparing a wise and witty speech and then never being called to make it. Yet, now, at the thought of leaving this Chamber, those frustrations were forgotten and memories of occasional past triumphs, of a maiden speech listened to with tears by the family in the gallery, of witty remarks delivered off the cuff that had caused the whole House to break into laughter, these flooded in and triumphed over the wish to score petty points.

So the Leader of the House was listened to in grave silence and so was the shadow Foreign Secretary, Paul Robinson, when he spoke briefly, thanking the Leader for agreeing to the emergency debate the following day, but promising to criticize, in the course of that debate, the Government with every weapon, every heavy gun, every shaft and arrow that the Opposition could muster.

'The behaviour of the Government has been disgraceful,' Robinson ended in a crescendo. 'They have authorized an attack on an unarmed plane belonging to a foreign government. They have lost the friendship of many powerful Arab states and their incompetence has led directly to the killing of a British citizen in Beirut. Such folly, such stupidity, such incompetence, such deceit can have only one result, the resignation of the Prime Minister and of the Foreign Secretary and the immediate calling of a general election. That is what we, the Opposition, will be voting for in the debate tomorrow. That is why we will vote against the Motion.'

It was a good finale and back-bench members of Robinson's party were moved enough to wave a few order papers above their heads and to give a modest cheer as he sat down. Desultory questioning followed and Anthony Onslow was asked whether either the Prime Minister or the Foreign Secretary would open the debate for the Government.

'That,' he replied, 'is not yet decided.'

Surprising, thought the experts in the press gallery, and they tried to read hidden meaning into this and sent their stringers running out with quick messages to political editors sitting in fortress headquarters in tower blocks. Did this mean that the Foreign Secretary was going to be sacked, or that the Prime Minister was resigning, or did it mean just what the Leader of the House had said, that the decision had not yet been taken? As the questions went on, Jock felt there was a growing sense of excitement. Whatever personal disasters lay ahead, MPs, like warhorses smelling gunpowder and hearing cannon-fire ahead, were preparing themselves with eagerness for battle. Jock shared in this sense of excitement until, as he was walking out of the Chamber, the Whip on the Front Bench looked up at him, beckoned to him to sit down by him, and whispered how badly he thought Jock had done in his interview with Martin Jevons:

'I heard bits of you on the radio at three o'clock. I thought Jevons had you really stitched up and you certainly didn't give the Prime Minister any help. In fact, I reckon you dropped him in the shit.'

Jock looked angrily at the Whip and thought it was intolerable for someone years his parliamentary junior to speak to him like that.

'You are showing the characteristic blindness of the Whips' office,' he muttered bitterly, 'all brawn and no brain. You haven't an idea of the difficulties involved.'

'And you haven't an idea of loyalty,' replied the Whip. Jock got up and walked out of the Chamber.

Well, that's the way it's going to be, he thought. The damage is done.

In Speaker's Court, he sent Joe away in the car and told him that he would not want him until around eight that evening and then he walked into Old Palace Yard and meandered between the double row of lime trees until he reached the gate on to Parliament Square. Acknowledging the policeman's salute, he walked through the gate, turned to the right and saw the headline in big letters on the top page of the news-seller's *Evening Standards*:

'SLIP BY PM KILLS HOSTAGE,' blared the *Standard*. Christ, thought Jock, that's my work. He bought a copy and read it as he walked. He felt no immediate urge to go back to his office, even if that were filled with the loyal and supportive noises of his private secretaries. So he strolled through King Charles Street, between the comfortable buildings of the Treasury and the Foreign Office, down the Clive steps and into St James's Park. Since his early days at the Foreign Office, he had always thought that the park, with its strangely shaped pool and its ducks and tourists and bandstand, was at the heart of Whitehall. He had often wandered round the lake before parliamentary Question Time, preparing his answers in his mind and trying to calm himself down. Now he wandered round it again, past the metal bridge and right up to the Buckingham Palace end, thinking that if Bruce Gordon won the general election and stayed Prime Minister, he was hardly likely to have a ministerial job any longer. And, if Bruce Gordon lost the election, he wouldn't have a job in the government anyway. A different story, though, if Huggins won the election. He didn't think Robert would let him down. It seemed to him that, one way or another, he was certain to leave the Foreign Office, just as he was beginning fully to understand and enjoy his job there.

That's typical, Jock thought. It always happens. How will Mary take it if I get sacked? She's been so keen, so determined on my climbing up the greasy pole. She'll probably want me to leave the House and try and get back into business, and I'll need to earn lots more money to pay the school fees. I've really buggered things up.

He came back to the Horse Guards Road end of the lake and, pushing nostalgia and worry behind him, walked across the road and towards the Foreign Office. If I'm going to go, I may as well enjoy my last few weeks there, he consoled himself. I might even make a pass at Anthea. He thought of the way her bottom swayed from side to side under a tight skirt, as she walked out of his office. Not a bad idea, he said to himself.

13

Wednesday 3 July: Evening

Squadron Leader Snowling had been brought up in a prudent household where his mother's regular motto was: 'Do as you would be done by.' He was a just man and he had tried to follow that motto all his life. He knew that he was a good Air Force Officer and, as he rose in that profession, he always congratulated his junior officers when they did well and, in turn, expected his seniors to give him credit when it was due. By those simple, straight standards, he had had a rotten day.

He had slept well, sorry to hear from Colonel Spacemead early in the morning that there had been no hostages on board the Libyan plane, but delighted for Spacemead that the SAS attack on the plane had not led to any more deaths. When he got up, a bit late by his standards, and walked across the base to the Officers' Mess for breakfast, he had half-hoped to find a message from his Air Vice-Marshal in Britain, congratulating him on a job well done the evening before. After all, he had been told to get the Ilyushin back to Akrotiri at all costs, but with minimum fatalities, and this was precisely what he had achieved. Two dead, Snowling knew well, was nothing to what might have been. He had gone to sleep, thanking God that the fuel tanks on the Ilyushin had not gone up in flames or that decompression in the plane had not killed everyone on board.

As he ordered his usual breakfast from the mess attendant, he had been irritated, first to find that there was no bacon, and then by the message that the waiter brought him. It was in a sealed envelope marked PERSONAL. When he opened the envelope, he found a long telex from London, telling him to reply immediately to a brigadier he had never heard of at the Ministry of Defence, giving many more details of what had happened in the interception, minute by minute after his little squadron left the Akrotiri Air Base at 5.15 the previous evening. He was told that the report he had filed the previous night was inadequate and he was particularly incensed by a paragraph in the telex that read:

CHIEFS OF STAFF DO NOT UNDERSTAND WHY IT WAS NECESSARY FOR YOU TO FIRE AT THE LIBYAN AIRLINER WHEN, BY CLOSE AND THREATENING FLYING WITH YOUR SQUADRON, YOU SHOULD HAVE BEEN ABLE EVENTUALLY TO REQUIRE THE LIBYAN TO CHANGE COURSE. VERY CLEAR EXPLANATION IS NEEDED FROM YOU. THIS MATTER HAS THE PERSONAL ATTENTION OF THE PRIME MINISTER.

Bloody hell, thought Snowling. I'm being used as a scapegoat. They're worried at the reaction from the Libyans now that no hostages were found in the plane and they're trying to shift some blame on to me. I won't stand for it.

He ate his breakfast in a hurry, went back to the office that he shared with Colonel Spacemead and sent off a long telex to London, copied to the Coningsby Station, explaining how, with fuel running out and the Libyan showing no sign whatsoever of changing course, he had had no option but to follow the orders, the written orders, he added, that he had and to try persuasion by the use of his cannon. He emphasized how carefully he had fired in order to avoid hitting the fuel tanks. 'I am glad,' he added immodestly, thinking that, if no one else was going to say it, he might as well say it himself, 'that I was successful in this.'

But all to no purpose. Telex followed telex, pressing him for more detail – precisely how many seconds had he fired for? Why did he not aim further back at the tailplane? Until Snowling felt that he was unable to convince anyone in London that he and his squadron had done precisely what they had been required to do and had done it expertly well.

Then his Commanding Officer rang him and said that, instead of taking the forty-eight hours' leave in Cyprus which they had been promised, he felt that Snowling and all the squadron had

207

better fly back to the Coningsby Station tomorrow, 'as there are a lot of questions that people want to ask you.'

'Very good, sir,' said Snowling as he put the telephone down, but he swore violently to himself, walked back to the office where Spacemead was finishing writing his report on the SAS exercise and suggested that, as he was not flying until the following morning, Spacemead and he should have a large drink together in the Officers' Mess.

They walked over the tarmac, talking casually. Spacemead said that he had sent off his men for the day to enjoy the beaches, and a number of them had been taken out to sea by friends in the Special Boats Service whom the Navy regarded as their natural answer to the SAS. They entered the long hut, with creepers growing up its planked walls and curling round the metal windows, and Space-mead turned in the door and sniffed the air appreciatively and said that he would not mind spending some time in Cyprus.

'Well, my chaps have no chance of that,' Snowling replied. 'We've all got to go back to flat old Lincolnshire tomorrow.' Over their drinks, Snowling elaborated his view that the generals or the politicians in London were looking for someone to blame for what happened last night, and, as he sank his second pink gin, he waxed lyrical about the follies of the Chiefs of Staff and the incompetence of the politicians.

'They're all the same,' he remarked. 'When something goes right, they want all the credit, and the politicians want to be seen in the papers pinning a medal on you, but when it goes wrong, they just don't want to know, do they, and they search everywhere for someone else to blame so that a minister can get up in the House of Commons and say,' Snowling put on his most pompous voice and tried to imitate the Minister for the Armed Forces whom he had met once at Greenwich and to whom he had taken an instant dislike,

' "I can assure my Right Honourable friends that it is none of my fault. The fact that two members of the Libyan air crew were killed can be laid entirely at the door of one Squadron Leader Snowling, DFC, and he will be appropriately reprimanded."

' "Hear, hear, hear," said the honourable Spoffinbottom who had never been in a fighter plane in his life.' Snowling looked gloomily at his glass.

'Come off it,' said Spacemead, laughing. 'It's not that bad. Your Air Vice-Marshal in London knows very well that you had no choice but to fire at the Libyan freighter. You only had a few more minutes to go before you had to turn back to Akrotiri, the wind was against you and was getting up, and your instructions were perfectly clear: get the aeroplane. If necessary, shoot it down.'

'Yes, but it's bloody annoying, isn't it? I did a good job and so did everyone, pilots and navigators, in the squadron. We did it professionally, and well, and with minimum loss of life.' Snowling started to turn red in the face with anger, as the sense of injustice grew and grew. 'But all we do, fuck it, is get blamed because the hostages aren't in the plane. Well, we don't have X-ray equipment on board our Tornados. We couldn't photograph the inside of the whole damned Libyan plane and see whether the hostages were there or not, stuck in the boot of that great big car, or tied up under a blanket on the back seat, or hidden in the toilet.

'I expect I shall end up flying transports to the Falkland Islands, Hercules and that sort of rubbish. All so that the Secretary of State for Defence, pompous prick, can assure the Libyan Ambassador that the officer involved has been removed to other, less demanding duties. Perhaps they'll try and sack me from the Service.' Snowling looked despairingly at the glass in front of him, picked it up, drained it and searched for a mess waiter to refill it.

'You know, I've never got anything but support from my general when something goes wrong in an SAS exercise,' said Spacemead.

'Lucky sod,' muttered Snowling.

'And, of course, things do go wrong regularly the way we operate. We work on surprise and instant reaction. We never have time, during an operation, to think and calculate. If we did, we'd all be dead.

'Take our attack on the air freighter early this morning. If some of the Libyan crew had had guns and had used them, it's certain that one or two of my men would have been killed as we entered the plane. And every one of their crew could then have been killed by our fire, so you'd have had at least twelve corpses, that's for certain, including the captain. We fire to kill because we can't afford the possibility of another bullet being fired at us from a wounded enemy. Fortunately, my bosses in Whitehall know this.' The waiter hovered over them and Spacemead ordered another drink for Snowling and himself.

'You've heard about Bob Janes's press conference this morning in Beirut?' He looked enquiringly at Snowling who nodded his head. 'Clearly, something went very wrong in London in inter-preting the information they intercepted from Beirut, but what about this now? No hostages aboard the plane but they have found . . .' Spacemead spoke slowly, emphasizing his words, 'bloodstains in the boot of the Mercedes.'

'What the hell?' said Snowling. 'What does that mean?'

Spacemead enjoyed the impression he had just made. 'That's woken you up. I heard just before you came into my office and bullied me into coming and having a drink with you.

'The Libyans sent a message saying that they would send another freighter here tomorrow to pick up the Mercedes and also the bodies of the two crew. It'll take a long time to make yesterday's Ilyushin airworthy again. I don't know whether Proudian himself will fly out tomorrow but, as they knew they were about to lose the car, the local boffins spent the whole afternoon going over the Mercedes inch by inch. You know, testing it for fingerprints in case these compared with those of known terrorists, and anything else that could be useful for us and for Interpol. Right at the end, they found bloodstains, at the very back of the boot. Right at the back. Of course, they could be old. It's very hard to tell, but London's sending out two pathology technicians immediately to test them.' Spacemead sounded thoroughly excited.

'Fat lot of good that will do,' muttered Snowling, subsiding back into his anger. 'All that will happen is that two white-coated boffins will have a holiday trip to Cyprus.'

'Probably, but they've got to have a final crawl over the car before it goes back to Gadaffi's headquarters. Then, they'll certainly never see it again.'

Greg Stevens, the Government Chief Whip, sat in his little drab room off the corridor that runs from the Members' lobby to the central lobby. This is the centre of the spider's web that forms the Palace of Westminster. Hither come messages from the Commons and Lords all afternoon and evening when the House is sitting, describing progress in Committee rooms, rows in the Chamber, problems with the Opposition, difficulties in persuading the Speaker to move from one piece of business to the next. And hither, too, comes a regular trail of Members of Parliament, seeking to enlist the Chief Whip's support or to listen to his rebukes.

Greg had just finished reading and pencilling comments on a list of members' names, that his deputy had brought in to him a few minutes before, when Dominic Anderson, the Prime Minister's parliamentary private secretary, and Anthony Onslow walked in from the passage.

'Dom tells me you've asked him to come and have a word and I thought I'd join him,' said Onslow. 'Is that all right? The House is on the adjournment debate and there's practically no one in the Chamber.'

'Of course,' said Greg. He poured them each a glass of whisky, to which he added a modest amount of water, and beckoned to them both to sit down in the sofa on one side of the room. He sat in a deep chair facing them, with a glass in his hand. The three of them knew each other extremely well and had been through many Party and parliamentary battles together over the last ten years. Normally, there would be no secrets between them, but Greg knew better than anyone that these were hardly normal times. Loyalties were about to be tested, friendships broken, new alliances formed that might survive the next election or that might not last overnight.

211

'Did you see *News at Ten?*' asked Onslow. 'I caught the end of it and I thought it was dreadful. ITN should lose their licence. We should remove it from them. They showed photographs of Bruce Gordon and Robert Huggins with selected extracts from their past speeches underneath the photos. The impression given, the impression that they were determined to give the viewer, blast them, was that they had been at each other's throats all their political lives and what had happened over the last twenty-four hours was just a consequence of their pathological dislike for each other. They didn't quite say that what's-his-name, Harry something, Harrington would still be alive if Bruce and Robert had got on with each other, but they damn well implied it.' Onslow picked up his glass, and scowled at the contents.

'The BBC *Nine O'clock News* was just as bad,' said Dominic Anderson. 'I saw it with, of all people, the Prime Minister himself. We were having a drink in his flat, and there was Jock Meldrum-Ross putting the knife right between the PM's ribs and saying that Harrington only got killed because the PM had lost some shitty Foreign Office telegram or other. I've never heard such balls in my life.' He took a large drink of whisky and added: 'Talk of disloyalty. The Prime Minister was furious. I've never seen him so angry.' He paused and added meaningfully, 'He said he would try and see Jock later tonight.'

'That's not very wise of him. I hope he doesn't. Much better sleep on it,' said Greg Stevens quickly. Then he paused and added, 'Look, I don't want to keep you up because tomorrow's going to be a hideously busy day. I just wanted to mention to you, Dominic, and you can mention it to the Prime Minister in the morning unless I see him first, that I'm really worried about the vote tomorrow night. I've asked the Whips to do a quick trawl and there are forty or fifty of our lot who, at the moment, are saying that they won't support the Government. They're making all sorts of different excuses.' He waved the list in the direction of Anderson and Onslow.

'Can I see those lists?' said Dominic quickly.

Greg smiled: 'No, dear boy, you know very well you can't. Of course, at the moment I've very little idea who from our side will definitely vote against and who will just abstain. The one thing that's certain is that it's going to be extremely close. I've talked to all the different Irishmen, all seventeen, and they're against us; everyone is furious about the hijacking of the Libyan plane, about the hostages not being on board but, most of all, about Harrington's murder. Getting the plane wrong was one thing, and perhaps excusable, but Harrington's death certainly isn't.'

There was an unhappy pause. All three men looked silently at one another and then drank thoughtfully. Greg Stevens got up and walked round and topped up the glasses of each of the two facing him. He left his own glass where it was and sat down and said: 'What do you think, Anthony? Your statement went all right this afternoon, but the House was in a very subdued mood. Tomorrow will be different.'

Anthony Onslow paused and wondered how much he should tell the Chief Whip. He had only been in his job for a month. He loved being at the heart of the daily procedure in the House of Commons and he wanted to postpone an election as long as possible. He had talked to a number of cabinet ministers during the evening and had tried, over a private dinner in his house, to persuade four of them to stay firmly committed to the Prime Minister. But he was far from certain about the position of the rest of the Cabinet and he did not know where, at the end of the day, the Chief Whip's own loyalties lay. To the Prime Minister or, in the final analysis, to the Tory Parliamentary Party? He decided to dissemble.

'I've talked to some of the Cabinet this evening. There'll obviously be a thorough discussion in Cabinet tomorrow morning but I think it'll be all right.'

'Thorough's not the word for it,' said Anderson. 'There'll be a bloody row.'

'Yes. All right,' continued Onslow. 'There's going to be a row, well there is already, isn't there, between Bruce and Robert and I imagine that, after the election, Robert will have to go. But I don't think there'll be too much other trouble. Tony Castle will

213

probably support Huggins in Cabinet, he usually does, and perhaps a handful of others. I've no idea about the peers, they're a law unto themselves, as always. God knows what the Lord Chancellor or the Leader of the Lords is thinking, but the others – really senior members – Piers Potter and Macintosh, they're obviously all right. We have to paper everything over calmly tomorrow, explain why we acted as we did with the squadron of Tornados and then get on with the business of government until the election. Harrington's death is damned unfortunate, but we all know that Beirut is an impossible place. Totally impossible.'

Greg looked across over the top of his glass at Anthony Onslow and guessed that he was only telling half of what he knew. After all, he thought, that is what most senior politicians do most of the time and, when life gets really tough, the half tends to turn into a quarter or even less.

'I wish it were quite as easy as that, Anthony,' he said. 'I hope it will be and, of course, I'll get the Whips' office tomorrow to lean on as many of our wild men as possible. But my first duty must, as always, be to keep the Party together.' He paused, 'The press conference the other hostage gave in Beirut this morning, what's his name, Bob Janes, that, I think, did a lot of damage. It made the PM seem incompetent. And then there are these strange rumours going around about Bruce, that he's not very well and that, since his wife died, he's gone a bit gay, asking young men to stay for the weekend and that sort of thing.' He looked enquiringly at Dominic who returned his gaze coldly.

'Oh, for Christ's sake, Greg, you haven't been listening to any of that rubbish, have you? You shouldn't listen to such ridiculous tales.'

'The Chief Whip, Dominic, has to listen to everything. You know that as well as I do. That's part of his job. We are, as Enoch Powell gracefully put it, the sewers of parliament. Through us the muck flows. And the fact is,' Greg looked across the room and half smiled: 'though adultery may be acceptable to the Tory Party, buggery certainly isn't.'

Anderson looked furious and rose to his feet. Greg put his glass down on the floor, got out of his chair and said: 'Don't worry, Dominic. And tell the PM not to lose any sleep. I'm sure we've been through worse crises although I don't remember when. Good night.'

The policeman gave no sign of being surprised when Jock Meldrum-Ross rang the doorbell of Number 10 at 11.30 that evening.

'The Prime Minister is expecting you, sir. He's upstairs in the flat. You know your way.' Jock said that he did and he was pointed towards the lift. He went up to the top floor and found, unusually, the Prime Minister waiting for him as he came out of the lift doors.

The Prime Minister did not smile or greet him but beckoned him to follow and led him down the passage to the drawing room. He sat down in his usual chair and told Jock to sit opposite him. In a cold and clear voice, the Prime Minister said that he was deeply disappointed in Jock. He had had high hopes for him and had planned, after the election, to promote him to the Cabinet but he felt that Jock today had let him down very badly and had committed the ultimate sin, that of disloyalty.

The Prime Minister paused and, without offering Jock a drink, walked over to the tray sitting on the bookshelf, poured himself a large measure of neat whisky and drank this in one gulp. He then walked back and sat down again and his watery, blue eyes fastened on Jock.

'I listened to what you said to that bloody little BBC reporter, Martin Jevons, and you went out of your way to put the blame for the hostage's death on me. You did not try to explain the disappearance of that damned telegram as a mishap for which you are, or someone else at the Foreign Office is, in fact, responsible. Instead, you clearly went out of your way to put the blame on me, the head of the Government, the person who appointed you to your present job.' Gordon paused, looked at Jock, and then said slowly and deliberately, 'I can't stand that and I don't want you to remain in my Government. I shall wait until after the debate is concluded

215

tomorrow evening and then I shall expect you to hand in your resignation to me. If you don't, I will dismiss you. I cannot say how disappointed I am in you for I had begun to expect a great deal of you. That's all.'

Jock searched for some words with which to reply but could not find any. He was not certain that a reply was appropriate, so he gulped and said: 'I don't think that's fair, Prime Minister, but obviously it's your decision.' He paused and the room was full of silence.

'Goodnight,' he added. He got to his feet and, as the Prime Minister still said nothing, turned and walked out of the room. He took the lift down to the ground floor and walked out, down the long corridor, past the pictures and past the sculpture that he knew so well, pausing, and looking at them, and thinking that, probably, it would be the last time that he ever saw them. He said goodnight to the policeman at the door and sent Joe away with the ministerial car, saying that it was a lovely night and he would walk back across the park to the flat. As he walked over the grass towards the big plane trees, moving in the direction of Birdcage Walk, he found his heart still thumping and, his bravery of earlier in the evening gone, he wondered what folly had caused him to put the copy of that ill-fated message from Beirut into his pocket and, then, to let it disappear. Unplanned, unpremeditated, it all was, he thought, as if some destructive devil had suddenly put ideas into his head. But it was too late to moan. He wondered, too, what explanation he should give to his constituency chairman when he rang him tomorrow night. God, that would be awkward, he thought.

Suddenly, ahead of him, walking toward Wellington Barracks, but at a slower pace than his, he noticed two women, one medium height with a mass of gently curled blonde hair flowing over the nape of her neck, the other fully six inches shorter, with dark hair cut short. They were walking slowly, arms linked together, and heads down in deep conversation. How extraordinary, that looks like Mary, Jock thought. What on earth is she doing in the park?

He broke into a run over the grass. There was a new moon and he could not see the women clearly until he was within thirty yards of them and then he shouted:

'Mary, Mary. Hi! It's me!' Mary turned towards him, breaking away from the girl, and Jock could see that she looked astonished at seeing him. He got the impression that she turned hurriedly towards the other girl and was still speaking authoritatively, even commanding her, as Jock ran up beside them both.

'Darling,' he put an arm round her and kissed her. 'What on earth are you doing here at this time of night?' and he looked enquiringly at the girl by her side.

Mary had regained her composure and kissed him warmly, full on the lips.

'Darling, this is Monique Renault. I told you about her, do you remember, the other evening?' Jock shook his head. 'Ah, yes, my dear. You've forgotten. Perdita Huggins introduced us last year. Monique is now living in Switzerland but she's come to London for a few days and we've had dinner together. It's such a lovely night that we thought we'd walk in the park before finding a taxi to take Monique home.'

Jock introduced himself to Monique who smiled at him. She had, he noticed, remarkable eyes, almond-shaped, he instantly thought, and a very strong chin.

'*Bonsoir, monsieur, Marie m'a beaucoup parlé de vous.*' Jock looked at Mary.

'I think,' Mary said, 'a year in Switzerland has made Monique forget most of her English,' so they talked in French gently, idly, and to no special purpose as they walked under the old plane trees. In Buckingham Palace Road, they hailed a taxi for Monique who assured Mary:

'*Je vous téléphonerai demain avant de partir pour Zurich. Mille fois merci pour une soirée très agréable et des renseignements très interessants.*' She got into the taxi and settled back into the seat without looking further at them.

'She looks like an Arab,' remarked Jock as absent-mindedly they walked back towards Victoria Street and then to their flat.

'Well, perhaps half Arab,' said Mary defensively. 'I think her

217

father may be Lebanese. She's great fun,' added Mary inconse-quentially.'

'She's pretty in a Middle East sort of way, but she certainly didn't learn much English while she was here,' Jock commented.

'They weren't here long, and then, sadly, her husband left her for another girl – a secretary in the French Embassy, I think.'

They turned into their block of flats.

'You look tired,' said Mary. 'I bet you've had a very busy day. Do tell me about it.'

'It's hell,' said Jock, as they got into the lift. 'I'll tell you upstairs.'

Once in their flat, Jock went quickly to the cupboard and got each of them a large drink, whisky and orange for Mary, neat whisky for himself. Mary was already sitting on the sofa, reading the evening paper. Jock handed her her drink and sat down close to her. She smiled at him and put her arm through his.

'Have you had an awful time, my darling? You look worn-out. Lots of my friends have rung me up this evening and told me that that BBC reporter, Jevons, was very difficult and became quite nasty to you, but you handled him brilliantly.' She gave his hand a comforting squeeze, and then asked with a note of caution creeping into her voice, 'Have there been any repercussions?'

'Yes, I'm afraid there have. I've got some rotten news.' He told her all about the short interview that he had just had and his peremptory dismissal by the Prime Minister.

'The bastard!' said Mary. Her stomach turned at the prospect of the uncertainties ahead and she thought for a moment. 'But I'm sure it'll come all right. The newspapers are baying for his blood and he will lose the vote in the House tomorrow. So then there's bound to be an election. He won't sack you then. It'd sound just like bad temper. Tell me more.' Mary got him another drink and led him through every detail of the day, as was her custom. Jock told her of the Whip's rude comments and his reply. 'It was silly of me,' he said, 'but I was so cross.

'You know,' he added, 'everything seems to go back to that

telegram I pocketed at Chevening and then lost.' Mary looked at him and shook her head.

'Darling, you simply mustn't blame yourself. You had to come down against the Prime Minister after what he leaked to the media about your involvement. I thought what was said at Cabinet committees was secret?'

'It should be,' said Jock gloomily. 'It certainly used to be.'

'Well, there you are. Gordon behaved dishonourably. The man's on the way out now and deserves to be, and you've made your decision, Jock. You've cast the die.'

Then Mary put her arms round Jock's neck, kissed him and insisted that it was time for bed. It was a hot and sticky night, with summer lightning turning darkness into day. Once they were in bed, they threw off the sheet and Mary, naked, started to undo the buttons on Jock's pyjamas.

'Let's drive politics away,' Mary whispered, licking the lobe of his ear.

'It's too darned hot,' muttered Jock.

'No it isn't,' said Mary, and they made love in a desultory, mechanical way that gave neither of them great satisfaction.

Afterwards, Mary rolled over on her side and fell asleep before Jock. She started to toss and turn and Jock heard her muttering and arguing in her dream. She seemed to be mentioning figures and, at one stage, he thought she was arguing about some money. She must be worrying about the cost of our holiday, thought Jock. They were still planning to take their children on a long summer swing through the Dordogne and the Lot-et-Garonne. He smiled to himself. Dear person. She shouldn't have to worry about such things, and he gave her shoulder a very gentle shake and she rolled over on to her right side and then fell asleep with a satisfied smile on her lips.

14

Thursday 4 July: Morning

There was thunder and lightning throughout the night. The trees in St James's Park, heavy with leaf, shook in the wind and two of the largest fell across the road in Birdcage Walk, hitting the roof of a passing taxi and causing great alarm to the two American tourists in the back who had been enjoying some of the most disreputable clubs in Soho.

Several excursion boats broke their moorings alongside the Embankment, swung out into the middle of the Thames and were swept rapidly downstream, causing the river police to sound their emergency alarms and to ask the BBC to broadcast on the early morning news a warning to all those travelling along the Thames between Tower Bridge and Albert Bridge. It was two hours before they managed to get lines aboard the boats and, by then, one had hit the middle pier of Westminster Bridge and knocked a keystone out of the supporting arch. The river police rang Scotland Yard immediately and warned their colleagues that traffic would have to be diverted from Waterloo past St Thomas's Hospital and from the Embankment to Millbank, whilst the foundations of the centre section of the bridge were checked.

'Christ,' said one policeman to another, on duty at the Whitehall end of Downing Street, 'it's like the end of the world. I've never known a shitty night like it.'

The Prime Minister had slept very badly. He had gone to bed after Jock Meldrum-Ross had left Number 10, taken two sleeping pills and fallen asleep whilst reading scurrilous comments about himself in *Private Eye*. As he drifted off, he wondered whether he should sue the magazine for libel. If he succeeded, and got a massive payment out of them, at least that would solve his pension problem when he retired.

He was woken by the noise of thunder a few hours later, stirred and reached for the watch on his bedside table. Damn, he thought, it's only four o'clock. He tried to get to sleep again but his mind started to race round the day ahead, the difficult Cabinet meeting, the long and careful speech that he would have to make in the House, the inevitable stream of television and press interviews, and the violence of the row between Robert Huggins and himself. He groaned to himself and wished, for a moment, that he was shot of the whole business. He remembered Henry V: 'He which hath no stomach to this fight, let him depart; his passport shall be made.' Christ, he thought, I still have some stomach left, even if it's riddled with ulcers. I must beat that sod, Huggins, but I wish I had someone, just someone, I could trust. Dominic's all right, but, even with him, I'm not sure that I really know what his game is. What does he want in the end? A job, a peerage? Not money at least. He's got enough of that. If only my darling were still alive. She'd hold my hand.

His thoughts wandered on as sleep became more and more impossible. He turned on the light, pulled over a black box that was sitting with three others on the table by the side of his bed, unlocked it with one of the bundle of keys that lay between his glass of water and the bottle of sleeping pills. He pulled out a heavy bundle of papers that came from the Treasury and that started with a long minute from the Chancellor on the likely fiscal effect of doubling the limit under which mortgages qualified for tax relief on interest payments. The Chancellor, in good Treasury style, weighed the pros and cons carefully and at great length so, long before the Prime Minister reached the paper's conclusion, his attention had wandered. He picked up a piece of paper and a pencil and drew a line down the middle. On the one side he wrote: 'FOR' at the top and, on the other, 'AGAINST'. He put his own name at the top of the FOR list and Huggins' at the top of the AGAINST list. He paused, chewed the end of his pencil and then wrote: Home Secretary and Chancellor in the FOR list. He paused again, took a sip of water and saw the long flashes of summer lightning through his curtained windows. Then he added, under

221

Huggins' name, Defence Secretary and Social Security. I'm behaving like a Whip, he thought, and he shrugged disdainfully at himself. Then he wrote down: Lord Chancellor and Lord Privy Seal in the first column. I'm sure they're both with me, he thought, and the last thing they would want is a lot of disturbance and long nights in the Lords just before August. Anything for a quiet life.

Gordon threw back the bedclothes, got slowly out of bed and walked over to the window. He half pulled back the curtains and saw that rain was now pouring down as he peered across Downing Street at the Foreign Office opposite. Strange, he mused, that my worst enemy should be just opposite me. He looked at the heavy, Italianate building and, for once, a hint of sadness swept over him. A pity, he thought. When we started, Robert and I were such good friends. We saw everything eye to eye, used to breakfast together and make plans for the next day in Parliament, the next pamphlet, even the next holiday. A shame that it all went wrong. He shut the curtains again, walked to the bathroom just outside his bedroom door, urinated, grimaced at himself in the mirror, and walked back to his bed. He sipped at the water glass and then picked up the pencil and wrote quickly under the Lord Privy Seal's name in the first column: Agriculture, Wales, Scotland and Chief Secretary. They're all young, he thought. They all owe me their jobs and I can promise them all promotion. I'm sure I can get those four. In the second column, under Huggins' name, he put Employment and then paused and then pencilled in a question mark after that word.

He counted the two lists and thought nine certainly for me, four certainly for Huggins or more or less certainly. We're twenty-two in the Cabinet, so I need at least eleven. Energy and the Chairman of the Party. Of course, they'll be all right. Damn it, they're two of my closest friends. He thought again: that gives me eleven for sure.

Gordon lay back on his pillows, started to feel sleepy and found difficulty in remembering other names in the Cabinet. DTI, he thought. Yes, Trade and Industry, no I don't think I can count on her. Then he remembered Onslow, the Leader of the House. He struggled up from his pillow, wrote Leader of the House in the first column, counted again and thought, twelve, that's all right. He picked up the black box, shovelled the papers back into the top of it and put it back on the side table. He turned out the light, listened for a few seconds to the rain hammering on the windows of his room, and fell into a dreamless sleep.

At precisely seven in the morning, the telephone rang by the bedside of the Home Secretary. He was sitting up in bed, three pillows behind his back and he was into the middle of his second large red box. Papers were strewn on the bed all round him and there was another box sitting on the floor beside him, expectantly, waiting to be opened. His wife had long ago given up trying to share a bed with him when they were in London and was wisely asleep in the little dressing room next door.

'Is that you, Piers? It's Ross Macintosh here. What a bloody night it's been. It's as if the gods wanted to destroy us. I hardly slept at all and I should think the Chief Constables have already been on to you asking for all sorts of special powers to clear streets and create even more traffic chaos than they usually do.' Piers heard the Chancellor of the Exchequer chuckle at the other end of the telephone and felt immediately annoyed.

'It's not a laughing matter, Ross. If the Home Counties are in anything like the mess in London, the local authorities will all come running asking for more money under some emergency rules or other and your precious Chief Secretary will have to find it for us. With his usual charm, he'll make a lot of noise about that.' He paused and then, in a milder tone, said: 'But I'm sure that's not what you rang about at this ungodly hour. What can I do for you?'

'You're right. Are we talking on a secure line?'

'I suppose so, insofar as any of our lines are ever secure, which they are not.'

'To be blunt, I think we must have a pact about the Cabinet meeting today.' There was a short silence at the other end of the line, and then Ross Macintosh continued, feeling his way. 'It seems to me to the advantage of both of us that Gordon should go on until the election. If he retires now, or is forced out as a result of the Cabinet this morning, you and I will each be in a fight against Huggins. I don't know which of us would win, but, personally, I think that your chances and mine will both be better after November when we have had time to do more planning and more lobbying. At the moment, Huggins' contacts with the backbenchers are much better than ours and he would get a great deal more support than he deserves.' Ross paused again, and then said, 'You and I may both be damaged by being seen as close supporters of Gordon, Piers, just too damn close. We could distance ourselves from him during the general election campaign. That would give us elbow-room.'

Piers Potter thought for a long time before speaking. Macintosh asked whether he had heard everything that he had said and Piers simply said that he had but he was damned if he was going to be rushed. Then he made up his mind. He agreed to follow the Chancellor's line and support Gordon both in Cabinet and to the press throughout the day. He thought Macintosh's arguments were right. But he had one condition to make: 'After today, if Gordon survives, I want you and me to share our planning and thinking right through the general election period. If we work together, we're both in the end more likely to bring Gordon down at the right moment when one of us, rather than Huggins, can succeed him.' He paused. 'Obviously, Ross, I'd give you any job you want in the Government if I become Prime Minister, and I assume that you would say the same to me.'

'Yes, of course,' Ross's voice sounded momentarily strained and shrill. 'That goes without saying.'

'All right, there's a bargain made. We had better tell our press officers immediately to start putting out supporting messages behind Gordon and implying that it is all the Foreign Office's fault. I'm sure we can pin the Akrotiri disaster on Huggins somehow.'

At 7.30, the telephone rang in Huggins' study at the top of Number 1 Carlton Gardens, the Foreign Secretary's London residence. Huggins had been up for two hours working on his red boxes and drinking black coffee as he rapidly read the minutes, files, submissions and copy telegrams that were now strewn all over his desk.

'Yes, Foreign Secretary here,' he said picking up the telephone.

'It's Jock Meldrum-Ross. I'm sorry to bother you at this hour.'

'Don't worry. As you can guess, I've been up since five or so, working.' Huggins spoke almost smugly.

'I thought I should tell you. I got a message late yesterday evening to go round to Number 10. The Prime Minister saw me there by himself and he sacked me on the spot, or at least he told me that he wanted to have my resignation after the debate tonight. If he didn't get it then, he'd fire me.'

'Good God,' said Huggins. 'The man's gone mad. Why is he sacking you?'

'He says that I let him down in my television interview with Martin Jevons at lunch-time yesterday. I blamed him for the loss of the telegram telling us not to mention Al-Fatah's name. He thinks I should have protected him or put the blame on you or me instead.'

'But why should you?' asked Huggins angrily. 'It was Number 10 who lost their copy. And I'm told that you were put on the spot by Martin Jevons. You didn't have any choice but to say what you did. Or, at least, that's what my private office have told me. I just haven't had time to see a tape of the interview myself.'

There was a long pause and then Jock said, 'Well, thank you for saying that, Robert. But there it is. There's nothing much I can do. I'll wait till after the vote tonight and then send him a letter, saying all the usual nice things and I'll have to think of something to say to my constituency chairman and the local press.'

'Don't do anything at the moment. Don't tell anyone except Mary,' Huggins almost shouted down the telephone. 'Do you think the Chief Whip knows about this?'

'I shouldn't think so,' said Jock. 'I got the impression that Gordon had made up his mind in a rush and was just charging ahead.'

'Sit tight,' commanded Huggins.

Anthony Onslow made a habit, whenever he was in London, of

walking every morning from his house in Great College Street through Dean's Yard, past Westminster Hall and so into St James's Park. He liked to walk round the pond in the middle of the park, gaze at the birds, look to see if the Royal Standard was flying over Buckingham Palace and thus, back up Birdcage Walk, right into Queen Anne's Gate and so to Great College Street. A walk of around twenty-five minutes that prepared him for the day. This morning he'd only got as far as the top of the park when he decided that it was all too wet and stormy and he retraced his steps, feeling disgruntled at being robbed of his quiet minutes of relaxation. As he opened the door of his house, he heard his wife answering the telephone upstairs in the kitchen and saying that he was out walking in the park.

'No I'm not. I'm just back,' he shouted up the stairs.

'Hold on, Greg,' he heard his wife saying. 'He's back after all. He's just come through the front door.'

Onslow put his umbrella down against the wall by the front door and ran up the stairs to the first-floor kitchen. He smiled at his wife and picked up the telephone.

'Onslow here,' he said. Greg Stevens apologized for ringing him so early and referred to their conversation late the previous night which he thought Onslow had obviously found a bit disturbing.

'You're Leader of the House, though,' the Chief Whip said, 'and you command a lot of respect among other ministers from every side of our Party and I'm frankly worried about some of the stories that have been circulating.' There was a pause then Greg Stevens went on: 'I thought you should know that the Prime Minister did call round Jock Meldrum-Ross late last night and has, apparently, sacked him, or told him that he must resign after the debate and the vote tonight. He certainly didn't consult me. I wish he had.'

'Good God. Why on earth did he do that? He should certainly have talked to you first,' said Onslow.

Stevens told him of the details that he had just heard from Robert Huggins and added, wearily, that Meldrum-Ross being sacked in this manner wouldn't help unity in the Party.

226

'He may not be the most popular person, and some of the Whips don't like him, but he's bright. And this will just look like the Prime Minister getting his revenge by sacking one of the Foreign Secretary's closest allies.'

'Yes,' said Onslow tersely. He put the telephone down, walked to the breakfast table shaking his head, sat down, picked up a knife and cut the top off the boiled egg in front of him without a word. The yolk dribbled down the side of the shell.

Tony Castle was still shaving when his wife shouted to him that Robert Huggins was on the telephone for him. He put down his old-fashioned razor, hastily wiped some soap off his mouth, and asked his wife which telephone Robert was on.

'The secret one in our bedroom,' she shouted back from the kitchen.

As Tony walked down the ill-lit corridor in Admiralty House, back to their bedroom, he laughed to himself at his wife's description of the telephone. In his judgement, no telephone line was ever secret and his experts from the security services were constantly bringing him new bugging and anti-bugging devices which they assured him would either protect his communications or enable him to arrange the interception of others'. Such confidence usually lasted about four weeks and then a successor device was produced that undid the work of the previous one, just installed at enormous expense. He picked up the telephone receiver which was lying on his crumpled pillow, said his name and asked for confirmation of who it was at the other end.

'It's Robert,' said the Foreign Secretary. 'I thought it'd be wise to have a word with you and a few other friends before the Cabinet meeting this morning. I use the word "friends" advisedly. I'm going to need them. The Prime Minister's clearly going to go for my throat and I shall retaliate in kind. You know the background as well as anyone, and I hope I'll have your full support.

'By the way, I gather that the Prime Minister sacked Jock Meldrum-Ross, last night. He didn't ask the Chief Whip or anyone

227

else about this but he just got furious that Jock hadn't supported him more during a television interview yesterday. I think the man is going off his head with jealousy or suspicion, or a mixture of both. Or perhaps he made a pass at Jock and got his hand slapped.'

'How extraordinary. Poor Jock. I always liked him. But don't worry, Robert, I supported the Akrotiri exercise all along. It didn't produce the result we wanted but that can't be helped. It was certainly worth trying and I shall say so, both in Cabinet and to the outside world.'

'Thank you,' said the Foreign Secretary and then Tony felt rather than heard him hesitate before he went on: 'I think we'll have quite a few other supporters round the Cabinet table who are very worried about Gordon and feel that he's gone more ga-ga than usual. There's even a story around that he's taken to rent-boys. I don't suppose for a second it's true, but I did want you to know, Tony, that I . . .' and again there was a perceptible hesitation: 'I appreciate your support very much indeed. If I were, either now or after the election, to become Leader of the Party and the Queen were to ask me to be Prime Minister, you could become Foreign Secretary, for example, if that's what you want.'

'No bribery now, Robert,' Tony laughed down the telephone. 'I enjoy being Defence Secretary very much but I'll remember your offer even if I don't take it up. Bye.' Tony went back to the bathroom and was smiling so much as he shaved that he nicked himself in the fold of his chin. Blast! he thought, that'll look good on television, and he asked his wife where she had put the Savlon.

'It's in front of you, on the basin. Under the mirror. Under your nose,' she remonstrated from the kitchen.

Isobel Turner handed Roderick a large bowl full of bran, Alpen and brown cornflakes as he rushed into the kitchen. She insisted that he eat all the contents of the bowl before he belted down the staircase in their tall, narrow house, off Clapham Common, and fell into the waiting official car. Roderick muttered a protest, accustomed to having his way in the private office at Number 10 and much more widely throughout the corridors of Whitehall. But Isobel would brook no refusal and reminded him of his gastric ulcer of last summer and how the doctor had insisted that he drink many glasses of water and eat a lot of bran to absorb the acid in his stomach which, doubtless, would be generated in large quantities during a day like the one he had ahead of him.

'You're being boring,' he mumbled but he dutifully sat down and started to chew his way through the wholesome pile in front of him. At a moment when his mouth was almost entirely full, the telephone by his side on the kitchen table rang and he picked up the receiver.

'Is that the principal private secretary?' a prim and precise voice at the other end enquired.

'Yes,' Roderick grumbled.

'It's Number 10 here. Hold on a moment, sir, and we will put Sir Peter Trout on the line.'

Roderick groaned to himself, grimaced at his wife and chewed rapidly. There were a few clicks and then Sir Peter's voice came through clearly and without hesitation:

'Trout here. I'm glad I caught you at home. I thought you might already have left for Number 10.'

'I was just about to,' said Roderick, conscious that he should have set off at least five minutes earlier.

Sir Peter, however, was not put off. As foreign affairs adviser to the Prime Minister, he had a great deal of seniority, knew it, and exercised it with relish. He explained at some length to Roderick how deeply worried all his contacts in the Middle East were by the events of yesterday and the day before. The Egyptian Ambassador in London, a real friend, Roderick was assured, had rung him a few minutes before to say that unless either the Prime Minister or the Foreign Secretary apologized profusely during the debate in the House that afternoon, there was a real risk of the Arab central banks concertedly selling their holdings of sterling and converting their reserves into dollars and Deutschmarks. The effect of this on the market would be horrific and the Chancellor would certainly have to put up interest rates by several points to defend the exchange rate.

'In addition,' Trout continued, sounding as if he relished the prospect of disaster, 'the Arab Ambassadors at the United Nations are planning to put forward an emergency resolution deploring the terrorist actions of the United Kingdom and suggesting that we should forfeit our permanent seat on the Security Council.

'That would be an unprecedented loss of face,' said the retired Ambassador.

Roderick listened with extreme care to Sir Peter's words and asked whether he got any impression that the Arab leaders were holding the Prime Minister more to blame than the Foreign Secretary, or the other way round. Sir Peter did not think that entered into their calculations. Rather, a very serious mistake had been made right at the top of the British Government, and a full public apology and, Sir Peter said, handsome financial reparation to Libya, were the only answer.

'I rang you because I thought you'd want to put this to the Prime Minister well before Cabinet starts at ten-thirty.'

Roderick Turner, without a trace of irony in his voice, thanked Sir Peter for his thoughtfulness and, disregarding his wife's querulous protestations, pushed his bowl of unfinished cereal away from him, left his glass of orange juice untouched and, picking up off the floor a shabby black briefcase from which the gold of the royal coat of arms was almost rubbed off, bounded down the stairs two at a time and into his waiting official car.

'Get us to Number 10 as fast as possible, Kevin, will you?' he asked. 'I'm already ten minutes late and it's going to be a terrible day.' In the car, he looked at the pile of newspapers stacked on the seat beside him, and then pushed them aside in irritation. He knew what they were all saying and he did not wish to read any more disastrous headlines. He started to wonder how he could best draft into the Prime Minister's speech for that afternoon a sufficient note of apology that would satisfy the Arab Ambassadors without immediately justifying the Opposition's demand for the Prime Minister's resignation.

★

The rain eventually stopped, and some members of the Cabinet walked from their nearby offices to Downing Street. As they turned into the street past the policemen, they were treated as if they were pop stars. Cameras were thrust at them, visitors from Bootle and Atlanta and Osaka and Fulham asked who they were and thrust autograph books at them, until the police cleared a pathway through the crowd.

'I feel like Mick Jagger,' said Anthony Onslow as he walked down the pavement of Downing Street with Angela Fawke, the Social Security Secretary.

'Well, you don't look like him. He's a lot thinner than you are, and younger, Anthony, and he's paid probably a thousand times more than you a year,' Angela Fawke grinned cheerfully back at the Leader of the House.

He ignored her. 'If I lose my ministerial job at the next election, I should perhaps try an alternative career. I used to have rather a good voice and I sang in a Bach choir before I got into the House.' Angela laughed. They were only about twenty yards from the door to Number 10, and on the other side of the road was a bevy of photographers with seriously big cameras and twenty reporters all pointing microphones in their direction.

'Whose side are you on today, Angela?' asked Onslow very quietly.

'I'm for Robert. I think he has justice on his side,' said Angela. 'What about you?'

'I was of the other persuasion, but I've had a lot of 'phone calls,' replied Anthony. 'I'm thinking.'

They both stopped on the doorstep of Number 10, turned smartly and in unison as if rehearsed by a ballet master, waved cheerfully at the waiting photographers, ignored the beckoning cries from the reporters with the microphones and then, in apparent harmony, turned back and walked through the open door.

The Chief Whip looked round the Cabinet room from his vantage point at the far end of the table. He counted quickly and saw that everyone was present, twenty-two members of the Cabinet including the Prime Minister – twenty men and two women. The only others in the room were himself and Sir Richard Endicott, the Head of the Civil Service and Secretary to the Cabinet, Roderick Turner and Dominic Anderson.

The routine business was dealt with quickly. Onslow, as Leader of the House, announced the business for the following week, the Chief Whip announced the whipping for the week and, in turn, the Leader read out the full text of the Motion which would be debated that afternoon. The Prime Minister, he said, would speak first, opening the debate. He would be followed by the Leader of the Opposition. The Foreign Secretary and Robinson, the Labour Shadow Foreign Secretary, would wind up the debate before the vote at ten o'clock. He looked down the table towards Greg Stevens and Greg, taking his cue, said that there was, of course, a three-line whip and that he expected all ministers and their parliamentary private secretaries to be present without fail. No excuses for absence would be accepted from any member of the Government. He hoped that members of the Cabinet would be present in the House for the opening and closing speeches, to support the Prime Minister and the Foreign Secretary. There was an approving murmur round the table. And then the Prime Minister, from the middle of the table, turned, looked down to his left and asked Greg how he thought the vote would go.

'It's a bit early to say, Prime Minister,' said the Chief Whip. 'As of late last night, forty of our colleagues or so had expressed serious reservations but we will work on them throughout the day and I've no doubt that we'll reduce that number somewhat.'

'Forty?' A muffled voice somewhere down the table expressed surprise and dismay.

'You'll have to work hard but we'll talk more about that in a few minutes after we've got rid of the other business,' said the Prime Minister calmly.

The Chancellor then gave a short and depressing commentary on the financial markets and the continuing pressure on sterling which had not lessened after the 1 per cent interest rise the previous week. Sterling was very weak that morning and there was widespread belief that the Arab countries were selling. There was desultory discussion about this and about the next item, the suggestion from the Employment Secretary that there should be a further review of unemployment benefit before the contents of the election manifesto were finally decided. Angela Fawke protested, as she knew she was expected to do, but agreement was reached with a minimum of argument.

Then the Prime Minister looked up from his papers which he had been studying with constant attention, his head tucked down, and said:

'We must move on to our discussion on what has happened in the Middle East in the last two days and the consequences of this. I want there to be plenty of time for everyone to express their opinion. Party politics will obviously come into this as the general election is so close and normally the civil servants would leave Cabinet at this stage, but, none the less, I have asked both Richard Endicott and Roderick Turner to stay with us because the outcome of the discussion is extremely important and could have constitutional implications. Sir Richard has agreed that he and Roderick should remain and they will keep minutes of our discussion.

'I am going to ask the Foreign Secretary first to give us his version of the events,' Gordon paused and Greg Stevens wondered whether any irony was intended. The Prime Minister went on: 'Foreign Secretary, please cover both the abortive attempt on the Libyan airliner south of Cyprus and the murder of one of our hostages in Beirut yesterday morning. I will then ask the Chancellor to speak about the financial implications, given the threats that I understand a number of the Arab countries are making; I will ask the Lord Chancellor to speak about any legal aspects in relation to charges of piracy and I will then throw open the discussion to every member of the Cabinet.' The Prime Minister looked over his left shoulder at Robert Huggins, sitting all too close to him, and Huggins picked up the notes in front of him and started to explain, once again, to the full Cabinet the

233

reasons for authorizing the RAF Tornados to intercept the Libyan air freighter over the Mediterranean Sea two days earlier, and to use their weapons, if necessary. He emphasized that, after careful consideration, the Cabinet Committee had been in unanimous agreement. The Cabinet prepared themselves for a long exposition.

At about the same time, the British Ambassador, 2000 miles to the south-east of London, was getting ready to leave Helen Harrington's flat on the fourth storey of a shabby concrete block in East Beirut. Benedict Adams was not a man to shirk his duty and, though dreading the tears and all the evident signs of human misery, he had gone to call on Helen and to try to share her unhappiness with her as soon as she was willing to see him. Throughout their interview, Helen had sat on the edge of a dilapidated sofa, with her two small children hanging on to her. The Ambassador noticed that the cover of the sofa was worn and that the stuffing showed through in several places. This upset him as they talked, and he wondered whether there was any way the Embassy could find some money to help the finances of the Harrington family. Perhaps he could do it through his own, small discretionary fund without the Accounting Officer noticing.

He had discussed the tragedy of what had happened at length, as seen from the information available to the Embassy, but there was very little new to add. Helen Harrington had already heard it all, either over the radio or from Bob Janes who, with his wife Sally, had been with her almost continuously for the last thirty-six hours. Throughout their talk her children clung on to her like ship-wrecked sailors hanging on to the only rock in the sea. At first, she was clear and brave and said that she understood the difficulties and, obviously, everyone had been trying their best to find and to release the two men but, slowly, as the conversation wore on, tears started to come into her eyes. Her shoulders sagged and her children clung even tighter to her than before.

Finally, she burst out that she could never understand why Al-

Fatah's name was mentioned publicly by the Prime Minister when it had been made so clear that that could be disastrous. The Ambassador looked embarrassed and shuffled his feet and said that it had been extremely unfortunate and there were doubtless circumstances and reasons not known to either of them. But, in the end, he could only agree with Helen's judgement.

After forty minutes, and feeling that his reservoir of sympathy had been exhausted, the Ambassador got to his feet to go, assuring Helen that he and all his small staff would be at her husband's funeral on Saturday and that the Embassy would do their utmost to help Helen's brother and sister-in-law, who were flying from London that day, to get past the soldiers at the airport and through passport control and customs as quickly as possible. Helen thanked him and, telling her children to remain on the sofa, she walked with the Ambassador to the glass-panelled door of the little flat. As he opened the door, she burst out to him that, all her life, she would never be able to forgive the Prime Minister for what he had done to her husband and their family. Their lives were ruined and always would be. Perhaps she shouldn't say that, she added, gulping back tears, but that was the way she felt and she did not think she would ever feel differently.

The Ambassador wondered whether to put his arm round her shoulders to comfort her but then thought that might be embarrassing. Feeling deeply unhappy himself, he muttered his sorrow and his farewells, turned away, stumbled and then walked down the narrow concrete stairs.

His driver and his security guards were waiting for him outside the apartment block. As he settled back into the rear seat of his Jaguar, he ran the back of his hand over his forehead, anguished over the meeting he had just had, again wondered how he could give some help to the Harrington family.

Then he picked up that day's Beirut paper and re-read the small paragraph on the front page, announcing that the British Defence Attaché had been released the evening before after a misunderstanding at Beirut airport the previous day. How many hours of argument and irritation went into that ludicrous episode, thought the Ambassador wearily as he turned to the middle pages which he had not yet read.

These were full, as always in Beirut, of crime and shootings by different terrorist and militia groups and he barely noticed a small paragraph, half way down one of the pages, saying that a young Lebanese couple were being sought by their families and by the police. They had been held up and seized from their car in West Beirut on Monday afternoon, while driving back from work, and had not been seen since. He was twenty-five and an electrical engineer, she twenty-four and a dental assistant. Typical, he thought. I'll have to put West Beirut out of bounds to anyone who hasn't got an armed guard with them.

As he settled back into the comfort of the Jaguar, the Ambassador read on and saw that there was reference to the fact that he would be opening an exhibition of Lebanese art and artefacts at the Trade Centre on Saturday and he reminded himself to check the security arrangements that evening, now that his presence had been noted and broadcast in the papers. The terrorism in the heart of Beirut was getting worse and worse all the time. Fortunately, he had now done two out of his three years there.

The Chief Whip looked at his watch. It was nearly 12.40. He knew that most of the Cabinet had, as usual, lunch engagements. Many of these were with journalists and, on this day of all days, they would not want to break those appointments. They would all be itching to explain their personal position in regard to the Cabinet meeting that morning and the debate that afternoon. They would be using the media to stake out their claim in whatever leadership battle might develop. The Cabinet meeting had gone on for over two hours, much longer than usual, and the press and the television reporters outside would already be commenting back to their editors that discussion must have been serious and bitter for the Cabinet to have lasted so long.

Bitter it certainly had been. In his six months as Chief Whip, he had never heard such charge and counter-charge as there had been between the Prime Minister and the Foreign Secretary. There was hardly a crime of which one had not accused the other: lying, concealing vital documents, breaking up the Parliamentary Party, leaking vital and secret matters to the press, ruining the Party's chances at the election – recrimination after recrimination, like thunderbolts, had been hurled between them. If it had been the Montagues and the Capulets, thought Greg Stevens, the swords would have been unsheathed long ago and the blood would have flowed.

Bruce Gordon and Huggins had been the main protagonists, and the fact that they sat right next to each other only made the interchange more embarrassing. But Tony Castle had been consistent and vehement in his support of Huggins, Piers Potter had been eloquent in defending the Prime Minister and Ross Macintosh vitriolic in his assessment of the effects on sterling of the mad folly at Akrotiri, as he kept on calling it. Every member of the Cabinet had spoken and it was only those who attended by custom rather than by right – himself, Dominic Anderson and the two civil servants – who had said nothing. Greg Stevens noted, though, that the civil servants had never stayed still. The notes that they had been scribbling must have caught every spoken word and he, in turn, had kept a tally of those who declared for the Prime Minister and those who spoke against. A typical Whip's task, he thought. He had ten down on either side with two undecided. He looked at his watch again and, at the same moment, he noticed that the Prime Minister was scrutinizing very closely a piece of paper that he held in his hand.

The Prime Minister had with him the pencilled list that he had made during the night. As the Chief Secretary, the junior Cabinet minister at the table, was sanctimoniously insistent in his support – you little creep, thought Greg Stevens, you think you can guess which way the wind is blowing – the Prime Minister looked at his note and reckoned that everyone on whose support he had counted, had spoken clearly in his favour with the exception of Onslow, the Leader of the House and Lord Privy Seal. To his

surprise, Onslow had been unclear and hesitant in his remarks, as
if he could not decide whom to support. He waited until the Chief
Secretary had brought his remarks to an end with all the sincerity
of a Uriah Heep, and then he looked down the table, first to his
right and then to his left and said:

'I must bring this discussion to a close. I've a lot of work to do on
my speech for the debate this afternoon and I have an audience
with the Queen at two.' An evident sound of surprise came from
some sitting at the table. 'Yes, Her Majesty agreed to bring the
time forward,' continued the Prime Minister, 'so that there was no
chance of my having to leave the House while the debate was still
continuing.'

The Prime Minister then paused and kept silent for some
seconds. Then he said, emphasizing his words, 'It's regrettably
clear that there is a fundamental disagreement between the
Foreign Secretary and myself as to where blame lies for what has
happened over the last two days. Bitter and unpleasant remarks,
personal attacks indeed, have been made round the Cabinet table
this morning. In many years, I've never known a discussion like
this one, and some of you may well feel that you cannot serve any
longer in my ministerial team.' The Prime Minister looked
directly at Huggins as he said this.

'But first, we've got to get through the debate this afternoon.
We've got to win the vote which, the Chief Whip has already
warned us, is going to be very close. I intend, therefore, to ask each
of you in turn whether you agree with the line that I shall take this
afternoon, in which I shall firmly put any blame for the misunderstanding,' Gordon chose the word carefully, 'about revealing the
name of the terrorists holding our hostages on to the Foreign
Office. I regret this, but I have no choice. I wish there to be a
collective decision coming out of this Cabinet supporting that line,
supporting me strongly in the House this afternoon and supporting me in any conversations that you have with the press and
media.'

The Prime Minister turned directly to Huggins on his left who
shook his head and said there was no way in which he could

support what the Prime Minister had just said. The Prime Minister continued, one by one, round the long table. The Energy Secretary and the chairman of the Party, sitting in the Cabinet as Chancellor of the Duchy of Lancaster, supported him, so did the Chancellor of the Exchequer and the Home Secretary when it came to their turn, and so did the junior cabinet ministers on whose support he had reckoned during the small hours of the night. But those about whom he had been uncertain, Trade and Industry, Employment, Health, Education, Transport, Environment and Northern Ireland; he did not win one of their votes. In their different ways they joined with Tony Castle, the Defence Secretary, in saying that they could not support the Prime Minister's story of what had happened.

The Prime Minister's hand began to tremble as he clutched his little piece of paper with his two pencilled lists on it. Christ, he thought, this is bloody close. He made a quick calculation. Eleven for him, ten against. He looked down to the far end of the table on his right. Oh yes, he thought, only Onslow still to vote. Well, he'll be all right. He turned and looked at Onslow and so did everyone else round the Cabinet table. There was total silence in the white-panelled room and even the pens of the two civil servants stopped moving across their notebooks. Onslow cleared his throat:

'Prime Minister,' he said. 'I had intended to support you. It was you who appointed me to my job as Leader of the House and it would be my natural instinct to return your confidence in me with loyalty to you. I don't really care,' he added slowly, 'what happened to the telegram about Al-Fatah. It's the sort of mistake that can happen in any government, but I have to say that I'm increasingly worried about your leadership of our Party and your judgement. I understand that you summoned the Minister of State from the Foreign Office round here late last night and you dismissed him on the spot.' The Prime Minister opened his mouth to speak, but then kept silent. 'I think that was foolish. It showed a bitterness, a wish for revenge that, I have to say, I can't tolerate. Perhaps it's for the wrong reasons, but I can't vote for

239

you this morning.' Onslow stopped, shuffled the papers in front of him neatly together, and looked straight down the table.

There was a collective sigh from other members of the Cabinet followed by a long silence. Then the Prime Minister turned to Richard Endicott at his right hand and said:

'Cabinet Secretary, what do you make the tally?'

Endicott knew the answer perfectly well but he counted the names on the paper in front of him again and then turned to the Prime Minister and said: 'I make it eleven either way, Prime Minister. That, of course, is including your vote as a vote for,' he paused, 'yourself.'

The Prime Minister suddenly smiled ruefully, coughed and then appeared to gather himself together before he spoke across the table.

'A tie. Under those circumstances I have a casting vote and obviously that vote is for myself.' He stopped, appeared to reflect for a long time, took a sip of water from the glass in front of him and then said, in slow and emphatic tones, 'I believe in what I have said this morning and I believe in the correctness of what I have done. You will all agree, as a Cabinet with collective responsibility, that it is intolerable if we appear divided to the outside world. Any question of that must stop. We cannot have eleven resignations today; indeed, I don't want any resignations. We must remain united until the election, four months away. With that in mind, I want all press briefing and press releases cleared through the Number 10 press office from now onwards and I shall insist on unanimity.'

He paused and then went on even more slowly: 'If the general election weren't so near, I would obviously take other measures as well but our first task must be, for the sake of the Party, to win the next election. I expect you all to be totally loyal to me with that in view. That is all. I am now going to work on my speech for this afternoon. Foreign Secretary, I will be grateful if your office would send me round immediately a full draft of what you are proposing to say in your wind-up speech this evening. We will check it here.'

Without pausing to allow anyone to speak, the Prime Minister got up, pushed his heavy chair back, and walked briskly towards the doors. Robert Huggins looked across the table at Tony Castle, raised his eyebrows but, for once, was at a loss for words. All along the table, members of the Cabinet shuffled their papers together and then silently, like sheep, shuffled themselves out of the room.

15

Thursday 4 July: Afternoon

At precisely five minutes before two, the Prime Minister's Jaguar swung through the open iron gates into the forecourt of Buckingham Palace. The Changing of the Guard was over for the day and only a handful of tourists remained, staring in through the bars of the railings at the guardsmen in their sentry-boxes. Time was, thought Bruce Gordon, as his car drove at five miles an hour diagonally across the forecourt, when the guardsmen and their sentry-boxes were outside the railings, properly protecting the Monarch. Now they are inside as if they themselves needed protecting, and any tramp is able to climb over the railings and pop into the royal apartments.

His car went through the arch on the south side of the Palace and into the interior quadrangle. It drove at a slow, ceremonial pace to the corner, made a right-angled turn then stopped half-way down the west wing. A uniformed attendant moved forward and opened the door of the Jaguar, and the Prime Minister got out to be greeted by an ADC in RAF uniform.

'You're earlier than usual today,' commented the ADC chattily, as they walked through the double doors, crossed a long gallery and then up the red-carpeted stairs in front of them. At the top of the stairs, Sir Brian Chumley was waiting, dressed as if the world never changed, in dark morning coat and waistcoat, white shirt with a silver-grey tie and striped trousers. The Prime Minister looked instinctively at his watch as Sir Brian came forward and saw that it was one minute before two. Sir Brian saw the half-furtive look, smiled and said that the Prime Minister was, as always, the epitome of punctuality.

'Was it Queen Mary who remarked that punctuality was the gift of princes?' asked the Prime Minister.

'It could have been,' said Sir Brian, 'or was it the politeness of kings? Of course, Queen Mary was a tigress for good manners and correct behaviour, and punctuality would have been all part of that.' They paused in their small talk as they sat down on a hard settee outside tall double doors of unstained mahogany. A uniformed attendant stood by the doors, motionless, as neither man gave any indication of the tumult and doubt that were in their minds. The Prime Minister longed to unburden himself to someone he could trust, but felt he could not involve Sir Brian, a courtier and apolitical, in his perplexity.

He took a deep breath and said: 'I always think that that Winterhalter over there is a very fine picture of Queen Victoria in her late middle age,' he pointed to the wall opposite them. 'Winterhalter captures her better at that age than any other Victorian portrait painter. He makes her look wise and serene and not too dowdy and round.'

'You're right. In my opinion, he's a very under-rated painter. There are particularly fine examples of his work at Windsor.' Sir Brian paused. Pictures, he thought, were as good a conversation-filler as the weather, and more predictable. Then he asked, 'How long have you got, Prime Minister?'

'I must be back in the House just before three-fifteen to answer questions. I suppose I should leave here not later than three if that is convenient to Her Majesty.'

'I will tell her.'

As Sir Brian said that, a subdued bell rang on the edge of the double doors and the attendant came to life, stepped forward, looked over at Sir Brian and opened the doors. Sir Brian got up immediately, walked forward into the further room and the doors shut behind him with a well-oiled decisiveness. The Prime Minister looked round him and thought that the furniture was arranged in discreet little clumps, rather like the Palm Court at the Ritz. The difference is, he considered, that there are many fewer pieces of furniture here but they are all priceless. The bell rang again, the attendant opened the doors and the Prime Minister got up, walked to the doors and bowed.

The Queen was standing about five yards in front of him, to the right-hand side of her desk and Sir Brian was a foot or two behind her. She gestured towards one of the Regency chairs between her desk and the windows and suggested that the Prime Minister sat there. She sat herself down behind her desk in the middle of the room. With its separate piers and the well-stacked papers on it, it looked like the desk of a working partner in a merchant bank and the Queen adopted an equally straight-backed and business-like attitude, as she turned to the Prime Minister and invited him to bring her up to date on political matters and the problems of the day.

Bruce Gordon half-smiled at those traditional words. He knew well that the Queen was always thoroughly well-informed on what was happening at Westminster and in Whitehall. Not only did she receive a daily letter from one of the Senior Whips describing the doings in the Commons, but he had no doubt that there was a constant stream of telephone calls every hour between Sir Brian and Whitehall mandarins and some ministers, too. He gave the Queen his own version of what had happened with the Libyan freighter and the later events both at Akrotiri and in Beirut. He told her of the threats from many of the Arab countries, especially the resolution at the United Nations calling for the removal of Britain's permanent seat on the Security Council. The Queen interrupted him at this point and asked whether this would be supported by the other permanent members, China, the USSR, France and the United States.

'We don't know, Ma'am, at this stage. It could be.'

'That would be exceedingly bad,' said the Queen and motioned to him to continue.

The Prime Minister reminded her that there was to be an emergency debate in the House of Commons that afternoon which he would open. As he trotted out the facts which he had now rehearsed so often, his mind half wandered and he looked round the room in which he was sitting and thought how, in its own way, it was a cosy place with many photographs on the occasional tables and the shelves, vases full of roses, a lot of books, and chairs which, though of formal elegance and of a certain age, were comfortably upholstered. It's a friendly room, he thought, and it looks very much as though it's used for working meetings and important discussions at which decisions are taken. It's not just a show-piece.

The Queen interrupted him again, thanked him and said that she imagined Middle East questions had been discussed widely at Cabinet that morning. She looked quizzically at the Prime Minister as she spoke. He assured her that such matters had indeed been aired and he informed her, tersely, that there had been some disagreement on interpretation and motivation between the Foreign Secretary and himself but, by and large, the majority of the Cabinet agreed with him and all would support the line that he proposed to take in the House that afternoon. It was necessary for there to be clear and open unanimity on the part of the Government if the current sterling crisis was to subside.

As the Prime Minister said this, the Queen, sitting with a ramrod back in her chair, turned to face him directly, looked at him through her spectacles and asked him to go into more detail about the divisions between the Foreign Secretary and himself. The Prime Minister did his best to gloss over these, saying that it depended on the view of whether the interception of the Libyan aeroplane was still justified even though no hostages were found on board. He thought it probably was not and had always been rather doubtful about what he described as the adventure, but the Foreign Secretary took a contrary view.

The Queen asked him about the missing telegram from Beirut of which there had been so much in the press and the Prime Minister, starting to resent what was beginning to be a cross-examination, explained that the loss of a copy of this telegram had been extremely unfortunate, but it was something that could happen relatively easily, given the flood of telegraphic traffic that there was these days. He had already asked for procedures in Whitehall to be improved. As he concluded, he thought how elegant the Queen was looking in a dress of shot green silk and three strands of large pearls around her neck. She always looked so much younger in real life, he thought to himself, than she does in her photographs. A pity she has to ask questions.

The Queen pulled her chair round towards him and crossed one elegant ankle over another. She thought for a moment or two and then said:

'Prime Minister, I'm sorry to say this but I'm not certain that you are giving me a wholly full and accurate picture of what happened at Cabinet this morning on this very difficult question of the hostages.' She spoke with resounding clarity. 'My information is that there was a long and heated debate. Certainly that is what has been picked up, too, by the *Evening Standard*.' She pointed at the lunch-time edition which lay on a satinwood Pembroke table by her. 'Of course, one does not believe the tabloids but I am told that, at the end of the meeting, you felt it necessary to ask for an individual vote round the Cabinet table to confirm that you had a majority of support. That is most unusual. In fact, the vote was eleven against eleven, with yourself using your casting vote in your own favour.' She paused and looked searchingly at the Prime Minister. He put a finger inside his collar, ran it round and meditatively scratched his neck.

'Ma'am, of course you're right technically, but it wasn't wholly necessary to have a vote. I knew the general mood of the meeting was with me but I thought it might be better to establish that I did have a majority. There had been some pretty hard words said at the meeting, and I thought a vote would clear the air.'

'I'm not certain that a vote of eleven to eleven, then decided by your casting vote, exactly clears the air,' the Queen said primly. She paused for a long time, looked at the blotter on the desk in front of her, then at the photograph of her father standing on the corner of her desk, and then she turned round and her blue eyes gazed directly at the Prime Minister's face. 'Have you thought of having a general election now?' she asked.

'Yes, Ma'am, I have,' Gordon replied, 'and I've come to the conclusion that it's not necessary. The summer holidays are almost on us and, in my judgement, it would be better to delay until after the holidays, till October or possibly until November itself.'

The temperature in the room seemed to drop rapidly and the

Prime Minister suddenly had a vision of a Tory Victorian Prime Minister, was it Robert Peel – he could not quite remember – coming and being berated by the Queen's great-great-grandmother, for insisting that the ladies of the Queen's bedchamber should be changed when the Whigs lost office. To the incoming Tories, these honorific posts at court were part of the spoils of an election victory but not so to the Queen's ancestor. Queen Victoria must then, the thought passed through the Prime Minister's mind, have put on much the same expression as Queen Elizabeth was now wearing.

'I was advised shortly before one pm of the hung vote in Cabinet this morning and, since then, I have consulted with Sir Brian,' she nodded in the direction of her private secretary, 'and my constitutional advisers. As a general election has to take place within four months and as the news of this serious split in the Cabinet is bound to leak, if it has not done so already, the advice they have all given me is that Parliament should be dissolved immediately. Without that, they think there will be great turbulence, with a consequent serious weakening in sterling. We are particularly worried about the prospect of our losing our permanent seat in the Security Council. That would be an irreparable blow to our international standing.' The Queen stopped, and the Prime Minister felt his heart beating. What the hell's coming? he wondered. Then the Queen continued slowly, 'As you well know, Prime Minister, it is your constitutional duty to advise me when to dissolve Parliament and to call a general election. It is my duty to listen but not necessarily to follow your advice. I could, for example, listen to you,' the Queen paused, looked again at the blotter in front of her, and went on, 'and then call on someone else, another leading Conservative Member of Parliament, to form a government. Obviously, that would not be ideal at the moment.

'I have, however, decided to follow my advisers' unanimous view and to ask you to announce the dissolution of this Parliament in the Commons this afternoon with the general election to be held, I suggest, on Thursday in four weeks' time, the last possible day really before we are all into the summer holidays and I shall be going to Balmoral.'

The Queen paused again and then said more briskly: 'Now, as I see it, you have two alternatives and I am being brief because I know you have to leave the Palace by three pm. Either you can decline to follow my wish, in which case I will ask the Foreign Secretary to form a Government but immediately to dissolve Parliament, or you will accept the view of myself and my advisers and announce this as your own suggestion that you have put to me, and which I have been pleased to accept.

'Presumably, you can do this when you speak in the House this afternoon? What is quite clear to me is that you cannot continue pretending that the Cabinet is united when, in fact, it is split,' and here the Queen raised her voice and emphasized her words, 'right down the middle.'

The Prime Minister looked at the Queen with amazement. Never had he expected to be overruled and overrun by the Monarch in this manner. He had, at times, confessed to his close friends that, whilst he admired the Queen for reading all the countless bits of political paper that she was sent, he thought that she lacked determination and initiative.

'She never seems,' he said, 'to have any new ideas of her own.' And yet, here she was, firmly telling him that he must dissolve Parliament, go to the country, probably lose his job, or else she would sack him. Even as he paused, a feeling of admiration swept through him, and then one of relief. The decision had been taken and he no longer had to hang on and pretend, and all of that lifted a burden from his shoulders.

He looked at the Queen, paused for a while and then smiled broadly. 'You have, of course, described the constitutional position correctly, Ma'am. In my judgement, a few months do not make any great difference and I accept your view about the election. It would be better, if I may say so, Ma'am, for you as well as for me if this was to come as my clear request to you, which you have graciously accepted.' The Queen inclined her head towards Bruce Gordon. 'I will therefore announce it in that way in the House of Commons this afternoon and the election will be on Thursday, four weeks' time.' He started to fumble in his pocket and to look for a diary.

'August 1st,' interjected the Queen.

'Thank you, Ma'am.' He paused and looked at the Queen, but she said nothing more. So Bruce Gordon got to his feet, thanked the Queen and Sir Brian for their advice, bowed his head and walked towards the double doors, where he turned and bowed again. The Queen pressed the bell on her desk and the doors were opened, as if by magic, when he was within a pace of them. As he stepped through them and muttered his thanks to the liveried attendant, he had the faint impression that he heard the Queen laugh gently behind him. He assumed that he was wrong and, accompanied by the ADC, hurried down the carpeted steps to his car.

Barely half an hour later, at 3.15 precisely, the Prime Minister was on his feet to answer questions. The first was from a Labour member and, as usual, asked the Prime Minister to tell the House of his engagements for the day. For once, the glove fitted the hand very neatly and the Prime Minister announced, reading from the written answer provided by his civil servants that, in the morning, he had presided over a Cabinet meeting and had had meetings with ministers and others and that he had just returned from his weekly audience with the Queen. He then paused and looked up from his written text, and the House suddenly had a sense that the unexpected was going to happen.

The Prime Minister looked at the benches opposite him and said:

'Mr Speaker, I wish to advise the House at the first opportunity that, during my audience with Her Majesty, I informed Her Majesty that it would be for the benefit of the country if uncertainty were removed and a general election were held before the summer holidays rather than waiting until October or November. I therefore suggested to Her Majesty that the House should be immediately prorogued. I can inform the House that Her Majesty has given her gracious consent to my advice. The general election will be held in four weeks' time on Thursday, August 1st. The

249

formal Dissolution of Parliament will take place next Monday and discussions will be held immediately between the usual channels concerning the business that can be concluded in both Houses by then.'

There was pandemonium around the Prime Minister as he sat down. Cheers and whistles and boos filled the Chamber and most of the press lobby stood up and, stumbling over each other in their urgency, rushed up the steep stairs from the gallery to telephone their editors. Once seated, the Prime Minister turned to his right and saw that the Leader of the House's mouth was hanging open as he gaped at him.

'What the hell . . . ?' stammered Anthony Onslow.

'I got bored,' replied Gordon half under his breath as he got ready to deal with the onslaught of the Leader of the Opposition.

July the Fourth was coming to an end at the eastern end of the Mediterranean. With a flaming sun setting behind the grey hills of Cyprus, and the mosquitoes beginning to buzz and the pink gins and the gin and tonics and the whisky and sodas being poured in the Officers' Mess at Akrotiri, nothing had changed. And yet, thought Squadron Leader Snowling as he walked in to meet Spacemead for a last time in the Mess, everything has changed. The certainty has gone, confusion everywhere. He tried to remember a speech from Julius Caesar he had learnt at school – '. . . and bloody treason somethings over us'. 'Triumphs over us,' that's it. 'Bloody treason triumphs over us.' He bought himself a soft drink from the bar and walked over to where Spacemead was already sitting. He gazed at him reflectively and wondered how Spacemead would react to what he was about to tell him. He started slowly,

'I've just spent an hour with the two boffins from London.' Spacemead looked up enquiringly. 'You know, the technicians you told me about.'

'Oh?' Spacemead asked. 'Have they found anything interesting?'

'You're bloody right, they have.' Snowling warmed to his subject. 'They've established that the bloodstains at the back of the Mercedes' boot are definitely of the same blood groups as those of the two air-crew who, Proudian said, were killed on the plane. Of course, that's not conclusive in itself. It's a common blood group that they both belonged to, O Rhesus (D) positive. But listen to what follows.'

'You're sounding like Hercule Poirot,' Spacemead muttered into his drink.

A hint of a smile lit up Snowling's face, and then he quickly became serious again, putting great emphasis on his words.

'The boffins are very puzzled. They say that the bodies of the man and the woman are quite smashed up as they could be, I suppose, from the Tornado's heavy cannon-fire or from the disintegrating turbine-blades. They've found no bullets yet but they think the angle of entry in the wounds is all wrong. It looks as if they were killed from close to and from directly behind them, as if someone had put a heavy pistol right to their backs and killed them. Now I certainly wasn't behind them. I was firing at the engine from above. And, in case that were not enough,' Snowling paused and took a long sip from his drink and enjoyed the suspense that he was creating, 'they're convinced from the dissecting, or whatever it is that they do with corpses, that the two were killed about twenty-four hours before we attacked the Libyan freighter. So,' Snowling paused again for effect and said: 'what do you make of all that?'

Spacemead screwed his eyes up, stared at Snowling and then looked round the walls of the bar at the photographs of previous commanding officers of the Base. Fifteen seconds passed in silence between the two men, with the only noise being that of the BBC World Service coming over some loudspeakers at the far end of the room. Then Spacemead scratched the back of his head and turned to Snowling and said:

'So we were deceived all along.'

'It looks like it. If the boffins are right, and they're convinced that they are although it will all have to be checked out in properly equipped laboratories in London, then the Libyans either guessed or knew that we would attack their freighter and get it to divert to Akrotiri. So they must have put two dead bodies into the Mercedes before the plane left Beirut Airport.'

'Shit,' said Spacemead, 'if I'd known that, I wouldn't have been so nice to Proudian and his crew last night. I'd have arranged for him and a few of his mates to be shot, too.'

The two men rose as of one mind and walked back to the bar together and ordered another round of drinks.

The debate ended quietly. Once the Prime Minister had finished his announcement of the election date, the fire went out of his words and the rights and wrongs of what had happened 200 miles south of Akrotiri and thousands of feet above the Mediterranean Sea, seemed much less important than they had before. Sympathy was properly expressed by all who spoke for Les Harrington and for his brave wife, Helen, and for their family, but when the Labour Leader of the Opposition accused the Prime Minister and the Foreign Secretary in the strongest terms he could find, of incompetence, of blundering and of mutual hatred, there was enthusiastic support for him from only a handful of members left on the back-benches behind him.

Already the thoughts of Members of Parliament were far away. They only had four weeks in which to prepare for an election; at stake was their own personal survival, their careers and their salaries and expenses. Most spent the second half of the afternoon on the telephone to their constituency chairmen, their agents and their families, cancelling holiday plans, booking halls for election meetings and ordering photographers to come and take the latest handsome pictures of themselves, spouses, dogs, cats and reluctant children.

The Prime Minister gave a long and detailed account of events. He explained, without too much reference to the secret interception of radio messages, that he and his fellow ministers had had every good reason to believe that the hostages were on board the Libyan freighter. He had already offered a broad apology to the Libyan Government and he assured the House that discussions would take place immediately for suitable financial reparation to Tripoli.

'They're murderers,' Sir John Williamson roared from the Tory back-benches, but the Prime Minister contented himself with commenting that, whilst he usually had every sympathy with the views of his honourable and gallant friend, on this occasion there was no doubt that some financial settlement would have to be made to the Libyans. He made no reference to the disappearance of a copy of a telegram between Number 10 and the Foreign Office.

The Foreign Secretary wound up the debate to benches that were almost empty. He emphasized the atrocities constantly being committed by terrorists in Beirut and deplored the death of Les Harrington.

'We always recognize the fine work done in difficult situations like that in Lebanon by Britons throughout the world who work for charities, who bring humanitarian aid and comfort to families in distress. And all of us in the Foreign Office who get to know these young people and who see them at work, feel deeply sad, as if we had lost a member of our own family, when one of these brave young people, engaged in decent work and trying to bring help to others, is mercilessly killed. Their death is a loss for us all.'

The few members present listened in a quiet, sombre fashion. There were no interjections, and no questions about the rift between Foreign Secretary and Prime Minister. Time had moved on. When the Opposition voted not to approve the Government's action, potential rebels and many Labour members had already disappeared into the night and the Government won by a majority of more than fifty. The Chief Whip went back to his office behind the members' lobby and told his team that they had better all go home and get ready to fight to keep their seats. God knows, he wondered, where we will all be in four weeks' time.

The Foreign Secretary walked out of the Chamber, after the vote, with Jock Meldrum-Ross, and he turned to him and asked him to come back to the Foreign Office with him.

'It might be helpful,' said Robert Huggins, 'if we have a chat about what we're both going to do next.'

As they walked into the Foreign Secretary's office, they were met by Alastair Crichton, the Under Secretary. He looked pink and flustered and out of sorts with his normal cool and immaculate self.

'I tried to get you in the House,' he said anxiously, 'but you had just got on to your feet for your speech. The officials in the box said they couldn't get a message to you. If I'd rung a minute or two earlier, it might have been possible but, once you were at the Despatch Box, it wasn't.' His voice tailed away with a sense of despair.

'What the hell are you talking about?' asked Robert Huggins. By way of answering, Alastair Crichton handed him a long telegram from Akrotiri that covered three pages, and he gave a copy to Jock. The three of them sat down in the sofa and chairs, facing the fireplace, overlooked by a grim portrait of Warren Hasting awaiting his trial for corrupt dealings with the East India Company. They read of the findings of the two pathology technicians that Snowling and Spacemead had discussed an hour or two before over their drinks in the Officers' Mess, and then they came to the conclusion, after paragraphs of technical detail, of the Commanding Officer at the Akrotiri Base:

IN MY OPINION, THE CLAIM BY CAPTAIN PROUDIAN THAT ROUNDS FROM THE RAF TORNADO HAD KILLED TWO MEMBERS OF HIS CREW, WAS A CAREFULLY PLANNED HOAX, INTENDED TO EMBARRASS THE BRITISH GOVERNMENT. I CAN ONLY REGRET-FULLY CONCLUDE THAT THE LIBYANS, FOR ONCE, SUCCEEDED REMARKABLY WELL IN THEIR OBJECTIVE.

Robert Huggins, the second he finished reading, turned to Jock: 'Do you see what must have happened?' he said speculatively. 'Just as we were intercepting their messages, they must somehow have managed to learn what we were planning. We've got foolproof codes, and I can't believe they managed to break those. So someone on our side, at GCHQ or in Whitehall, must have been feeding them information.

'When they learnt that we were going to go for the Ilyushin but they weren't going to be given our two hostages by Al-Fatah, they took matters into their own hands. They planted two dead bodies in the plane, Lebanese they had murdered before the plane left Beirut.' He paused, and thought, and then said with more confidence, 'Yes, that's it. They encouraged us to believe that they would take our hostages out to the airport in the boot of the car. Instead they took two dead bodies and, I suppose, once they were airborne, they got them out of the car, straightened them as best they could, and spread them out in the aisle of the aeroplane. The Tornados came along just as they expected and the Libyans put up a good charade, pretending they were going to be tough and fly on to Tripoli until one of the Tornados fired into their plane. Then, horror of horrors, as he turned back to Akrotiri, the captain of the Ilyushin claimed to the world that the British had killed two innocent crew members.

'God,' Huggins suddenly started to get angry and he turned to Alastair Crichton and shouted. 'Do you bloody well realize that if you had got this information to me before I got to my feet in the House, I could have made the best, the most exciting speech of my life? I would have exposed the Libyans as frauds and cold-blooded murderers, and I'd have had the whole House cheering me on.'

Alastair Crichton shrugged his shoulders and regretted that he had no control over the speed with which telegrams were delivered from Cyprus.

'You don't understand, you don't understand,' Huggins yelled at him. 'This was a chance of a lifetime, to show up this dreadful hoax, to expose the Libyans for the murderers that they are, not murderers of Harrington in Beirut, but murderers of two totally innocent young Lebanese. It would have saved my career. Put me into the history books. Probably made me Prime Minister.' He buried his head in his hands and his shoulders shook. Then he looked up and said more quietly to Jock: 'You realize, don't you, that Gadaffi has got us by the short and curlies with the whole Arab world for once on his side? They're all denouncing us as pirates and bullies and they're sympathizing with the poor little Libyans. But if, tomorrow, we tell the world what we've just learned, that the whole thing was a hoax and that these two on the plane were brutally murdered a day earlier, Gadaffi will say that we're lying and that we've just made the story up to save our faces. And more than half the world will believe him.'

Robert Huggins got up from his chair, turned and walked

towards the long windows and stared out into the dark, over St James's Park. He clenched his hands together and sighed and then he turned back and asked Crichton,

'When did the Prime Minister get this news?'

'At the same time as you, Foreign Secretary,' said Crichton. 'Presumably at the moment that he left the Chamber after the vote.'

A hundred yards away, the Prime Minister was also sitting at his desk with his head in his hands. He, too, thought of the political triumph that he would have had in the House if the information in the telegram in front of him had reached him a few hours earlier. How he would have enjoyed himself. How he would have laid into the evil of the Libyan regime. How he would have had his backbenches roaring in approval! These thoughts went sadly through his mind and then he thought of the minute size of his majority in Southampton West. He picked up the telephone on his desk and asked the Downing Street exchange to get him the Foreign Secretary, wherever he was. A minute later, his telephone rang and he picked it up and said:

'Robert? Yes, it's me, Bruce. Yes, I've just read the same telegram from Akrotiri as you. We've been fooled, haven't we? Someone's been working behind our backs. Someone must have been feeding information on our plans to the Libyans all along.' He paused.

'Look, is Jock with you? Good. Tell him not to bother about resigning. There's no point in him doing that now. What's your majority in that crappy seat of yours in Portsmouth?' Bruce Gordon paused again and listened and then laughed and said:

'Fifteen hundred? You're even worse off than me. I'm eighteen hundred. It'll be tough for both of us.' He was about to end the conversation when he added reflectively: 'If only we'd had this information a few hours earlier. God, what we could have done with it. It could have won us the election.' He put down the receiver, walked to a window and looked out across the park at the distant, floodlit prospect of Buckingham Palace.

16

Saturday 3 August

Susan Moberly looked across from the driver's seat at her husband sitting beside her on her left. She had insisted on driving so that he could relax after a long night in the aeroplane but she smiled to herself and thought that she need hardly have bothered. James Moberly, despite six hours in the plane flying economy class – a typical Ministry of Defence meanness, Susan thought – still looked as if he had come out of a bandbox. The trousers had a knife-edge to the crease and the Green Jackets blazer was beautifully brushed and pressed, even if closer inspection would reveal a little fraying at the cuffs. The brown hair, turning a gentle grey around the ears, was parted and combed as though he had just come from an interview with his commanding officer. He doesn't change, she thought, and I'm glad that he doesn't. But, goodness, I hope he's not going to find life in England just too dull.

Their two children, aged eleven and nine, were bouncing about on the back seat. They had kissed their father enthusiastically as he came into the arrivals lounge an hour ago and had looked at his two suitcases, wondering whether there was a present there for them but they were too polite to ask. When he had kissed them back, they both thought that his moustache felt a bit funny.

'Like being kissed by your hamster,' said the younger girl to her sister afterwards. But, by now, they had lost interest in their newly returned father and were already wondering how long the car journey would last to the cottage their parents had rented for the next three weeks in North Wales.

'How long will it take us to get there, Mummy?' asked the older sister.

'I really don't know, darling. It depends on how busy the Severn

Bridge is. If it isn't blocked, we should get there in about four hours.'

'That's an awfully long time.' Her sister yawned her agreement. 'How many miles do you think it is?'

'I've told you that already. I think it's about two hundred and fifty.'

'How many have we been already, Mummy?' the younger sister picked up the interrogation.

Susan looked at the odometer in front of her and answered that, so far, they had been forty-five miles since leaving home in South London.

'Oh, I'm getting so bored,' came the complaint in unison from the back seat.

'The car's so hot and stuffy.'

'I expect I'll be sick soon,' the younger sister remarked in a conversational tone.

Colonel Moberly sighed very slightly, almost imperceptibly, but Susan noticed and turned to him and said:

'You must be very tired, darling. It was a long flight, and it's a big change coming back here after your months in Beirut.'

She's a decent sort, thought Moberly. It's good of her to try and cheer me up. I only wish I didn't feel so gloomy about the future. He smiled half-heartedly at her.

'We haven't really had a chance to talk about the two days you were in prison, held by those dreadful Lebanese soldiers. Do tell me all about it,' said Susan.

He was grateful for this, and he found that the opportunity to talk at great length to his wife about the unpleasantness of being in prison, and about his indignation at being arrested in the first place, helped him to unwind and to get some of his frustration and sadness out of his system. He also told her in much more detail than he had done in his letters how he had tried unsuccessfully to chase the car that they thought might be used to get the two hostages out of Beirut and how he, himself, had been attacked and nearly captured.

'The sad thing is,' he added, 'that it's me who seems to have been blamed for everything going so wrong. I was blamed by the Ambassador for chasing the car. I was blamed by the politicians back here for not finding it and not discovering definitely whether the hostages were in it or not. Yet I did my best and goodness knows where my next posting will be. They'll probably send me to the Falkland Islands.'

Susan laughed and said that, if he did go there, she would love to come too. She thought the South Atlantic sounded rather a glamorous place but then she asked him how he thought the Lebanese had known he was at the airport perimeter fence, keeping watch on the Libyan air freighter.

'I don't know,' he replied. 'It's possible that they just picked me up by chance. Someone was driving round the perimeter road, perhaps, and just saw me there and I may have been a bit indiscreet, with my binoculars in my hand. But I have a funny feeling that some of the Lebanese knew all along what we were up to. When I was in prison and being questioned fiercely and violently, one of their officers even hit me several times with his swagger stick.' Moberly sounded properly indignant. 'But some of them just laughed at me when I told them my story of looking for our two hostages. They laughed as if they knew I had been set up. You know, like the Indians used to do, tying a goat to a tree in order to tempt and then catch and kill a tiger.'

'I've never thought of you as a goat, darling, more like a sheep perhaps.' Susan, as soon as she said it, wondered whether this sounded unkind and put her left hand over from the steering wheel and squeezed his knee affectionately.

'Perhaps we were sheep. Or lambs led to the slaughter,' Moberly remarked gloomily. 'That goes for all of us from the Ambassador downwards. You know,' he added reflectively, 'there was a great hoo-ha in the Beirut press about a young couple who were seized from their car the afternoon before I was caught at the airport. They were never heard of again – no ransom note, no bodies, nothing. I've wondered whether it could have been them who were killed, put into the boot of the embassy car and then on to the plane.'

259

'Poor devils,' said Susan, 'how dreadful. They'd done nothing wrong.'

'No, they were just in the wrong place at the wrong time. I suppose I was, too.'

Susan thought James was in danger of getting too gloomy, so she suggested that they all play a game and asked whether they would prefer the alphabet game or animal, vegetable and mineral. After a lengthy dispute on the back seat, the vote went for the animal game and this occupied them for most of the way down the M4 towards the Severn Bridge. Once they were in Wales, the children started to doze off and their parents switched on the radio and listened to the very last of the election results coming in from Northern Ireland where, unusually, there had been two re-counts.

Jock was sitting in the drawing room of their London flat with the Saturday newspapers strewn all around him. There was not one political commentary or analysis of the results that he had not read and, like a gambler unable to go home after a very long session at the roulette wheel, he looked around for yet another piece of exciting information to analyse and to digest. His own result, in Kensington and Fulham, had been declared around one in the morning on Friday. His majority had fallen slightly, by about 2000 votes, but he still had a very comfortable victory over his Liberal opponent, with Labour coming a close third. That worry behind him, he had thought, without break, for the last thirty-six hours about his own position in the Government. Would the telephone ring for him or not? Mary knew from the agonies of previous elections just what to expect. She had tried hard to keep him occupied, had taken him for a long drive to Suffolk to see his mother and father on Friday afternoon, so that he could tell them all about the election and not listen every second for the ring of the telephone. When they had come back to London, they had gone out to an expensive, celebratory dinner, just the two of them, and had not come home until just before midnight. The dinner was not a great success. They had both been preoccupied and Jock felt several times that Mary was not giving him her full attention as he poured out his concerns about the make-up of the new government.

'The telephone certainly won't ring now,' said Mary crossly and longing to go to bed. 'Even a new Prime Minister must have some sleep.'

'I'll just listen to the midnight news,' said Jock, 'in case there's any change in the overall majority.' But the smooth, young lady with blonde hair and the very large mouth, who read the midnight news as if it were an invitation to a potentially indecent party, confirmed that the overall Conservative majority was still expected to be ten, after the two re-counts the following day in Northern Ireland. Tony Castle had come back from Windsor Castle after his audience with the Queen at about 8 pm and had gone straight on to Conservative Central Office in Smith Square for a rousing celebration party where the television cameras filmed him waving at the crowd and being warmly embraced by women, young and old, all wearing large blue rosettes. Someone had quickly painted a banner which read, blue letters on a large strip of white sheet, 'My kingdom for a Castle'. Mary, who was watching the television over Jock's shoulder, dressed in her nightie, muttered:

'I suppose it would be quite funny if the Queen had actually said that to Tony. Come on, darling, it's bed time.'

And now, of course, the political editors in the Saturday press dissected and analysed at great length the Queen's decision to send for Tony Castle after the defeat of both Bruce Gordon and Robert Huggins in the election, and to ask him to form the new Government. There were two more senior ministers, Piers Potter and Ross Macintosh, either of whom, the political editor of *The Times* thought, might have been constitutionally the more correct choice. But in these unique circumstances, when the governing party was re-elected but the Leader of that party was, himself, defeated in the election, the Queen was exercising her unique constitutional privilege, that of choosing, after a general election, whosoever she considers most suitable to form the new Government. The choice is hers and hers alone, although clearly she took good constitutional advice, *The Times* thundered. If she were to get it wrong, this would weaken the position of the Crown but the choice of Tony Castle, five years younger than either Potter or Macintosh, with a more sympathetic manner, and not so tarnished by the policies of his predecessor, was likely to prove popular and successful. *The Times*' conclusion was endorsed by the other broadsheets, although the *Sun*'s headline read MONARCH'S GAMBLE and the *Mirror* said DISASTROUS CHOICE FOR PM.

'Funny, both Bruce Gordon and Robert being defeated,' commented Jock to Mary for the twentieth time. 'Of course, they had marginal seats in Portsmouth and Southampton and I always knew that Robert thought he might be beaten. I suppose, the difficulty was that the row about who was to blame for Harrington's death went bickering on and on. Labour kept on coming back to the point throughout the election; it was about the only point that they had to make, and that's why the swing against those two was higher than the average.' He paused and looked through the *Financial Times*. 'Even the *FT* seems to like the idea of Tony as Prime Minister. He's been sensible in his Defence Reviews, and they think that he's very popular with other European Defence Ministers and that may help us in our negotiations with the French and the Germans, for co-operation over a European rapid assault force.'

Mary had heard all of this many times in the last two days and knew that Jock was only talking for talking's sake in order to keep his mind away from the telephone. So she turned to the huge pile of congratulatory letters, cards and other mail on the desk. She was half-way through opening one envelope when the telephone rang. Jock leaped to his feet, scattering the newspapers from his lap on to the floor, rushed over to the desk and picked up the receiver.

'Hello, hello,' he said.

'Keep calm,' muttered Mary.

'Yes, it's me. I mean, Meldrum-Ross.' He put his hand over the mouthpiece and whispered to Mary: 'It's the switchboard at Number 10. The Prime Minister wants to speak to me.'

'Of course, I guessed that,' smiled Mary.

'Yes, yes. Good morning, Prime Minister, and many congratulations on your victory and particularly on being asked by the

Queen to form a government. Many congratulations indeed.' Jock almost gabbled his words and Mary whispered to him to slow down. She could hear the voice talking at the other end of the line but could not pick up what was being said. She turned again to the envelope in her hand, looked at it carefully and walked quickly to the window, her back towards Jock.

'Of course, I would be delighted, and honoured, Prime Minister.' Mary pulled a typewritten letter out of the envelope, together with a card. She saw that the letter came from the Union Banque Suisse, Zurs, Switzerland and was headed: 'Strictly Personal and Confidential'. She skimmed through the two paragraphs, picking out the reference to the opening of the new bank account, and giving a secret identification number of eight figures, and she saw that an initial deposit of £100,000 had been made a week earlier. The card simply said: '*A bientôt*, Monique'.

'Chief Secretary to the Treasury. That sounds marvellous, Prime Minister. As you say, it is a start. Holiday? Yes, we were just going to take the children off for a few weeks in France.' There were further words from the other end of the telephone. Mary read her letter again, and slipped it and the card back into its envelope, which she put into the pocket of her jacket. Then she heard Jock finishing the conversation:

'Thank you again, Prime Minister. I will wait for a telephone call from the Chancellor, but we'll certainly be back from holiday by the end of August.' He hesitated and then added: 'Good luck, Prime Minister.' The line went dead and Jock, flushed, his eyes glowing alight with pleasure, announced:

'That was the Prime Minister.' Mary started to smile and then stopped. 'He's made me Chief Secretary to the Treasury. He says "that's a start". Ross Macintosh is staying on as Chancellor of the Exchequer. I suppose he and I will get on all right. Of course, I don't know anything much about finance but I can learn. He then told me to go away with you for a long holiday. Most of August, he suggested, with the children. He said there will be a hell of a lot of work when I get back and I'd better be refreshed and ready for it.' He paused and smiled at Mary. 'That's wonderful, isn't it,